GH

D1139181

PRIVATE
BEIJING

THE PRIVATE NOVELS

Private (*with Maxine Paetro*)
Private London (*with Mark Pearson*)
Private Games (*with Mark Sullivan*)
Private: No. 1 Suspect (*with Maxine Paetro*)
Private Berlin (*with Mark Sullivan*)
Private Down Under (*with Michael White*)
Private L.A. (*with Mark Sullivan*)
Private India (*with Ashwin Sanghi*)
Private Vegas (*with Maxine Paetro*)
Private Sydney (*with Kathryn Fox*)
Private Paris (*with Mark Sullivan*)
The Games (*with Mark Sullivan*)
Private Delhi (*with Ashwin Sanghi*)
Private Princess (*with Rees Jones*)
Private Moscow (*with Adam Hamdy*)
Private Rogue (*with Adam Hamdy*)

A list of more titles by James Patterson appears at the back of this book

WHY EVERYONE LOVES JAMES PATTERSON AND THE PRIVATE SERIES

'Great action sequences…
breathtaking twists and turns'
ANTHONY HOROWITZ

'An **unmissable**, breakneck ride'
JAMES SWALLOW

'**Exhilarating**, high-stakes action'
LESLEY KARA

'An exhilarating and **totally
satisfying read**' NB MAGAZINE

'A **breakneck fast**, brutally
good page-turner' DAILY MAIL

'Hits the ground running and the
pace never misses a beat'
DAILY EXPRESS

'Yet another fine outing from the
master of thrillers' CITY A.M.

PRIVATE BEIJING

JAMES PATTERSON
& ADAM HAMDY

CENTURY

1 3 5 7 9 10 8 6 4 2

Century
20 Vauxhall Bridge Road
London SW1V 2SA

Century is part of the Penguin Random House group of companies
whose addresses can be found at global.penguinrandomhouse.com.

Penguin
Random House
UK

First published in the UK by Century in 2022

www.penguin.co.uk

A CIP catalogue record for this book is available from the British Library.

ISBN: 978–1–529–13606–7 (hardback)
ISBN: 978–1–529–13607–4 (trade paperback)

Typeset in 12.25/18.25 pt ITC Berkeley Oldstyle Std by Jouve (UK), Milton Keynes
Printed and bound in Italy by Grafica Veneta S.p.A.

The authorised representative in the EEA is Penguin Random House Ireland,
Morrison Chambers, 32 Nassau Street, Dublin D02 YH68

*For the brave members of law enforcement who
work so hard to keep us safe*

CHAPTER 1

THE LIGHTS OF Beijing, city of twenty-two million souls, stretched as far as the eye could see and shimmered and danced in the July heat, adding a touch of magic to the darkness. Shang Li loved this city, his home, and paused at one of the viewpoints on Qiaobai Road to admire the sight of one of the most populous places in the world. All those lights, all those people, mostly living in harmony, striving to improve their lives, working, resting, playing.

The city hadn't swallowed up the surrounding hills and mountains yet, but offshoots could be found in the intricate folds of the green surrounding valleys. There were reservoirs and power plants, quarries and industrial parks, and shops and restaurants to serve the workers. One day, Li suspected, the city of patriotism, innovation, inclusiveness and virtue—its core values—would extend even further. He wasn't normally a cheerleader for official designations, but thought his city's values a model for all to live by. He was a true patriot, always strived to do better, harbored no hate in his heart, and tried to be virtuous. But if everyone else in the city below lived by those values, he would be out of a job.

He couldn't linger over the view so resumed his journey along the deserted winding road. He had been summoned by colleagues who wouldn't have wasted his time if there was nothing to see. He'd instructed them to alert him only if the target of their surveillance did anything out of his ordinary routine. His colleagues knew how much importance he set on family time. He'd been halfway through dinner with his wife Su Yun and their children Mai and Han when Jinhai had called.

Li slowed his gunmetal grey Changan CS75 SUV as he approached the signpost for Yunhu Forest Park, making a left onto an otherwise deserted track. It cut through a copse of trees so thick even the pervasive glow of the city lights was obscured. He drove for two hundred yards until the track reached the edge of the vast Miyun Reservoir, which stretched away into the darkness. He turned off the headlights as he followed the bank for another five hundred yards before slowing as he rolled into a large parking lot. There was one other vehicle there, a blue LDV 9 van, parked near the perimeter fence, overlooking Zhonghang University. The distinctive red-roofed campus buildings stretched away to the south and west, looking eerily unpopulated at this time of night.

Li stopped next to the van and got out of his vehicle. The warm July air hit him along with the strong scent from the pine and juniper trees edging the northern side of the lot. He hurried to the van, opened the side door and climbed in to find his three-man surveillance team crowded in the back. Kha Delun, a former army lieutenant who'd been discharged due to a leg injury, was on comms, and Ling Kang, ex-Beijing Police, operated the controls of a surveillance drone. Jiang Jinhai, the head of the team, watched the drone footage on-screen. He had joined Li's unit from Guoanbu, the Ministry of State Security, and was a quiet, methodical man.

"What have you got?" Li asked, sliding the door shut behind him.

"Zhou drove all the way out here to stand around an empty university campus," Jinhai replied, gesturing at the screen. "It's not exciting, but it's certainly out of the ordinary."

Li nodded. He had asked to be notified of anything unusual and this certainly qualified as odd behavior from David Zhou, one of Beijing's richest and most powerful men, currently standing on his own in a courtyard between three lecture halls. Flecks of grey in his perfectly styled short hair spoke of his years of experience, but his trim physique gave no hint of his age. He had weathered well, despite Beijing's demanding and pressurized business environment. He wore a dark tailored suit that would have looked at home on a Milan catwalk, and seemed to be checking his surroundings nervously. It had to be someone or something important that had brought him all the way out here without his personal protection team.

"What's he doing?" Li asked.

Jinhai shook his head and shrugged.

"Waiting," said Kang.

"But for what?" Li wondered.

What would bring David Zhou out here? They'd been following the man for a while now and knew his habits. He spent his days in the office and in the evenings took business meetings in some of Beijing's finest restaurants. His life isn't completely mundane, Li told himself, thinking of Zhou's visits to the strange old woman in Pinggu District, one of Beijing's poorest neighborhoods. Those trips seemed to support their client's theory that David Zhou was a man with something to hide, as did tonight's solitary excursion.

Li noticed movement on-screen and felt the tension rise as the others too registered a shadow moving toward Zhou from between two campus buildings. A man emerged from the gloom. He wore dark trousers and a black hooded top with rolled-up sleeves. The two figures nodded tersely to each other.

"Zoom in on his left wrist," Li suggested, and Kang changed the zoom on the drone camera to focus on the hooded man's arm.

There was a distinctive tattoo of twin dragons entwined around a third, more ferocious firebreather.

"Does anyone recognize that?" Li asked.

The others shook their heads, and he wondered whether the tattoo was just a one-off or a symbol with underlying, as yet unknown, significance.

"I wouldn't have come if I'd known it was you I'd meet." Zhou's words to the newcomer were broadcast through the van's speaker system.

Li moved closer to the comms unit to hear the conversation being picked up by the directional microphone pointed at their target. Who was Zhou meeting? Why the secrecy?

"You had to come," the hooded man replied. "You know the game is almost over. One of us will define China for a generation."

"It will not be you," Zhou responded angrily. He started to back away.

"You're wrong," the hooded man countered. "Your being here tonight has handed me victory."

On-screen, Zhou stopped in his tracks and turned to face the other man, face creased in puzzlement. "How?"

Li heard a sound outside the van. An animal?

The side door suddenly slid open and a masked figure tossed something into the cabin.

"Grenade!" Li yelled, but there was nowhere to take cover.

The masked man slammed the door and the central locking snapped shut.

Li thought of Mai and Han, his wonderful children, and of his beautiful Su Yun. He prayed they would not feel his loss too deeply.

Jinhai grabbed the grenade and rushed to the back door, but before he could do anything more, the device detonated.

There was no explosion. Instead it released a cloud of noxious gas that made Li cough and splutter. He'd taken a couple of lungfuls before he realized he should hold his breath. He grabbed the handle of the side door and tried to release it, but their assailant had overridden the system. It was no good, they were trapped, and whatever was in his lungs was doing its work. He saw the rest of his team fall and felt his own body weaken as the gas took him into oblivion.

CHAPTER 2

TWO FORENSICS TRUCKS stood on the far side of the parking lot, next to a couple of Beijing Police vehicles in their black-and-white livery and three unmarked SUVs. Uniformed officers performed a fingertip search of the area while crime-scene analysts in white full-body hazmat suits checked the interior and exterior of the blue van. Sunlight dappled the woodland between the parking lot and the reservoir, where more police officers performed a ground search.

Zhang Daiyu had been to many such scenes before, but what made this one different was her personal connection to the victims. Years on the force had taught her to control her emotions, but it proved difficult to keep a lid on her grief as she parked beside one of the forensics trucks. She cut the engine and took a moment to compose herself, glancing in the rear-view mirror and wiping away the tears that threatened to brim over. Through the rear window of her Honda CR-V she saw someone approaching. She quickly climbed out. Chen Ya-ting, a former colleague in the city's police department, came toward her. He'd called and suggested she come to the scene. He wore the sky-blue shirt, black tie and black trousers that had once been Zhang Daiyu's uniform too. As he reached her he removed his peaked cap and ran his hand over his tufty black hair. His usually cheerful face looked somber.

"Zhang Daiyu," he said. "I wish I could say it was good to see you, but not in these circumstances."

"Thanks for calling me," she replied. His sorrow only made things harder and she fought back more tears. Kha Delun, Ling Kang and Jiang Jinhai were her colleagues, and she thought back to all the moments she'd spent with them—laughing at Delun's lame jokes, arguing over the best noodle stands with Kang, or discussing cases with Jinhai, who was always the most serious of the trio. She couldn't bear to think they were gone.

"We believe the assailant or assailants used knockout gas before shooting them. We found the canister in the van."

"And Shang Li?" she asked.

Her boss had texted her to say he was on his way here because Jinhai had summoned him.

Chen shook his head. "No sign of him. We found drag marks near the van. They're patchy, but they lead over the parking lot to the bank of the reservoir. We have divers in the water searching for him."

Shang Li was the warm, generous man who'd recruited Zhang Daiyu from the Beijing Police. She knew his wife and children, and didn't want to be the one to break this terrible news to them. She prayed Chen was wrong in assuming her boss had been drowned.

"What were they doing out here?" he asked.

"Following a lead," she replied.

"That sounds a lot like detective work," he countered.

Private detectives were officially illegal in China, but they existed thanks to a loophole that permitted consultants and advisers to help individuals and organizations solve operational problems. Anything overtly investigative was against the law, and would be punished, but Zhang Daiyu and Chen went way back and she knew there was no need for pretense between them, not least because they were standing a few yards away from a van full of surveillance gear.

"This lead have a name?" Chen asked.

Zhang Daiyu was saved from answering by a shout from one of the officers involved in the fingertip search.

"Sir, I've found something," she said, rising from the ground. She hurried over and showed Chen a tiny USB drive in the palm of her gloved hand.

He thanked her and carefully put on a pair of latex gloves before taking the small data-storage device. Zhang Daiyu followed him to the nearest forensics truck. The blast of air conditioning was welcome relief from the mid-morning heat.

There were two crime-scene technicians working at neighboring benches, analyzing and bagging evidence recovered from the scene.

"Check this for prints," Chen said to the nearest technician, a young woman whose face was the only visible part of her body. The rest of her was concealed beneath a hazmat suit. The technician nodded and sprayed light-sensitive fluid onto the USB, before holding it under a UV lamp. She shook her head.

"No prints or biological material. You want me to bag it for analysis?"

"Thanks. I'll take a look at it first," he replied.

He beckoned Zhang Daiyu over to a workbench in the corner of the truck and popped the drive into the USB port of a laptop. The screen came to life and the computer automatically opened a file window.

"All the hard drives in the surveillance van have been erased," Chen revealed. "Whoever did this was trying to cover up something."

There was a single video file contained in a folder. He played it.

The screen filled with surveillance footage shot by a drone, showing a man standing in a courtyard on the nearby university campus. His face was familiar to Zhang Daiyu, and she knew Chen too would recognize him as one of Beijing's richest men.

"David Zhou," he said.

The footage ended, freezing on an image of Zhou's face.

"Was this your lead?" Chen asked.

There wasn't any point in denying it. Not now. So Zhang Daiyu nodded.

"Then I think we've found our suspect."

She couldn't argue. They'd been hired to investigate David Zhou, and now three members of the surveillance team were dead and the head of the Beijing office was missing, presumed drowned.

"I'm going to have to let the boss know," Zhang Daiyu said. "My American boss."

She pulled a phone from the pocket of her trousers and called Jack Morgan.

CHAPTER 3

THE MUSIC WAS so mellow I could feel the stress of the day melting away. A. Ray Fuller was on stage with his band, eyes closed, lost in a world of smooth sound, transported by the riffs of his electric guitar. The bass, drums and keyboard accompanied his perfect fingerwork brilliantly, and the sight of a group of artists so into their craft brought a smile to my face.

I looked across at Justine, nodding her head to Fuller's easy jazz rhythms, and she caught my eye and smiled. It had been a long day. I'd been stuck in the office, dealing with admin from our national and international branches, and Justine had been immersed in the Griffith Strangler case, helping LAPD profile a serial killer who was preying on young women around Griffith Park. We were both feeling drained and beleaguered by the time we called it a day, and to breathe some life back into us, I'd suggested we catch Fuller's show at Vibrato, a jazz dinner club in Beverly Glen.

The lights were low but the flickering candle on our table illuminated Justine's face, and I was reminded once more how lucky I was. She was beautiful, with wavy brown hair that fell to her shoulders and eyes that shone with intelligence. The fatigue of the day behind her now, she seemed so alive. We'd had our ups and downs, but after all our difficulties, love had triumphed. We'd found a way of being together that worked for us.

A server deposited our drinks on the table—a couple of high-balls. I nodded my thanks and the server made his way back through the crowded restaurant to the packed bar. The other patrons were similarly rapt in the music so I drew looks of irritation when my phone rang. I felt like an idiot because we'd been asked to turn them off at the beginning of the performance and I thought I'd switched mine to silent. I signaled an apology to those around us and the band, who didn't drop a note. Fuller shook his head and smiled as I silenced my phone.

I recognized the name on-screen—Zhang Daiyu, number two in the Private Beijing office—so I got to my feet, hurried through the maze of tables and answered as I reached the main entrance.

"Jack Morgan," I said.

"I'm sorry to trouble you, Mr. Morgan."

Zhang Daiyu spoke fluent English—she'd been educated in England if I remembered her personnel file correctly.

"It's not a problem, Zhang Daiyu. What can I do for you?"

I was outside now, near the valets who parked for the retail complex in which Vibrato was located.

"I have bad news," she replied. I thought she might be crying. "Three of our colleagues were murdered last night. Kha Delun, Ling Kang and Jiang Jinhai are dead, and Shang Li is missing, presumed dead."

My stomach plummeted and I thought for a moment I might vomit. My head felt light. I leaned against the storefront next to Vibrato to steady myself. Then I checked my phone to make sure the call was really coming from Zhang Daiyu and this wasn't a sick prank.

I'd experienced many such losses in my life, from fellow Marines who had died during my time serving as a pilot in Afghanistan, to colleagues, clients and others lost while I was heading up Private, but no matter how many times I experienced bereavement, nothing blunted its merciless edge. The pain of grief was not something I'd ever grow accustomed to, and the thought of three—possibly four—of my staff meeting violent, premature deaths hit me hard.

"I'm so sorry to hear that, Zhang Daiyu," I replied, trying to stay professional and supportive.

I sensed movement nearby and turned to see Justine emerge from the club. She wore a puzzled expression, which turned to one of concern as she read my expression.

"Who is it?" she whispered.

"Zhang Daiyu," I replied. "Three of our operatives in Beijing were murdered, and Shang Li is missing, presumed dead. I'm going to have to fly out there." I returned to my call. "Zhang Daiyu, I'm coming to Beijing. I'll leave tonight and will send you my flight details as soon as I have them."

"I'll be waiting for you when you arrive," she assured me before hanging up.

I slipped my phone into my pocket and caught Justine's eye. She looked bewildered and uncertain. Her green dress billowed in the warm July breeze, the fabric dancing like leaves on a tree. She looked gorgeous. Fragile and wounded, too, but I knew why. My last two overseas trips had been highly dangerous. I almost hadn't made it back. She would be feeling the same sorrow as I did over the tragedy in Beijing but would also be worried about me. It pained me to leave her. If there had been any other way, I would have chosen it, but right now my leadership was needed to get Private Beijing through this.

"Jack—" Justine began.

"I've got to go," I cut her off. "Three of our people are dead and the head of the office there, my friend and business partner, is missing. They need me."

An anxious look on her face, she fixed her eyes on me and nodded slowly. "I know. I don't like it, but I know you must go."

She turned toward the valets and produced a ticket stub from her purse.

"Excuse me, sir," she said to the guy who'd parked her Mercedes, "I'm going to need this." She glanced at me. "You'd better settle up inside." She nodded toward the restaurant. "I'll drive you to the airport."

CHAPTER 4

THE TINY APARTMENT that acted as their operational base was starting to develop a stale smell. Jessie had tried to describe this phenomenon to friends who worked outside of law enforcement, but never quite managed to describe the complexity of the aroma. It was like a T-shirt worn by a sweaty man for a week had been left to get to know an old French cheese on a warm afternoon and then spent the evening being dunked in beer: an acrid, yeasty, fungal smell that permeated everything.

She and Lewis Williams had been working the night shift during the surveillance operation, and she couldn't tell whether their take-outs or Roscoe and Patton—the two Private operatives on day shift—had contributed most to the gross smell.

The studio apartment was barely large enough for a single adult, so the four of them working in paired shifts was overload for the confined space. It had air conditioning, but the window didn't open. The apartment was the best they could get at short notice and the solitary sealed window overlooked West 75th Street and gave them a decent view of the penthouse on the top floor of the redbrick building opposite. One of New York's finer pieces of real estate, the penthouse belonged to Ivor Yeadon, the man their client had hired them to investigate.

Yeadon was an Ivy League-educated hedge-fund manager whose life involved gliding effortlessly from one high-end venue to the next. They'd followed him to dinner in some of Manhattan's finest restaurants, dates at the theater, drinks with colleagues, cocktails with his old college buddies. Jessie had been leading the investigation for a couple of weeks and was intensely jealous of this man who seemed to have everything. He worked out in the gym regularly, which kept his body trim, he had a dazzling million-dollar smile, and sported a glorious golden tan. He also had a far more interesting love life than Jessie did and seemed to be seeing three women regularly, as well as a couple of others he took out on a date or to lunch now and then.

Tonight Ivor had invited one of his steady girlfriends to his apartment for a take-out and drinks. They'd eaten and were now kissing on the couch.

Lewis was watching through a pair of field glasses, but lowered them when Ivor and the girl started to remove their clothes.

"Want to play cards again?" he asked.

He and Jessie played poker for matchsticks whenever Yeadon was entertaining one of his girlfriends. His love life was of no interest to the investigative team. Private had been engaged to discover whether Yeadon was supplementing his massive income by selling confidential client information for profit.

Jessie turned down the volume on the speaker that picked up signals from the listening devices Lewis and Roscoe had installed around the penthouse apartment. She had no desire to hear their sex noises as things grew hotter and heavier over there.

"Yeah," she said with a sigh. "Let's play cards."

Lewis pulled a boxed deck from the pocket of his crumpled jeans. Like Jessie he wore black denims, but unlike hers, his T-shirt was in grey-and-black camouflage whereas hers was navy blue. They'd chosen dark colors to reduce the risk of being spotted through the tinted windows.

They moved away from their vantage point by the dining table and sat on the edge of the bed, within easy reach of the living area, kitchen and bathroom.

"Deal?" Lewis asked.

Jessie didn't answer. Her attention had been drawn to the apartment's front door. She watched as someone outside depressed the handle.

Had Roscoe or Patton forgotten something?

Puzzlement turned to panic when the door swung open and she saw a masked man enter, gun in hand. Lewis registered her horror and turned in time to see the gunman fire two shots. One bullet hit Lewis in the throat and the other caught him in the mouth, shattering his teeth. He made a terrible shrill, screaming sound, which shocked Jessie and spurred her to action.

She leapt across the bed and barged into the shooter as he fired a third bullet that hit Lewis in the forehead.

Jessie drove her shoulder into the masked killer's chest and he dropped the gun. He tried to grab her, but she punched him in the face and he staggered back. She saw him reach for the pistol and didn't waste any time. She raced through the front door and sprinted away.

CHAPTER 5

JESSIE BURST INTO the corridor and headed for the elevator lobby, almost sixty feet away. As she picked up speed, she fumbled awkwardly in the pocket of her jeans for her phone. She used her other hand to bang on every apartment door she ran past.

"Call the cops!" she yelled. "And stay inside. There's a shooter in the building. Call the cops!"

She repeated the message over and over until a bullet whipped through the air inches from her head. She quickly glanced back to see the masked gunman sighting her, trying to get a good shot. He fired again, and the suppressor fitted to the end of the barrel gave a muted crack as the bullet zipped toward her. This one caught Jessie in the right arm. Blood sprayed everywhere as the bullet tore an exit wound. She stumbled and dropped her phone while she fought the excruciating pain burning up and down her arm.

She found her footing and barreled on as another shot cracked and a bullet whistled past her. She saw the stairs and pushed through the fire door, hardly breaking stride as she started down the carpeted steps on the other side.

She flew down the staircase, bouncing off the walls and the guardrail, gathering speed, running and jumping, going so fast she was on the verge of toppling over. Above her, the gunman burst into the stairwell. She heard him thunder down in pursuit.

When she reached the ground floor, she turned away from the lobby and instead burst through the fire door and sprinted down a long bare concrete corridor toward the emergency exit. She was a couple of yards from freedom when she heard another crack and felt searing heat in her left side. She heard the bullet strike the metal door ahead of her and looked down to see blood soaking into her T-shirt from a wound just above her hip. Hot panic flooded through her. She was experienced enough to know a bad wound when she saw one.

Death was close on her tail. She felt weak and desperately wanted to lie down, but knew that was just the prompting of her wounded body. She pressed on and fell through the fire exit. An alarm sounded the moment she spilt onto the busy street. On instinct she dodged to the right as another bullet whined past where she'd just been standing and shattered an apartment window. Someone screamed, and passers-by gave her a wide berth when they saw the blood spreading across her T-shirt.

"Help me," Jessie said to a thin man in a baggy suit.

He took a bullet in the chest before he could respond, collapsing with a look of shock on his face.

She glanced round to see the gunman by the fire exit, pistol in hand, aiming at her. More people screamed and scattered as he shot again. The bullet flew past, inches away from her face. She looked around in desperation. She was growing weaker. Darkness gnawed at the edge of her vision.

She saw a city bus slowing as it headed south through the intersection with Central Park West. She ran for the corner, some fifty yards away. Fleeing passers-by provided her with some cover as they scattered in every direction, shouting and screaming, and the gunman struggled to get a clear line. Jessie made it to the corner and slammed her fist against the side of the bus as it was starting to pull away from the stop. The driver stepped on the brake, bringing the vehicle to a jarring halt.

Jessie ran to the passenger doors as they opened on a rush of air.

"Go!" she yelled, climbing aboard.

The driver, a bearded man in his fifties, looked perplexed, but that quickly gave way to shock when he saw her condition. He was about to say something when a bullet burst through one of the side windows, shattering it, before embedding itself in his windshield, creating a pocked crater of frosted glass.

"Go!" Jessie commanded once more, but the driver had already hit the gas. She was flung into a passenger's lap when the vehicle lurched forward.

Sirens sounded in the distance. Jessie gasped out an apology to the passenger who'd caught her and rolled into the empty seat beside him. She eyed the gunman from the relative safety of the departing bus.

"Central control," the driver said into his radio, "shots fired at the intersection of Central Park West and Seventy-fifth Street!"

He brought his dispatcher up to speed. Even though Jessie wanted to listen, the words didn't seem to make any sense. Her body felt numb and distant from her; she just wanted to rest. People were fussing over her. Was someone tying a tourniquet?

She wasn't interested in them or their frantic words. She kept what little focus she had on the gunman hurrying away from the intersection, west along 75th Street.

The last thing she heard was someone say, "She's losing a lot of blood," but she didn't know which of the blurry, increasingly distant faces had uttered the words. Her vision was going. A few seconds later, her mind went blank.

CHAPTER 6

THE SUN WAS shining as brightly as ever but Los Angeles had lost its luster. Justine steered her black Mercedes S65 into the parking garage beneath the Private building on Wilshire Boulevard. She'd taken Jack to the airport the previous evening and had returned to her empty apartment with a feeling of foreboding. As far as the world was concerned, Jack epitomized the action hero. No one else saw him as she did: The moments he drifted back into his memories and the pain of the past was written on his face; the nightmares when he spoke indistinct but fearful words; and the terrors from which he woke screaming, but with no recollection of the horror that had prompted them. Even though they didn't live together, they were not often apart. She knew him better than anyone else did, but realized she would never fully understand him. He would rush headlong into danger when others would shy away, confront it without hesitation. Three murders and a disappearance in Beijing suggested Jack was going into danger there, and Justine could not help but worry about him.

She pulled into her parking space just as her phone rang and she saw Rafael Lucas's name flash on-screen in the center of the dashboard.

"Rafael," she said when she answered his call. "I'm just parking so we might lose signal. Can I call you back?"

"Sure," he replied. He still had more than a trace of a Spanish accent, a legacy of his upbringing there in the region of Cantabria. "If you're not with them, you might want to loop in Sci and Mo-bot."

He was referring to Maureen Roth, Private's tech guru, and Seymour Kloppenberg, the agency's forensics expert.

"I'll see if I can get hold of them," Justine replied, but the line had already gone dead. She took the elevator up to Private's offices on the fifth floor, emerging into the lobby where Michelle and Dewayne, the two cheerful receptionists, normally sat, but Justine was early and the pair weren't in yet.

She found Mo-bot in the computer lab on the fourth floor. Maureen Roth, known to everyone at Private as Mo-bot, was a technology genius. Her tattoos and spiky hair suggested a cool, aloof rebel, but she had the warmest heart, and many at the firm, Justine included, thought of her as their second mom, someone they could go to with any problem. The rest of Mo-bot's team weren't in yet, so the lab was otherwise empty.

"Morning, sunshine," Mo-bot said, turning her attention away from lines of code. "I hear Jack has gone to Beijing. What a tragedy. Those poor people."

"Yes," Justine agreed. "It's awful." She was silent for a moment out of respect for their fallen colleagues before continuing, "Rafael Lucas wants to talk to us. Says we should loop in Sci."

"I'll call him," Mo replied as she hit the speaker button on the phone on her desk.

"Hey, beautiful," Sci said after a couple of rings.

Private's chief criminalist, Seymour Kloppenberg, was nick-named Dr Science—or Sci for short. He ran a team of twelve forensic scientists who worked out of a lab in the basement of the building. He was an international expert on criminology and consulted for law-enforcement agencies all over the world, ensuring Private stayed current with the very latest scientific thinking. A slight, bookish man, Sci dressed like a Hells Angel biker, which often unsettled the agency's more conservative cli-ents. He enjoyed restoring and customizing old motorbikes, and Justine thought that right now she could hear a powerful engine idling somewhere in the background.

He and Mo-bot had been among Jack's first hires and their mutual professional respect had evolved into a deep friendship.

"Flattery will get you nowhere," Mo-bot replied. "And we don't have time for your forked-tongue smooth talk. Rafael wants to speak to us."

"No problem." Sci adopted a more serious tone immediately.

The idling engine noise fell silent.

"I've got Justine with me. I'll call Rafael."

"Hey, Sci," Justine said as Mo-bot dialed the number. It rang a couple of times before he answered.

"Hello."

"Rafael, it's Maureen Roth. I've got Justine with me, and Sci is patched in."

"Thanks for calling," he replied. "I've got bad news, I'm afraid."

He sounded tired and downbeat. Whatever it was must be serious because he paused for a long while.

"You still there?" Mo-bot asked.

"Yes. I'm sorry," he replied. "Jessie Fleming and her partner Lewis Williams were shot last night. Lewis died at the scene, but Jessie managed to escape and is under police guard in an induced coma in Mount Sinai Hospital."

"Jeez," Sci remarked. "You're kidding."

"I'm afraid I'm not," Rafael responded.

"Oh, God." Mo-bot sighed sadly.

"That's unbelievable," Justine said. "This can't be a coincidence, can it? Another attack on our staff so soon after what happened in Beijing. What's Jessie's condition?"

"Touch-and-go."

Justine couldn't be certain, but it sounded as though he was crying.

"Any leads on the shooter?" Sci asked.

"None," Rafael replied. "That's why I'm calling. With Jessie in a coma and Lewis dead, the team here needs leadership."

Justine looked at Mo-bot, who nodded.

"I can move some things around."

"Same here," Sci chimed in.

Justine had submitted her profile of the Griffith Park Strangler last night and was between assignments.

"I think we can make something work," she told Rafael.

"Thank you," he said, his relief palpable. "Send me your flight details. I'll meet you at the airport."

He hung up.

"Beijing and now New York? You're right to be alarmed, Justine," Mo-bot observed. "I don't like this."

Justine nodded. It could have been a coincidence, but two attacks on Private personnel in the space of twenty-four hours was more than unusual. And what if this was only the beginning?

CHAPTER 7

I'D SLEPT FOR most of the Air China flight from LAX to Beijing. One of the flight attendants woke me to say we were beginning our approach. The first-class cabin remained dark as people raised their window blinds. A moment later, the cabin lights came on, rousing the last of the heavy sleepers. Beijing was fifteen hours ahead of LA and the flight had taken a little over twelve hours. We'd be landing just after 1 a.m. local time.

I raised my blind and looked out of the window as the aircraft banked so the wing on my side was pointing toward the ground. Seen from the air Beijing was magnificent, shimmering with millions of lights that stretched into the distance like a galaxy of stars. It was roughly twenty times the size of New York, and it was impossible not to be in awe of the sheer scale of Chinese industry. It was hard to believe this would have been considered an underdeveloped economy less than four decades ago.

The pilot made his announcement in Mandarin and then in English, informing us of the local weather conditions—warm—and our estimated time of arrival—1:06 a.m.

We were at the gate a minute early, after a very smooth landing, and soon I was walking through the huge terminal building with my overnight bag slung over my shoulder. Even at this late hour, the airport was well staffed and my journey through customs and immigration was quick and painless. I still had time to run on my most recent business visa and was accorded a warm welcome by the immigration officer who dealt with me.

"*Xièxie nǐ,*" I said to the man, who smiled indulgently at my poor pronunciation of "thank you."

Once I was through immigration, I checked my messages and found one from Justine. She sounded distressed, so I called her as I made my way through the terminal building.

"Jack," she said, answering after a single ring.

I could hear a lot of background noise at the other end of the line. "Where are you?" I asked.

"Just about to board a plane to New York. I'm with Sci and Mo-bot. Jessie Fleming and Lewis Williams were shot last night while you were in the air."

I stopped in my tracks, my mind reeling.

"Jessie is alive, but Lewis . . ." Justine hesitated. "He didn't make it."

I sighed deeply and fought back grief that threatened to overwhelm me. How could this have happened? Passengers from my flight hurried by, oblivious.

"Rafael has asked us to assist."

I couldn't reply.

"Jack? Are you there?"

"I'm here," I assured her. "I'm sorry. I just . . . you caught me off-guard. Rafael's right. You need to help steady the ship and get Jessie whatever care she needs. Send our condolences to Lewis's family and implement the death-in-service procedures."

"Will do," she said. "I spoke to Zhang Daiyu and let her know."

"Good. Send a message to all offices to let everyone know what's happened. We might need to be more vigilant."

"Exactly what I thought," she replied. "Two attacks in twenty-four hours can't be a coincidence, can it?"

"I don't know." It was extremely unlikely, but not impossible. Our work was dangerous.

I suddenly became aware of the sounds and sensations of the airport around me. "I have to go. Zhang Daiyu will be waiting."

"Be careful, Jack."

"You too," I replied, before hanging up.

I pocketed my phone and took a moment to compose myself. Lewis was a popular young investigator, and this loss would be felt keenly by everyone in New York. Jessie was the head of Private New York, a brilliant detective I'd recruited out of the FBI. I prayed she would pull through. Part of me wanted to be there with Justine, Sci and Mo-bot, bringing whoever did this to justice, but I felt a similar obligation to my Chinese colleagues too. I pulled myself together and re-focused.

I had no checked baggage so made my way through the vast hall to Arrivals, where I saw Zhang Daiyu almost as soon as I stepped beyond the automatic doors. She stood in a crowd of drivers holding placards with American names on them, and friends and family members waiting with bleary eyes and smiles of eager anticipation for the first sight of their loved ones. Zhang Daiyu nodded and made her way along the barrier to meet me.

"Mr. Morgan," she said.

"Please call me Jack," I replied.

"Zhang Daiyu." She offered me her hand in formal greeting and I shook it.

We'd spoken a little during Shang Li's monthly briefings, but never met in person before. I was familiar with her exceptional record while serving in the Beijing Police. She'd worked organized crime and had faced down some of China's most dangerous gangsters. She was five feet five and slightly built, with short black hair cut into an angled bob. She wore a dark pantsuit and flat shoes that looked as though they'd be good for running. Some people might overlook or underestimate her, but not me. Even if I hadn't been familiar with her service record, she had steel in her eyes. The world had tried to break her and had failed. Like a tempered sword, she'd come through the flames stronger and sharper.

"I'm sorry to hear about what happened in New York," she said.

"Thanks. It's been a difficult twenty-four hours for all of us."

"Do you think the incidents are connected?" she asked.

"I don't want to jump to conclusions at this stage. I'm so sorry about Kha Delun, Ling Kang and Jiang Jinhai," I said. "And Shang Li of course."

"We don't know he's gone for good," she responded. "I can't believe they would kill . . ."

Her voice wavered and for a moment I thought the tears that filled her eyes might spill over.

"I can't believe they would kill him and not leave him to be discovered with the others. Why would they do that? But I don't want to jump to conclusions either."

There were many reasons for taking someone away before killing them. Interrogation, for example, but despite my misgivings about Li's fate, I didn't want to dispel her comforting illusion.

"We need to find out what happened to him," I said. "And we need to make sure all our colleagues get the justice they deserve."

"Thank you," Zhang Daiyu replied.

She had obviously been shaken by the killings and fell silent for a few moments.

"I've made arrangements for your hotel," she said finally. "Is this all your luggage?" She pointed to my holdall.

I nodded. "I travel light. I slept on the plane, so I'd rather get straight into things if that's okay with you. My hotel can wait."

"Your reputation is justified. Shang Li says you never stop." She smiled wryly before getting back to business. "The crime scene will not tell us much more than the police have already found. I wasn't personally involved in the Zhou investigation, but I spent the afternoon reviewing the file and the surveillance data. I think I've identified an anomaly. He is one of the richest men in Beijing and yet he visits an address in Pinggu District."

I looked at her blankly.

"It is one of the poorest neighborhoods in Beijing. Agricultural. They are peach growers. A man like David Zhou has no business being there."

"I like anomalies," I replied. "Let's start there. Unless you need to rest?"

"Three of my friends are dead, Mr. Morgan, and Shang Li is missing. I'm like you: I never rest on a case. Especially not this one. I'll fill you in on the Zhou investigation on the way."

CHAPTER 8

DISTANCE CONCEALS MANY flaws, and down here among the wide highways that cut through the urban sprawl, you could see that Beijing wasn't so different from any other city. Beneath the glare of the shimmering lights were the signs of poverty, particularly once we'd left the heart of the city with its new neighborhoods and gleaming towers of apartments and offices. Out here to the north-east of the center were old buildings showing signs of neglect. Simple homes from a time before the phenomenal growth China had experienced in recent decades.

Zhang Daiyu steered her dark blue Haval H6 SUV through the streets of Beijing like she knew them well. She'd served in the people's police force for twelve years before Shang Li recruited her to join Private, but if she'd ever declared to him her reasons for leaving a highly respected position on the force, Shang Li had never shared them with me.

She came off the 2nd Ring Road onto North Linyin Street and we headed up a wide, deserted street lined with supermarkets and apartment blocks. The shops were all shuttered and shared the same air of pervasive neglect as the apartment buildings.

"How's Su Yun?" I asked.

"She's taken the news as expected," Zhang Daiyu replied as we stopped at a set of traffic lights. We were in the only vehicle on the road. "Badly. Like me, she refuses to believe he's dead."

"Do we have someone with them?" I asked.

"I put a six-operative team on Li's family so there's someone with them at all times."

Zhang Daiyu was good. Effective even in the face of personal loss. Years of experience had taught me how to compartmentalize and the importance of maintaining detachment in such situations. She clearly had the same ability.

The lights changed and we started moving again. Another hundred yards along Linyin Street and Zhang Daiyu turned right onto Xinkai Street, which was flanked by apartment blocks that looked as though they dated from the 1980s.

"It's over there," she said, pointing to a cluster of four blocks around a square set back from the road.

She turned off and followed an access road that took as around the square. The open area was a couple of hundred yards wide and weeds grew there. There were even graffiti tags daubed here and there, something I hadn't seen much of in the heart of the city. There were a few vehicles parked to the sides of the road, all old and decrepit, and the four twenty-story blocks were covered with faded and flaking gray paint. This was the kind of neighborhood where hope was strangled by impoverished reality. I'd seen places like this all over the world.

Zhang Daiyu parked outside the third block along and we got out and headed toward the building. It was a warm night, humid and close, and the sheer number of open windows suggested the apartments were stifling. There were only a couple of lights on and the whole square was deathly silent, making our footsteps sound like cannon blasts in the stillness.

"The apartment is on the eighth floor," she said as she pulled open the front door.

I followed her into a lobby that smelt of bleach. A blemished painted metallic cat—the ubiquitous Japanese *maneki-neko*, popular throughout Asia—waved one paw from a spot atop a long row of mailboxes. It was a symbol of good fortune. As we walked to the elevator I hoped some of it would rub off on us.

"I checked the apartment address against the civic and criminal registers," Zhang Daiyu said as the creaking elevator rose. "It is supposed to be unoccupied, which is itself unusual. Empty properties are reassigned quickly in Beijing."

The doors opened and we stepped into a dim corridor lit by a couple of bare bulbs. The walls and floor were concrete. The ceiling had been painted a cream color, now gray with years of ground-in dirt.

"This one." Zhang Daiyu stopped at the fifth door along from the elevator.

She knocked and rang the bell. There was no answer, so she

tried again. Still nothing. She produced a set of lock-picking tools and set to work.

A few moments later, the lock clicked. Zhang Daiyu checked the coast was clear before pushing the door open. I followed her inside and we crept along a short pitch-black corridor. My senses were alert for sounds and movement, but I could hear only the hum of a distant fan.

Zhang Daiyu pushed open the door at the end of the corridor and suddenly there was a blinding light and the sound of someone shouting. When my eyes adjusted to the dazzle from a bare bulb hanging from the ceiling, I saw a short overweight woman in her fifties, wearing a nightdress, urging us to stay back. Despite her appearance, I took her very seriously because of the razor-sharp meat cleaver she brandished at us.

Zhang Daiyu spoke to her quickly in Mandarin. Whatever she said calmed the woman. She still eyed me with suspicion but lowered the cleaver while Zhang Daiyu kept talking.

The woman responded to whatever had been said and then shook her head. Her words sounded different to Zhang Daiyu's.

"What language is she speaking?" I asked.

"It's Beijing dialect, local to the city. She says her name is Meihui," Zhang Daiyu revealed. "She claims to be a spiritual adviser. A wise woman. She says she's never heard of David Zhou."

"Show her a picture," I suggested.

Zhang Daiyu nodded and produced her phone. She flipped to a press photograph of Zhou and showed it to Meihui. The older woman shook her head.

"You sure this is the right address?" I asked.

Zhang Daiyu nodded.

"Shang Li runs a tight ship. He certainly doesn't have amateurs working for us," I responded. "If the case files say they trailed David Zhou to this apartment, then I believe them." I fixed Meihui with a stare. "Which means she's lying."

CHAPTER 9

I TOOK A step toward Meihui, my hands held in the air, my smile unwavering, indicating I meant her no harm. She backed away and raised the meat cleaver menacingly, while rattling off some angry words.

"She says she will call the police," Zhang Daiyu translated.

I lowered my hands and took a long look around the apartment. "Tell her we would welcome the police."

Zhang Daiyu frowned but relayed my words.

Meihui's eyes narrowed and I could tell she was trying to decide whether I was bluffing.

"Okay, Mr. American. I will call them," she said, surprising me by breaking into English.

She moved toward an ancient pushbutton phone mounted on the wall beside the equally ancient refrigerator. The kitchen and living room were a tiny combined open-plan space, and Meihui had filled them with the accumulated clutter of decades. The kitchen was packed with pots and pans, and produce burst out of the old, dilapidated cabinets. The furniture in the living room was from the eighties. There was a straight-backed armchair next to a more comfortable-looking easy chair that both faced an outdated television. A deep-pile rug separated the two seats. There was a smell of incense and sweet spices about the place.

Meihui watched me walk further into the apartment so I could see into the bedroom, which was overwhelmed by clothes and clutter. I glanced through another doorway into the bathroom. Meihui frowned and spoke rapidly to Zhang Daiyu.

"She says she doesn't want the police coming here and asking questions about her business."

"I didn't think she would," I replied. "Spiritual counselor, right? Wise woman? What is it you really do here?"

While the West had come to rely on digital surveillance, many countries in Asia and Africa still did things the old-fashioned way and maintained extensive human-intelligence networks. A spiritual counsellor would be a valuable tool in the collection of intelligence. People would confide in a simple old lady who was only trying to help. Of course, I couldn't prove she was anything more than someone trying to serve her community, but experience had taught me to recognize when someone wasn't being honest, and Meihui was giving all the signs.

"Why did David Zhou come here?" I asked her.

"I don't know this man," she replied.

"Come on. We both know that isn't true," I countered.

"You have no power here, Mr. American. You both need to leave."

I shrugged and surveyed the apartment again. "A wise woman needs to be good at reading people. A detective needs to be able to read people and places. You're lying, that much is clear."

She muttered something. I didn't need a translation to recognize a curse.

"Go!" she said.

Sometimes it's the simple things that give people away. In this case it was two bowls and four chopsticks drying beside the sink, the indentation of a man's shoe on the thick rug, and the raised toilet seat in the bathroom.

"Where is he?" I asked, and immediately heard movement coming from the bedroom.

I ran through the doorway and Meihui started shouting. There were more noises, this time clearly coming from inside the closet. I crossed the cramped, cluttered room and pulled open the sliding door to reveal nothing but clothes hanging from a rail. I brushed them out of the way and banged on the back of the closet, discovering it was hollow.

I searched around for a catch or button but couldn't find anything. Brute force would have to do. I barged the rear panel with my shoulder while Zhang Daiyu restrained an angry and animated Meihui. To my surprise, the rear panel rotated around a central pivot to reveal a hidden room behind complete with windows and a fire escape. I stumbled into the secret room, which contained a single bunk and some magazines and books, and burst through the fire door at the back.

Zhang Daiyu shouted something after me and followed as I rushed onto an exterior platform that linked all the apartments on this floor. There were metal fire stairs at either end. When I leant over the safety rail at one end of the platform, I saw David Zhou racing down the steps closest to me.

"Take the elevator," I told Zhang Daiyu, who nodded and retraced her steps as I started running.

By the time I reached the stairs, Zhou must have had a three-story lead. He wore the same dark tailored suit I'd seen in the video, and his formal shoes clattered on the metal steps, waking some of the neighbors as he raced down toward the street. Lights flickered on in apartments around us and a few faces appeared in nearby windows. A couple of people had phones to their ears and I had little doubt they were calling the police.

I sprinted down the stairs, taking them two or three at a time. I'd gained on Zhou, so that by the time he reached the street I was only a floor above. As he cleared the fire escape, I vaulted the rail and leapt through the air to land bodily on the man. He grunted as the wind was knocked from him, but the moment we hit the deck he lashed out with a flurry of punches that startled me. He kneed me in the ribs and I rolled clear, smarting from his blows. He got to his feet, haring away from me along the path beside the building. I got up and gave chase.

I'd underestimated the guy. This was no out-of-shape business executive.

I closed the gap and shoulder-barged him in the back, knocking him off balance. He stumbled a couple of steps, but before he could fall, Zhang Daiyu rounded the corner and delivered a knockout punch that floored him. David Zhou landed flat on his back, out cold.

"Let's get him in here," I said, grabbing him and starting to haul him toward Zhang Daiyu's SUV

But we were too late.

The square was filled with the sound of sirens, and then came flashing lights as the first of a trio of police vehicles screeched to a halt.

Zhang Daiyu raised her hands and I followed her lead. As the first officers leapt out and sprinted toward us, I turned to her and asked, "Are we in trouble?"

"Probably," she replied with a wry smile. "But it's nothing I can't handle."

I looked at the stern-faced officers, who were now yelling commands at us, and hoped she was right.

CHAPTER 10

RAFAEL WAS WAITING for them in the terminal building at JFK. The lawyer looked haunted and exhausted, but forced a feeble smile as Justine, Mo-bot, and Sci approached him.

"I'm sorry to drag you over here, but with Jack out of the country I didn't know what else to do," Rafael said. There was a tremor in his voice. "Thanks for coming."

Justine hadn't heard or seen him like this before. He was normally so suave and confident.

"We're not going to let this slide," Sci replied. He'd spent the flight firing off emails to his New York Police Department contacts, asking for information on the investigation. "One of my buddies tells me the case has fallen on the desk of Detective Luiz Salazar out of the Twentieth Precinct. Says he's a good man."

"I didn't know that," Rafael replied. "We're all pretty shaken by this. I'm not at the top of my game."

His stubble and sweats spoke to that. Justine had never seen him out of a three-piece suit before and now here he was in gray sweatpants and a matching hooded top, looking as though he'd just stepped out of a grimy gym.

"We'd like to swing by the precinct and see what they've got," Mo-bot told Rafael.

"You don't want to freshen up? Shower? I got you some rooms at the Langham," he said.

Mo-bot shook her head. "Every minute counts. We want to catch whoever did this."

Justine remembered the Langham Hotel from her last time in New York. It was where she'd picked up that wonderful phone call from Jack in Afghanistan, a call that had yanked her out of a pit of sorrow and brought her back to life. The place where that had happened would always be special to her.

"I'd like to visit Jessie," she said.

"She's in an induced coma," Rafael reminded her sadly. "She won't be able to give you anything."

"I'd still like to see her. Let her know we're here for her. Even if she doesn't respond." Justine also hoped Jessie might by now be showing the first signs of recovery and could even give them a clue.

Rafael nodded with no show of enthusiasm. "We can drop off Mo and Sci on our way. My vehicle is in the garage across the street."

He led them outside the terminal to the multi-story opposite, and a few minutes later they were in his white BMW X5, overnight bags loaded in the trunk, speeding through the airport complex.

It took a little over ninety minutes to reach the city, and they fought late-afternoon traffic all the way. Sci and Mo-bot were in the back. Sci was lost to his phone, and Mo-bot had her laptop open and was tapping away intently. Justine envied people who could read and write in transit. She felt a little queasy just looking at Mo-bot.

While the other two worked, Justine had tried striking up a couple of conversations with Rafael, but they'd quickly died out. It was clear grief and anxiety had taken hold and trapped him with his thoughts. They spent most of the journey in silence, Justine taking in the sights as they made slow progress to West 82nd Street.

Manhattan was an island with heart and soul. It had taken both to muster the energy and ingenuity needed to build the canyons and peaks here that rivalled anything the natural world had to offer. Huge monuments to industry towered over the city, casting it in shade, reaching for the heavens, embodiments of human ambition.

Rafael parked outside a building that looked like a concrete bunker, next to a line of NYPD patrol vehicles.

"We'll leave our bags with you," Sci said, and Rafael nodded.

"Stay in touch," Mo-bot advised Justine.

"Will do."

Mo-bot and Sci jumped out and headed for the main entrance. Rafael pulled away and drove along 82nd Street. They joined Columbus Avenue heading south and drove downtown to Mount Sinai, a huge redbrick hospital that occupied most of 59th Street between Ninth and Tenth Avenues. Rafael parked nearby and they walked toward the hospital.

He stayed silent and seemed to grow more and more distressed as they neared the building. This had to be difficult for him. As Private New York's lawyer, he had almost daily contact with Jessie and the two of them were friends.

"She'll be okay," Justine said, touching his shoulder.

"I hope so," he replied. "I can't bear to think about what happened to them."

They went inside, got directions from a receptionist, and navigated the soulless corridors and monochrome wings to reach Jessie's room a few minutes later. A nurse showed them in before leaving to give them some privacy.

Justine approached Jessie's bed, shocked to see the state of her colleague. Purple shadows surrounded Jessie's sunken eyes, and her lips were an icy tint of blue. She was hooked up to monitors and drips, giving no sign that she knew she had visitors.

Justine took her hand, which was cold and clammy.

"Jessie, it's Justine. I hope you can hear me. I want you to focus on getting better. We've got this."

Justine was surprised to find herself growing emotional. This could have happened to any of them. It could have been her in that bed, or Jack, or Rafael. Jessie didn't deserve this any more than they did. Like the rest of the Private team, she'd only ever tried to do good.

"We're going to find the person who did this," Justine assured her colleague. She looked at Rafael and saw his eyes were full to brimming. He nodded at her emphatically. "We're going to find them and bring them to justice."

CHAPTER 11

DETECTIVE LUIZ SALAZAR, a grizzled, streetwise cop in his late thirties, had offered to drive Mo-bot and Sci over to the crime scene. Deskwork had probably put a little beef on Salazar, but there was enough of a hard edge to his six-foot muscular frame to suggest he could still handle himself. The shootings had taken place in a small apartment that had been rented for a month by Private New York. Rafael had emailed Mo-bot and Sci the case files, which revealed Jessie and Lewis had been investigating Ivor Yeadon, a degenerate hedge-fund manager whose employers believed he was selling corporate secrets to fund an increasingly out-of-control drug habit. Of course, Yeadon or one of his associates was prime suspect in the shooting. Some might say he'd have to be dumb to kill the people surveilling him, but after a lifetime spent hunting criminals, Mo-bot knew the simplest, sometimes stupidest, explanation was often the right one.

Mo-bot wasn't famous, not like Sci. He lectured on forensics all over the world and ran special courses with the FBI and police departments around the country. Sometimes he was brought in to consult on difficult investigations, bolstering his reputation and building up a bank of favors with field offices, police departments, and district attorneys all over the United States. His semi-celebrity status earnt him a warm welcome from Salazar, who seemed to appreciate the prospect of superstar support. The two men bonded almost immediately and spent the short journey talking about Sci's motorbikes and Salazar's silver Dodge Charger, which had a custom engine and lowered suspension. The detective was seriously proud of his personal transport, which growled like a lion through the Manhattan streets.

Mo-bot didn't enjoy the limelight, which was just as well because her work took place in the shadows. She had several hacker aliases to ensure she stayed current on the latest cyber threats and intrusion and detection technology. She knew she was regarded as the mom of Private to Sci's dad, and didn't mind playing the nurturing role to atone for her more mischievous activities. She couldn't stay current without a little black-hat hacking every so often. After the events that had almost led to the destruction of the Private Moscow office, she'd taken a particular interest in Russian Intelligence agencies and infrastructure and, a few months ago, had managed to successfully disable the FSB email system for almost a week.

They pulled up outside the redbrick building on 75th Street where the Private surveillance team had been based, got out of Salazar's formidable vehicle and followed him inside, taking the elevator up to the twelfth floor.

"You check building security?" Mo-bot asked.

Salazar nodded and produced his phone. "And every camera in a five-block radius. We got these."

He opened his photos and flipped through some images of a masked man entering the building then chasing Jessie out of it, plus a couple of photos of him on the street.

"And then?" Mo-bot asked.

"He disappears. Either got in a vehicle or changed his clothes. Man in a ski mask would get noticed," Salazar said wryly.

Mo-bot scoffed. "You think? Can you access the camera footage remotely?"

Salazar nodded. "It's on our VPN."

"I have a little piece of code that might help," she said, patting her laptop case.

The elevator car opened and they walked along the corridor to a door that had been sealed with police tape. Salazar pulled this away and opened the padlock that had been fixed to the door.

They went into a tiny studio apartment – bed, kitchen, and living space, all in one room with a nano-shower cubicle off to one side. The window offered an excellent view of the penthouse opposite, but Mo-bot's eyes weren't on the building across the street. She was looking at the bloodstains and little marker flags that showed where bullets had hit the floor and walls. She shuddered at the thought of the horror perpetrated here against people she cared about.

"Okay to use this?" she asked, indicating the kitchen counter.

"We've been through the place so you're good," Salazar replied.

Mo-bot took her laptop out of its case and it switched on as she opened it.

"Can you log in?" she asked Salazar.

He came over and went to the NYPD Twentieth Precinct private network and logged in. He found the case file and opened the folder that contained hundreds of clips of video lifted from cameras around the building.

"This is everything we could get half an hour either side of the shooting," he said.

"Thanks," Mo-bot responded. She took control of her laptop and went to a folder marked "Gaiter."

She highlighted the video footage and ran it through the Gaiter program.

"Neighbors see anything?" Sci asked.

Salazar shook his head. "They heard the chase and a woman yelling, but no one saw anything useful." He looked over Mo-bot's shoulder. "What is that?" he asked, pointing at the Gaiter status bar, which showed the program had almost finished analyzing the video files.

"No two humans walk the same way. Our gait is as unique as out fingerprints, so I created an AI program that's studied millions of gait patterns from video footage taken around the world and has taught itself to identify a person solely from their gait," Mo-bot replied. "Pretty cool, huh?"

She was used to the stunned reaction she received from people when she gave them these glimpses of the future, and Salazar didn't disappoint.

"We've got six matches," she said, looking at the search results.

She scrolled down a tile display of six individuals who featured in multiple videos. One was the masked man.

"This looks like our shooter. He takes off his mask between that camera and this one." She pointed at stills from two different sites. "Unfortunately, he's got his back to the camera when he removes the ski mask."

"Wow," the detective remarked in awe. "You just saved us hours of legwork."

"You think you could share the case files?" Sci asked, taking advantage of the goodwill their breakthrough had engendered. "We can see what else we can help with."

Salazar nodded. "Sure. Once you've signed a contractor NDA, I'll send you everything we've got."

Mo-bot smiled as she clicked the still and Gaiter opened the relevant video file: a short clip taken from a traffic camera at a distance. The shooter walked away from the camera for a little while before pulling open a wire-mesh gate and hurrying into an alleyway beside an apartment building.

"You see it?" Mo-bot asked.

"Yeah," Sci replied. He was at her shoulder, totally absorbed in the footage, which had started playing again from the beginning.

"See what?" Salazar asked.

Mo-bot waited until the suspect pulled open the gate.

"See how he reacts here?"

She saw Salazar register the significance this time.

"He nicks himself on the gate."

"Right," Sci said. "We don't have a visual, but we just might have his DNA."

CHAPTER 12

THE LAST TIME I'd been locked up, I'd shared a cell with a downed US airman called Joshua Floyd in an outpost on the Afghan–Pakistan border. This time I was alone in a six-by-eight cell in a police station in the Pinggu District of Beijing. Zhang Daiyu and I had been manhandled into custody and booked for offences I didn't understand. We were separated early on and the officers who processed me didn't speak English, so despite my protests that I didn't know why I was being held, I was frog-marched to a cell in the custody block. This had no windows and my watch and phone had been taken along with my passport and wallet, so I'd passed the hours on a steel bunk, listening to the sound of a leaking toilet, and eventually lost track of time. I only knew night had turned into morning when I heard activity in the corridor outside.

I'd spent most of the restless night thinking about David Zhou.

He'd proved to be a handful, and his attempt to flee spoke to his guilt, or at least to his playing some part in the murders and Shang Li's abduction. I was annoyed I hadn't been quicker. All I needed was some time alone with the guy, but that now looked very unlikely. Zhang Daiyu had been right to pick out the wise woman's apartment as an anomaly from the surveillance file. Normal people didn't have secret rooms hidden in their homes, and it was clear from Meihui's reaction and her circumstances that she was pretending to be something she was not. But I wasn't clear what she really was, or why Zhou was hiding there. Intelligence, perhaps? Or maybe organized crime?

I heard footsteps and the buzz of an electric lock being activated. I got to my feet as the door was pushed open by a lone uniformed officer I hadn't seen before. He looked mean, like he'd been forced to spend his life doing tax returns.

He yelled something unintelligible to me and signaled me to follow him.

"I'd like to speak to the American Consul," I replied. "Or my firm's Beijing attorney, Duan Yuzhe."

My words prompted an angry repetition of the command, so I sighed and got to my feet.

The officer's uniform was new, but the black trousers and blue shirt weren't a great fit, so he looked like a little kid playing dress-up in his father's clothes.

The police station couldn't have been more than a few years old, but already seemed worn and tired. I followed the officer through the cell block, retracing the journey I'd made the previous night. Another officer stood guard by a steel gate and nodded before running a key card over a reader. The lock buzzed and the guard pulled the gate open, allowing us to pass into the main booking hall.

I saw Zhang Daiyu immediately. She was talking to a man in Beijing Police uniform. He was in the same light blue shirt and black trousers, but his fit perfectly. He was clean-shaven and had a thoughtful-looking face.

Zhang Daiyu smiled as I approached them. "Mr. Morgan, good morning."

"I thought I told you to call me Jack," I replied. "Did you spring me?"

She nodded at her companion. "This is Chen Ya-ting. He's leading the investigation in the murders. He . . . clarified things with the officers here, so the misunderstanding that led to our arrest could be corrected."

"Mr. Morgan," he said, offering me his hand. "I've heard a lot about you. I'm sorry for the loss of your team."

"Thanks," I said. "And thank you for getting us out."

"Some of my colleagues lack nuance," he said. "They like cracking heads and stamping on people, but that isn't the way of modern police work, is it? You should never have been in custody. They should have thanked you for locating and apprehending David Zhou."

I immediately liked the guy. "These things happen. I want to ask you about Shang Li. What's your working theory?"

Chen Ya-ting looked at Zhang Daiyu and shook his head slowly. "We think maybe they put his body in the reservoir. We found some footprints by the water's edge."

"Why would they do that?" I asked. "And leave the others in the van?"

He shrugged. "To conceal evidence maybe. Who knows what was going through the mind of whoever did this?"

I frowned, pondering the fate of my business partner and friend. "And David Zhou? Where's he?"

"He's been taken to Qincheng Prison for questioning."

"It's a high-security facility," Zhang Daiyu explained. "Reserved for enemies of the Chinese people."

"Political prisoners?" I remarked.

"We don't have such things in China," she responded playfully.

"Why would they take him there?" I asked.

She shrugged and Chen Ya-ting shook his head in reproof.

"In China one is not encouraged to ask about such things," Zhang Daiyu remarked. "Qincheng is the preserve of people who have powerful enemies, and those enemies become hostile to anyone who asks troubling questions."

"I need to talk to him," I said.

Chen scoffed: "Even I can't see him. Any requests for information must be submitted to the Qincheng authorities. It is impossible for anyone from the outside to see the prisoner."

Zhang Daiyu looked thoughtful for a moment. "I wouldn't be so sure. There might be a way . . ."

CHAPTER 13

DETECTIVE SALAZAR HAD shared copies of everything he had with Justine and the Private team, on the understanding the transfer of information would be a two-way street. Mo-bot had told Justine about Salazar's reaction to the Gaiter program, and how it seemed to have convinced him to take a collaborative approach. The two victims were Private employees, so the organization had standing and a strong interest in finding the perp, and Salazar was smart enough to recognize the resources he'd have at his disposal if he collaborated with an investigation that was going to happen anyway.

Justine leant back and rested her head against the couch. She was alone in the meeting room on the thirty-fifth floor of Private's building at 41 Madison, a thirty-six-story black-glass-and-steel skyscraper that stood on one corner of Madison Avenue and East 26th Street, overlooking Madison Square Park.

Mo-bot had been worried the room might trigger painful memories because it was here that Justine had erroneously received the news that Jack had been killed in Afghanistan, but she liked the place precisely because of that dark association. She'd never felt lower than she had at that moment, and had decided then she would do anything to ensure others never felt the same way. Besides, the memory of how low she had felt came with its corollary of learning Jack was alive, and that had been one of the happiest moments of her life, something she never wanted to forget.

Justine tried to set aside her personal feelings and consider Salazar's case notes the same way she'd look at any investigation. This wasn't a robbery or an abduction gone wrong. The killer had entered the apartment with the express intention of killing. His actions were either personally motivated—unlikely given the speed and lack of gratification shown during the shooting— or professional. Justine suspected he'd been hired or otherwise instructed to kill Lewis and Jessie, and that marked Ivor Yeadon as an obvious instigator, but would anyone, even a degenerate financier, be stupid enough to commission a double homicide on their own doorstep?

Mo was currently in the Private New York computer lab, reviewing video footage from a wider range of cameras, trying to use Gaiter to see if she could get an image of the suspect's face. Sci was in the forensics lab, doing his own analysis of a DNA sample they'd collected from the wire gate. The suspect had indeed snagged his hand on a broken link in the mesh and left a small trace of blood. NYPD had taken a sample and Sci had managed to get a usable swab from what was left. He was running it against the databases Private had access to while he waited for news from Salazar. Sometimes Justine envied Mo-bot and Sci and the certainty of their respective disciplines. When Mo-bot hacked a network or confirmed an image search, the result was unequivocal. And when Sci got a DNA match or identified a suspect from a fingerprint, the outcome was definitive.

So much of Justine's work was speculative, making educated deductions based on what she knew of human psychology and behavior, and sometimes it felt as though she was trying to find her way in the dark. Even when her profiles helped law enforcement or her colleagues at Private, she rarely focused on the elements she'd got right and instead obsessed over the characteristics or behaviors she'd called wrong. In this way her work was less a science and more an art, and sometimes, like now, she found herself frustrated by the lack of certainty. She wished she could give the team something concrete to work with.

Her thoughts were interrupted by Sci, who came in buzzing with energy.

"I didn't get any ID matches, but I did manage to run genealogy."

A match would have been too much to hope for, Justine thought, trying to hide her disappointment. Genealogy would at least give them something. Many years ago, Private had invested in the same capabilities as the numerous DNA genealogy companies.

"The suspect comes from mainland China," Sci went on. "Looks as though one parent originated from the Beijing region."

He had got Justine's attention. It might have been a coincidence, but it supported her initial suspicion when she first heard of the New York attack—the two incidents had to be linked.

CHAPTER 14

AFTER WE WERE released from police custody, Zhang Daiyu and I had taken a taxi from Pinggu District to the Private building located near Dengshikou Station in the financial heart of Beijing. In truth, we didn't lease the entire building, just the twenty-eighth floor of the striking tower, but I always referred to it as our building because it was such a landmark for me. My dad would never have believed I could take the tiny business he'd left me and turn it into a huge international operation. Of all our offices, Beijing was perhaps the one that most symbolized our reach. There were many US corporations that couldn't operate in China, but I'd managed to navigate local law, find myself a partner in Shang Li, and launch a successful private detective agency in a country that officially prohibited them.

Justine had left me messages so I took the opportunity to call her. I knew she'd be worried.

"Jack," she said, her relief palpable. "Where have you been? Your phone has been switched off."

"Jail," I replied. "But I'm out now."

"Jail on your first day is an achievement even for you," she responded. It was meant to be a joke, but her voice lacked conviction.

"I know. I'm sorry."

"Sci has given us a lead. According to DNA analysis, it looks like Lewis and Jessie's shooter was ethnic Chinese."

She had my complete attention. This was confirming that there might be a link between the two attacks.

"We're going to keep digging," Justine said.

"Same here. We're on our way to the office now," I replied. "Let's keep each other updated."

"Will do," she responded. "Stay safe."

"You too," I said, before hanging up.

Zhang Daiyu gave the polite smile of someone who'd been pretending not to listen as I pocketed my phone.

When we arrived at the office, she introduced me to the team of eighteen field operatives and ten administrative staff. The mood was somber, which wasn't surprising, since they had lost three of their own, and possibly a fourth, their boss and my friend.

I thanked them all for their hard work and expressed my sympathies for their fallen colleagues' friends and families before Zhang Daiyu took me into her office.

"They will have appreciated your words," she said. "I know I did. Now I'm going to make some calls to see if I can get us in to speak to David Zhou," she told me. "Make yourself at home."

"I'd like to review the surveillance tape, if possible," I responded. "See what Li and the team found on Zhou."

"Of course."

She set me up on her computer and I checked the photographs, video, and audio recordings of David Zhou, which had been captured by the team over the preceding two weeks. While I was doing this, she made her calls.

After a while, my own phone rang. I didn't recognize the number, but it was from Beijing.

"Jack Morgan," I said when I answered.

"Mr. Morgan, this is Lin Su Yun, Shang Li's wife. You left a message for me. I'm sorry it has taken me so long to return your call, but I have not been able to talk to anyone. My family. The children . . ."

I had phoned Shang Li's wife shortly after arriving in Beijing.

"You don't need to explain, Su Yun. I can only imagine what you're going through. I'm so sorry about what's happened. I wanted to arrange a time to visit to see if you need anything."

"I need my husband," she said.

"The police think—"

"I know what the police think," she replied. "They're wrong."

I hesitated. Denial was the most common initial response to bereavement. There was an outside chance Shang Li was still alive, but with three dead colleagues, even if he'd been alive when he'd been taken from the van, there was little chance of him being allowed to live for very long.

"Do you have someone you love?" Su Yun asked me.

I was silent, thinking about Justine.

"If you do, you'll know you can feel them in your bones. They are part of you, like your eyes or your heart," she told me. "Would you know if your heart stopped, Mr. Morgan? Mine is still beating. He's somewhere out there. Find him for me."

"If he's alive, we'll find him," I assured her.

"My husband speaks highly of you, Mr. Morgan. We will meet when he is by your side and we can celebrate his safe return."

"Until then," I replied.

"Thank you, Mr. Morgan," she said before hanging up.

"Su Yun called," I explained to Zhang Daiyu when she finished her call.

"How did she sound?"

"Defiant," I replied.

Zhang Daiyu joined me at the computer and we sat in her modest office reviewing the investigation material for a couple of hours. She briefed me on what she'd already found and pointed out interesting highlights, like David Zhou's frequent visits to Meihui. I built up a picture of an extremely successful financier with some unusual connections. Along with Meihui, there were regular visits to a street vendor in Pinggu who sold cheap radios and to a *chow fun* stall in Dongcheng District.

"What do you think?" I asked.

"Intelligence or criminal," Zhang Daiyu replied. "Maybe both."

"What was he doing on the university campus the night they were all killed?"

"The police think Zhou knew he was the target of surveillance and that he lured the team somewhere they would be vulnerable," Zhang Daiyu revealed. "They believe he planned the ambush to prevent us from discovering whatever it is he's up to."

I didn't think he'd be so stupid, but Zhang Daiyu's phone rang before I could respond. She got to her feet and answered, pacing her office while listening to whoever was calling. I'd noticed there were few personal touches in her office. No photos of family or friends, just a framed picture of her in her Beijing Police dress uniform hanging alongside some sort of certificate. Shang Li had told me she was dedicated to her job, and nothing I'd seen so far led me to believe otherwise.

"Okay," she said after she'd hung up. "Let's go. I've got you into the most secure prison in China."

"So long as I can get out," I replied, getting to my feet, wondering how she'd managed to do something so difficult. Chen Ya-ting had said even he couldn't get into Qincheng. Just who was this woman? I asked myself, studying her.

I didn't like the wry smile she gave in response to my joking comment. "Now *that* I can't promise."

CHAPTER 15

IT WAS LATE afternoon when we arrived at one of the most notorious prisons in the world. Qincheng is a huge facility located in the Changping District, on the edge of Beijing in a valley 3,000 feet above sea level, making the air thin and the sun powerful. Ten cell blocks were arranged in the outline of a square that dominated the surrounding fields. The main entrance featured a large pagoda surmounting two gatehouses, but we weren't heading there. Zhang Daiyu steered her H6 SUV along the perimeter road, and we passed beneath some of the highest watch towers I'd ever seen.

"Some people joke that it's a holiday resort for high-ranking party officials who get caught doing bad things," she said, "but those people are wrong. It's an awful place. The walls of the cells are padded to prevent inmates taking their own lives by smashing their heads in. It's no holiday resort."

I looked at the high concrete wall beside us and wondered what horrors lay on the other side. Built in the late 1950s, the prison had a fearsome reputation for breaking political prisoners and dissidents. The very existence of such a place was an affront to America's core ideal of freedom of expression. Independence of thought had made the US an economic and military powerhouse but China had taken a different route, governing through a single party, prizing social order and cohesion above all else, subjugating individual rights to the needs of the community. Qincheng was the embodiment of this difference in approach.

I couldn't help but wonder who Zhang Daiyu had been talking to when I'd been reviewing the case files back at the office. She must have some powerful connections. I hoped they were trustworthy.

We pulled into a small parking lot near the south-eastern corner of the prison complex. A guard in a gatehouse waved her on and she took one of the few empty spaces.

We got out and crossed the perimeter road, heading for a solid steel door.

"If anyone asks, you're FBI," she said, and I shot her a surprised glance.

"Why?" I asked.

"Just trust me. You're with the Bureau, here on an international exchange," she remarked, pressing a buzzer beside the door.

She looked into a video camera beside the buzzer and spoke in Mandarin. A moment later, the huge four-inch-thick steel door slid open on rollers and I followed her inside.

A pair of young corrections officers sat behind a twenty-foot-long bullet-proof glass window that gave them a commanding view of the staff entrance. I couldn't understand a single word they said to Zhang Daiyu, but I didn't need to. They were stern and officious, clearly making her jump through hoops. I smiled blankly and looked around the lobby, which was as wide as the bullet-proof window and about twice as long. There was another smaller steel door in the south wall, opposite the entrance, and near it a custody officer in black pants and white shirt stood beside a walk-through metal detector while a colleague sat by an X-ray machine. The room was painted battleship gray, the drab shade successfully conveying some of the misery and hopelessness that the inmates of this penal institution must feel.

Zhang Daiyu's voice rose and suddenly took on an imperious edge. She barked at the men behind the thick glass, and whatever she said had the desired effect. One of them responded meekly and waved us toward the south door.

"What did you say?" I asked as we headed for the metal detector.

"I reminded them my uncle doesn't tolerate inefficiency," she replied.

"Who's your uncle?"

"The deputy governor of this prison," she revealed casually, and I felt a surge of relief at the revelation.

She deposited her keys, purse, and phone in a tray and pushed it into the X-ray machine. I put my wallet, phone, and passport into another and pushed them into the machine, before following her through the metal detector. The corrections officer put on a fresh pair of latex gloves for each of us and conducted a fingertip search inside our mouths. He then removed his gloves and patted us down. If Zhang Daiyu objected to being touched by a man, she didn't show it. The surveillance and search protocols made Qincheng one of the most secure places I'd ever visited.

Finally satisfied we didn't pose a risk, the officer waved us on, and we gathered our effects from the X-ray machine.

The south door buzzed and swung open automatically as we approached.

"Your uncle is deputy governor?" I asked.

"It's not something we ever talk about in our family. People would seek to exploit the connection for good or bad," she replied. "There he is."

We stepped into a long corridor secured at both ends by large metal doors, each of which was monitored by three video cameras. A tall slim man in a black suit stood waiting for us.

"Uncle Yuhang," Zhang Daiyu said, as he stepped forward. "This is my boss Jack Morgan. Jack, this is my uncle Ma Yuhang."

"Pleased to meet you, Mr. Morgan," he said, shaking my hand. "We must be quick. There is a shift change in ten minutes. You must be out before guards who are less loyal to me take their posts."

Zhang Daiyu nodded and Ma Yuhang led us toward the steel door at the eastern end of the corridor. He used a key card to open it and rapidly led us through a network of corridors. It was a bleak place, and even though I only caught glimpses of dead-eyed prisoners and grim-faced corrections officers, I knew life here was hard, and could understand why the cell walls might be padded.

Zhang Daiyu and Yuhang talked quietly until we reached our destination, a short corridor with five doors either side. Nine of these stood open and I could see into small unoccupied interview rooms. The tenth door was closed and there were two corrections officers standing guard outside it.

Ma Yuhang issued an instruction and the officer nearest to us opened the door and allowed Zhang Daiyu and me inside.

David Zhou, the man I'd seen in the surveillance footage from the night of the murders, the man who'd almost got away from me at Meihui's apartment, was seated at a table in the center of the interview room. His arms and legs were shackled and the chain that linked them had been secured to a metal loop anchored to the floor. He wore a blue boilersuit and a defeated expression. He glanced up at us as we entered and shook his head wearily. I saw fresh bruises on his face.

Zhang Daiyu spoke in Mandarin as she sat down opposite him. I recognized the word "Private" and saw a flash of recognition on Zhou's face. I remained silent and leant against the wall while I scrutinized him. He'd fallen a long way from the luxurious lifestyle of only a few days ago.

"I have nothing to say to either of you," he replied in perfect English. "I don't care who you are or what you're here for."

"The police think you murdered our colleagues," Zhang Daiyu responded. "If you didn't, you need all the help you can get."

Zhou sneered at her. "You're not here to help me. I have nothing to say."

"I don't think you'd be stupid enough to kill the men who were tailing you," I chipped in. "But even if you weren't involved, you were there that night. You can tell us what happened. One of our colleagues is missing. The police think he's dead. We need to know what happened to him."

Zhou glanced at me. I could tell he had something to say, but he stayed silent.

"Let us help you," I told him. "If you're innocent, we will find who really did this and you'll walk."

"If you find who really did this, you will end up dead," he replied. "I didn't know your organization was following me until the police informed me I was being charged with luring your colleagues there to be murdered. I'm innocent but I'm no fool. Look around you. See where we are. I'm here because someone has declared me an enemy of China. I'm rich, powerful, and have friends. If they can do this to me, what do you think they will do to you?"

"Appreciate your concern, Mr. Zhou, but we can take care of ourselves," I replied.

He scoffed. "You think it's safe to go into the cave because it's dark and you can't see what's inside. If you knew, you would run." He sat back in his seat, stretching the chain to its limits "Run! Run away from the darkness while you still can."

Then he hesitated for a moment, his expression visibly softening.

"I don't know what happened to your colleague but you should expect the worst."

He barked something I did not understand and one of the custody officers opened the door, speaking to Zhang Daiyu.

"He wants to know if we're finished," she said.

I was about to reply but before I could say anything, David Zhou cut me off.

"Yes, we're finished."

CHAPTER 16

ZHANG DAIYU'S UNCLE chivvied us back to the lobby, eager to beat the shift change. We were searched again and our belongings X-rayed before we were allowed out.

"What do you think?" she asked me as we crossed the perimeter road to the parking lot.

"He's claiming innocence," I replied, "which isn't surprising. And he's suggesting someone is out to get him. Someone with the power to put him in there."

"He doesn't trust us," she observed.

"I don't blame him. I wouldn't trust anyone if I were in his shoes. Whether he's innocent or guilty, one wrong word might get him killed."

Zhang Daiyu nodded and we got in her SUV.

The heat had become stifling in the late-afternoon sun, and

I was glad when she started the engine and the first breaths of ice-cold air-con hit me, soothing away the heat and humidity.

Zhang Daiyu drove us out of the parking lot and gave a cursory nod to the gate guard before we joined Huaichang Road, a large and busy highway that would take us out of the valley and back into the city. We sped through fields, past industrial estates and factories, into suburbs that grew denser the farther west we went.

"So what now?" she asked.

I never got to answer her question. Instead, when I looked over I saw something that froze my blood. A motorcycle had drawn alongside the driver's side of the H6. Both rider and pillion passenger were in black helmets with opaque visors, and the second man was pointing a QCW-05 suppressed submachine gun directly at Zhang Daiyu. I had only had a split second in which to act.

I grabbed the steering wheel and jerked it right, hard.

"Down!" I yelled.

She cursed. She hadn't seen the threat, and only looked left when I pushed the wheel that way in an attempt to side-swipe the bike.

Muzzle fire blinded us and there was a terrible rattling sound followed by the crack and crash of shattering glass. The bullets missed their target, flying in front of Zhang Daiyu before smashing the windscreen. My maneuver of turning toward the bike had startled the motorcyclist, causing him to go heavy on his brakes. It looked as if the two assassins had been left behind..

Zhang Daiyu cursed again and took the wheel, but she

couldn't see very well as the remnants of the shattered wind-screen blocked her view.

I slid off my jacket, wrapped it around my arm and punched and swept away the cracked white glass, creating a hole through which we could both see the road ahead.

"Turn off here," I said, gesturing to an exit ramp to our right.

I turned my head and saw the bike directly behind us.

She stamped on the brakes. As she followed up and spun the wheel, the rear window erupted under a burst of machine gunfire.

There was a cacophony of horn blasts and the screech of tires as we cut across another lane of traffic. Craning my neck around, I saw the bike follow. The pillion rider was reloading.

We shot onto Changcui Road, a broad street that cut through the surrounding residential area. We went east, passing beneath the highway, racing by low-rise apartment blocks and houses to either side of the street. There were vehicles parked the whole way along, and a few shops and restaurants at the base of the buildings flanking us, which drew crowds of diners. This was no place for a chase; too many lives would be put at risk.

"Stay close to the side of the street," I said, signaling left. "And get ready to stop."

I glanced back to see the man on the pillion raise his gun.

"Emergency stop . . . now!" I yelled, and Zhang Daiyu stepped on the brakes again.

The tires screamed as they bit into the road, and the motor-cyclist had no choice but to swing right to try and avoid us. As the bike came past, I flung open my door and the bike tore it off. The collision had the desired effect, though, and the door became tangled beneath the bike's wheels and frame and took it down. The CFMoto 650GT and its riders skidded along the road for thirty feet before hitting a parked truck.

I leapt out and started running to the machine gun that had been dropped halfway between us and the crashed bike. The dazed driver and pillion man struggled to get to their feet as they came to their senses. Then the gunman started sprinting toward the fallen weapon.

I had to beat him to it, I had to, or Zhang Daiyu and I were both dead.

CHAPTER 17

I DROVE MY legs as fast as they would go, glancing back moment-arily to see a dazed Zhang Daiyu still sitting in the driver's seat of her H6, struggling to come round. She wasn't in any state to help me so I sprinted on, my feet pounding against the concrete road surface, chest heaving, arms pumping through the air, but it wasn't enough. The gunman was closer to the weapon and his gloved fingers coiled around the grip, which he swung up to level the muzzle at me.

I stopped dead.

I couldn't see his face, just my own reflected in his opaque visor.

So this was how I was to die. Killed by a stranger for reasons unknown. Gunned down in a foreign land.

I was three feet away from the muzzle. I was as good as dead.

No one could dodge a bullet at this range, and the moment I moved, the gunman would fire.

I saw the motorcyclist get to his feet and stagger away. Only then did I become aware of the groups of onlookers gathered on the sidewalks and others at their windows. My death would have an audience. I might not have had any chance of beating these odds, but I was damned if I was going to go down without a fight.

The gunman held his aim for what felt like an age.

I tensed my body, ready to make my move.

Then the gunman surprised me by shifting his aim toward Zhang Daiyu.

"No!" I yelled. I barreled forward and drove my shoulder into his midriff as he pulled the trigger.

The shots flew high and wide, clattering into the awning over a storefront. I pushed on and the gunman and I went down. I rolled clear, got to my feet and kicked the man in the ribs. He caught my foot and swept his round to kick my supporting leg out from under me. I fell heavily, knocking the wind from my lungs as I landed on my back.

I rolled and got to my feet. The gunman was already up and had Zhang Daiyu in his sights again. She'd staggered out of the van and was coming toward us. Why was he trying to kill her and not me? He'd had a direct shot and had spared my life.

I didn't have time to answer the question. I rushed him as he opened fire and knocked the gun off target. Bullets sprayed the adjacent building, thudding into the concrete and shattering windows. I unclipped the gunman's helmet strap and pulled it off as he hit me with the butt of the machine gun. As I fell back I took the helmet with me and saw the face of the man I'd pulled it from—young, scarred, with jet-black hair that had been shaved close to his scalp. He came at me again, but I held the helmet by the strap and swung it at him. The hard plastic shell caught him on the side of the head, and he dropped the gun and staggered back, dazed. As he clutched at his head, I saw a tattoo on his wrist: twin dragons coiled around a larger one. I heard the roar of an engine and glanced over his shoulder to see a black Mercedes E-Class racing up the street. An older man, mid-forties, also heavily scarred, leant out of the passenger window and yelled something, and the gunman turned and ran toward the speeding vehicle.

I stooped and grabbed the submachine gun, but there was no way I could take the shot. There were too many innocent bystanders in the line of fire, and besides, I didn't have the same legal argument of self-defense if he was running away—if Chinese law even allowed for self-defense with a lethal weapon.

I dropped the gun and produced my phone to take pictures of the gunman as he jumped into the vehicle. I then concentrated on getting images of the license plate as the Mercedes sped away.

There was a great deal of commotion around us now and people had their phones out and were filming. I could hear the wail of approaching sirens and hurried over to Zhang Daiyu.

"Are you okay?" I asked.

She looked dazed and was bleeding from a head wound, but she managed to focus on me and nodded.

"We need to get out of here," I said.

She nodded again so I took her arm and led her down a cluttered alleyway that ran between two restaurants. It looked like the perfect place for us to disappear.

CHAPTER 18

I COULDN'T RISK taking Zhang Daiyu to her apartment or the hotel room that had been reserved in my name. It was obvious we'd been targeted. She was dazed but I didn't think she was suffering from concussion, which was just as well because we couldn't risk seeking medical treatment either. I pressed her for a suggestion as we ran away, and when we emerged from the network of alleys she gradually began to recover her senses sufficiently to get her bearings. We were on a busy street packed with grocery stores and at the end was a food market.

"Two blocks south," she mumbled. "On the corner of Dongcui and Changcui Roads there is a hostel for workers."

The effort of speaking was almost too much for her. She staggered and leant against me for support. I held her and guided her through the busy streets until we found the building she'd spoken of.

Four floors high and a block wide, sweeping curved balconies ran the width of every floor, providing an exterior walkway that offered access to the rooms, each of which was marked by a numbered red door.

There were a couple of old men sitting outside the building, smoking pipes. They eyed us up and down as I steered Zhang Daiyu inside. The lobby reminded me of an old cinema with red drapes, gray marble floor, and metalwork everywhere. Pipe smoke wafted through the open double doors, giving the place a musty scent. An old woman wearing half-moon glasses and traditional Hanfu dress sat behind the reception desk opposite a gold spiral staircase.

"I'd like a room, please," I said.

The woman rattled off a reply in Mandarin. She seemed to be alarmed, and I guessed she was concerned for Zhang Daiyu's safety.

"My friend needs rest," I said.

She replied with growing agitation, bordering on anger, then picked up her mobile phone and shouted to the men outside as she dialed a number.

What was I thinking? Bringing a semi-conscious woman to a hostel while I was unable to speak the language and assure people I had Zhang Daiyu's best interests at heart? The two pipe smokers came in and approached me warily as the old woman put her phone to her ear.

I hated to do it, but I shook Zhang Daiyu.

"Hey. I really need your help here," I said, trying to rouse her. "Please, say something to them. Tell them it's okay."

To my great relief, she came to and managed to muster the energy to reply. Her voice was weak and faltering, but her tone was soothing. I couldn't understand what she said, but the old receptionist nodded and ended her call. She spoke sharply to the two smokers, who ambled back outside.

I produced my wallet and handed over notes until the receptionist was satisfied. She gave us a key to room 15.

"*Xièxie nǐ*," I said.

She smiled and I led Zhang Daiyu up the spiral staircase and through a door that took us onto the first-floor balcony. We walked along until we found room 15, and I supported her while I got the door open.

I ushered her into a tiny hostel room with a double bed, chest of drawers, and a dilapidated shower and toilet cubicle. I put her on the bed, and, like a child's doll, her eyes shut the moment she was horizontal. Soon her breathing grew heavy with sleep, I sat on the end of the bed and watched her, wondering why someone had targeted her.

Was it this investigation or something else? I realized I knew very little about the woman I was working with, and the thought that I might not be able to trust her took root in my mind. Was Ma Yuhang, the deputy governor of Qincheng Prison, really her uncle? I only had her word for it. Had she really been able to gain access to China's most secure prison because of a family connection? Or was there something else at work here? Could she be involved in something that had put Private at risk? If the gunman had been sent to stop our investigation, why hadn't he shot me? What if he had been sent to kill a co-conspirator instead? Someone who knew too much about what was really going on.

I sat for hours, watching and puzzling over these questions. After a while I used the bathroom and washed my face. As I gazed at my reflection in the mottled, rusting mirror I came to a decision. I needed to find out more about Zhang Daiyu.

I checked she was comfortable, took her purse, grabbed the room key, and locked the door behind me. It was dark outside and the city was quiet. My watch said it was 1:06 a.m., but I wasn't worried about the lateness of the hour because I was heading somewhere I knew I would always be welcome.

CHAPTER 19

BEING IN A strange city, particularly one in which you can't speak the language, is a little like disappearing. You can never be an active, full participant and are relegated to the status of an observer, but even in that role you have limitations because you can't fully understand what's happening around you. It's both liberating and disconcerting.

It's freeing because you're not bound by social expectation, so once it became clear to the taxi driver that my conversation was limited to what I could output through Google Translate, he gave up trying to talk to me and the two of us traveled through the city in silence.

Being an alien leaves you with this daunting feeling you don't quite belong, don't really understand the world around you, so you could drift or be driven into danger without at first realizing it. I had no idea whether the driver was taking me where I wanted to go, but there was little I could do about it. According to the map on my phone we were heading in vaguely the right direction and that would just have to do.

So I looked out my open window, relishing the feeling of the cool breeze against my face, admiring billboards I couldn't understand, catching glimpses of Beijing night owls on the street in vehicles we passed, or backlit in their apartment windows.

I needed something familiar, someone who could ground me in a world I knew. I needed Justine. It would be lunchtime in New York. We hadn't spoken since the call in the cab on the way to the Beijing office this morning so I dialed her number, but it went through to voicemail.

"It's me. Just checking in. Love you."

I hung up and caught the driver's eye in the rear-view mirror. He smiled blankly and I nodded back.

Thirty minutes later we stopped near Dengshikou Station and I paid the driver and jumped out. I walked the short distance to the Private building. The reception area was lit up but deserted, so I used Zhang Daiyu's key card to gain access through the side door. I took the elevator to the twenty-eighth floor and her key card got me into the office.

There was a cleaning cart in the lobby, which meant there was probably a janitor around, but other than that the place was empty. I typed the phrase "I work here. I'm visiting from America" into Google Translate so I'd have a calming explanation if I met a startled night worker.

I went to Zhang Daiyu's office and started by searching her desk. I was looking for something, anything, that might point to why she was targeted. Why would they try to kill her and not me? Was she mixed up in the deaths of her three associates and potentially Li's? Or was there some other reason? I used the photo-translate function in Google to read documents I found, but there was nothing unusual.

Her office was full of exactly the sort of things I'd expect for a senior manager at Private: case reports, personnel files, financial statements, and key performance indicators. I felt something of a heel for investigating a member of staff like this, but I had a nagging feeling I had learnt not to ignore; the sense I was missing a huge piece of the puzzle.

I was about to attempt to access Zhang Daiyu's computer when I heard a noise outside, followed by a curse. Probably the janitor. Then came a very clear electronic beep and, even though I couldn't understand the language, what was unmistakably another curse word. I rose from Zhang Daiyu's desk and crossed the room silently. I eased the door open a crack and felt my heart leap into my throat when I saw a face I recognized.

Standing in the corridor no more than thirty paces from me, dressed in blue overalls, was the gunman who had attacked us on our journey back from Qincheng Prison. He now had a dark bruise on the side of his face where I'd hit him with his motorcycle helmet. He rubbed his close-cut black hair and focused on the object in his hand. He was holding a slab of C-4 and a detonator. I watched in horror as he slid the explosive device under a filing cabinet.

CHAPTER 20

HE MUST HAVE sensed movement because I wasn't even breathing. He turned and our eyes locked in one of those predator–prey moments, though I wouldn't have been able to tell you who was which.

He was young, fit, and determined, with fire in his eyes, but he was clearly surprised to see me. He quickly turned away and sprinted back through the office toward the lobby. I chased after him but was unable to close the gap as we raced through the building. I was a few yards behind him when he reached the janitor's cart near the elevators.

He thrust his hand into one of the boxes of supplies and I ran at him, suspecting he was reaching for a weapon. I collided with him as he pulled out a gun and we both toppled over.

I grabbed his arm and directed the weapon away from me as he squeezed the trigger. The shot went wide, but the crack of close fire set my head ringing. I rolled off the man and twisted his arm as I moved, forcing him to make a choice between dropping the weapon or suffering a fractured arm.

He chose to keep his arm intact and dropped the gun. As I reached for it, he hit me with something hard and sent me sprawling onto the weapon. My head was swimming but I managed to look round and see the collapsible baton in his hand. He raised his arm for another strike, but I fumbled under me and managed to get hold of the gun. I could hardly focus, but I pointed it in his general direction and fired twice. The shots missed their mark, but they prevented another assault. Instead, he turned tail and ran.

I tried to shake off my grogginess, but he had got me good. I staggered to my feet and set off in pursuit. With each step, my surroundings came into better focus and I raced into the elevator lobby and pressed the call button. I could see one of the other cars descending and guessed the gunman was in it.

As my car rose from one of the lower floors, I was struck by the thought there might be genuine night-shift workers in the building, so I ran to the fire alarm located beside the elevators and pulled it. A klaxon sounded and was swiftly followed by a continuous ringing and a pre-recorded announcement in Mandarin.

The door opened. I ran inside and hit the button for the lobby. I slid the pistol under my belt and checked my distorted reflection in the stainless-steel control panel as the elevator descended. There was something on the side of my face, and when I reached up to brush it away, I felt the warm cloying texture of clotting blood. I looked at my fingertips, which were coated red.

The moment the car reached the ground floor and the doors opened, I was out and running. There were a few cleaners and other service staff making their way to the main exit, and outside more were mustering at evacuation points.

I ran out of the main entrance onto the street and looked in all directions, trying to spot the fleeing gunman. To my surprise he wasn't running anymore. He stood on the corner of Kaiyuan Street, beside a stationary black Mercedes E-Class. The same one that had spirited him away earlier. He smiled when he was sure I'd seen him and showed me something small and metallic in his hand.

There was no mistaking what it was.

"Bomb!" I yelled, urging the last stragglers forward to the nearest evacuation point.

I looked over their shoulders to see the gunman press the button on the detonator.

High above us, multiple explosive devices detonated. Huge fireballs tore through the building, bursting from its sides like dragon's breath.

I looked round to see the Mercedes E-Class speed away as the first slivers of glass and debris rained down on the sidewalk yards away from us. The ground shook and rumbled and finally settled as high above us a firestorm raged in what had once been the Private office.

Someone had struck another blow at my organization. Someone who, for whatever reason, wanted me alive to witness the carnage. I would make sure that decision proved to be a huge mistake.

CHAPTER 21

JUSTINE WAS CARRYING the Cobb salad she'd bought from Upland, a bright diner a block away, when she took the elevator back to her office. She had spent the morning finalizing her profile of Lewis's killer, and everything about him pointed to a highly motivated professional. Sci and Mo-bot were checking cameras for more footage of the man, but once he went through that gate he seemed to vanish into the ether.

Justine hadn't spoken to Jack in a while, so as the elevator car rose, she pulled her phone from her purse and was surprised to see she had missed a call from him forty minutes before, a little after she'd set out to buy lunch. She must not have heard the phone above the Manhattan traffic.

She called Jack as she stepped out into the Private lobby. She could tell something was wrong the moment he answered.

"Justine, are you okay?" he asked.

"Of course," she replied, suddenly on edge. "Why wouldn't I be? What's going on?"

She could hear sirens and the noise of multiple vehicles in the background at his end. Where was he? What had happened?

"There's been an explosion at Private Beijing. Zhang Daiyu was injured earlier today. One of the men who attacked us planted high explosives in the office. It's gone, it's all gone."

Jack sounded agitated and distressed. She suddenly felt sick with worry.

"Are you OK? Where are you now?"

"I was at the office when the bombs were planted—I tried to capture the attacker. I was there checking Zhang Daiyu's background—I thought someone might be targeting her for some reason—but it's clear now they're out to get Private. I want you to alert all our offices around the world. Ask them to sweep the buildings."

"Okay, I will," Justine replied. "Are you sure you're alright? You weren't injured?"

"Nothing major. Don't worry about me. We need to stay focused." He sounded almost frantic. "After what happened to our surveillance team, it would be fair to assume the New York office might be the next target."

"I agree," Justine replied. "I'll get the building searched immediately and put out an alert to all our other offices."

She went through the lobby doors into the office and hurried toward the computer lab.

"What's your next move?" she asked.

"I'm on my way back to Zhang Daiyu. I left her somewhere safe. I'll lay low until she's back on her feet."

"Jack, please be careful."

"Of course, but I should tell you—something weird is going on. The guy who attacked us earlier had a clear shot on me and didn't take it. And when I showed up at the office, he was shocked but waited until I had left the building before he detonated the bombs. I don't think these people want me dead, though I can't figure out why."

"Well, that's something, at least," Justine said as she entered the computer lab. "I still want you to be careful though."

"I will be," he replied. "Get the offices swept ASAP."

"I'm on it. Love you."

"Love you too," he echoed before hanging up.

Sci and Mo-bot were seated by one of the terminals. There were five tech specialists dotted around the room, all of whom had their headphones on and were rapt in concentration.

"What's up?" Mo-bot asked as Justine approached. "You look like someone dumped the weight of the world on your shoulders."

"Private Beijing was just blown up. Jack wants us to notify all offices and have them searched," Justine revealed.

"You're kidding," Sci remarked. "Is he okay?"

Justine nodded. "He's fine, but he thinks this could all be part of a coordinated attack on the organization."

"It's looking increasingly likely," Sci observed.

"I'm messaging every head of country now," Mo-bot said, typing on her computer.

"I guess we better evacuate," Sci said, getting to his feet. "Everyone out," he yelled at the tech specialists. "Someone pull the fire alarm."

Justine followed him out, silently praying Jack's suspicions were wrong.

CHAPTER 22

JUSTINE, MO-BOT, AND Sci conferred in Madison Square Park across the street from the Private building. Sci and Mo-bot were talking about the investigation and what they would do next, but Justine wasn't really following their conversation, too distracted by what had happened. They'd evacuated the office and notified the other businesses in the three floors immediately below their top-floor premises, who'd also taken the decision to ask their staff to vacate the building. So far over two hundred people had congregated in small groups around them, all trying to avoid the punishing July sunshine by crowding together under the shade of some overhanging trees.

Twenty minutes after they'd evacuated the office, building security had located three suspicious packages during their sweep and called the New York Police Department Bomb Squad, who'd instructed them to evacuate the rest of the building, adding to the crowds in the park and surrounding streets.

If those packages proved to be bombs, Private's sanctuary would have been violated, and Justine could hardly bring herself to think about what might have happened if Jack hadn't warned them.

Sci abruptly stopped talking and his eyes shifted across the busy street.

"Well, I'll be . . . Susan Evermont. She's an old buddy of mine. NYPD forensics."

He pointed to a smartly suited woman in her early forties who was talking to some detectives just inside the police cordon that had been established around the building.

"Come on," Sci suggested. "Let's go see what we can find out."

He didn't wait for a reply but headed out of the park. Mo-bot and Justine followed. They crossed the intersection, but as they approached the cordon a uniformed police officer moved to intercept them.

"Hey, Susan," Sci yelled over the young officer's shoulder.

She glanced up and smiled the moment she caught saw sight of Sci. He had that effect on people, charming and disarming.

"It's okay," she said, walking over. "Let them through."

The uniformed cop stood aside, and Sci ducked beneath the police tape. Mo-bot and Justine followed.

"How the heck have you been, Sci?" Susan asked him.

"Still breathing," he replied. "This is Justine Smith and Maureen Roth."

"Pleased to meet you." They shook hands. "You work with this reprobate?"

"For our sins," Mo-bot replied.

"This your building?" Susan asked.

Sci nodded. "You find anything?"

"It's not official, but the chatter suggests we've got three C-4 blocks on timers that were set to detonate in forty-five minutes."

Justine felt sick. Jack's warning had saved them, and if it hadn't been for his intervention, they might all have been killed. Private had made enemies over the years, but this was a new level of horror. Mo-bot looked as though she shared Justine's shock, but for some reason Sci was beaming like a child who'd come downstairs on Christmas morning to find a bumper haul of gifts under the tree.

"Bomb Squad are disarming now. You know what that means?" Susan Evermont asked him.

"Treasure trove," Sci replied.

"You're not even fazed someone tried to kill us, are you?" Mo-bot remarked.

"No point getting upset about it. They failed. This is good news. People don't tend to be careful with fingerprints around bombs because they expect any evidence to be destroyed. Devices like these are usually full of forensic clues so we should be happy we found them before they went off."

"For the forensics?" Justine asked.

Sci nodded.

"Rather than because we avoided being killed?"

"Well, that too," he responded, and Justine smiled.

He was obsessed, but it was part of his charm. She really hoped he was right and the devices contained evidence that would lead to whoever was trying to kill them.

CHAPTER 23

I GOT CLEAR of the area around the Private Beijing building before the police had a chance to establish a cordon and managed to hail a taxi that dropped me off five blocks from the hostel. It was almost 3 a.m. and everywhere was still and silent, making me feel even more isolated and alone. I was hiding in a strange city, hunted by people who wanted to destroy my organization and kill my colleagues. I didn't know who to trust or where to turn and everything around me felt unfamiliar and unwelcoming. I heard distant noises—an animal rooting through trash perhaps—and others that were unidentifiable and closer echoed along the deserted street.

Office blocks lined both sides of the road, interspersed with the occasional shop, house or apartment block. The district was a little rundown, its flaws even more apparent in the dead of night. Rust ate away at the roller shutters that covered entrances.

Corporate signs and logos were cracked and some had flickering lights. Most of the buildings looked as though they hadn't been painted or cleaned in years.

I picked up my pace, eager to get back to the hostel, and made it another block before my phone rang.

It was Justine.

"Hey," I said.

"NYPD found three devices," she replied instantly, and I stopped in my tracks and tried to center myself. Someone was targeting Private, someone dangerous, someone who didn't care if people got killed.

"Is everyone okay?" I asked.

"Yes. We evacuated the building and the bombs have been deactivated. Sci is pleased because he thinks he will be able to pull some evidence from the devices."

"He's probably right," I replied. "I want you to notify every office about exactly what was found. Tell them to move to a war footing. I want heightened security measures across the board."

"Will do," she assured me. "Where are you now?"

"On my way to somewhere safe. Back to Zhang Daiyu. You?"

"Mo-bot and Sci are setting up a mobile command unit in one of the staff trucks so we can continue operations remotely until NYPD clears the building."

"Call me if anything else is found," I suggested.

"I will," she replied. There was a pause and then: "I love you, Jack."

"Love you too."

She hung up and I slipped my phone into my pocket. I wanted

nothing more than to be with her, curled up in bed in my home in LA, but first there was ugly work that needed to be done. The comfort and peace of being back with her would have to wait.

I hurried to the hostel, let myself into the deserted building and went to our room. I unlocked the door and eased it open silently. I went inside to find Zhang Daiyu exactly where I'd left her. She was breathing heavily and seemed to be deep asleep. I shut the door quickly and sat in the gap between the bed and the shower-room wall. I rested my hands on my knees and put my head down on my forearms. Soon the soothing sound of Zhang Daiyu's regular breathing, rising above the silence, calmed me and I drifted off to sleep.

CHAPTER 24

A HUBBUB OF voices invaded my restless sleep. I woke to hear a group of men passing the door to the room. I was immediately alert and on edge but calmed down after a moment when the voices drifted by. They were most likely workers on their way out to start the day. I rolled onto my back and found Zhang Daiyu leaning over the edge of the bed, looking down at me.

"You were talking in your sleep," she said.

As was often the case, my dreams had been of fire and death. I'd seen more than my fair share of both and carried the searing recollections with me. From the battlefields of Afghanistan to the streets of Berlin, from the slums of India to the palaces of Moscow, death had stalked me and those close to me, and the bombing of Private's Beijing office had stirred bad memories. One moment I was back in Afghanistan, trying to rescue fallen comrades from my downed Sea Knight. But as the flames raged around me, when I looked down at the body I was pulling from the wreckage, instead of one of my Marine platoon I saw the face of Karl Parker, an old friend, the man who'd been assassinated in the New York Stock Exchange while I stood beside him. Trauma sometimes played out like that, disregarding the constraints of time and location, creating a doubly disturbing kaleidoscope.

I felt uneasy at the enforced intimacy between Zhang Daiyu and me. From the expression on her face, it was clear she felt it too.

"I'm sorry, I didn't mean to . . . you didn't say anything coherent, just a jumble of words. I didn't mean to make you uncomfortable."

"It's okay," I assured her. Military service and field operations as a detective had taught me not to be precious about the awkward situations that often arose.

I sat up and stretched. "How are you feeling?"

"My head is sore and my bones ache," she replied, "but other than that, not too bad. At least I'm still breathing."

I smiled. She had a dry sense of humor.

"Thank you for saving me," she said.

I nodded. "The guy who tried to shoot you planted bombs at our office last night. I interrupted him while he was priming the detonators."

"Bombs? What the . . . Did you call the Bomb Squad?"

I shook my head. "He managed to detonate them."

She gasped.

"Our office here has been destroyed. Everything's gone."

Zhang Daiyu took a moment to absorb the news.

"Was anyone hurt?" she asked at last.

"I don't think so," I replied. "I managed to evacuate the building in time."

My phone rang and I saw Justine's name flash on-screen. "I need to take this," I told Zhang Daiyu.

"Searches of the other offices haven't revealed anything," Justine said as soon as I answered.

"That's a relief. But we still need everyone to be on high alert," I said. "Enhanced security across the board until we find out who is behind this and why they've targeted us. We don't know what their next move might be."

"We're on it," she replied. "Jack, please be careful. I want you to come back to me in one piece."

"I will," I assured her before hanging up.

Zhang Daiyu was busy on her phone sending texts.

"Most of the team already know about the office," she remarked without looking up. "The authorities want us to come in for questioning."

"How do you feel about that?" I asked.

"I think this would be a bad time to start trusting strangers."

"I agree."

"Do the other offices know?" she asked.

I could tell something was on her mind.

"Yes. I spoke to Justine last night and told her to alert everyone."

"What were you doing at the office?" Zhang Daiyu asked, giving voice to what was troubling her.

I felt that I'd betrayed her by going looking for evidence she was somehow involved in whatever was going on. The attack on the New York office proved my initial suspicions were unfounded; it was Private that was being targeted rather than her.

"I had some things I wanted to check out."

"Okay," she said. "Do you have any thoughts on why we're being targeted like this?"

I shook my head. "No. But although this has spread wider than Beijing, it began here. We need to review all cases from the last six months."

"I can ask Huang Hua to recover the case files from the Cloud," Zhang Daiyu replied. "It will take a few hours perhaps."

"Good to know."

"I'll get him on it now," she said, tapping furiously into her phone. "I'll instruct everyone to work from home until further notice. The IT team will implement our remote working protocols."

"This started with the investigation into David Zhou," I observed. "I want to rule him in or out of this. He's either been very unlucky or he's part of whatever's going on, and I need to know which. Who was our client?"

"Molly Tan," Zhang Daiyu replied. "She's a technology entrepreneur. She owns China's second-largest online auction site and retailer. She and David Zhou have a history of being on opposite sides of deals."

"OK." I nodded. "I think we need to pay Ms Tan a visit."

CHAPTER 25

IT WAS GONE 8 p.m. and Justine was still in the Private New York office, working in the conference room on the thirty-fifth floor, trying to put together a profile of the person who had planted the bombs intended to kill her and her colleagues.

She had developed a couple of scenarios. In the first, whoever planted the devices was the same person who shot Jessie and Lewis. The second possibility was that they were separate and unrelated people. Bombers tended to be meticulously careful individuals with little appetite for encountering death up close. Someone capable of gunning down two people in close contact had a very different attitude. But if there was one person who combined the discipline and technical knowhow needed for bomb-making with an appetite for close combat, then that suggested someone with military or paramilitary training.

Justine had written up two different profiles but it had taken her much longer than normal because she had found herself frequently distracted by her concern for Jack. Speaking to him hadn't helped. He had sounded dead tired and worried, and she hated to think of him fighting for his life in an unfamiliar city. She had, however, heard good things about the Beijing office's number two, Zhang Daiyu, and hoped she lived up to her reputation.

There was a knock at the door and an Atlas Security officer entered. He wore a gray uniform shirt and was accompanied by an English Springer Spaniel sniffer dog, held on a short leash.

"Sorry to disturb you again, ma'am," he said. "We're doing another sweep."

"Go ahead," Justine replied, watching as the security officer allowed the dog to sniff the corners of the room in search of traces of explosives.

It spent a while under the table and its handler opened the cupboards built into the storage unit behind her. She watched the dog check inside the large piece of furniture, tail wagging.

"Looks like he's enjoying himself," Sci said.

The forensics expert was standing in the doorway, leaning against the frame.

"He knows he gets a treat if he does a good job," the security officer said. "You're clear," he told Justine, and he and the dog squeezed past Sci to leave the room.

"I have news," Sci said, shutting the door and taking a seat at the boardroom table. "NYPD has been able to trace the detonators to a demolition firm based in Connecticut. Ryedale Engineering. Guy called Seth Ryedale runs the place. Mo-bot is working up a background on him and the firm. Detective Salazar has asked us to give him a clear run and not to make contact until lunch-time tomorrow at the earliest. They want to question Ryedale and search the place for evidence. They don't want us doing anything to tip him off."

"We can do that," Justine replied. "We need to cooperate wher-ever we can."

"How's Jack?" Sci asked.

"He's doing okay," she said. "Considering."

"And you?"

"I'll be glad when he's home."

"We all will," Sci agreed.

"Is Mo-bot in the computer lab?"

Sci nodded.

"I'll join her," said Justine, getting to her feet. "See if any of the staff at Ryedale Engineering fit the profiles I'm working on."

CHAPTER 26

ZHANG DAIYU AND I took a taxi from the hostel to Chaoy-ang Park, one of the most exclusive neighborhoods in the province. The place was alive, humming with traffic and activity, and watching from the cab window I really got a sense of the magnitude of Beijing. We drove through individual areas the size of Manhattan, city-sized districts within this sprawling metropolis. It wasn't spread out like Los Angeles but as densely populated as New York. Everything was on a different scale here. Twelve-lane highways crisscrossed the city, and the flowing lanes of traffic became a moving blur of colors as automobiles, buses, and trucks raced about their business.

Zhang Daiyu put her head back and shut her eyes. I didn't disturb her, partly because she looked as though she needed the rest, but also because I didn't want to discuss the case in front of the taxi driver. So I kept my gaze on the city, watching our surroundings as we turned off the 4th Ring Road and joined Chaoyang Gongyuan Road, a wide tree-lined boulevard that ran to the south of Chaoyang Park. This neighborhood reminded me of Fifth Avenue in New York, or some of the upmarket cross streets near Central Park. Sidewalks were packed with rich people carrying shopping bags branded with the names of the luxury boutiques that lined the street. Designer clothes from every corner of the globe were displayed in the windows of these exclusive shops. Dark-suited doormen ushered the big spenders into these temples to capitalism.

It seemed odd to have such conspicuous consumption in an ostensibly communist country. We left the retail district and took a right onto the broad perimeter road that ran alongside the grand park. We were heading into the residential part of the neighborhood and it managed to make Manhattan look impoverished. Skyscrapers lined the perimeter of the park, overlooking the broad, exquisitely manicured green space. Each building was newer and more impressive than the last, glass-and-steel megastructures that featured garden balconies, huge atriums and multi-level penthouses. The cab drew to a halt outside a gold-and-black tower that stood at least fifty floors high. I nudged Zhang Daiyu, who stirred.

"I think we're here," I observed.

She nodded, said something to the driver, and handed him some money.

We climbed out of the cab and started toward the building.

"You okay?" I asked her.

"Exhausted," she replied. "But okay."

We entered the building through an automatic glass door and stepped inside a huge atrium complete with a flourishing rock garden and waterfall. We were greeted by a doorman in a traditional black suit. Zhang Daiyu spoke to him, and he made a phone call before directing us to a bank of elevators off the huge lobby.

We went up to the forty-eighth floor, where we stepped out into a marble lobby with two doors: a service corridor and a double-width oak door that gave access to the only apartment on this floor. The huge door opened as we walked toward it, and a woman I recognized from Google image searches greeted us formally then bowed her head in apology.

"I'm sorry," she said in perfect English. "Where are my manners? You must be Jack Morgan," offering me her hand as she spoke. "I'm Molly Tan. My doorman told me you'd like to ask me some questions. Please come in."

She stood aside and ushered us into a hallway with a marble floor and wooden cabinets lining the walls.

She took us into a huge vaulted living room with double-height floor-to-ceiling windows that offered a breathtaking view of the vast city. There were several seating areas, some more formal than others. She took us across to an informal arrangement of sofas and armchairs near the window. A woman in a blue silk dress placed a tray of small bowls and a teapot on a low table before quickly withdrawing into an ante-room.

"Please sit," Molly invited us. She took an armchair and offered us tea as we both sat down on a sofa opposite her.

"Thank you for agreeing to see us," I said.

"Of course," she replied. "I'm a client of Private. Anything I can do to help after the terrible attacks."

"You know about them?" I asked.

"They have been in the news. The police are eager to question you, I understand? But I know how complicated these situations can be and I am sure you will talk to them at the appropriate time."

She pushed a delicate porcelain cup toward Zhang Daiyu, who nodded her thanks.

"Would you like tea?" Molly asked me as she filled another.

"No, thanks. We'd like to talk to you about David Zhou," I said. "You hired us to investigate him and his business dealings. Why?"

"Mr. Zhou and I have crossed paths many times," she replied indirectly, picking up her cup.

She sat back, looking every inch the billionaire in a black couture dress hand-embroidered with red, pink, and gold finches in a beautiful swirling design. Her long black hair was arranged in an intricate up-do and her makeup was flawless, accentuating her delicate features.

"We were both supposed to be part of a syndicate of investors taking over an international shipping business, but I did not wish to risk tarnishing my reputation by association. I'd heard things about Mr. Zhou and his business partners. Thought I should do due diligence before entering any business deal as his associate."

"What sort of things had you heard?" I asked.

"That he is connected to the underworld. That he comes from an old Triad family," Molly replied. "The kind of rumors that can be unsettling for a businesswoman who cares about her own reputation."

I looked at Zhang Daiyu. Nothing like that had ever come up in our background investigation of David Zhou. Had Molly Tan been fed misinformation? Or was she lying to us?

"What's happened to the deal?" I asked. "Since his arrest."

"It's lost momentum," she replied. "We're all waiting to see what happens to him. Whether he needs to be replaced."

"There was no mention of this deal in our original terms of engagement," Zhang Daiyu remarked.

"I did not wish to risk word of your inquiries reaching my fellow investors and spooking them," Molly replied.

Something was off here, that much was clear. She wasn't being entirely honest with us.

"There was no mention of it in our background investigation either," Zhang Daiyu countered.

"In our world these things are agreed with a phone call and a handshake," Molly replied. "The lawyers do the paperwork when we are ready to sign. We weren't yet at that stage when I spoke to you. Particularly not after I heard the rumors about Mr. Zhou."

"Who told you about them?" I asked, and she looked momentarily taken aback.

"I can't say. Not without breaching a confidence."

"Why us?" I asked. "Why choose Private? There are plenty of other agencies in Beijing."

Molly didn't get a chance to answer me. The hallway door opened and two children spilled into the room, chattering to each other. They were accompanied by a slim man in a tailored suit. Molly rose and spoke to them in Mandarin and the children ran over and gave her a hug. Both boys, they were between ten and twelve years old and wore matching school uniforms.

"Mr. Morgan, Detective Zhang Daiyu, these are my boys Ru and Yan."

"Hello," I said.

"Mr. Morgan is American," Molly explained to them.

"Like Iron Man," Ru, the elder of the two, noted.

I chuckled. "Not quite like Iron Man."

"Close enough, I'm sure," the man said, joining us. He was a few years older than Molly, his hair frosted with grey.

"This is my husband, Bryan Meng. Jack Morgan and Zhang Daiyu from Private," Molly introduced us.

"The detective agency," Bryan remarked. "You're famous for all the wrong reasons."

He gave his wife a sharp-eyed glance to convey that he wasn't as sanguine about hosting fugitives as she seemed to be.

"Give us a few minutes, please, darling," Molly said. "We're nearly done here, aren't we, Mr. Morgan?"

"Almost," I replied.

"Come on, boys," Bryan said, and the two kids followed him through a door that led to a large kitchen.

He closed it behind them.

"So?" Molly remarked.

"You were going to tell us why you chose Private," I reminded her.

"Because you're the best, Mr. Morgan. Your reputation is unrivaled. Will that be all?"

"Don't you want to know if we found anything?" I asked. "On Mr. Zhou, I mean."

"Why?" she responded. "He's in prison. The deal is on hold. He'll either be found guilty and go away for a very long time, or he'll be cleared and his business activities will resume. In either case, he no longer poses any risk to me. The police investigation will resolve the matter one way or the other. When you are able, you should please arrange for me to be sent the final bill for your work."

I nodded. "Of course."

She wasn't going to give us any more, and I had as much as I needed—hints that she was lying. Which meant she was either involved in the strike against Private or had something else to hide.

"Then our business is concluded," she said.

"I guess so," I replied.

Molly got to her feet. "You must contact me if anything else comes to mind. Here are my details." She pulled a card from under a coaster on the table. It had obviously been placed there in readiness for delivering this brush-off.

"Thank you," I said, taking it. "We're sorry to have intruded on your family time."

"That's quite alright."

She walked us back to the elevator.

"Good luck with your investigation," she said. "I hope these problems you're having go away."

The elevator door opened and Zhang Daiyu and I stepped in and said goodbye to Molly Tan, who watched us out of sight.

"Thoughts?" I asked when we were on our way down.

"She's hiding something," Zhang Daiyu replied.

I nodded. "Nothing she said stacks up. I can't shake the feeling we're being used for something. We should run surveillance on her. Look into the business deal she talked about and find out the real reason she hired us to dig into David Zhou."

CHAPTER 27

JUSTINE WAS DESPERATE to interview Seth Ryedale and ask him about the member of his workforce identified by Mo-bot as a possible suspect, but they hadn't wanted to make an enemy of Luiz Salazar. A cooperative NYPD detective was invaluable to them, so she and Sci made good on the bargain they'd struck with Salazar and didn't arrive in Connecticut until after lunch the following day. Sci was driving the New York staff vehicle, a red Nissan Rogue. Justine was in the passenger seat, worrying about Jack. He had texted to say they were following up a new lead and had requested some support from Mo-bot to help the Beijing team restore their systems and implement remote working. Mo-bot was currently back at the office in Manhattan making it all happen.

They turned off the Connecticut Turnpike just outside Bridgeport and drove into an industrial estate of warehouses and factories. Sci followed the GPS instructions until they saw the large black sign announcing Ryedale Engineering that hung on a high chain-link fence. Behind the fence was a parking lot and an aluminum-sided warehouse with silver-tinted windows. This was the source of the detonators that had been found in the Private office.

Sci drove up to the gatehouse. A security guard came out and greeted them.

"Afternoon, sir, ma'am. Who are you here to see?"

"Seth Ryedale," Sci replied.

"Do you have an appointment?"

"Tell him it's about the bombs found in Manhattan."

"Your names?"

"Seymour Kloppenberg and Justine Smith. We're from Private. The bombs were found in our office."

"Just a moment."

The guard returned to the gatehouse and made a phone call. He spoke briefly to someone before he re-emerged.

"Go ahead," he said. "Visitor parking is near the entrance."

"Thanks," Sci responded as the guard raised the barrier and allowed them to pass.

There were forty or so vehicles parked in the lot, and all six visitor spaces were empty. Sci pulled into the one closest to the door and they headed inside.

"Mr. Kloppenberg, Ms. Smith," a man said the moment they entered the lobby through the silver-tinted sliding doors. "My name is Seth Ryedale. I run this place. I'm so sorry about what happened."

Ryedale was a tall, muscular man in his early forties. His boots, jeans, and sky-blue T-shirt made Justine think of a ranch hand, and the rough stubble that covered his chiseled jawline only added to the illusion.

"The cops told me they think the detonators came from here, so as you can imagine I'm pretty bummed out by all this."

"Can we talk somewhere private?" Sci asked. Seth shook his head.

"Look, I don't mean to offend you but I've already told the police everything I know. If you've got any questions, take it up with them."

"You sure you don't want to go somewhere private?" Sci pressed.

Seth shrugged. "We've got nothing to talk about."

"Then we'll do this here," Sci replied, nodding at Justine.

"Our investigation has revealed you have an employee here who is using a Social Security number flagged as part of a data theft from the Commerce Bank of Boston," she began.

"What the hell?" Seth remarked, lowering his voice so as not to be overheard by the receptionist.

"You can see why we wanted to do this in private," Justine said.

"Fake social security?" asked Seth.

"Probably bought online," Sci chimed in.

"Who?" Seth asked, his expression hardening.

"Francis Johnson," Justine replied.

"Francis?" Seth scoffed. "He's one of our accounts clerks. He's a nerd."

"Nevertheless," Justine said, "he's the first person we want to talk to."

"Do the cops know?"

Sci shook his head. "Not yet. We will share the information with them if it comes to anything."

"Why didn't my vetting firm spot this?" Seth asked. "Or the cops?"

Justine shrugged.

"We have extensive resources," Sci replied. "The cops will probably see the anomaly when they start looking at your employee records. We have methods that speed up the process for us."

Justine knew he was referring to an AI search algorithm Mobot had designed to spot identities that had been implicated in large data thefts.

"Maybe I need to come to you next time," Seth said.

"We'd be happy to hear from you," Justine replied. She handed him a business card, which he examined thoughtfully. "Can we talk to Mr. Johnson?"

"He's not come in today."

"You think you could give us an address?" Sci asked. "And a photograph?"

"You bet," Seth replied. "It would be my pleasure."

CHAPTER 28

MY HEART WAS racing as we finished our climb to the top of
the fire stairs. Part exhaustion, part anxiety, it thundered like a
jackhammer while I watched Zhang Daiyu circumvent the alarm
that should have automatically sounded when she opened the
fire door. She used a portable device to maintain the illusion of
a closed circuit as she cut into the alarm wires before pushing
the door wide.

We went through, and behind us came Huang Hua, the head
of private Beijing's tech team. He was thirty-six, but his long
foppish black hair and upbeat demeanor made him seem much
younger. Like Zhang Daiyu and me, he was dressed in black and
moved like a shadow as we crossed the roof.

Zhang Daiyu had managed to get blueprints for Molly Tan's
building and she and Hua had identified a point of entry through
the ventilation system. He had secured the necessary equipment

from an emergency stockpile he kept at home. We had driven to Molly's building, arriving just after 3 a.m. and breaking in through a service entrance to the rear of the high-rise.

The wind hit my face as Zhang Daiyu led us across the roof, and when we neared the edge, my legs went weak at the sight of the fifty-story drop. Beijing was so far below us it looked like a never-ending, glittering toy town.

"It's this one," she said, dropping to a crouch beside an air duct.

Hua and I joined her. He dropped his tool bag, produced an electric screwdriver and used it to remove the mesh that covered the duct. Next he reached into his bag for a small flight case and opened it to reveal a tiny drone nestled in custom laser-cut foam.

"The drone carries six bugs," he said, pointing to half a dozen tiny surveillance devices on the device's undercarriage.

He took the drone out of the foam, switched it on, and used the small remote control with inbuilt video camera to conduct a test flight before sending the device into the air duct. Six tiny rotors, each about the size of a dime, worked to keep the drone steady as it descended through the ventilation system. When Hua saw "48" appear on-screen, signaling the device had reached Molly's floor, he moved it horizontally, guiding it along the vent network until it reached her apartment.

He piloted the drone toward another mesh, and on-screen I saw the hallway Zhang Daiyu and I had entered by the previous day. He didn't plant one of the bugs there, but instead piloted the drone further into the network until he reached the next mesh.

He set it down next to the metal guard, and I saw the large sitting room beyond that.

"Odd," Hua said, and used the remote to direct the camera away from the living room, pointing it parallel to the mesh. "I thought I saw something when it landed."

There, a few inches away from our drone, was a tiny bug, an audio-visual surveillance device like the ones attached to our aircraft.

"It's another bug," he confirmed.

"Someone else has been spying on her," Zhang Daiyu remarked.

"Can we find out who?" I asked.

"I can try," he replied. "It's sloppy work. These things are magnetic. Designed to be removed once an operation is concluded. This should have been recovered by whoever planted it."

"Maybe it's still running," I suggested.

Hua checked a small signal display next to the main monitor on his remote control and shook his head. "It's not giving off a signal. The batteries are probably dead."

To illustrate what he meant, he used the remote to release the first bug from the drone's undercarriage. The moment it detached, it showed up as an AV signal on the remote's display and Hua was able to toggle between the audio-visual feed of the bug and the drone on the main monitor.

"Even if we couldn't decrypt the signal, at this range we would pick it up," he said. "Let me see if I can grab it."

He piloted the drone forward a few inches and there was a click as the bug snapped into place in the vacated bay on the undercarriage.

"Got it."

He flew the drone through the rest of the ventilation network and deposited our surveillance devices. There were other bugs in every room and Hua collected five more of them before piloting the drone back through the maze of ducts and up to the roof. He powered down the device and picked it up to examine the bugs on its underside.

"Same model as ours," he observed.

"Guoanbu?" Zhang Daiyu asked, referring to the Chinese Intelligence service.

"Maybe." He nodded. "Hard to say for sure at this point, but at least we now have eyes and ears on Molly Tan."

He cycled the remote-control screen through images being broadcast by the six bugs he had placed throughout her penthouse.

I was determined to find out what she really knew. And besides that, I was more than intrigued to learn that someone had been spying on her well before we had placed our bugs. Who could that be?

CHAPTER 29

JUSTINE AND SCI had been parked outside the small house on Howard Avenue, Bridgeport for a couple of hours, waiting for any sign of Francis Johnson, the man who'd used a false Social Security number to get his job at Ryedale Engineering. According to his employee record, Francis was five feet ten, one hundred and seventy pounds, and his photo showed a hawkish man with short brown hair and a crooked nose, the result, he'd claimed in his job interview, of a childhood fall from a bike. Justine had emailed the Ryedale Engineering staff photo to Mo-bot who was running an image search against mugshot databases.

The Private staff vehicle was parked thirty yards south of Francis's house on the opposite side of the street, giving Justine and Sci an unobstructed view of the property. Howard Avenue was in a blue-collar neighborhood of modest, well-kept one- and two-story homes on small lots. Most of the houses were clad in painted timber or aluminum and nearly all flew the Stars and Stripes from their porches or beneath the eaves of their roofs. The sight of the red, white, and blue displayed on the street reminded Justine of Jack and the service he'd given his country. She couldn't wait to see him.

She had thought about calling him, but it was one of those situations where she didn't want her personal feelings to cloud her professional judgment. She was worried about him, but other than the temporary relief and joy of hearing his voice, didn't think anything useful would come of a conversation at present. She had no new information and Jack had assured her he'd call as soon as he had something worth sharing.

"He'll be okay," Sci remarked. "Jack, I mean."

Justine nodded. "I wasn't thinking about him."

Sci smiled mischievously. "Really?"

"Well, maybe. But you're right," she replied. "He will be okay." She heard the uncertainty in her voice and wanted to change the subject. "Where is this guy?"

They had tried the house a couple of times, ringing the bell and knocking on the front door, but there was no answer. The lime-green 1982 Volkswagen Golf parked in the driveway was registered in the name of Francis Johnson, suggesting wherever he was, he'd left without his usual means of transport.

"You want to take a look around the place?" Sci asked.

"Break in?"

Sci nodded.

"And if he walks in on us and calls the cops?"

"You can keep look out," Sci replied playfully.

"I don't think we're there yet," Justine said. "I'd rather wait."

Despite their seniority, Sci and Mo-bot could sometimes behave like a pair of rebellious teens. Perhaps it was their decades of experience that gave them the confidence to do so?

Justine's phone rang and she pulled it out to see Mo-bot's name on-screen.

"Mo," she said. "You're on speaker with me and Sci."

"The man posing as Francis Johnson doesn't have a criminal record," Mo-bot responded, "but I was able to identify him from an old photograph on Facebook. His real name is Billy Bostic."

"Why's he using a fake ID if he's clean?" Justine asked.

"Maybe because his brother, Joe Bostic, has a long criminal record for illegal gun sales and dealing in unlicensed explosives," Mo-bot replied. "Any vetting agency would find the link and no employer would take the risk of allowing him anywhere near detonators or high explosives."

"What better way to access product than to have your brother on the inside of a firm like Ryedale?" Sci remarked.

"Does the brother have any history of violence?" Justine asked.

"No," Mo-bot replied. "At least none that I can see on his record. He looks like a dealer. Nothing more. Why?"

"I want to know if he's likely to pull a gun on us if he finds us inside his brother's house," Justine said, and Sci smiled. "Thanks."

She hung up.

"You're going to get your way. Come on," Justine said, opening the driver's door. "Let's go take a look inside."

CHAPTER 30

THEY CROSSED THE street toward Francis Johnson's, or rather Billy Bostic's, two-story wood-clad home. They walked past the green Volkswagen Golf and went to the back gate. Justine reached over the top and glanced around to make sure no one was watching. She felt for and found a bolt, drew it back and opened the gate. She and Sci hurried through and he closed it behind them. They went along a narrow path between the house and the neighbor's fence and found the back door near the far corner of the building.

"I brought my tools," Sci said, reaching into his back pocket for a leather wallet that contained his lock-picking set, but as he touched the handle it moved, and when he tried the door, it swung open without resistance.

Justine and Sci exchanged a glance of surprise before heading inside. She took point and moved slowly into a modest kitchen.

The place was reasonably clean apart from two partially eaten plates of food surrounded by takeout cartons, which covered the small table. The ripe smell filling the room suggested the food had been there some hours and was beginning to turn.

"Two diners. Interrupted," Justine whispered, and Sci nodded.

They crept through the small kitchen and went into a hallway that linked the room to the front door. There was a solid wooden floor that was pockmarked and scored with age, and the walls were covered in old wallpaper that peeled here and there. The once-colorful bird pattern that adorned the paper had faded with age. There were no photographs or artwork anywhere to be seen. The living room lay to their right and Justine saw two couches and a TV through the open doorway.

A set of stairs stood to their left and she and Sci crept up to the second floor. Justine strained her senses, but all she could hear were their footsteps and the creak of the floorboards beneath them. The bare walls beside her bore the outlines of the pictures that had once lined the staircase. She couldn't shake off the nervous tightening around her stomach as they neared the top.

Justine recognized the smell when she stepped onto the landing. The sweet ripeness with a hint of the putrid stench that was to come as decay set in.

She hurried into the bedroom directly opposite the staircase and found the bodies of two men splayed on the floor. She recognized one from his Ryedale Engineering employee photograph, Francis Johnson, otherwise known as Billy Bostic, and guessed that the man lying next to him, who bore more than a passing resemblance, was his brother Joe.

Both men had been shot in the head at close range.

"We'd better call this in," Justine said.

Sci had already produced a pair of latex gloves. "Go ahead. I'll see what I can find before the police get here."

CHAPTER 31

"AND YOU DIDN'T touch or disturb anything when you found the bodies?" Otis Urban, one of the detectives leading the murder investigation, asked.

It was late afternoon by now and Justine was feeling the heat as she gave her statement to the detective. He was a short, slight man with dark hair and a heavily stubbled jaw. He had an air of intensity that reminded Justine of a hummingbird. His black suit was lined with mustard-yellow silk, which added to the mental image she had formed.

They were standing in the shade of a beech tree in the neighboring garden, but even in the shadows it was hot on this sweltering day. Justine could see Sci being interviewed by Urban's partner, Siobhan Sullivan, in a garden across the street.

Howard Avenue had been cordoned off and Bostic's house was now a crime scene, with forensic experts checking every inch of the interior and grounds. Police officers and plain-clothes detectives were canvassing the neighborhood, talking to locals about what they might have seen or heard.

"We came straight out and called 911," Justine assured Urban.

She didn't feel comfortable about misleading the detective, but Sci had insisted there was no need for them to know he had spent quite a while combing the crime scene. He had been careful, he said, and insisted that their knowing the truth would only complicate matters. A good defense lawyer would be able to say the scene had been compromised, even though Sci had been meticulous as ever.

Urban checked his notes. "Okay," he said. "I think I've got everything I need for now."

"You know where to find me if you need anything else," Justine said.

The detective nodded. "Thanks," he responded before moving toward the house.

Justine watched Sci wrap up his interview and saunter over to join her.

"Boy, it's hot," he remarked.

"You tell them what you found?" Justine asked.

"Yeah," Sci replied. "Nothing."

She responded with a skeptical look.

"I'm serious," he said. "They might recover some DNA or microfibers, but I doubt it. Looks like a professional hit. And if we hadn't identified the brother from the photo on Facebook, we would have no idea who they really were. Their wallets and phones were taken. Probably destroyed."

"You think they were killed by whoever bought the detonators?" Justine asked.

Sci nodded. "Most likely. Trying to cover his or her tracks."

"Makes sense," Justine agreed. "But we have nothing to go on."

"I didn't say that," Sci replied with a twinkle in his eye. "I sent Mo-bot some information. We'll see what she can do with it."

Justine eyed him with suspicion and shook her head. He and Mo-bot had earnt their reputations as legends within their respective fields. If anyone could find this killer, it was them.

CHAPTER 32

I WAS SITTING watching the footage being transmitted by the drones, listening to the restful sound of Zhang Daiyu sleeping. Hua had set us up in one of the Beijing office's surveillance vans, a black LDV 9 with screens, audio receivers, and data-capture systems that made the most of the information being transmitted by the bugs he'd hidden around Molly Tan's apartment.

Hua had taken away the defunct bugs we had discovered in the apartment for analysis. They were standard-issue CREPTO, the same model and design as the ones he'd installed. Intelligence agencies and private security companies throughout Asia used them.

Zhang Daiyu and I stayed in the van, which was parked around the corner from Molly Tan's building. We decided to split the day into shifts and I was on point first, monitoring the apartment while Zhang Daiyu slept in a cot at the back of the vehicle.

She was due to relieve me at 8 a.m., but she was exhausted and still suffering from the after-effects of the street attack, so I planned to let her sleep in if she didn't wake naturally.

Her breathing was deep and rhythmic. It would have sent me off to sleep too had it not been for the years of training that kept me alert and focused on the mission. There would be a time for sleep, but this wasn't it.

The apartment was completely still. Molly and her husband were in bed and their two boys were fast asleep in their bedrooms. She was one of the richest women in China, if not the world, but when it came to the fundamentals of life, her needs were the same as everyone else's.

I'd never really had to worry about money, not in the way people operating at the margins of society do, but I'd been exposed to the challenges faced by families who weren't as fortunate as the Tans. I wondered how many children could be fed and clothed with Molly Tan's fortune. Retaining just half of it would still have left her a wealthy woman, but how many lives might the other half have changed? I wasn't usually big on politics, but inequality on this scale was hard to ignore. It was of course built into the capitalist system, and was one of the distinguishing features of a functioning democracy, but China claimed to be something else. Yet still there were people like Molly Tan living here, who had so much when countless others had so little.

I couldn't quite square this in my mind.

I allowed my thoughts to wander for a time, to avoid the lure of sleep, but eventually I forced myself to focus on the job in hand: watching the Tans' apartment. Nothing much happened and I settled into the rhythm of the sleeping household, disturbed only by the occasional deep breath or snore.

Then, at a little after 5 a.m., the peaceful scene was interrupted by something completely unexpected. I saw the living-room door open. The live video feed from the surveillance device in the air vent above the living area showed two men in ski masks creep into view.

They were both carrying pistols fitted with long suppressors and I had little doubt they had come to murder Molly Tan.

CHAPTER 33

"ZHANG DAIYU, WAKE up," I said, and she stirred immediately. "We've got a problem."

I pointed to the screen showing the two masked men creeping through Molly Tan's apartment. One was slight, the other tall and muscular. They were both dressed in black and moved with the grace of leopards.

She rolled off the cot and hurried over to join me as I pulled out my phone and dialed a number.

On a second screen, I saw Molly roll over in bed, fumble for her vibrating phone, and answer me.

"It's Jack Morgan. Don't hang up," I said. "You need to move fast. There are two men in your apartment. They have guns and they're coming for you."

I saw her sit bolt upright.

Behind me, Zhang Daiyu was making another phone call and

rattling off information in Mandarin. I guessed she was on the phone to the police.

"Do you have a panic room?" I asked.

"Yes," Molly replied.

"Go there now," I said. "Do not switch on any lights."

"Okay," she replied. She sounded terrified but had the presence of mind to act, whispering to Bryan.

On-screen, they got out of bed and hurried from their room. Molly went right and Bryan went left. They ran into their children's bedrooms and grabbed their sons.

The masked men were almost through the living room, near the corridor leading to the bedrooms.

"Hurry," I told Molly.

She and her husband plus the two boys emerged into the corridor at the same time. They all ran away from the door to the living room, heading for what looked like a dead end.

One of the masked men opened the door to the bedroom hallway and his companion crept inside with his pistol in the ready position.

I switched surveillance devices to pick up Molly and her family reaching the end of the corridor. She touched a section of marble wall, which illuminated around her palm, and a large panel in the wall retracted.

The light of the palm scanner drew the intruders' attention. The leader shouted something and opened fire as Molly and her family ran into the panic room. Shots flared in the darkness and bullets struck the panel as it slid back into position. The gunmen sprinted toward it as it sealed itself shut, but before it locked flush, the first gunman shoved his pistol between panel and wall, jamming the mechanism.

"They're not giving up," I said to Molly. "Do you have access to the entryphone system?"

"Yes," she said.

"The police are on their way," Zhang Daiyu told me.

On-screen, the gunmen were packing the gap between the panel and wall with what looked like explosives. "We can't wait for them to arrive. We don't have time. They're gonna blow the door."

I opened the side of the van and jumped out. Zhang Daiyu followed me. We sprinted across the street and raced toward Molly's building.

"Zhang Daiyu and I are coming in. Open the door," I said as we neared the block's main entrance.

A buzzer sounded and the door closest to us clicked open. I pulled it wide and Zhang Daiyu and I sprinted across the cavernous, deserted lobby.

"Which elevator?" I asked.

"Four," Molly replied, and the doors opened.

We ran inside, and with a growing sense of frustration I watched the doors slowly close.

I hoped we'd make it in time.

CHAPTER 34

THE ELEVATOR TOOK us to the forty-eighth floor, and we raced across the lobby toward the open front door. We were a few feet away when the sound of an explosion thundered out of the apartment, the building shook and the lights flickered. Zhang Daiyu and I stopped running and exchanged looks of concern

"Molly?" I said into my phone. "Are you okay?"

There was no answer.

"Molly," I repeated more urgently. "Are you there?"

"They're coming," she said, her voice tinny and distant-sounding but still enough to trigger a wave of relief in me. I was glad to hear she was alive. "We're going into the service corridor. It's off the elevator lobby. Third panel is a secret door."

"Third panel," I said to Zhang Daiyu. "Check that side."

I scoured the wall on the left while she felt around on the right. I heard a catch pop as I pushed a panel of marble, and when I pulled the three-feet-wide section of wall open, saw a dimly lit corridor beyond.

"You go this way," I said. "Find the family. I'll take the apartment."

Zhang Daiyu nodded and went into the concealed corridor. I shut the panel behind her and ran through the front door of the apartment.

I crept into the huge living room. No movement. Clear. I sprinted across the wide space and ran into the hallway leading to the bedrooms. At the far end, you couldn't miss the devastation around the entrance to the panic room. A huge hole had been blown in the wall. If Molly and her family had been close to the explosives, they would have been done for.

I raced toward it. The gunmen couldn't have got—

The taller of the two assailants stepped through the hole. I was no more than three paces away, and he was just as surprised as I was. But I recovered more quickly and his hesitation gave me the opportunity I needed.

I drove my shoulder into his gut as he tried to raise his pistol. The force of the impact knocked the gun from his hand, and it clattered to the floor. He pummeled his fists into my back as we tumbled through the hole. We landed on the rubble and wreckage of the explosion.

On my feet first, I sensed movement behind me. Across the smoke- and dust-filled ruins of the panic room, I saw the second gunman raise his pistol. He was no more than ten feet away and would have had an easy shot if his companion hadn't tried to tackle me at that precise moment.

I grabbed the big man's shoulders and spun him in front of me as the gunman opened fire. A brace of bullets hit my captive in the chest, and he cried out and groaned before going limp. I pushed him ahead of me and drove him at the second gunman, who swiftly sidestepped.

I tackled him as his companion landed on the floor, dead. We traded blows and wrestled. I held his arm to stop him using his pistol. He kicked at my legs, but I sucked up the pain and headbutted him. He staggered back, dazed, but didn't drop his gun. While he came to his senses, I ran back to the blast hole and found his accomplice's gun. I pivoted, raising the pistol as the masked gunman focused.

"Drop your weapon!" I commanded.

The panic room was fifteen feet square, strewn with the remains of a couple of bunk beds, some supplies, a video and communication console, and computer gear. There was no sign of any separate exit. Molly and her family's escape route was a mystery that had frustrated their would-be assassins. It also meant the gunman thought there was only one means of escape—through me.

He raised his gun and fired wildly, forcing me to reply. His aim was off, perhaps because of injuries, but mine was true and I hit him twice in the chest. He went down instantly.

I hated taking another's life but here I had no choice. Yet another death to haunt my dreams, but at this moment I couldn't let emotion get the better of survival instinct. I quickly used my phone to photograph both dead men in the flickering light of the ruined panic room. I didn't recognize either of them. When I'd taken pictures of their faces, I pulled back their sleeves and saw the same tattoo as on the man who'd planted the bombs at the Beijing office and attacked us on our way back from Qincheng Prison: two dragons coiled around a third larger one. There was no longer any doubting it: this was gang insignia.

I heard distant sirens. Lots of them. I dropped the gun amid the wreckage and hurried out of the apartment. I took the elevator down to the ground-floor lobby, where I found Zhang Daiyu with Molly Tan and her family.

"What just happened?" Molly asked me. "How did you know about those men?"

"They won't be a threat to you or your family again," I replied, ignoring the question.

The sirens were getting closer now.

"We need to leave," Zhang Daiyu said.

"We owe you our lives, Mr. Morgan," Molly said. "If there's ever anything I can—"

I cut her off before she had a chance to finish her sentence. "Tell me the truth. Tell me why you hired my firm to investigate David Zhou."

Molly looked toward her husband, who stood a few feet away with their children. The boys were distressed and he was doing his best to console them. He nodded to her.

"A man came to my office a while ago," she said. "He had photographs of my family taken from inside our home. He said he would kill us if I didn't hire your people to investigate David Zhou." She hesitated. "I'm sorry. He told me not to tell anyone. I didn't think people would get hurt."

"Seems they were going to kill you anyway," I said. "Did you know him? The man who came to see you?"

She shook her head, so I produced my phone and showed her the photos I'd taken of the dead gunmen.

Her eyes lit up with recognition when she saw the picture of the man I'd shot.

"That's him."

"Do you know who he is?" I asked.

"No. I'm sorry."

"I do," Zhang Daiyu said to me. "And I'll tell you if we can just get out of here."

The sirens were very close now. I nodded.

"What should I tell the police?" Molly asked.

"The truth," I replied. "Tell them we saved you and your family. It might do us some favors."

Zhang Daiyu started running and I followed her.

Within moments we were back in the Private surveillance van, heading away from what was certain to become a very busy crime scene.

CHAPTER 35

JUSTINE AND SCI were in the tech lab at Private New York, watching Mo-bot analyze a data set she'd pulled from the cell mast near the house where Billy Bostic and his brother had been found. Rafael had heard about the murders on the local news and had joined them.

Justine had always thought the handsome Spaniard something of a good-time socialite, but the attack on Jessie and Lewis, the discovery of explosives at Private, and now this double homicide had brought out a different side to him. He leant against the desk, dark and brooding, smartly dressed as ever in a three-piece suit. His initial shock and grief had given way to somber resolve, and this was reflected in his switch back to more formal attire.

Justine's phone rang and she was relieved to see it was Jack calling.

"Hey," she said. "How are you?"

"Okay," he replied. "You?"

"Same. We think we found the guy who sourced the detonators for the bombs in the New York office."

"He talking?" Jack asked.

"Not really. He's dead. His brother too. Looks like a professional hit."

Jack exhaled sharply.

"Mo-bot is working on something to try and track the killer."

"We ran into more heat here," Jack revealed. "Someone just tried to kill one of our clients. Molly Tan. She hired us to check out David Zhou. Turns out someone blackmailed her into engaging Private. The whole case was a set-up."

"Are you serious?" Justine exclaimed.

"Deadly. Zhang Daiyu recognized one of the men from her time with Beijing PD. His name was Wang Yichen—"

Justine cut him off. "Was?"

"He's dead now," Jack replied. "Zhang Daiyu told me he was a low-level enforcer. Street muscle for an underworld kingpin called Liu Bao."

"You want us to dig into this guy? See what we can find?" Justine asked.

"Yeah. The team here is on it, but let's see if there is any international intel on Liu," Jack replied. "I'm also going to send you photos of a tattoo. Two dragons wrapped around a larger one. The guy who shot at Zhang Daiyu and me, and planted the bombs in the Beijing office, had one, and so did the two men who attacked Molly Tan and her family. Zhang

Daiyu doesn't recognize it, so we've got the team here looking into it . . ."

". . . And you want us to see if it's showed up in any FBI or Interpol reports," Justine finished his sentence.

"Exactly," he replied.

"We'll get on it as soon as I have the photos," she assured him.

"So we've got Private being targeted on two continents by assailants with similar MOs. I wonder if the similarities extend to the way they set us up?"

"You think maybe the client who engaged us to investigate Ivor Yeadon was also coerced?" Justine asked, referring to the Wall Street financier Jessie and Lewis had been surveilling.

"Maybe," Jack responded. "It's worth checking out."

"Will do," Justine said. "You be careful, Jack. Anyone who's prepared to kill a family—"

"Won't think twice about a war dog like me," he interrupted. "I'll be careful. You too."

"Love you."

"Love you too," he replied, before hanging up.

"Jack?" Sci asked. "How is he?"

Justine nodded. "He's okay. He wants us to talk to the client who engaged us to investigate Ivor Yeadon." She turned to Rafael. "Who was it?"

"His name is Lawrence Finch. I've spoken to him already. There's nothing unusual about him. He's a dead end."

"I might just check him out again," Justine said. "See if any of our new information sparks anything."

Rafael nodded slowly and looked as though he was about to

respond, but Mo-bot leant back in her chair and pointed at one of the three monitors in front of her.

"There we go."

"There we go what?" Sci asked.

"So I ran the cell-mast data for all phones pinged in the area around Howard Avenue, between nine and eleven p.m., which, based on the abandoned meal and the state of the Bostics' bodies, is when Sci estimates the shooting took place," Mo-bot explained, obviously quite pleased with herself.

"I then cross-referenced with the masts near the apartment where Jessie and Lewis were shot and with the mast nearest this building a week prior to the discovery of the bombs. There is only one phone that's been to all three places during those times."

Justine looked at the screen Mo-bot was pointing to and realized it showed a birds-eye view of a location. There was a street, a building, and a little flashing beacon marking the position of the cell phone in question.

"Even the most ruthless killer can be careless," Mo-bot remarked. "And no one would expect anyone to do this kind of analysis. Given the fact the phone has kept moving after the Bostics' deaths, we can safely assume it doesn't belong to them."

"You're a superstar," Sci remarked.

"It was your idea," she replied.

"When the mutual admiration fest is over, shall we figure out what we're going to do?" Justine said.

"I think we should check out whoever owns this phone," Rafael suggested. "We don't have enough to involve the police. There's no probable cause. Could be coincidental."

Sci nodded. "It's circumstantial so far. Any decent attorney could argue this person's presence at the locations was pure coincidence. But in our experience, how likely is that?"

"I say we check it out and see if we can get any other evidence," Rafael said.

The lawyer wasn't part of the investigative team, but his instincts were good.

Justine nodded. "You and Sci find this phone and identify its owner," she told Mo-bot. "I'm going to talk to our client, Lawrence Finch, and find out why he engaged us to investigate Ivor Yeadon."

"You don't want us to tag along?" Mo-bot asked.

"I think the dream team already has their hands full." Justine smiled, and got replies in kind from Sci and Mo-bot.

"I'll help them, Justine," Rafael suggested. "I want to help bring this guy to justice."

They all exchanged nods.

"Okay," Mo-bot said. "Let's go see if we can catch a killer."

CHAPTER 36

JUSTINE HAD TRIED Lawrence Finch at his firm, Leyland & Co., but had been told he was working from home, so she'd checked his address on the Private client-engagement file and taken a cab uptown to a fully serviced apartment block off Third Avenue, near Union Square Park.

She spent the cab ride learning as much as she could about their client. According to LinkedIn, various reports on TheStreet and other purported insider blogs, Finch was a fast-living, high-flying banker with over $10 billion under management in his fund.

Fifteen minutes after she'd left Leyland & Co., the cab pulled up outside a striking contemporary building with smoked-glass windows, golden metalwork, and more than a hint of Trump Tower about it.

Justine paid the driver and a doorman in a green half-coat and matching pants helped her out of the cab.

"Visiting, ma'am?" he asked.

"I'm here to see Lawrence Finch," she said, crossing the sidewalk. They were on the shaded side of the street but Justine could still feel the heat pressing in on her.

"Is he expecting you, ma'am?" The doorman's smile was well practiced and didn't waver.

"He is," Justine lied. "He's in apartment 17A, right?"

"That's right, ma'am. You can go straight up."

The doorman walked Justine into the lobby and nodded to the building concierge, who stood behind a black marble desk on the other side of the glittering, gilded space.

"Visitor for Mr. Finch," the doorman announced, and something about his tone suggested an unspoken message. She guessed Finch must have a lot of female visitors.

"Far elevator," the doorman said, gesturing at a trio of gold doors. "Seventeenth floor. Mr. Finch's apartment will be on your left."

The far elevator door opened as Justine approached.

"Thanks," she told the doorman, who smiled and nodded.

There were no buttons in the elevator. A moment after she stepped inside the car it started to rise. There was a gentle chiming sound as it reached the seventeenth floor. When the door opened, Justine stepped out into a large lobby. There were only three doors visible, all black and double-width, discreetly numbered. Apartment 17A was to her left but when she rang the buzzer there was no answer.

She waited and tried again. Still no response.

She tried the door and was surprised to discover the big gold handle gave at her touch. The latch clicked open. Her stomach churned with a sense of déjà vu as she recalled the discovery of the bodies at the house on Howard Avenue. Justine pushed the door wide and instantly knew something was wrong. The apartment was still and silent and there was the familiar and unmistakable sweet smell of decay.

Justine took out her phone and moved forward. She was in a wide, bright hallway with windows overlooking Union Square Park. She moved toward a set of double doors at the end of the hall but stopped when she passed an open archway to her right. It looked like a home office, but it wasn't the desks, shelves full of books, or multi-screen trading station that caught her eye. It was the body on the floor.

Justine dialed 911.

She stepped further into the room and could see the body wasn't in an advanced state of decomposition. She could clearly identify it as Lawrence Finch from his LinkedIn profile and news articles. He was lying prostrate, his face turned toward her. Both hands were stretched out ahead of him and three bullet wounds had stained his white T-shirt with blood. He was in boxer shorts, suggesting whoever had shot him had disturbed him in the night. Justine was no forensics expert, but she'd been around Sci long enough to know the basics. She nudged Finch's left arm with her shoe and saw it move easily, which meant rigor mortis had subsided. Judging from the lack of bloating, puffiness, or serious decay, he'd been dead between forty-eight and seventy-two hours. She moved to get a better view of Finch's hands and saw they were reaching into a circular safe that had been concealed beneath a retractable floor tile.

She noticed a trail of blood from the desk to the safe.

Finch had dragged himself across the room after being shot. Why? What was so important? What would make a man expend such effort in his dying moments?

Justine knew she shouldn't touch anything, but she had to know what would drive someone to such lengths. She crouched down and pulled his hands from the safe. They were cold and clammy. She recoiled in disgust. Experienced as she was in being around death, she still didn't find it easy.

There were thousands of dollars in the safe and a couple of large Swiss watches, but neither Finch nor his killer seemed to have been interested in them. Justine found a digital Dictaphone in Finch's right hand, and when she prized it from his stiff fingers saw it had been recording for ten hours. She stopped the device and rewound it to the start of the recording.

She heard heavy rapid breathing.

"My name is Lawrence Finch," said a man's voice. "I've been shot. The gunman, he . . . he was Asian . . . Chinese, I think. But . . . but I'm convinced it has something to do with the investigation into Ivor Yeadon."

Justine listened intently.

"The man who got me into this. The man who . . ." Finch took frequent gasping breaths. "He said I would be exposed. He'd tell the world about my sex addiction. He said . . ." Further gasps. "Said I'd be ruined. His price was me hiring Private to investigate some guy called Ivor Yeadon. Never even met him."

More shallow, rapid breathing. "Man who blackmailed me into hiring Private thought he was anonymous, but I took a photo of him. It's . . ." Justine could tell he hadn't long left by this point, and prayed he'd managed to finish. Some indecipherable words followed. Then something she could understand. "Photo . . . in safe."

There was a thud, and then the recording went silent.

Justine stopped the Dictaphone. She reached inside the safe and felt around but found nothing. She craned over Finch's body and saw something: a curled photograph pressed against the side of the cylindrical interior.

She pulled it out and turned it over to see a face she recognized. Shot surreptitiously, the image was taken from a low angle and was slightly blurred, but there was no mistaking who it was.

Rafael Lucas.

Disbelief was quickly followed by a wave of nausea. She put out one hand to steady herself.

Rafael?

No, he couldn't be involved in this, could he? Why? How?

She took out her phone and dialed, her hands trembling, already fearing the worst.

If Rafael was part of whatever was going on, Sci and Mo-bot were heading into a trap.

CHAPTER 37

THE PHONE MO-BOT had traced was located in a building on 60th Street near Eighth Avenue, in the heart of Brooklyn's bustling Chinatown district. Trucks lined the sidewalks delivering catering packs of food and crates of beverages to the restaurants and supermarkets that jostled for space in the vibrant neighborhood. People crowded the sidewalks, testing the fruit and vegetables on display or vying for outside seating at the restaurants.

Sci steered the Private pool vehicle along the crowded street, taking in the hustle and bustle, trying to ignore the enticing scents that were invading the Nissan Rogue's ice-cold air-conditioning system. Dinner would have to wait. They had a job to do.

He glanced over at Mo-bot, studying her laptop. Rafael was in the back and Sci caught his eye for a moment before the Spaniard turned his attention to his cell phone. He seemed on edge, no doubt nervous about what they might face when they encountered the owner of the phone.

"It's that one," Mo-bot said, pointing to a block of apartments above a restaurant. The block was 1980s redbrick with large curved bay windows in white steel frames. It would have looked Art Deco were it not for the giant green-and-gold letters that dominated the side of the building. They left no one in any doubt that the restaurant was called the Golden Lotus.

"There are a bunch of short-term rentals in the building," Rafael said, consulting his phone. "They're listed on Airbnb and a few other sites."

"Fits the bill," Sci remarked. "Out-of-town gun for hire. This is a busy neighborhood. People won't notice someone new coming and going."

Sci steered around a delivery truck and turned right into an alleyway that ran alongside the Golden Lotus. They could see inside the restaurant through the large bay windows. The interior was also decorated in green and gold and was packed with diners. Servers deftly navigated their way around the tables carrying platefuls of food.

Sci pulled into a small parking lot behind the restaurant and they all took a moment to study the building.

"Do you know which apartment?" he asked.

Mo-bot shook her head. "But I do have a way of finding out."

She opened a small flight case she had brought with her and produced a tablet computer that looked little larger than a normal phone.

"This device will home in on the target phone's Bluetooth

signature when we get within range. We walk the building and we'll find him."

"Shall I wait out here?" Rafael asked. "Keep a look out for anyone entering after you?"

"That makes sense," Sci agreed. It was fair enough if Rafael didn't have the stomach for walking into the unknown, he wasn't even meant to be in the field. "Call me if you see anything suspicious."

Rafael nodded and Sci and Mo-bot got out. Mo-bot switched on the Bluetooth tracker as they hurried across the street. The sweet–savory smells from the restaurant were strong now, and Sci's stomach started growling at him. Some people say heat kills the appetite, but he had always found it stimulated his and this summer evening was sending it into overdrive.

They found the entrance to the apartment block next to the Golden Lotus's staff door, and Sci used his lock-picking tools to get them inside. A small lobby lined with mailboxes led to a set of stairs. A tiny box elevator stood to one side, but neither of them moved toward it.

"Stairs?" Sci asked. He had no desire to be trapped inside a metal coffin in enemy territory.

Mo-bot nodded and they started up the steep staircase.

The interior was a mix of redbrick and white plaster turned dirty gray by time. The smell from the restaurant filled every nook. In his current frame of mind, Sci would have found living in this block complete torture.

They reached the second floor and walked along a corridor that ran through the center of the building. Mo-bot checked her device every step of the way and shook her head when they reached the end. They retraced their steps and climbed to the next floor.

They had made it to the second apartment on the third floor when Mo-bot raised her hand.

"I think it's this one," she whispered.

Sci's phone vibrated in his pocket. He pulled it out, expecting to see Rafael's name, but was surprised to see Justine's.

"I can't talk right now," he whispered, turning away from the door so he wouldn't alert whoever was inside.

"You don't need to talk," she replied urgently. "Just listen. I think Rafael might be involved in this. If he is—"

"We're walking into a trap."

Sci heard a door open and turned toward it. His stomach dropped as his eyes drew level with the broad chest of a heavyset Chinese man with a crew cut and pitiless eyes. He was holding a matt-black machine pistol.

CHAPTER 38

"INSIDE," THE GUNMAN said. He was barefoot, wearing a gray muscle vest and loose black trousers. It didn't look like he'd prepared himself for a fight and he had the air of someone who hadn't had time to set a proper trap. Had Rafael warned him? Phoned him from the parking lot? The thought fueled Sci's mounting sense of indignation and anger.

He knew death waited for them in that apartment and there was no way either of them could afford to cross the threshold.

"It's for you," he said, offering the gunman his phone.

The man frowned, and the ease with which the lines of his face manifested the expression suggested he spent too much of his life feeling displeased. Sci thrust the phone at the guy with both hands, aware that a mistake now would get both him and Mo-bot shot. Someone willing to plant bombs and assassinate people wouldn't be shy of pulling the trigger in an otherwise deserted corridor.

As he thrust his phone across the space between them, Sci simultaneously reached into the long inside pocket of the phone case for his Hail Mary fall-back. This was a Life Card. About the size of a credit card, it was a single-shot collapsible pistol he kept next to his phone in case he was ever robbed. He'd been working crime scenes long enough to know that a single shot could make all the difference.

The gunman shook his head, rejecting the phone and waving his gun at Sci. "Inside."

In one movement Sci slid the Life Card out of the case, popped the button that activated the tiny trigger and shot the suspect in the thigh. The gun's report sounded like a firecracker, but the bullet was potent enough and tore into the gunman's leg, causing him to cry out.

"Run!" Sci shouted, grabbing Mo-bot by the arm and heading for the stairs.

Most people would have dropped what they were holding and clutched at their leg, but not this guy. He was too well trained. He cursed in Mandarin and opened fire. The pain and shock caused by his wound must have thrown off his aim because the bullet missed them and bit into the wall beside the stairs.

As they started down them Sci glanced back over his shoulder. The gunman had lurched along the corridor after them, dragging his wounded leg behind him, firing at them. They disappeared from view as they ran past the turn in the stairs, but still bullets chewed the brickwork beside them, throwing clouds of dust everywhere. The gunman was leaning over the safety rail of the stairs and firing at random into the stairwell. His gun wasn't a firecracker, it was a cannon, and the sound of it drew residents to their doors.

Sci and Mo-bot could see faces peering out at them as they reached the second-floor landing.

"Get back inside! Lock your doors! There's a gunman!" Sci yelled. "Call the cops!"

More bullets came from above, cracking the hard tile floor but wildly off target. The guy was firing blind, unable to see them. The sight and sounds sent the residents back inside. Numerous doors slammed shut at once.

Sci and Mo-bot ran down the stairs and through the first-floor lobby, bursting out into the alleyway. Sci was disgusted to see a look of surprise on Rafael's face when he looked over at them. The normally suave lawyer tried to compose himself as Sci and Mo-bot raced across the parking lot. Sci had expected him to run, but the guy was clearly going to try and brazen it out. He stayed in the back of the Nissan Rogue as Sci and Mo-bot jumped in the front. Sci hit the ignition button, gunned the engine and drove out of the lot.

A new barrage of pistol shots started as they reached the alleyway access, coming from a third-floor window above them. A few bullets thudded into the hood, but they didn't slow down the Nissan. Sci floored it and swung onto Eighth Avenue, putting as much distance between him and their would-be murderer as possible.

The murderer's accomplice was a different matter. Sci wanted to keep Rafael as close as possible.

"Take this," he said handing Mo-bot the Life Card gun. Rafael wouldn't know the single shot had been used. "If he so much as moves, shoot him."

"What the hell is happening?" Rafael asked.

"Yeah," Mo-bot said. "What the hell is happening?"

"He betrayed us. He betrayed all of us," Sci revealed, glaring at Rafael in the rear-view mirror. "He sold us out to the shooter back there. The man who killed Lewis, who put Jessie in the hospital. The man who tried to kill us all."

Sci glanced at Mo-bot and saw her eyes widen as the implications sunk in.

"You're crazy," Rafael tried, but Sci could sense his lack of conviction.

"Shut up. If he tells one more lie, I want you to shoot him."

Mo-bot nodded and turned in her seat to face Rafael. She pointed the tiny muzzle at him.

"I know what you did. Soon everyone's going to know. I can hardly bring myself to look at you right now." Sci was seething. Calm and analytical as he normally was, it was hard not to take an attempt on his life personally. "How could you do this? How could you betray your friends?"

The lawyer's facade crumpled. Tears welled in his eyes.

"I'm sorry," Rafael said "I'm so sorry. I didn't know. I . . . He lied to me. Blackmailed me. You don't understand. I didn't know what he had planned. I'm sorry. Please believe me, I didn't want to be part of this."

"I'm not interested in your excuses," Sci replied. "I'm interested in what you know. We're going to go somewhere nice and quiet and you're going to tell us everything."

CHAPTER 39

NO ONE HAD followed them when they'd left Brooklyn. Thirty minutes later they were driving through open countryside, near Plainfield, New Jersey. Fields and woodland surrounded them and there were very few vehicles on the quiet country road as they headed west. Sci felt as though he was on the very edge of the world, that anything might happen here.

Mo-bot had called Justine to let her know they were okay, and tell her of their plan to interrogate Rafael, the traitor.

He exuded nervous tension as they turned off a farm track onto a rough gravel road that cut through a wooded area. After a quarter of a mile, Sci pulled to a halt on the verge.

Mo-bot turned to face Rafael and Sci did likewise. Mo-bot handed him the Life Card pistol, which he held aimed at Rafael's gut. There were tears in Rafael's eyes and his hands were trembling. This was not a man who would have to be forced to confess.

"So, here's what's going to happen," Sci said. "You're going to talk and we're going to listen."

There was a moment's hesitation.

"Well, get talking," he added, brandishing the gun.

Rafael gulped and nodded.

"Alison was taken two weeks ago," he said, referring to his wife. "She was snatched from the street."

Sci saw Mo-bot register the significance of Rafael's words and guessed where this was going.

"I got a call from the Chinese man . . ."

Rafael broke down sobbing and took more than a moment to pull himself together.

"I'm so sorry. I'm . . . There's nothing I can say to excuse my actions, I know, but I got a phone call from the man you just saw in that building. He calls himself Angel. He told me to meet him if I ever wanted to see Alison alive again. He knew everything about us, about our families. He said I was being watched at all times. I wanted to come to you, to Jack. I wanted to go to the police, but he told me she'd be killed if I spoke to a single person. I didn't know what to do. I didn't know . . ." He trailed off, broken, and took some deep breaths before resuming. "He wanted information, but when I met him—"

"Where?" Sci asked. "Where did you meet?"

"A mall in Pelham, at the food court," Rafael replied.

Busy and anonymous, Sci reflected.

"When I met him, he told me he wanted someone on the inside, providing information, steering things a certain way.

I didn't know what he was going to do to Jessie and Lewis, I swear it!"

"But you knew what he wanted to do today," Mo-bot cut in, and Rafael looked ashamed.

"He said he'd kill Alison if his mission didn't succeed. He said he'd kill her." Rafael wiped his eyes. "I didn't know what to do. What was I supposed to do?"

Sci ignored the question. "What mission?" he asked.

"I don't know. He told me to make sure you came to New York. All of you: Maureen, Seymour, and Justine."

"He named us?" Mo-bot asked.

Rafael nodded. "I'm so sorry. I never thought it would be like this."

"What about the protocols we have in place for coercion and duress?" Mo-bot said. "God, Rafael, we're your friends!"

"I wasn't thinking about protocol, I was thinking about my wife! I'm sorry. I thought I had no choice. I know you can never forgive me, but I'm sorry. I truly am."

"Did you give up Lewis and Jessie?" Mo-bot asked. "Did you give this Angel their location?"

Fresh tears sprang to Rafael's eyes as he nodded.

Mo-bot shook her head wistfully. "You're going to have to answer for that." She turned to Sci. "What do you think?"

"We need to find Alison." He paused. "We find her, Angel won't be far away."

"Agreed," Mo-bot said. "He'll have flown the apartment by now, but he has to stay close to his hostage. She must be somewhere near to where we were."

"He give you any proof of life?" Sci asked Rafael.

"I get to speak to her once a day."

"Then she's definitely alive. Let's find her, save her, and catch this guy," Sci said. He glared at Rafael. "Then you're going to answer for what you've done."

CHAPTER 40

"THIS ISN'T THE kind of place I'd expect to find street criminals," I said as Zhang Daiyu and I crossed a broad plaza.

It was mid-morning and we were in the financial district of Beijing, near its economic heart, heading for the Liu Investments building, which could only be described as an architectural marvel. Constructed from glass, steel, and composite materials, the silver structure stood twenty storys high, shaped like an eye with curved steel edges that glittered in the hazy morning sunshine. It wasn't the largest building in the district, but it was the one that most easily caught the imagination. It was situated in a landscaped plaza with gently contoured walkways, clearly designed to be the focal point.

Zhang Daiyu and I had returned to the workers' hostel and slept for a few hours, me on the floor, her in the bed, before resuming our investigation. On the drive over, she had briefed me on what she knew about Liu Bao, the man who'd once been the underworld boss of Wang Yichen, the guy I'd shot at Molly Tan's apartment. Liu had started out as a street criminal, which was where she'd first encountered him. He'd been implicated in the drugs trade, but was clever and slippery. Zhang Daiyu and her colleagues had never been able to build a case against him. He quickly climbed the ladder to become a gang boss—a combination of ruthlessness, intelligence, and a reputation for honoring his word led to his stratospheric rise. Liu Bao had transformed himself from street thug to moneyed villain. He now owned an investment firm that made risky, highly speculative bets around the world, but Zhang Daiyu suspected the business was just a front to launder money from Liu's criminal activities, which she believed had now expanded to include international arms dealing. Zhang Daiyu suspected Liu Bao was protected. She didn't see how someone so obviously crooked could rise so high without some powerful guardian angels.

"This is exactly where you will find gangsters," she told me, gesturing to the skyscrapers that surrounded us. "And monsters. Criminals have always been attracted to money and there is much more of it here than there is on the street."

She was right, of course, and I nodded as we entered the Liu Investments building. Security was very obviously tight, with manned gates, metal detectors, and an X-ray machine blocking the path to the elevators. We went to a long wooden reception desk that lay to our right and Zhang Daiyu spoke to the receptionist, who smiled, nodded, and gestured toward a seating area beside an indoor lily pond filled with koi. Half a dozen security guards in beige suits were posted around the place, eyeing staff and visitors.

We sat in silence, watching a soundless video on a huge wall display. It showed inspirational scenes of people at work, dramatic Chinese landscapes and images from industrial manufacturing processes. Glossy and well produced, it was all style over substance. The Liu Investments logo appeared at the end.

After a few minutes, a woman in a white blouse and green pencil skirt came to greet us.

"Mr. Morgan, Detective Zhang Daiyu, Mr. Liu will see you now."

She took us through security and we rode an attended glass elevator to the twentieth floor, passing through the very center of the eye. There was no chit-chat, although our guide did smile at us politely throughout. Distant, but not cold.

We emerged into a large seating area that was open to both sides of the building, offering dual-aspect views of the city. There were two women dressed similarly to our guide at desks near some imposing double doors. They looked up but didn't smile as our guide took us through into Liu Bao's office. He had the same magnificent dual view of the city, but his office was much larger than the lobby where his assistants worked. There were three separate seating areas, each with leather couches and chairs, a boardroom table, sculptures, traditional Chinese art. Behind a huge desk that stood midway between the two glass sides of the building was Liu Bao.

He said something to our guide, who withdrew, then he stood and came toward us.

"I would offer you a drink but you would only refuse, perhaps thinking it was laced with some toxin or other."

He smiled in a way that made it impossible to tell whether he had just made a joke or a threat.

Money could solve a lot of problems but it couldn't solve Liu Bao's biggest challenge, which was that even in this opulent, impressive space he reeked of violence and death. His nose had been broken in the distant past and he hadn't bothered with corrective surgery. His muscles shifted like a wary animal's under the camouflage of his black tailored suit. His eyes were as dead and empty as an ancient haunted house, as though nothing in the world could ever bring him joy.

I knew a pitiless sociopath when I saw one.

"I'd offer you a seat but you probably wouldn't take that either." Liu Bao drew closer to me. "You are a very proud man, Mr. Morgan."

I knew he was trying to test me, maybe goad me, but I was wise to his game.

"We ran into an old pal of yours . . . Wang Yichen," I said.

I didn't expect a reaction and he didn't give me one.

"It doesn't matter how long I spend on the right side of the law, some people will always see only my past." He looked pointedly at Zhang Daiyu. "I have put it behind me. I wish others would too. I haven't seen Wang Yichen in many years."

Zhang Daiyu responded with a single scornful word.

"You can call me a liar if you wish, but that doesn't affect the truth of my statement," Liu Bao said. "And truth is what matters. You work for this man now. You are not a police officer anymore.

You work for a private citizen. An American. And like America, his power rests on his ability to convince people he is powerful. It is a trick of the mind. When you realize a country that has lost in Vietnam, Iraq, and Afghanistan cannot be powerful, you understand why they want you to believe a lie."

"Power comes in many forms," I said. "It doesn't have to stem from fear."

"I'm not afraid of you," Zhang Daiyu told Liu Bao sharply. He just smiled. "You're old school. A believer in Chinese might and the supremacy of the party. You represent a dying belief system. The people want rights along with responsibilities."

"A dying belief system?" he scoffed. "There is nothing but life in *my* China. It is only now that we are beginning to take our proper place in the world, and I am happy to make my own small contribution. Through my businesses, of course."

"What happened to Shang Li?" I asked. "Where is he?"

Liu Bao smiled and I wanted nothing more than to wipe the expression off his smug face, but I restrained myself.

"I don't know anyone of that name. If you've been careless with the security of your friends, Mr. Morgan, I'm afraid I can't help you."

Zhang Daiyu touched my arm, to soothe more than restrain me, but she needn't have worried. I'd been goaded by men like this before and I knew better than to let them get to me.

"You sit here atop your little mountain, indulging yourself in dreams of empire and conquest," I told him. "Your view of geopolitics isn't my concern. But if I find out you were involved in what happened to Shang Li and his team, and the targeting of me and my people, there isn't a force on earth that will save you from me."

Liu Bao looked at Zhang Daiyu and grinned derisively. "See? They need you to believe they're powerful. That's why the era of America is over. They have no way of backing up their threats."

He held the smile as he turned to face me. I glared at him in reply.

"Let's go," I said. "We're done here."

I headed for the door and Zhang Daiyu followed. I had everything I needed from this visit.

His body language, the subject matter, even the triumphant tone of his voice, told me he was involved in what was happening.

Now all I had to do was prove it.

CHAPTER 41

ZHANG DAIYU AND I said nothing while our guide escorted us out of the building. As we rode the elevator to the first floor, I found myself reflecting on a world that rewards men such as Liu Bao. He was a criminal and I strongly suspected he'd had a hand in the deaths of my colleagues and the trouble we'd faced ever since, but he sat on top of the world, while so many good people struggled to get by. Someone with power protected and facilitated Liu's interests because he was useful to them or shared the same beliefs. A person simply couldn't accumulate such wealth and influence in a country like China without back-up from friends in high places, and I wondered who they were and how he was useful to them.

Our guide smiled as we reached the first floor. She led us through the lobby to an exit.

"Goodbye," she said, and continued smiling as she watched us leave.

"I hate that man," Zhang Daiyu said the moment we stepped outside. "I hated that we could never get to him when I was in the police, and I hate him now. He was almost taunting us."

"Agreed," I replied. "We should put him under surveillance."

"He was always so careful."

"Then we need to be on point. We've got to find out what he's up to and why he's involved in a plot to target Private."

Zhang Daiyu nodded. "I will talk to Hua."

I will always be grateful for two things about that day: the gentle summer breeze that took the edge off the humid heat, and the bright sunshine. That same breeze also applied just enough force to the bullet aimed at Zhang Daiyu's head to send it wide, slamming into the concrete slabs ten paces behind her, and the bright sunshine glinted off the scope of a sniper's rifle on the roof opposite, allowing me to fix the gunman's position once I'd recovered from my surprise at the attack

"Shooter!"

I grabbed Zhang Daiyu's arm and we raced toward the thirty-story tower from which a steady barrage of semi-automatic gunfire was issuing. People around us scattered, screaming, as bullets tore up the slabs, filling the air with dust and the crack and whine of deadly danger. As we neared the building entrance, security guards were rushing to bolt the doors shut. We made it to the cover of the large canopy that protruded from the second floor and blocked the sniper's line of sight.

Then the shooting stopped.

"You okay?" I asked Zhang Daiyu. She nodded. I glanced around. "The shooter won't use the main entrance of his building to escape. Let's check the sides and rear. I'll take the north-west corner. You take north-east."

"Okay," she replied, and started east, staying close to the building.

I hurried west. The shooter couldn't risk being caught on the roof, and I could see that inside the lobby security guards had started checking people's identities. A full-scale building search was a risk for a man with a gun. He would likely try to escape, but the front entrance was locked and under scrutiny, creating too high a chance of capture.

I ran along one side of the building, past three fire doors to the rear north-west corner where I stopped. I could see another three fire doors opening on to the busy street behind the building, where life was carrying on as though nothing had happened. There was a huge, bustling market further along the street, which was drawing crowds, and through the flurry of pedestrians I caught sight of Zhang Daiyu on the opposite corner, her eyes switching rapidly between her side of the building and the rear. I did likewise, watching for suspicious movement. We'd be in trouble if the building was evacuated, but that was unlikely unless the gunman posed a threat to those inside, and in the chaos of the moment, building security probably hadn't yet established the shooter was on their roof. I watched and waited.

In my mind the shooting had confirmed Liu Bao's involvement. No one else knew we were here.

He had the knowledge and resources required to organize a quick hit, and when I got my hands on the shooter, I was going to make him tell me everything.

CHAPTER 42

THREE MINUTES LATER, the rear middle fire door opened and a man in a gray boilersuit emerged, hands in his pockets, walking nonchalantly though his eyes told a different story. They were the eyes of a predator scanning its surroundings for rivals, and they found one in me.

He looked my way and held my gaze for a moment. The tattoos on his face and neck were more typical of a criminal than a janitor. He raised his right hand and almost arrogantly ran his fingers through his hair. I saw the tattoo on his forearm: two dragons entwined around a third. It was the same design I'd seen on the gunman who'd attacked us near Qincheng Prison and on the men who'd tried to kill Molly Tan.

I looked beyond the sniper and saw Zhang Daiyu heading his way, but he didn't seem the slightest bit concerned. He flashed me an arrogant grin before crossing the busy street and weaving through the crowd on the other side. I heard police sirens as I ran to intercept him. Glancing to my right, I could see flashing lights further down the road.

The sniper was running in my direction and I would have cut him off if it hadn't been for the Mercedes S-Class that screeched to a halt to avoid colliding with me. It had almost stopped, but the impact was enough to knock me down, giving the sniper the chance to get ahead of my position. I jumped to my feet, waving away the angry shouts of the Mercedes driver, and chased the sniper through the crowds.

Zhang Daiyu was about fifteen paces behind me. The two of us closed the gap on the sniper, who kept glancing over his shoulder. He was heading for Chenxingcai Market, a large bustling hall with an outer perimeter of crowded shops, near the junction of Canzheng Hutong, a broad ten-lane highway, and Naoshikou Street, a quieter road lined with retail outlets. The sniper pushed his way into the packed market, Zhang Daiyu and I in pursuit.

He pressed through the throng that packed the aisles between the bountiful food and textile stalls. We went after him. The place was buzzing with the hustle and cacophony of trade. The sniper sprinted round a lychee stall and headed for a side exit that led to a quiet backstreet.

I ran behind the display table, cutting into the stallholder's space, and closed the gap to about ten paces. By the time we reached the street, I was almost within touching distance.

I pressed on, legs burning, lungs heaving, and closed the gap between us.

I grabbed the gunman by the shoulder, but as I pulled him

round, he surprised me by shoving a pistol in my face. I slapped it away instinctively and it discharged into an adjacent wall. The loud gunshot set my ears ringing, and the sniper caught me with a heavy blow to the head, which sent me staggering back into Zhang Daiyu's arms. My vision blurred and my head rang as I watched the man sprint down the sidestreet and disappear round the corner.

"I'm okay," I said to Zhang Daiyu. I took a moment then ran on.

When we reached the intersection, I looked east to see a motorcyclist yelling at the gunman, who was riding away on a stolen bike.

I looked at Zhang Daiyu and shook my head in frustration.

"So close," she said.

"It's not a total failure," I replied. "I spotted he had the same tattoo as the others.'

"We still have no idea what it means. I've checked with Chen Ya-ting and he hasn't come across it before either," she replied, referring to the Beijing detective who was investigating the case of Shang Li and his team. "For us and the police never to have encountered it, well, it's either new or very, very secret."

"It does tell us one thing, though," I replied. "This guy attacked us outside Liu Bao's office. No one else knew we were coming here, which means he was almost certainly sent by Liu. And the tattoo connects him—and Liu—to everything that's happened to Private so far."

"We still need to find out why he wants us dead," Zhang Daiyu reminded me.

I nodded and rubbed the back of my head gingerly.

We started back the way we had come. When we reached the main market, my phone rang. I glanced at the screen, saw it was Justine calling and answered.

Nothing could have prepared me for what she was about to say.

CHAPTER 43

"JACK," JUSTINE SAID. "I'm in the executive meeting room at Private New York with Seymour and Maureen. We have Rafael Lucas with us. There's no easy way to put this."

She was flushed with anger and adrenaline in anticipation of what she was about to say. Part of her still didn't believe their associate could have done this.

"Rafael betrayed us. He was coerced by a Chinese national into the plot against Private New York. He gave this man, known as Angel, Lewis and Jessie, and he just tried to walk Mo and Sci into a trap."

Rafael was seated on the sofa near the door, head in his hands. He was trembling and couldn't meet the gazes of those around him. Mo-bot and Sci sat on opposite sides of the boardroom table, avoiding looking at the man responsible for such treachery.

Jack was silent for so long Justine worried the line had gone dead.

"Go on," he said at last.

His dead tone told her he was seething.

"He says his wife was abducted—"

"She was," Rafael cut in. "He has her and he says he'll kill her if I don't do everything he wants."

"Quiet!" Mo-bot shouted at him. "We'll tell you when we want to hear from you."

Jack sighed, his pain audible.

"You sold out your friends for nothing," he said, and his words hit home. Rafael sagged visibly. "You've got blood on your hands, and he still has your wife. What did you think was going to happen? The nice man would keep his word and bring her home if you were a good boy and did as you were told?"

The question seemed to suck all the air from the room. Rafael choked back a series of sobs that made his chest heave.

Private had procedures for such eventualities. Rafael wasn't strictly part of the agency, but he worked for Private and knew the correct protocols. If he'd come to them when Alison had been taken, they would have worked with the cops and FBI to find her, and would have had a good chance of recovering her by playing on Angel's need to complete his mission. But now the assassin would probably guess Rafael had been compromised, which would place Alison at greater risk. Whichever way you looked at it, Rafael had made the wrong choice, and Justine wondered whether that realization had sunk in yet.

"Have you informed the police?" Jack asked.

"No," Justine replied. "We're going to see what else he knows before deciding what to do."

"I've told you everything," Rafael protested, his voice breaking pathetically.

"And you'll tell us again and again and again until we're satisfied you have nothing else to give," Sci snapped.

There was another heavy silence.

"It goes without saying, do not let him out of your sight," Jack said.

"Don't worry about that," she assured him before hanging up.

"Tell us again what happened?" Sci said, activating the voice recorder on his phone. His tone was flat, like someone who'd suffered a bereavement. "I want every detail this time. Don't leave anything out, no matter how small. We need something we can use to find Alison."

"She went for dinner," Rafael began, "with friends. Annabelle's on Sixty-third Street. He must have been following her for a while because he knew to take her when she was near home. We live on the Upper East Side, on a quiet street, and there isn't much traffic at night. He knew the best place to snatch her."

Justine couldn't help but feel some sympathy for the man as his voice failed him. Alison's kidnapping and the use of her as leverage was clearly torture to him. It had pushed Rafael beyond breaking point.

"He called me after he took her," Rafael said once he had composed himself. "When we met, he told me what he needed. I had no idea what he had planned. I wouldn't have . . . I couldn't . . ." He choked out the words then his voice drifted into silence.

"How has he been communicating with you?" Mo-bot asked.

"Sendal," Rafael replied.

"It's a secure messaging platform," Mo-bot explained.

"Why did he target me?" Rafael asked, giving way to self-pity, which was offensive to them in light of the harm his poor judgment had caused others.

"Because you love your wife," Justine replied dispassionately, as though she was delivering a profile. Her voice did not once betray the depth of her personal feelings about what this man had done. "Anyone could see that in the photos of you together. You were identified as a weak link. Someone they could break."

Rafael and Alison Lucas regularly featured in New York society pages. She hailed from a notable Manhattan family, so they were an easy target, and the newspapers and magazines were full of useful nuggets of personal information.

Rafael looked away, ashamed.

Mo-bot stood and approached Justine.

"Little conference outside?" She nodded toward Rafael. "I don't want him listening in."

Justine followed her into the corridor, which was quiet due to the lateness of the hour. It was shortly after 11 p.m. and the city beyond the floor-to-ceiling windows was shutting down for the night.

Mo-bot closed the door behind them. "If he's using Sendal we can trace him . . ."

"But?" Justine asked, noting the pregnant pause at the end of Mo-bot's sentence.

"But Jack's going to need to call in a favor."

CHAPTER 44

WE WERE ON Wangfujing, a busy street in the Dongcheng district of Beijing, near the Forbidden City. It was lined with modern stores, and here and there street hawkers were preparing food carts and stands for their lunchtime trade. The smell of hot pots, noodles and spiced meats filled the air as we made our way back to the workers' hostel, but I wasn't interested in food. I was still reeling from the news that Rafael Lucas, a man I'd considered to be a friend, had betrayed us all. He'd sentenced Lewis to death, put Jessie in hospital, and jeopardized the safety of everyone in Private New York.

I told Zhang Daiyu what I'd learnt and she looked at me in shock. She didn't know Rafael, but I think she could sense my hurt and disappointment.

"Do you think he had anything to do with what happened here?" she asked when I'd finished briefing her.

"I don't know. Justine, Sci, and Mo-bot are questioning him now. They'll send me anything relevant," I replied. "We need to stay focused on Liu Bao."

I said the words as much for my benefit as for hers. It would have been all too easy to dwell on the betrayal, to obsess over what Rafael had done, but I couldn't afford to indulge myself in what would have been a perfectly natural reaction. I had to put an end to this and make my organization and my people safe again.

Zhang Daiyu made a call as we walked away from the market. She asked Huang Hua to meet us at Liu Bao's office late that night with a surveillance package. We would bug his place and see what we could get on him and his associates.

Zhang Daiyu and I caught a cab a block later and didn't speak as the vehicle joined the 2nd Ring Road. I was tired and, despite my determination to move on, still shellshocked by the news. How could a colleague I'd considered a friend do this to the people he worked closely with? I considered myself a good judge of character but would never have foreseen this kind of betrayal. My mind swam with questions. Had Rafael also played a part in what had happened here? Did he have even more blood on his hands? I gazed absently at the passing city and tried to puzzle out what had happened. Shang Li's team had been killed, leaving the Beijing office leaderless. David Zhou had been put in the frame for the attack, but the real trail led to Liu Bao, an underworld figure who'd blackmailed Molly Tan into engaging us. Meanwhile in New York something similar had happened and it seemed a Chinese national was involved, strengthening my theory that the attack linked back to here.

My phone rang and I pulled it from my pocket to see Mo-bot's name.

"Go ahead," I said.

"Can you talk?"

"I can listen," I replied.

"Good enough. We got a lead from the traitor. He and Angel have been using Sendal to communicate."

"The secure messenger?" I asked.

Zhang Daiyu's interest was piqued but she said nothing. Our taxi driver kept his eyes fixed on the road.

"The same. Not many people know this, but Sendal isn't as secure as you might think."

"I assume everyone can read anything I write online."

"Wise man. Well, maybe not you then, but the average Joe or Josephine won't know that the National Security Agency has back doors into most messaging systems. The men in black can read your every word. So, I was wondering if you could reach out to Secretary Carver and call in a favor . . ."

She was talking about the Secretary of Defense. He owed me a couple of favors, but I wasn't much for cashing in markers. Mo-bot knew this, so she gave me some added incentive.

"The lawyer might deserve what's coming to him, but his wife doesn't."

She was right as usual. Rafael might have betrayed us, but his wife was an innocent.

"Does he know what this is all about?" I asked.

"No."

"Was he involved in what's happened in Beijing?"

"He says he has no idea, and he didn't give Angel anything on the operation over there," Mo-bot replied. "I believe him. He's cooperating fully. He's desperate to get Alison back. If we can find this Angel, he might be able to tell us why we're under siege on two fronts."

She was right again.

"I'll make the call," I assured her.

CHAPTER 45

I MADE THE call from the cab, and the Secretary of Defense phoned me back just as we arrived at the workers' hostel on Changcui Road. I first encountered Eli Carver during the Moscow investigation in which I had saved his life, and then again after rescuing Joshua Floyd from Afghanistan, events which had given me special access to one of the most powerful men on earth.

"Secretary Carver," I said as I followed Zhang Daiyu through the lobby. "Thanks for calling back so quickly."

"One of these days I'll persuade you to call me Eli."

"One day . . ."

"I can tell today isn't going to be that day, Jack. What can I do for you? It's late here, so I'm guessing it's urgent."

"It is," I replied. "My tech specialist says the NSA maintains back doors into all the major messaging platforms."

"I can neither confirm nor deny that, Jack."

"I don't need to know, sir, but what I do need is the location of a device used to coerce one of my employees."

"Everything okay?" he asked. "I'm told you're in China."

It didn't surprise me that he knew exactly where he was calling me.

"I'm taking care of some business, sir."

"Like Moscow?"

"It's shaping up that way, sir."

"Sorry to hear that."

"So am I," I agreed.

"Try not to raise too much hell."

"That I can't promise, sir."

"Send me the number of the person being coerced and I'll see what I can do," Carver said.

"Thank you, sir."

Zhang Daiyu and I had reached our room by the time I hung up.

"He's going to do what he can," I told her.

She unlocked the door and I followed her inside, conscious once again of just how small the place was. Zhang Daiyu was attractive and, as far as I was aware, single. And we were living in each other's pockets. I didn't need to continue to stay with her to make sure she was okay, as I had when we first arrived at the hostel.

"I think I'm going to see if they have another room," I said.

"I'll do it, Mr. Morgan," she replied.

"It's Jack. We've faced too many bullets together for 'Mr. Morgan.'"

She smiled. "It will be easier if I try for another room, Jack."

She left and I went into the bathroom, got undressed, and stepped into the tiny shower. The tiles were cracked and broken, and the water was on the chilly side of tepid, but it felt good. I emerged revitalized. I dried myself and got dressed, making a mental note to buy new clothes at the first opportunity.

"You don't hum," Zhang Daiyu said when I stepped into the room. "I was told Americans always sing or hum in the shower."

"I have a special exemption," I replied, toweling my hair dry.

"They don't have any rooms available," she revealed. "Looks like you're stuck with me for a while."

"We could go somewhere else," I replied.

"The manager and I have reached an arrangement. Our stay will be handled with complete discretion. I'm paying him double the room rate and have promised a bonus if we make it out of here in one piece."

I wasn't thrilled with the prospect of more nights on the floor, but she was right to suggest we stay. Anywhere that could be trusted to keep our presence secret was worth an uncomfortable sleep.

I sat on the bed and put on my shoes. She leant against a rustic dresser. The shower had revived me, but I was still starving.

"What makes you do this?" she asked. "I know your background. You don't have to work like this, exposing yourself to danger."

"My father gave me this agency. It was nothing but a name. He wasn't like me. He was a gambler. Destructive. He was in it to make money, but never did. Not really. I prefer to try and help people. Private is a force for good. I do this because I can."

It was hard to tell whether she thought me brave or foolish, and I've often wondered about the distinction myself.

"What about you?" I asked. She'd proved herself to be brave and loyal, so I wasn't suspicious of her anymore. I genuinely wanted to know more about her. "Why did you leave the police?"

"Politics," she replied, and I thought for a moment she wasn't going to go any further, but she kept talking. "I came from a small village near Dazhou in Sichuan. My father was a chicken farmer. One day some money went missing from the local market and he was accused of taking it. His life was ruined and he faced jail, but the local police inspector proved it was another man, saving my father and bringing the true criminal to justice. I wanted to be like that, but when I got to the city, I discovered it is all about politics and ambition and sometimes even corruption. I thought about returning home, but I saw Private was recruiting and your ethos and mission appealed to me."

"I'm glad you joined," I said.

"So am I."

"Shall we get something to eat while we wait?" I asked, but before she could answer, my phone rang. There was no caller ID. The screen was blank.

"Hello."

"The information you want is at one-six-seven-three-four dot com," a man said. "It will be there for three minutes. One-six-seven-three-four."

The line went dead and Zhang Daiyu looked at me in puzzlement.

I said, "I think Carver just gave us our suspect."

CHAPTER 46

JUSTINE WAS EXHAUSTED. It was after 3 a.m. and she was on her way back to the office from a coffee run when Jack called. She stepped out of the elevator, put the tray of cups on the reception desk, and answered the phone.

"Jack. How are you?"

"We're okay," he replied.

There had been a time when she'd been jealous of her female colleagues, but she and Jack trusted each other implicitly now. Their relationship had been strengthened by his time away in Afghanistan.

"Carver came through. I need to speak to Mo," he said.

Justine left the tray of coffee and hurried through the security doors, along the corridor to the executive meeting room. Mo-bot was working on her laptop at the boardroom table, and Sci and Rafael were asleep on couches against the walls.

"It's Jack," Justine said, handing Mo-bot the phone.

"I'm putting you on speaker," Mo-bot said.

"Carver identified the device that was being used to send Rafael messages. It was a Raid-Box," Jack revealed.

Mo-bot leant back in her chair and exhaled loudly. "Sheesh. A Raid-Box. Guoanbu-issue ghost device designed to be untraceable."

"Guoanbu?" Rafael asked. He looked groggy as he stirred.

"Chinese State Security," Mo-bot explained.

"Alison has been abducted by Chinese State Security?" he asked, his concern palpable.

Sci was lying on the couch behind the door and stretched as he woke.

"Not necessarily," Mo-bot replied. "Could be someone who has access to their tech."

"Raid-Boxes are supposed to be impossible to trace unless you have the machine number, aren't they?" Sci remarked.

"Guess what Carver's people gave me?" Jack said.

"You're kidding?" Mo-bot responded, suddenly coming alive. "Jack Morgan, you're a genius."

"I just made a phone call," he countered.

"How did they get the machine code?" she asked.

"Who knows what the Pentagon is really capable of?"

"I thought I did," she remarked. "With the machine code, I can run a crawler to watch local ISPs and see if he uses the Raid-Box anywhere within two hundred miles of the city."

"Good," Jack said. "You let me know when you find him. And call the cops. We need to bring them in on this."

"Police?" Rafael asked.

"Yes," Jack replied. "You made a bad choice. The chips are going to fall where they fall."

Rafael nodded slowly and Justine saw a look of defeat sweep across his face. He had accepted there would be a full legal reckoning. Jack had made their decision for them.

"I'll get started," Mo-bot said. "We'll call you as soon as we've got anything."

"Good luck," he responded before hanging up.

CHAPTER 47

ZHANG DAIYU AND I grabbed some *zhajiang mian* fried-sauce noodles from a stall near the hostel. We ate standing on the street not far from the grinning, wiry old man who kept up a steady trade serving his sweet-smelling bowls to the locals. I had never tasted anything so good in my life. Partly a consequence of hunger, but also a testament to the chef's skill with the spices that went into the hot sauce covering the noodles.

"Good, right?" Zhang Daiyu remarked.

"I can't tell you how good," I replied.

She spent time on the phone, briefing Huang Hua, who was leading the surveillance effort on Liu Bao. We had a team of six operatives working in rolling shifts and Hua had put together an equipment package ready for installation that night. I didn't care about the cost. I wanted the man who had targeted my organization and killed my colleagues.

After my call with Justine, Sci, and Mo-bot, Zhang Daiyu and I went to a local clothes shop and refreshed our wardrobes. I bought underwear, black jeans, and a gray T-shirt, and was dressed like many of our fellow residents in the hostel. The only thing missing was the ubiquitous blue worker's jacket, but it was far too hot for outerwear. Zhang Daiyu was in a pair of black trousers and a red blouse, which she managed to make look like designer wear despite the fact it had been cheaper than our noodles.

"I want my own clothes," she grumbled between mouthfuls. "I feel as though I'm in my mother's wardrobe."

"You look great."

"Thank you, but you don't have to be kind. I suppose I can't go home until this is over?"

I nodded. "Seems that way. These guys are serious."

Her phone rang and she pulled it from her pocket and answered rapidly before hanging up.

"Come on," she said, hurrying back to the stall to hand her bowl to the vendor. "The surveillance team has spotted someone of interest visiting Liu's office. A man with the triple dragon tattoo on his arm. If we hurry, we can support them. They don't have the resources to watch Liu Bao and tail this new target."

I nodded and handed my bowl to the chef, who smiled his thanks.

Thirty minutes later, after a cab ride, we reached the financial district and asked to be dropped off a few blocks from the building. We walked to Guangcheng Street, where we found Hua's Private surveillance van parked in a multi-story between two office blocks. The van was on the roof of the building and had a partial view of Liu Bao's eye-shaped headquarters.

Zhang Daiyu rapped on the side door and someone let us in. Hua was alone, monitoring a variety of screens.

"Good," he said. "I think you're in time. We haven't seen him come out."

"What are you running?" I asked.

"Six fixed cameras monitoring the entrances and exits, two operatives on the main entrance."

"Good."

"We haven't been able to install anything inside, but we'll fix that tonight."

I was impressed. They'd managed to get up and running very quickly.

"We've tried directional mics, but they seem to have counter measures running," he said. "A lot of corporates used counter surveillance to prevent industrial espionage. We'll learn more when we get inside later."

"Can you show us the guy?" I asked.

Hua nodded and took a seat on one of the stools in front of the main console. He gestured for Zhang Daiyu and me to sit next to him. I was grateful for the van's independent cooling system, which kept the air conditioning running even with the engine off—essential for long field operations in the heat.

Hua scrolled through some video footage of the main entrance to Liu Bao's building, which captured everyone entering and leaving.

"Where are the cameras?" I asked.

"Lamp posts. Bollards. Two button cameras on the agents," he said, pausing the footage on a man in black slacks and a white shirt with rolled-up sleeves. "Zhang Daiyu told me about the tattoo so I thought this might be relevant."

I nodded and studied the man on-screen. He had short hair and a gentle demeanor. He was slim and moved gracefully, a far cry from the criminals we had encountered so far, but he sported the same tattoo as them. The likeness of two small dragons curled around a much larger one was emblazoned on his left wrist.

"Recognize him?" I asked Zhang Daiyu.

She shook her head.

"He's coming out," Hua told us. "Should I re-task the agents who are watching the building?"

He gestured to a smaller monitor showing a live feed of the main entrance. The man with the intricate tattoo was walking out.

"No," I replied. "Keep them on Liu Bao. Zhang Daiyu and I will take this guy."

CHAPTER 48

HUA KEPT ONE of his agents on the target until we reached the plaza outside Liu Bao's headquarters. I felt uncomfortable being back in the space where we'd been attacked only the previous day, but no one knew we were here and we moved through the plaza without incident. Hua communicated with Zhang Daiyu by text to give her directions. We caught sight of the man heading down Jinchengfang Street, and she and I worked an overlapping tail to minimize the chances of him getting wise to being followed.

Zhang Daiyu took point for a while and I got ahead of the guy. I guessed he'd go straight on at the intersection with Taipingqiao Avenue, but he turned right so I crossed the street and followed from the other side. After a while, Zhang Daiyu went ahead of him and I took the tail. We carried on like this for twenty minutes, looping around the city until he reached Ganjiakou subway station. He went down the steps into the huge station, and I followed him and joined a queue at a kiosk to buy a ticket. Zhang Daiyu came down and took the lead then. She used her transit pass and tailed the guy through the subway barriers in front of the steps to the platform. When I finally got a ticket and made it downstairs, I couldn't see her or our target anywhere.

I walked along the platform, which was packed with travelers, and caught sight of Zhang Daiyu standing behind a pillar. The target was talking to her. She waved her index finger discreetly, signaling me to walk on, and I stopped a short distance away, close enough to help, but sufficiently far to be a disinterested commuter. As the only Westerner in a crowd of locals, I was aware I stood out, but that might have worked to my advantage. What foreigner would be crazy or dumb enough to take on someone from a gang?

I heard the rumble of the Line 16 train rolling into the station, and when I looked through the crowd I saw our target finish talking to Zhang Daiyu and turn toward the platform edge. She headed for the exit, texting as she walked.

My phone vibrated and I checked my messages to see one from her.

He made me. He knows I was following. Be careful.

The crowd on the platform waited patiently as the train rolled to a halt. Zhang Daiyu gave me a last glance from halfway up the stairs, but I didn't react. The target might have had accomplices in the crowd conducting counter-surveillance.

When the doors opened, the calm was broken as droves of people left the train, to be replaced by almost as many from the platform. I was one of them. I pressed my way into the carriage, which was uncomfortably full. I made sure I could see the target throughout our journey north and held on to a handrail as the train rolled on.

We went five stops to Wanquanheqiao where I followed the guy out of an increasingly crowded train. I tailed him through the station and we emerged into a modern part of the city. New buildings nestled in parkland, and mature trees dotted the neighborhood. We walked past a university campus and entered what looked like a government district. There were police everywhere and grand, imposing buildings with ministerial signs. The national flag of the People's Republic of China fluttered here and there. I felt distinctly out of place as I followed the target along Xinjiangongmen Road.

We neared a fortified compound of imposing buildings that was dominated by a tall concrete pill-box block. The complex was surrounded by high walls, wire fencing, and guard towers. There were cameras everywhere and police vehicles stationed in the street, which had been cut from four lanes to one by some concrete bollards.

As we neared the high-security compound, I tried to identify it, but the small sign on the main gate was indecipherable to me. While my eyes were on it the target walked behind a parked van. I moved to catch up but couldn't see him anywhere.

"I will tell you what I told your colleague Zhang Daiyu."

The target startled me by appearing at my shoulder. He must have gone round the van.

"You can waste your time following me, but you can't change

your fate, Mr. Morgan. You are out of your depth. You don't even know what this place is. It is the headquarters of Guoanbu, our Ministry of State Security. I'm going inside. You, well, you should go back to America. Enjoy life while you still can."

"Nice tattoo," I said, nodding at the dragons emblazoned on his forearm.

He stepped forward menacingly and thrust his arm toward me. "This? This isn't a tattoo," he snarled ferociously. "This is your doom."

He turned and walked toward the main gates, leaving me stunned by his audacity.

I texted Zhang Daiyu.

He made me too. Meet you at the hostel.

CHAPTER 49

EXHAUSTED, JUSTINE HAD given up trying to sleep in the office and had checked in to the New York Edition, a hotel located a block south of the Private building. She hadn't felt safe going to the Langham, the hotel Rafael had booked for her, in case he'd given the details to Angel. So she lay on the freshly made bed in her clothes and hoped sleep would take her, but even though she was beat, her mind was racing and wouldn't allow her to let go of the real world.

She still couldn't believe Rafael had betrayed them. She thought about him locked in the main meeting room, imagining the crushing guilt he must have been feeling. She wondered what she would have done if Jack had been taken. Would she have done the right thing? Or would she have cracked like Rafael had? She hoped she would have been better than him.

Her mind drifted to Jack, and she marveled at the ease with

which he confronted danger that would have paralyzed most other people with fear. She had no doubt he'd have done the right thing if she'd been abducted.

He'd have torn the world apart to get her back.

Even the thought of him made her feel better and settled her mind. She soon found herself drifting through daydreams of him. There was nothing specific, just flashes of memory; a day at the beach, lunch at Geoffrey's in Malibu, hiking in Topanga Canyon.

She woke to the sound of her phone ringing and pulled it from her pocket.

"Hello," she said without checking the caller ID. She could hardly open her eyes.

"It's me," Mo-bot said. Had she been working all night? "We've got something."

"I'll be right there," Justine replied and Mo-bot hung up.

Groggy and dazed by lack of sleep, Justine pulled herself to her feet. She felt worse than before she'd slept, but she went to the bathroom, splashed water on her face, and gave herself a stern look in the mirror that said, "Push on."

Jack wouldn't let fatigue slow him down and Mo-bot worked through her exhaustion. Justine knew she could do the same. She grabbed her purse and left.

It was a little after 5:40 a.m. It had rained while she slept, so the air was lighter and fresher, and the breeze helped energize her.

A few minutes later, after a short walk north through the stirring city, she was in the office, which was eerily silent until she reached the corridor outside the executive meeting room. She could hear Mo-bot speaking.

When she entered, she saw Sci and Mo-bot sitting at the long table. Rafael was on the sofa with his head in his hands. He looked haunted, like a man who now realized he had made entirely the wrong decisions.

"You've engaged local law?"

Jack's voice came through the speaker console at the center of the table.

"Yes," Mo-bot replied.

She and Sci had changed clothes at some point in the night, and Justine felt a little scuzzy, wearing the same ones as yesterday.

"We've informed them of Alison's abduction. Told them the suspect is linked to the attack on Lewis and Jessie and should be considered dangerous."

Mo-bot registered Justine's presence.

"Justine's here. The Raid-Box was activated an hour ago. I traced it to a warehouse in Brooklyn. NYPD are putting together a squad. They told us to stay clear but . . ."

"It's a free country," Jack suggested. "Hi, Jus."

"Hey. How are things over there?" she asked.

"Getting interesting," he replied.

Sci whistled. "That's never a good thing."

"I don't want to talk about it over the phone, but I've sent you all a secure message bringing you up to speed," he responded.

"What do you want us to do when we reach Brooklyn?" Sci asked.

"Surveillance only. Make sure this guy doesn't leave until the cops arrive."

"And Rafael?" Justine asked.

"NYPD officers are en route as we speak," Mo-bot replied. "They're taking him in for questioning."

Justine now understood the aura of pain and defeat around their associate. He was facing his reckoning. He'd be in police custody in a matter of minutes.

"They'll want statements from all of us at some point," Mo-bot said.

"You're not to engage this Angel," Jack cautioned. "Under any circumstances. Let the police do their job."

"Understood," Mo-bot replied.

"Keep me posted," he said before hanging up.

CHAPTER 50

THE WAREHOUSE LOOKED exactly the sort of place a person would plot murder. It was located on a rundown industrial park near Maspeth. The site was full of what Justine referred to as mystery businesses; small firms that traded in specialist goods like air-conditioning parts or vending machine coin-sorters. These were businesses that never seemed to grow or shrink, and it was a mystery to her how they survived. The warehouses that housed them were poorly maintained with flecks of rust on pipes, cracked windows, and crumbling concrete.

The building Mo-bot had identified as Angel's location was worst of all. Situated at the rear of the industrial park, near the Long Island Expressway, it looked as though it had been des-erted for years. A wire fence surrounded the lot but had been cut in places. The main gate was secured by a rusty chain and padlock, and beyond it was a parking lot that had been cracked and broken by a forest of weeds. The warehouse itself had four loading bays for large trucks and might once have been a food-distribution center, judging by all the wire-mesh cages rusting in a heap to one side of the yard.

Sci had driven them to the location and parked in the lot of the warehouse opposite, which belonged to a flooring adhesive firm. It was just gone 7 a.m. and was still too early for any of the surrounding businesses to be open. Sci and Justine sat in the front of the Nissan Rogue and watched Angel's warehouse while Mo-bot worked on her laptop.

"He's still there," she said, nodding toward her screen.

As if on cue, Justine saw an NYPD SWAT team double-time across the adjacent parking lot. They had come from somewhere behind the neighboring building. Two of the eight men carried bolt cutters and used them to widen a gap in the wire fence.

They moved through, their distinctive black uniforms making them look like shadows as they ran across the overgrown parking lot in the hazy early-morning light. Only the letters "SWAT," imprinted on the back of their body armor, made them seem real.

The lead officer used his bolt cutters to break a chain that secured a side door. The team entered the warehouse.

The tension was almost too much to bear. Justine could hardly breathe. She caught glimpses of the SWAT team moving through the building, although it was hard to be sure, they were difficult to spot in the dark windows.

"This guy isn't going down without a fight," Sci said, echoing her thoughts.

She was expecting fireworks.

Less than a minute after the team entered the building, a convoy of police vehicles, a SWAT truck, and some unmarked sedans rolled into the parking lot of Angel's warehouse, following a lead vehicle that crashed through the gates, snapping the rusty chain.

"This is it," Mo-bot said. "Let's see if we can get a few words with the guy."

She got out and hurried across the lot, Justine and Sci following.

Justine could tell something was wrong the moment they reached the parking lot in front of Angel's warehouse. Uniformed cops milled around with the despondency of baseball fans who have just seen their team get thrashed. The SWAT team emerged from the warehouse and started removing their helmets.

Luiz Salazar peeled away from a group of cops and marched over.

He didn't seem happy.

"Nothing," he said. "The place is completely empty. Either your man is a ghost or he's just played you and us for fools."

"That's impossible. There's a signal coming from inside the building," Mo-bot responded.

"I don't know what to say. The place is deserted," Luiz responded. "Completely empty."

"Any sign of Alison Lucas?" Justine asked.

"No sign of anything but rodents," Salazar replied. "I appreciate the tip, and I know you guys have a great reputation, but I really could have done without this result today."

"I'm sorry," Mo-bot said. "I was sure he was here."

Justine had never seen her look so shaken. Someone had got the better of her, an event so rare Justine couldn't remember the last time it had happened.

CHAPTER 51

"WE'RE MOVING OUT," Salazar yelled, walking back to his colleagues.

There was a lot of radio chatter and activity, and the cops started getting into their vehicles and leaving. Justine watched the speedy withdrawal with a sense of despondency. What now?

Mo-bot hurried after Salazar, who opened the door of his Dodge Charger.

"You mind if we look around?" she asked. She wasn't giving up.

"Knock yourself out," he replied. "I don't think the landlord is going to press charges for trespass."

He slid behind the wheel, and moments later became part of the convoy of vehicles churning up dust as they left the scene.

"You think they missed something?" Sci asked.

Mo-bot nodded. "I missed something, maybe they did too."

Justine followed her and Sci toward one of the loading bays. The roller shutter had been left open by the cops and Sci jumped onto the loading platform and turned to give Mo-bot a hand up.

Justine pushed herself onto the ledge and ducked beneath the shutter to follow them inside. She saw Mo-bot produce her phone and activate an app.

"The signal from the Raid-Box definitely came from here," she said. "My guess is he used some kind of relay, maybe another Raid-Box, as a cut-out to protect his true location."

Justine sensed a change in Mo-bot's voice, as though something had brought her back to life. She studied the app on her phone intently.

"He could cloak the cut-out and without the machine number I'd never find it," she said, gesturing around the gloomy warehouse. "We could spend weeks searching this place and still come away empty-handed."

Justine didn't relish such a prospect. The building was dark and reeked of rodent infestation.

"It could be hidden in the walls," Mo-bot went on. "But the cut-out isn't the only piece of equipment he'd have hidden here."

She walked purposefully, heading for what might once have been administrative offices at the back of the building.

"He'd want to know if the location had been compromised," she said, pushing open an interior door. "So he'd probably install a motion detector or camera somewhere. And they'd give off a signal. A signal this app I built is designed to detect!"

She brandished her phone as she led them into an old office, full of relics of whatever firm had once been here.

"Over there," she said, gesturing at a green glass bottle in the corner of the room. "Trash to the casual observer or the cop in a hurry. But if you look closely you'll see a motion detector inside."

Justine picked up the grimy bottle and saw Mo-bot was right. There was a device inside.

"And here," she forced open the bottom drawer of an ancient rusting filing cabinet, "is the relay device broadcasting the motion detector's signal that is showing up on my app." She gestured at her phone.

Justine peered over a rotting wooden desk to see a tiny device that looked like a WiFi signal booster box hidden in a filing-cabinet drawer.

"Can you trace the destination?" Sci asked.

Mo-bot nodded. "Call Salazar and tell him we can give him a real location."

Sci stepped away to make the phone call, while Mo-bot adjusted the settings on her app.

"He's close," she said.

She was now alive with the thrill of the chase and her energy was contagious. Justine had almost forgotten the disappointment of earlier.

"He's four streets away," Mo-bot said. "Looks like a house in a residential neighborhood."

Sci returned and was less than enthusiastic.

"Salazar says he's not going on another snipe hunt."

"What?" Mo-bot asked. "I've got the guy this time."

"I think he's caught heat from the higher-ups for ordering a mass deployment without verifying the intel," Sci replied. "He says we should get proof it's Angel."

"So we're on our own?" Justine asked.

"Yeah," Sci said. "We're on our own."

CHAPTER 52

JUSTINE RAN BACK to the Nissan Rogue with Sci and Mo-bot trailing her.

"Give me the keys," she yelled, and Sci tossed them over.

She jumped behind the wheel and started the engine, while Sci and Mo-bot, older and less fit, got in the car, panting for breath.

Justine put the Nissan in gear and shot out of the parking lot.

"Stay on this road," Mo-bot said from the back seat. It curved out of the industrial estate.

"Next left," Mo-bot said.

Justine swung the wheel and took a narrow left turn that led them out of the industrial estate into a rundown residential neighborhood. Two-story aluminum homes lined the street, standing behind rows of rusty pick-up trucks and old cars.

"Next right," Mo-bot said.

Justine slowed as they approached the mouth of another residential street. When she turned the wheel and cleared the house on the corner, she saw a face she recognized: Angel, sitting behind the wheel of a utility vehicle that was reversing down the driveway of a dilapidated bungalow.

"There he is," Justine said. "Put your seat belts on."

Sci was already clipped in, but Mo-bot hurriedly snapped her buckle in its anchor.

"Hold on," Justine said.

"Don't do anything crazy," Sci responded.

"Too late for that," she countered, accelerating toward the cab of the target vehicle.

Angel saw them at the last moment and reached down to grab something—probably a weapon—but he wasn't fast enough. The Rogue hit the black Chevrolet Express just by the driver's door. The impact sent the vehicle spinning into the road.

The airbags in both people carrier and utility deployed. While Justine's deflated she composed herself.

"Everyone okay?" she asked. Sci and Mo-bot nodded tentatively.

Justine got out to find smoke billowing from the Nissan's engine, which had been exposed after the hood crumpled on impact. The front bumper had become part of the Chevrolet. She hurried to the driver's window of the other vehicle and saw the cab was empty and the passenger door open. Angel was twenty yards away fleeing toward Grand Avenue, a busy road that connected the residential neighborhood with the Long Island Expressway. He had a pistol in his hand.

Justine was about to set off after him when she heard a voice yell, "Help me!"

She ran to the rear doors and flung them open to discover Alison Lucas lying on the flatbed. She'd been bound but had managed to work her gag loose.

"Alison!" Justine had met Rafael's wife at a couple of corporate events. "Thank God you're okay."

"Justine?"

She glanced round to see Sci and Mo-bot emerging from the Nissan. Sci looked the least dazed.

"We found Alison. Keep her safe. I'm going after Angel," said Justine.

Sci grimaced as he nodded.

Justine glanced west to see Angel run around the corner. She set off after him at a sprint.

CHAPTER 53

JACK HAD WARNED them not to engage Angel, but adrenaline flooded Justine's system and she didn't stop to think about whether it was wise to be chasing such a dangerous man alone.

She sprinted to the corner, grateful she limited high heels to evening dinners and cocktail parties. Her trainers slammed the sidewalk as her legs pounded out a rapid beat. She reached Grand Avenue, a broad street flanked by a run of local stores, most of which weren't open yet. Their parking lots were largely empty and Justine saw Angel running across the nearest one toward the road, where a steady stream of commuter traffic was building.

He glanced over his shoulder and fired a couple of wild shots at her in an attempt to discourage her and slow her down.

They had the opposite effect and spurred her on. That this man could be so casual about inflicting death, that he could so callously maim and kill her colleagues, that he could try to bomb them all . . . these things disgusted her, and she felt her anger mount when she thought about everything he had done.

Angel reached a line of traffic waiting at the intersection with Flushing Avenue. He ran toward the lights and opened the driver's door of the vehicle at the very front. He brandished the pistol as he pulled a startled man from the driver's seat. Angel gave Justine a taunting look over his shoulder, jumped in, slammed the door shut, and sped away.

Deflated, she slowed to a halt, put her hands on her hips and drew in deep breaths of air. She had let him get away and a sense of failure hit her hard. Then she heard the roar of an engine and the screech of tires approaching. She turned to see Salazar's Dodge Charger shudder to a halt. He leant across the cabin and opened the passenger door.

"Get in! We can still catch him."

Justine jumped in the passenger seat and Salazar stepped on the gas. "I couldn't authorize another deployment," he said. "But that doesn't stop me taking a cruise back this way."

He reached for his radio as the Charger shot forward.

"Dispatch, this is Salazar. I'm in pursuit of a black BMW 325, license plate 2240 PMA, heading south-west on Flushing Avenue. Request immediate back-up and a two-mile perimeter with intercepts."

He reached under his dash for the cherry, lowered his window and stuck it to his roof. With the light flashing, he set his siren going and shot head-first into oncoming traffic, which swerved to avoid him.

The radio came alive with instructions from the dispatcher as further police vehicles were deployed in the area.

"I figured it was unlikely you guys would be wrong twice in one day," Salazar said, without taking his eyes off the road.

Justine put her hand to the dashboard as though the gesture could ward off the vehicles speeding toward them.

Salazar seemed unfazed by the sanctioned game of chicken and kept his course as traffic veered out of the way. The engine roared and through the open window Justine caught the smell of gasoline, motor oil, and rubber as the detective put his powerful ride through its paces.

They closed the gap between them and Angel, who didn't have the advantage of lights or sirens, and was fighting slow-moving traffic on the correct side of the road. Justine wasn't sure he'd seen them, but when they got within fifty yards he left them in little doubt he'd been caught by surprise. The BMW jerked across the median and accelerated suddenly, taking advantage of its path being cleared by the Charger's sirens. The BMW raced toward the next intersection with 61st Street and Justine saw two patrol vehicles blocking the roads north and south.

Salazar surprised her by suddenly turning right and veering across the road. The Charger mounted the sidewalk and sped toward the intersection, Justine praying they wouldn't hit any-thing. Most of the stores were set behind parking lots, but there were a couple of diners that were flush to the sidewalk, and all it would have taken was for one early-morning breakfaster to step out at the wrong time . . .

She realized she was holding her breath and gasped when

she saw the reason for Salazar's seemingly reckless maneuver. One of the uniformed cops blocking the intersection unfurled a Stinger with split-second precision, leaving Angel no time to react.

It didn't stop him trying. He stepped on the brakes as the BMW rolled over the strip of metal spikes, which punctured all four tires. Angel couldn't have picked a worse time to have his foot on the brake pedal. The tires burst and the rapid deflation, plus the wire rims hitting the asphalt, sent the vehicle out of his control and into a violent spin. Justine watched the BMW careen across the intersection, whirling like a spinning top, until it came to an abrupt halt when it collided with a lamp post on the corner. The hood crumpled, airbags deployed, and smoke started billowing from the engine.

Salazar parked near the officer who'd deployed the Stinger, jumped out of the car, and ran toward Angel.

Justine followed and saw the fugitive pawing at the driver's door, struggling to get out.

Salazar drew his pistol and aimed it at the fugitive.

"Freeze!" he said. "You're under arrest."

Angel said something Justine couldn't quite hear.

"What did he say?" she asked, and Salazar shrugged.

"Diplomatic immunity," Angel said in English through the open driver's window. "I'm a member of the People's Republic of China's diplomatic mission to the United States and I claim immunity."

Salazar shook his head.

Justine couldn't believe it.

Even when injured, with blood flowing down the side of his head, trapped and at gunpoint, Angel had the wherewithal to make sure he was always one step ahead.

Unless she could think of something fast, this killer would walk unchallenged onto a plane to China, never to be seen again.

CHAPTER 54

THE COP WHO had deployed the Stinger came running over with his partner and they checked Angel's condition.

Salazar moved away to confer with Justine, whose mind was working furiously.

"We can take him in," the detective said, "but if he really is with the Chinese mission, he'll get sprung pretty quickly."

"What if I take him?" Justine asked, an idea forming in her mind.

More police were arriving now, and the occupants of the growing lines of vehicles snarled up in every direction were out, taking pictures and filming the scene on their phones.

"Citizen's arrest or whatever," she suggested.

"You mean, abduct him?"

"I mean hand him over to people who might be able to do more than NYPD."

Salazar hesitated. "What kind of people?"

"Government people. Guys who deal with this kind of thing day in, day out."

Salazar nodded slowly. "You know these people?"

"Yeah," Justine replied.

"You are full of surprises." The detective surveyed the scene and came to a decision. "This site isn't secure," he said to the two cops checking Angel. "We need to take him in."

"There's an ambulance en route, detective," the officer who'd deployed the Stinger said.

"We can't wait," Salazar countered.

"I need medical attention," Angel said groggily.

"Officers, I want you to secure the perimeter until forensics get here to check this vehicle. Divert traffic away from this intersection and keep the scene as uncontaminated as possible," Salazar instructed.

Justine could see the doubt on the men's faces. There was nothing of value to be gleaned from a stolen vehicle but they didn't voice this. Instead, they stepped away and allowed Salazar to take Angel by the arm.

"Hey! No! I need medical attention," he protested.

"You are under arrest for the theft of an automobile, reckless endangerment, and resisting arrest," Salazar said. "You have the right to remain silent. Anything you say can and will be used against you in a court of law. You have a right to an attorney. If you cannot afford an attorney, one will be appointed for you. Do you understand those rights?"

"Diplomatic immunity," Angel said.

He put up a weak struggle as Salazar pulled him out and handcuffed him. The man looked genuinely injured and kept lurching to the left, wincing in pain.

Salazar frogmarched him to the Dodge Charger and forced him onto the back seat. Justine got into the passenger seat as Salazar slid behind the wheel.

"I hope you know what you're doing," the detective said as he started the engine.

Justine made a phone call as they were waved through the cordon. She dialed the special number Jack had been given for if he ever needed anything.

"Yes?" a man said.

"I need to speak with your boss," she replied, taking care not to use any names within earshot of Angel. "It's a message from the man who saved him."

"Hold, please."

The line went silent.

"You can't do this," Angel remarked. "I have rights. You must follow the proper procedure."

"You killed one of my colleagues," Justine said. "You tried to kill many more of them. Was that proper procedure?"

"This woman is delusional, detective. Hysterical even. Do not listen to her. Take me to your precinct. Do your job."

"Play your games on someone else, pal. I'm not listening," Salazar responded.

"Hello, Miss Smith," Secretary Carver said when he came on the line. Justine was impressed because she hadn't announced herself. "What's the message?"

"There is no message, sir. I'm with an NYPD detective and we have in our custody a Chinese national who is claiming diplomatic immunity. We suspect he was responsible for the murder of at least one of our colleagues, planting a bomb in our offices and the abduction of the wife of another of our colleagues."

"Lies," Angel said.

"Open your mouth again and I'll shut it for you," Salazar said, and the prisoner glowered at him.

"The detective believes if we take him in, he will lawyer up and be sprung within the day. I was wondering if there was another way."

"Another way?" Carver asked.

"Another way," Justine repeated.

"I don't know anything about that. I'd recommend following due process," he replied. Justine's heart sank. There was a brief pause. "Do you have an address? I'd like to send some of our people over to ensure the gentleman gets to the right place."

Justine smiled. His earlier remark had been for the benefit of anyone who was intercepting the call.

"Of course, sir. I apologize for suggesting otherwise."

She gave him the address of the property where they'd found Angel trying to escape.

"Thank you," Carver said. "They won't be long."

"Thank you, sir," Justine said before she hung up.

"What did he say?" Salazar asked.

"We're to take him to the house he was using," Justine replied.

"You're going to regret this," Angel said. "I have a long memory."

"The psychopath rarely feels fear," Justine remarked, "but

he does experience humiliation. Is this bravado because you've just been humiliated? If so, you're only humiliating yourself further. I've been threatened by men who make you look like the Tooth Fairy. You're not scaring anyone here, so you might as well shut up."

Angel seethed but fell silent.

Justine's phone rang and she saw Mo-bot's name flash on-screen.

"Mo," she said.

"Justine, thank goodness you're okay. Where are you?"

"On our way back to the bungalow. You still there?"

"Yeah," Mo-bot replied. "Your way back?"

"I'm with a certain NYPD detective and we're bringing you a gift. We'll see you soon."

CHAPTER 55

ANGEL FELL SILENT for the remainder of the short journey back to the bungalow where they'd found him.

Sci and Mo-bot had pushed both damaged vehicles, the Nissan Rogue Private staff vehicle and Angel's utility, into the driveway. Salazar parked his Dodge Charger beside them. He grabbed the handcuffed Angel and manhandled him into the building where they found Sci and Mo-bot waiting with Alison. Justine could have kicked herself for not warning Mo-bot to make sure Alison was kept away from Angel. She could see the trauma writ large on the woman's face.

"What's he doing here?" she asked. "Get him away from me. Get him away!"

"Alison, I'm sorry. It was thoughtless," Justine said, going to the distressed woman.

Her hair was lank, face dirty, dress crumpled from days of wear.

"Come with me. Let's get you out of here." Justine put her arm around Alison and ushered her toward the bedrooms.

"You are all dead people," Angel said.

Justine didn't see the blow but she heard it. When she turned around she saw Salazar stepping back and Angel hunched over, cradling his jaw.

"Ignore him," Justine told Alison. "He's overcompensating. He won't be in any position to hurt anyone."

Alison nodded. She was a beautiful woman with delicate features, but looked tired and drawn, which was hardly surprising given her ordeal.

Justine took her along a short corridor that led away from the living room. She stayed clear of the door that had an open padlock on it, and when she saw Alison's reaction was glad she had.

"That's where he kept me," the other woman said, as tears filled her eyes.

"It's okay. He can't hurt you anymore," Justine assured her, leading her into a small bedroom that was completely empty.

"Where's Rafael?" Alison asked, the moment Justine shut the door.

How could she answer without crushing Alison's spirit?

"That's the same look Maureen and Seymour gave me," she remarked. "They wouldn't say anything about him. What's going on? Is Rafael dead?"

"No," Justine replied, and Alison sagged with relief. "He made a bad decision. Angel used you to blackmail him into betraying his colleagues."

"No." Alison tensed again, her face drawn. "No. He wouldn't do that. No. Not even for me."

"I'm afraid people were hurt, killed, because of his actions," Justine said, putting a hand on Alison's shoulder.

"No!" she yelled, brushing the hand away. "He's a good man. He wouldn't help that monster."

"He thought it was the only way to get you back."

Alison broke down completely then, sobbing, and Justine put her arm around her to try and console her.

They stayed like that for a while until Alison's tears subsided.

"I want to see him," she said, inhaling long gulps of air between her waning sobs.

"I'll see what I can do," Justine said, rising. "Wait here."

She left Alison alone in the bedroom and went into the living room. The place was run down and sparsely furnished with cast-offs. It reeked of misery.

Justine signaled Salazar, who stood over Angel. The powerful assassin was now seated on the floor, hands cuffed behind his back. Sci and Mo-bot sat on a ragged blue corduroy couch.

"Can I talk to you?" Justine said, and Salazar came over. "She wants to see Rafael."

The NYPD detective nodded. "Understandable. I can arrange it."

"You hear that?" Justine asked. There was a thrumming sound at the edge of her perception that rapidly grew louder.

"It's a chopper," Salazar said.

He went outside and Justine followed to see a small helicopter loom larger as it descended fast. Soon it was wheels-down on the street, bringing neighbors to their windows. Four men in dark suits emerged from the sleek black bird. One of them ran to meet Justine and Salazar. He was about six feet one with wild blond hair.

"Miss Smith, Detective Salazar, my name is Tate Johnson. I'm an independent contractor with the Department of Defense. Secretary Carver sent me to take care of a problem." He yelled to make his voice heard above the sound of the rotors.

Sci and Mo-bot hustled Angel out of the house.

"That's the suspect," Justine replied. "Known only as Angel."

"We'll see what we can find out," Tate said, before nodding to three colleagues.

The men ran over and took custody of the assassin.

"The Secretary asked me to pass on his thanks," Tate announced. "To both of you."

Justine nodded and watched him and his colleagues force Angel into the chopper. There were more neighbors at their windows now, and a few out on their lawns, and they were treated to the sight of the chopper rising into the sky.

As the sound of the powerful engines died away and the helicopter became a speck, Justine hoped Carver's people would be able to find out why a Chinese hitman had been briefed to target them, so that she, Jack and the rest of the Private team could escape the web that had ensnared them.

CHAPTER 56

IT TOOK A day for Hua and his team to get full surveillance on Liu Bao up and running. Hua was young, but he was as careful and methodical as a seasoned veteran, and went to great pains to ensure his electronic surveillance wouldn't be detected by any counter measures Liu's people might employ.

He was very ingenious: replacing the target's toothbrush in his penthouse apartment with a replica that contained a listening device, hacking into the webcam on Liu's laptop and compromising his digital personal assistant at home and in the office. Within twenty-four hours, Zhang Daiyu and I had eyes and ears on most of Liu Bao's life.

And what a life it was.

Money had washed him clean of the dirt of the street, but success hadn't changed everything about him. He clearly had a drug problem, which he indulged in the company of the girls who visited his home and office. His penthouse apartment was located on the top three floors of a magnificent tower block in Chaoyang, the diplomatic district, which was full of fashionable restaurants, clubs, and bars. His home was as much of a status symbol as his office block.

But for all the trappings of power and success, Liu Bao's life looked empty to me. Full of distractions but lacking in meaning.

Zhang Daiyu and I had established a makeshift command center in our room in the hostel. It consisted of three laptops Hua had provided us with, each connected to the Private backup server network by high-speed wireless dongles that fed us Liu Bao's movements and conversations. In addition to the digital surveillance we now had a team of eight agents working in shifts. There was no higher priority for me than finding out why Liu had targeted Private, and ensuring that he and the people who had killed so many of our colleagues were punished.

"Any idea where he's heading yet?" I asked Zhang Daiyu as I came through the door with dinner: a couple of cartons of noodles. Liu Bao had left his apartment with his security detail shortly before I'd gone to get our food.

"It's a drinks reception for the American Friends of China Business Consortium," she replied, shifting slightly so I could sit on the bed next to her.

I handed her the spring chicken noodles she had ordered while watching Liu Bao on-screen mingling with people in cocktail dresses or black tie.

"How did our agent get inside?" I asked.

"Fake Beijing Police identification," Zhang Daiyu revealed, and I frowned.

That was definitely beyond our permitted activities in China, but the situation was sufficiently desperate for us to be flexible about interpreting the law.

Liu Bao was glad-handed and had his back patted by many people as he walked around the room. It made me wonder how many of Beijing's rich and powerful knew about his background as a street criminal. Would they have cared or was money the great absolver?

On-screen, he made a beeline across the room for a guy who could only be American. He had carefully combed, wispy blond hair and was carrying a few extra pounds beneath his tux. There was a Stars and Stripes pin fixed to his lapel.

Liu Bao greeted him warmly, and the two men smiled as they engaged in friendly chatter together.

"Do we know who that is?" I asked.

Zhang Daiyu shook her head. "We can find out."

"Looks like they are friends," I remarked.

"I'll ask Hua to find out who the American is."

Her phone rang as she was texting the request and she answered. She listened for a short while before hanging up.

"Interesting," she said, and I was immediately intrigued. "That was a friend I've been trying to speak to ever since you followed that man to Guoanbu headquarters."

She put her noodles down, untouched, and got to her feet.

"Come on," she said. "We need to go. She wants to meet us tonight."

CHAPTER 57

WE TOOK A taxi to the park in front of the Temple of Heaven, one of a series of former imperial halls set in beautifully land-scaped parkland. Zhang Daiyu told me the place was popular with kung fu and tai chi schools in the morning, but it was virtually deserted when we arrived at 9:45 p.m. We headed for a circular three-tier pagoda.

"This is the Hall of Prayer for Good Harvest," Zhang Daiyu said as we approached.

"Your friend obviously has a good sense of irony," I remarked. "Who is she?"

"Her name is Ma Fen and she works for the Guoanbu."

"Chinese State Security?" I asked, and Zhang Daiyu nodded.

"If she's caught talking to us it would mean prison for her," she said.

I wondered why her friend would risk her liberty and life for our investigation.

We hurried across the park toward the Hall of Prayer for Good Harvest. As we drew closer I could see the bottom tier of the pagoda was painted deep red and the upper levels dark blue. The building was set on a mound lined with balustraded terraces. We had no need to make the climb though. I saw a tiny lone figure at the foot of the terraces, near the steps to the grand hall.

Ma Fen couldn't have been more than five feet two, and she was so thin I thought I might lose sight of her if she turned sideways on. Despite her slightness, there wasn't a hint of weakness about her. Even in the dark her eyes shone with intelligence and determination.

Zhang Daiyu and Ma Fen exchanged a warm greeting then the intelligence officer turned to me.

"Mr. Morgan. It's an honor and a pleasure."

"Nice to meet you, Officer Ma," I replied.

"Call me Fen, please," she told me. "Some people say you're a criminal. Others say you're dangerous."

"What do you say?" I asked.

"I think you're a hero. I read about what you did in Moscow. That was no easy thing. And now you are here in Beijing. Causing trouble. Liu Bao and his friends want you very badly."

"That's flattering, I guess," I replied.

Zhang Daiyu said something to her in a murmur.

"Zhang Zhang here sent me the photographs of the man leaving Liu Bao's office. The man you followed to Guoanbu," Fen said. "His name is Fang Wenyan and he is a mid-ranking field operative. He is in the ascendancy."

"Ascendancy?"

"There is a never-ending battle for the soul of China," Fen explained. "On one side there are those like me who believe we should look inwards and solve our domestic problems as a nation. And then there are those like Liu Bao and Fang Wenyan, who believe in empire and conquest. They think power comes from engaging in the affairs of the world. I and others like me think China can set a better example by disengaging from global power struggles. No offense, but America knows only too well the cost of geopolitical meddling and misadventure."

"I wouldn't call it meddling," I protested.

It certainly hadn't felt that way when I'd been deployed to Afghanistan. We were on an important mission to wrest control of the country from an evil regime that harbored and supported terrorism, but now after twenty years that same regime was back in power with the tacit approval of our leadership. Maybe there was something in what she'd said?

"Okay, not meddling," Fen conceded. "I'm not here to hold a debate. Let's call it pursuing an international agenda. Liu Bao and his friends won't be happy until China rules the world."

"Is he Guoanbu?" I asked.

"Who can say? Fang Wenyan might be his handler or just a well-connected friend. Either way, he's not to be underestimated."

"Do you recognize this?" I asked, producing my phone and showing her a photo of the tattoo we'd seen on so many of our assailants.

She studied the image of the three dragons emblazoned on Wang Yichen's arm, and shook her head. "I've never seen it."

"The men who have attacked us all carry this mark," Zhang Daiyu explained.

"A secret society perhaps?" Fen suggested. "Or a gang?"

She'd reached the same conclusion as Zhang Daiyu and I.

"Whoever they are, they're sufficiently clever to have gone undetected by the apparatus of the state," Fen remarked. "Which means they're dangerous."

She hesitated before continuing.

"China used to be an ideal. It used to be an objective, a utopia of equality, but now we're just like you, Mr. Morgan. Here a person can satisfy their greed even if that means they have too much while another starves. We have imported the worst of American thinking—the greed, ambition, dishonesty—but unlike America, here there are no checks and balances. This is a single-party state. Control the party and you control everything. That makes the men you face far more dangerous than anyone you've ever encountered. There is nothing to hold them back."

She turned to leave.

"America is more than greed, ambition, and dishonesty," I insisted. "There is community, faith, kindness, and so much more. There are good people everywhere. And bad."

She smiled wistfully, as though she didn't believe me.

"Well, you certainly found the bad ones here. And I wish you luck with them."

CHAPTER 58

JUSTINE'S PHONE RANG at 8:27 a.m. and she woke feeling half stunned from a dreamless and all too brief sleep. She answered the call.

"Hello."

"Miss Smith," Detective Salazar said. "If you bring her down to the precinct, I can get Mrs. Lucas five minutes with her husband."

"We're on our way," Justine said, running her hand over her face as she rose from the chair.

She hung up and crossed the room to rouse Alison.

After Angel had been flown away by helicopter yesterday, Salazar had arranged for an ambulance to take Alison to Presbyterian Hospital, and Justine had gone with her. A uniformed female police officer, a specialist in violence against women, had taken Alison's statement while she was waiting for the results of medical tests. Justine had been relived to discover Angel hadn't been overtly violent toward her during her ordeal locked in one of the bedrooms of the run-down house, though she had been manhandled when he'd snatched her off the street.

She had finally been discharged at 3 a.m. but couldn't stand the idea of going home while Rafael was being held in custody, so Justine had taken her to the New York Edition and shared her own hotel room.

Justine had sat in an armchair and watched Alison toss and turn in bed. She was deeply distressed, but it was hard to tell whether she was more traumatized by the abduction or by her husband's incarceration. It had been around 6 a.m. when Alison finally fell into a deep sleep, which allowed Justine to drift off too.

Ten minutes after waking, after a change of clothes, they were in a cab heading for the Twentieth Precinct. Justine had given Alison a green T-shirt and blue jeans, which clashed with the high heels she'd been wearing when she had been abducted. They were bright silver, embellished with sequins and tiny crystals. Lovely with the silver cocktail dress she had been wearing for her night out with friends, but impractical for daytime.

"I'm not sure I can do this," she said when the cab pulled up outside the precinct after fifteen minutes fighting the morning traffic.

"It's not going to be easy," Justine responded. "Your husband did what he thought was right, remember."

She found the words hard to utter because she felt they somehow betrayed the memory of Lewis, and Jessie, too, who was still hospitalized as a result of Rafael's actions. But Alison was an innocent in all this and she deserved some comfort.

They went into the precinct. Salazar was waiting in the quiet lobby.

"Good morning, Miss Smith, Mrs. Lucas," he said. "Follow me."

He used a key card and punched a code into an alphanumeric pad to get through the lobby security door into the operations area. Justine and Alison followed him past offices into a plain corridor that led to the holding cells and interview rooms.

There were four doors to Justine's right, each leading to an interview room. To her left was a double door that gave access to the cells.

"He's in here," Detective Salazar said, stopping outside the second door.

Alison took a deep breath, closed her glistening eyes to compose herself, and then nodded.

Salazar opened the door and she stepped inside.

Justine saw Rafael try to rise from his chair, but his hands were cuffed to an anchor on the table in front of him.

Justine couldn't see Alison's face, but she saw her shudder and tears filled Rafael's eyes.

Salazar closed the door but Justine could still see the couple through the observation window. Alison sat opposite her husband, although it seemed to Justine that she had partly collapsed, as if her legs had given out on her as she sank into the chair.

"What a mess," Salazar remarked. Justine nodded. "We're still figuring out what to charge him with because he was under duress. The DA will make a recommendation."

Justine was deeply conflicted. Rafael had been put in an awful position by a man who was a proven killer. He'd made some bad choices but wasn't an inherently bad man, nor a willing accomplice. She didn't envy the people who had to unpick the legal points here and felt nothing but sympathy for Alison. She was another of Angel's victims and would have to live with the consequences of his evil actions for the rest of her life.

Justine simply hoped Secretary Carver's people would break him and then decide on the best way for him to be punished.

CHAPTER 59

I WOKE UP to find Huang Hua standing over me.

"You really need better security," he said.

He was holding a laptop, which he took to the desk where Zhang Daiyu and I had our makeshift operation center. She was stirring now and sat up in the loose T-shirt and leggings she'd bought to wear as pajamas.

"Good, you're awake. I have something you need to see," Hua said.

He set up his laptop in front of the others he'd given us.

Zhang Daiyu said something sharp in Mandarin and he smiled.

"In English, Zhang Daiyu. Don't be so antisocial." He turned to me. "She wants to know how I found you and how I got in." He powered up his machine. "Getting in was easy. I just told the receptionist I was going to visit some friends, and I found you because I put a tracking device on my machines in case they were stolen." He gestured at the computers he'd given us. "I didn't mean to disturb you. I can come back later if you're busy."

His insinuation wasn't lost on either of us.

"They don't have any other rooms," Zhang Daiyu explained.

He held up his hands. "No need to explain. I'm not here to talk about you, I'm here to tell you about Gavin Hudson."

"Gavin who?" I asked.

Hua opened a file on his laptop and showed us a photograph of Liu Bao and the blond man with the Stars and Stripes lapel pin we'd observed at the reception the previous night.

"This is Gavin Hudson," Hua revealed. "He's a junior staffer at the US Embassy."

Hua opened another file and scrolled through Gavin's personnel records and official photographs.

"How did you access his State Department records?" I asked.

Hua made a face that reminded me of Mo-bot's expression when I doubted her abilities to fix a problem. It was as though I was suggesting his skills weren't up to the simple challenge of circumventing US Government security.

"The American State Department has rules and guidelines about in-country relationships," Hua went on. "Thankfully, Gavin met his sweetheart during his last rotation in Washington."

He showed us another photo, this one of an athletic brunette in a dark pant suit, posing for an official photo.

"This is Daisy Wells, a freelance technology reporter with by-lines in *Wired*, the *Atlantic,* and other well-established publications. She passed State Department vetting without any problems." Hua paused. "But there *is* a problem."

He brought up a photo taken from one of the surveillance cameras planted in Liu Bao's penthouse. It showed three women, and I recognized one of them as Wells.

"We thought she was a call girl. It is the perfect cover, with the number of women Liu has coming and going from his apartment. I think she's feeding him information on Hudson, or else taking instructions on how to manipulate him. Whatever she's doing, I'll bet Gavin Hudson has no idea she knows Liu Bao."

"Then I think we should tell him," I said, and Hua smiled and nodded his agreement.

CHAPTER 60

GAVIN HUDSON LIVED in Beijing's diplomatic quarter, not far from Liu Bao's penthouse apartment. It was one of the most heavily monitored places on the planet. The Chinese authorities wanted to know what the rest of the world was doing, and the various diplomatic missions kept tabs on each other, keen to understand which countries were trying to gain an advantage with Asia's superpower.

Hua drove Zhang Daiyu and me in the LDV surveillance van. It was early, but life in this part of the city was already in full swing. Embassy staffers were out jogging, hawkers were setting up their food stalls, and noisy trucks were making deliveries to local shops and restaurants. We arrived in Xiayuan Park, the complex where Hudson lived, and Hua found a space in the parking lot opposite the apartment building.

We left the vehicle and headed across the street toward the

block. There was an American guard on the gate. Civilian dress of dark trousers and a short-sleeve white shirt, but his ramrod posture, crewcut, and piercing stare screamed Marine Corps to me.

"Can I help you, sirs? Ma'am?" he asked, as we approached the open gate set in a green mesh fence. Behind it lay manicured gardens and a modern apartment block twenty floors high.

"We're here to see Gavin Hudson," I replied.

"Is he expecting you?" the guard asked.

"You with the Corps?" I gambled. "I was a pilot. Flew Sea Knights in Afghanistan."

"Good for you, but that don't make us brothers."

He obviously took his job very seriously, so I tried another tack.

"Mr. Hudson has got himself into some trouble with a local gang boss. It's compromised him and he's going to want to know about it."

"That's an embassy security issue, sir."

I began to wonder if the guy was a former Marine or a failed one. He lacked the imagination and initiative typically found in the Corps.

"We'll inform the embassy once we've spoken to Mr. Hudson," I replied. "Just call up and ask if he'll see us. Tell him it's about his finance friend."

The guard studied me for a moment and then nodded. He pulled a wireless intercom from his pocket and dialed a number. He stepped away to talk and returned a few moments later.

"You can go up. Fifteenth floor. Apartment fifteen-zero-eight."

"Thanks," I replied.

Zhang Daiyu, Hua, and I walked up the short path leading to the main entrance. The building was painted dark gray with wooden trim on the balconies and windows and there were matching panels artfully positioned on its fascia.

We went inside the air-conditioned lobby and saw another guy in dark trousers and short-sleeve white shirt standing beside a desk. He eyed us as we walked toward the elevator but said nothing.

"Friendly," Hua remarked.

We took an elevator up to the fifteenth floor and emerged to find Gavin Hudson waiting for us in a small lobby. There was a display of tropical flowers on the table behind him that filled the air with a sweet scent.

"Who are you people?" he asked.

Hudson was dressed in running shoes, sweatpants, and a T-shirt. We were obviously keeping him from his morning exercise.

"My name is Jack Morgan," I replied. "I run a detective agency called Private. These are my colleagues Zhang Daiyu and Huang Hua. We'd like to ask you some questions about your relationship with Liu Bao."

"Questions? Are you serious? I don't have time for questions," he responded.

"Okay," I said slowly. "Then we'll take it to the CIA section chief at the embassy."

"Take what?" Hudson asked, suddenly concerned.

"The fact that your girlfriend is an associate of Liu Bao. She's visited his apartment in the company of other women we believe are call girls. Do you have any idea why she might do that?"

It was as though I'd hit him. He staggered a little and the color drained from his face.

"Daisy?" he asked. "You're talking about Daisy?"

I nodded.

"Shit!" he said. "You better come in."

CHAPTER 61

SHOULDERS SAGGING AND with an air of bewilderment and defeat, Gavin Hudson led us down the corridor to his apartment.

It was decorated like an upmarket hotel, with eye-catching pieces of furniture, engaging abstract art, and beautiful coffee-table books displayed around the place: stylish but lacking the feel of a proper home.

He shut the living-room door behind us.

"Have a seat."

He gestured to two sofas facing each other either side of a glass door, which opened onto a large balcony. I could see the seemingly endless city beyond.

"I'm assuming you have proof of this allegation," he said.

I signaled Hua, who pulled his tablet computer from a

shoulder bag and handed it to Hudson. The embassy staffer scrolled through the photos of Daisy and Liu Bao.

He shook his head in dismay. "She introduced me to him. Claimed she'd met him during an interview for a magazine. Said he would be a good contact for intel on trade and finance. How did this get by State?"

I shrugged.

"I hardly know the guy. We've had a beer a couple times. That's it," Hudson continued.

"Sounds as though they were just getting started on you," I replied.

He looked relieved. If it had gone any farther, something like this could have ruined his career. Or made a traitor of him.

"Daisy?" he said, rising. He put his head through a doorway. "Daisy honey, could you come in here?" He was grimacing, but his voice gave away nothing much, just the slightest edge to it.

I wasn't expecting her to be in the apartment and exchanged a look with Zhang Daiyu, who seemed calm about the unexpected encounter. It would be a good opportunity for us to put Wells in a tight spot.

Hudson returned to his seat opposite us and a moment later Daisy Wells came into the room, dressed in an oversized T-shirt and little else, having obviously just woken up.

"Honey?" she asked Hudson, still coming round. "Who are these people?"

"Private detectives," he replied. "They say you work for Liu Bao."

She tried to conceal the shock she felt at the accusation but wasn't entirely successful.

"What? Bullshit!"

He showed her the photos on Hua's tablet and she crumbled almost immediately.

"He recruited me out of college. Said he needed a cultural advisor."

She sat next to Hudson and put her hand on his knee, but he moved away.

"I know I should have told you, honey." She started to cry. "I never meant for this to happen. He told me to befriend you in Washington. That you'd be coming to China soon."

"So he has good sources," Zhang Daiyu observed. "To know about US State Department postings in advance."

"I didn't realize that . . . I didn't know what he wanted. I still don't. As I got to know you, Gavin, I fell in love, but by then I was trapped. Liu threatened to expose me to you . . . to the embassy . . . unless I kept doing what he told me to do. I begged him to stop but he refused to let me go. He said I was to introduce him to you and help you understand that your future lay in furthering China's interests."

"Honey trap," I remarked. "One of the oldest tricks in the book. He got to Daisy with money and used her to get to you."

"Have you been sleeping with him?" Gavin asked her.

The silence that followed told him everything.

"How could you do this?" he asked, his face flushing red.

For a moment his anger surged and I thought I might have

to intervene, but as I tensed his rage subsided and was replaced by sorrow.

"I'm so glad you caught this," he said to me. "Thank you."

"You'll report it?" I asked.

"Report it?" Daisy echoed, concern in her voice.

Gavin nodded.

"Mr. Hudson has an obligation to report any compromised contact to his superiors," I explained. "They'll bring in specialists to assess the situation."

"I didn't mean . . . I'm sorry. I . . ." She was sobbing now.

Gavin's eyes were full of sadness. It was clear that life as he'd known it was over. He would almost certainly be transferred back to Washington for a time. If she was lucky enough to escape charges, Daisy would not be going with him. The State Department would put an end to their relationship.

"If I can ever repay the favor . . ." he said.

"We would like any non-sensitive intelligence she might be able to offer that relates to Liu Bao's operations," I replied.

"But I don't know anything," Daisy protested. "He always kept me in the dark. I should never have taken his money."

"No, you shouldn't," I agreed.

"What about Private?" Zhang Daiyu asked. "Did he ever say anything about an investigation agency called Private?"

Daisy wiped her eyes and thought for a moment.

"Yes," she said. "I heard him talking on the phone once. He said Private would be targeted. An example would be made of them."

I looked at Zhang Daiyu and could see she was equally troubled by this revelation.

"He said that?" I confirmed. "An example would be made of them?"

Daisy nodded.

Why would a powerful Beijing mobster with connections to Chinese Intelligence want to target my detective agency?

CHAPTER 62

WE LEFT GAVIN and Daisy to deal with the mess Liu Bao had made of their lives and took the elevator down from the apartment.

Daisy had been searching for easy money after college, and Liu, seeing an opportunity in a beautiful, intelligent journalism major, had taken a long-term bet she would be useful. I'd encountered this sort of strategic planning before, in Moscow, but few people could countenance the thought process involved in formulating espionage operations on a ten- or twenty-year time scale. Like the old urban myth of the frog growing accustomed to being boiled in a pot, by the time Daisy realized there was something sinister about Liu Bao's intentions, she was in too deep and had been sufficiently compromised for him to have leverage on her. Now Liu had started the same process with Gavin Hudson, finding something he desired—in this case Daisy—and using her to compromise him. Thankfully, we'd exposed the plan at an early stage and Gavin was unlikely to suffer any long-term adverse effects on his career.

Daisy was a different matter. The State Department might decide to prosecute, or they could flip her and run her as an asset to get intel from inside Liu Bao's organization. Either way, it was clear by the time we left that her relationship with Gavin was over.

"I still don't understand why Liu would target us," I said as the elevator took us down to the ground floor. "We've never crossed paths with him before, right?"

"Never," Zhang Daiyu agreed.

"Who can be sure though?" Hua added. "He has interests everywhere. He's brokered arms deals in Eastern Europe and Africa, financed mining activities in Asia and Australia, and has technology investments in North America. He has interests in energy production and mining in South America. A different branch of Private might have crossed his path and not even known it."

Hua was right, but this felt too targeted to be retaliation for something that hadn't even registered on our radar.

"I think we need to go back to the beginning," I said. "I want to talk to David Zhou again. Do you think you can arrange it?"

Zhang Daiyu exhaled sharply.

"Maybe you don't know how difficult it is to get into Qincheng," she replied.

"Maybe I don't," I said. "But I do know how capable you are, so if I ask the impossible it's because I know you can do it."

Hua said something I did not understand and she smiled.

"He says your American football coach psychology is very effective. In the old days you would have got a peasant to try and steal pearls from under the emperor's pillow."

"Thanks," I said.

"It's not a compliment," Hua responded flatly. "Crimes against the emperor were punishable by death. I was suggesting to Zhang Daiyu that you are dangerous."

I didn't like what he was implying but had to admire his honesty.

The doors opened. We stepped out into the lobby.

"I'll see what I can do," Zhang Daiyu said. "The emperor's pearls had better be worth the risk."

"I hope so," I replied. "Now we have new information to trade and understand more of what's going on, I hope we can convince Zhou to tell us the real reason he's been sent to prison."

CHAPTER 63

HUA RETURNED TO his surveillance team, and Zhang Daiyu and I spent a tense day at the workers' hostel on Changcui Road. I was meant to be reviewing the files Hua had put together on Liu, but in truth passed the hours waiting for Zhang Daiyu's phone to ring and trying to glean nuggets of information from her strained conversations.

Her uncle had said her request to get into Qincheng Prison once more was impossible to arrange, but Zhang Daiyu didn't give up and enlisted the help of her aunt, his wife, to convince Ma Yuhang that a meeting with David Zhou was essential for his niece. It became a family effort. There were calls from Zhang Daiyu to uncle and aunt, then between husband and wife, until finally, shortly before lunch, Ma Yuhang conceded he would try to get us in again.

The passing hours turned afternoon into evening, and it was a little before 6 p.m. when he finally rang and Zhang Daiyu listened to a few terse sentences from him. She replied gratefully and hung up.

"Seven-thirty p.m. exactly," she said to me. "That's when we have to be at the gate."

Time seemed to slow during the sixty minutes before we had to leave, but eventually we were in a taxi heading for Qincheng. We presented ourselves at the same heavy door we'd used on our first visit, but this time our experience was different.

At 7:30 p.m exactly Ma Yuhang opened the door to us in person and furtively ushered us inside. He said something to Zhang Daiyu, who translated to me, "Shift change. We need to be quick. Like before."

I glanced into the operations room to see one prison officer behind the thick bullet-proof glass. He was facing in the other direction, studying an information poster pinned to a wall, and I got the impression he was deliberately looking the other way as Ma Yuhang led us inside. We bypassed the X-ray machine and metal detector, both of which were unmanned.

Her uncle spoke to Zhang Daiyu in hurried tones that bordered on hostile at times. We moved further into the prison, heading along the same corridor we'd walked before. Ma Yuhang used his key card to open the heavy security doors and within minutes we were outside the interview room where we'd first encountered David Zhou.

Ma Yuhang spoke to Zhang Daiyu and she translated for me

"We have a few minutes only," she said. "He's called in many favors to get us this far, but they will only last so long."

I nodded to him. "*Xièxie nǐ*."

Ma Yuhang bowed his head in reply, but clearly wasn't happy. He opened the door and ushered us inside.

I have no idea how long David Zhou had been waiting in this bare gray concrete room that reeked of fear and misery, but he looked surprised and somewhat relieved to see us. He fidgeted with the shackles that tethered his wrists to the table.

"You seem less hostile than previously," I told him.

"I thought I was about to meet my end," he said. "So anyone other than an executioner is a most welcome sight."

Ma Yuhang shut the door behind us and stood guard outside. Zhang Daiyu and I took seats opposite Zhou.

"I was sitting here trying to make my peace with death but failing badly. I really don't want to die. Life is too good." He smiled sadly.

"You're expecting people to reach you in here?" I asked.

"Why not?" he replied. "You did."

"People like Liu Bao?" I asked.

We didn't have a lot of time and I was going to have to risk sharing some of the intel we'd acquired if I was going to get David Zhou to trust me.

He looked surprised and a little impressed. "Liu Bao is a mere foot soldier."

"Pretty powerful foot soldier," I remarked.

"You only say that because you haven't seen the power of the men he serves."

"We know he's connected to the Guoanbu," I revealed.

"He is Guoanbu," David countered. He looked around the room uncertainly and added softly, "As am I."

I exchanged a surprised glance with Zhang Daiyu. My surprise was two-fold. I was shocked to learn this prisoner worked for Chinese State Security, but also that he'd trusted us with the information. Assuming it was true, of course. He had no reason to lie to us and my instincts told me I could trust him, but I had learnt long ago that nothing is ever what it first seems.

"I met Liu Bao the night your people were attacked. He told me I was finished and that my demise would be used as an opportunity to take out another enemy."

"Private," Zhang Daiyu observed.

"Why would he consider us an enemy? Why would he use us to take you out?" I asked.

Zhou had relaxed a little now. Gone was the taciturn, suspicious man we'd encountered during our first visit to Qincheng. He seemed almost relieved to have someone to talk to. I could only imagine how hard his life was in this place.

"I have no idea why your business was targeted," he replied, "but he wanted me gone because I have been tasked by my superiors with bringing him to justice. For months I have been investigating him for embezzling state funds as part of his operations. I was authorized to engage with him and build sufficient trust that he would use me to process the finances for an arms deal in Africa."

"Process the finances?" I asked. "You mean money laundering?"

Zhou nodded. "I was able to prove the money he received

for the arms deal was not the same amount he returned to the Guoanbu bosses. There was a thirty-million-dollar shortfall, but before I could present the evidence, I was arrested for the murders of your colleagues. I have not heard from my superiors, so I can only guess they have been purged or convinced to remain silent. I underestimated Liu Bao and I regret that deeply. He is far better connected than I could ever have imagined. There's a war going on. A war for the heart and soul of China."

"We heard," I responded. "Someone told us there is a battle raging within Guoanbu."

"What's happening here to me, to you, is a manifestation of that battle," Zhou confirmed.

"But what do we have to do with it?" I asked. "Private has no interest in such things."

"I don't know, but you are involved whether you like it or not," he replied. "Liu Bao and his sponsors believe in the power of the individual. In your country people would say they were right-wing, but such terms have little meaning here. They believe in self-enrichment above all else, and as a result they support the idea of Chinese empire and conquest. This isn't about spreading ideology. This is about unparalleled greed."

"I still don't understand where we come in," I remarked.

The door opened and Ma Yuhang stepped in and said something to Zhang Daiyu.

"We have to go now," she translated. "Or else we will become permanent residents."

She got to her feet and I did likewise.

"I can't help you. I don't know why Liu Bao chose to target

you. Private never came up during my investigation," David Zhou said hurriedly.

"Thank you, Mr. Zhou," I said. "I hope you receive justice."

He nodded and smiled as Zhang Daiyu and I followed Ma Yuhang from the interview room.

Zhang Daiyu's uncle was on edge and kept chivvying us along as we made our way through the building. There were two more prison officers by the entrance and one of them approached us and asked a question. I couldn't understand Ma Yuhang's reply but I recognized its tone. He bawled the man out, overcompensating with a show of authority to hide the fact he himself was doing something illegal. The tirade worked and the officer backed off, chastened.

Moments later we were outside and Zhang Daiyu and her uncle exchanged hurried words.

"He says never to ask him to do this again," she translated.

I bowed and thanked him formally. He didn't acknowledge this, instead hurrying inside and slamming the heavy steel door.

"Did you get what you needed?" Zhang Daiyu asked.

"Well, we now know we're caught up in some kind of power struggle within Chinese Intelligence, but I don't feel any closer to understanding why Private has been sucked into it."

"Liu Bao knows," she remarked.

"Right," I agreed, as we walked away from the prison. "So our challenge is to figure out a way to get him to share his secrets."

CHAPTER 64

JUSTINE WOKE TO the sound of her phone ringing. She'd taken a sobbing Alison Lucas home to her midtown apartment after the visit to see Rafael in custody. She didn't know what Alison and he had said to each other, but the poor woman was deeply traumatized. She had refused Justine's offer to stay and support her. Alison said her sister would be arriving on the red-eye from Chicago, so Justine had returned to her hotel room at the New York Edition and collapsed into bed.

She thought about calling Jack, but they weren't like a normal couple who could exchange news of their day on unsecured telephone lines or by text. They faced danger at every turn and there was no telling how a tiny nugget of intercepted information might be used against them, so she lay on her fresh sheets, naked to maximize the chill of the air conditioning, trying to counter the baked-in heat of the scorching summer. She'd gradually been lulled to sleep by the humming of the fan and the muted sounds of the city.

She didn't recognize the number on her ringing phone when she squinted at it, slowly waking. She rubbed her eyes before she answered.

"Hello?"

"Miss Smith, it's TJ, we met the day before yesterday."

Justine recognized the voice of Tate Johnson, the man who had taken custody of Angel.

"I have good news and bad, but I'd like to share it with you in person. There is transport waiting downstairs. It will bring you to me."

"Give me five," she replied before hanging up.

She tried Mo-bot and Sci, but their phones were off and there was no answer from their rooms, so she rolled out of bed, took a hurried shower, and got dressed in light linen slacks and a white cotton blouse she'd purchased after taking Alison home. She grabbed her bag and hurried from the room.

When she reached the lobby, she was greeted by two men in dark suits.

"Miss Smith," one of them said. "My name is Cotton and this is Mr. Richardson. Mr. Johnson sent us."

Justine felt a sudden pang of uncertainty. What if these weren't Johnson's men? What if they'd been sent to abduct her? How did they know where she was staying? She hadn't told anyone other than Sci and Mo-bot that she'd switched hotels.

"How did Mr. Johnson and I meet?" she asked.

"Outside the house on Sixtieth Street. We touched down in

a chopper. Mr. Richardson and I were inside the aircraft ready to provide operational support. You were with your colleagues and Alison Lucas," the man replied. "We're the good guys, Miss Smith. We found you by tracing your phone."

Justine nodded. She wasn't entirely sure, but there was no such thing as perfect safety and these guys seemed on the level.

They took her outside to a black Escalade with a third man behind the wheel. Richardson climbed in the front passenger seat and Cotton got in beside her.

Justine checked her phone as the large SUV got underway. It was a little after seven, the city was only just coming to life, so they made swift progress through the quiet streets.

"Where are we going?" she asked.

"Forty-second Street," Cotton replied, as though that explained everything.

They were at their destination a few minutes later, which turned out not to be 42nd Street proper, but rather a service alleyway that ran behind the buildings on the south side of the street.

Cotton and Richardson stepped out of the vehicle.

"This is it, Miss Smith," Cotton said.

Justine followed them, suppressing her misgivings about what could turn into a dangerous situation.

Cotton led them to a metal fire door, which opened when he neared it. Another man in a dark suit gave him a nod of recognition and allowed them to enter.

They took a service elevator to the tenth floor, and Cotton walked them down brightly lit, carpeted corridors to an apartment at the front of the building. The door opened as they approached. Another man nodded a greeting as they went inside.

Justine followed Cotton and Richardson into a large living room that had been converted into a sophisticated surveillance center. Every surface was covered in flight cases that contained computers and electronic equipment Justine couldn't identify.

Three women and two men sat at workstations monitoring audio, video, and data feeds. At the heart of it all was Tate Johnson.

"Morning, Miss Smith," he said, offering her his hand. "Sorry for waking you but time is of the essence." He hesitated. "There's no easy way to say this, but we had to let Angel go."

Justine was dismayed. She experienced a rush of anger driven by a sense of betrayal. How could Carver's people have released a man who'd done so much harm?

"Back-channel pressure on the State Department began almost the moment we took him. It would have developed into a full-blown diplomatic incident and there was no way our man was going to talk, not without the kind of pressure we don't do in these parts anymore, so we had to cut him loose," Tate explained.

Justine felt a little sick. They had gone through so much to catch Angel, and their efforts had been rendered void by those who cared about politics more than people. Her disappointment must have shown.

"That's the bad news," Tate said in a soothing tone. "Here's the good news."

He took her to one of the many windows that were covered by thick drapes. He pulled one back a crack and gestured toward a building opposite. It was an imposing structure with extensive security; guards were posted all around the large gray-stone structure, there were cameras on every surface and counter-surveillance devices on the roof.

"That's the Chinese Consulate," he revealed. "They conduct regular security sweeps of all the surrounding buildings, but we have a short window of opportunity until the next one. Angel arrived eight minutes ago."

Tate moved the drape back into position. "If he's debriefed, we'll hear everything he says."

One of the operators at the surveillance terminals leant back in her chair and signaled to him.

"Sir, I have him. He's making a call on a secure line. It's to Beijing, sir."

"Put it on speaker," Tate said. "Let's hear what he has to say."

CHAPTER 65

ZHANG DAIYU AND I were in the surveillance van parked a short distance from Liu Bao's building. It looked as though he had settled in for the night at his penthouse. Several guests had arrived for dinner, including Fang Wenyan, Liu Bao's contact from the Guoanbu. Hua had identified some of the other guests as mid-level government officials and promised us a full background work-up on everyone, but he was dead on his feet and needed rest, so I had sent him and the physical surveillance team home.

Zhang Daiyu and I sat in front of the surveillance console, and she translated some of the chatter around the sixteen-seater dining table. It was mostly about sport and sports cars, and they drank nothing but champagne as the caterers served the meal. We heard a regular popping of corks and the talk grew more raucous.

"He's got a call," she said, putting the audio feed from the apartment on speaker.

I heard background hubbub and Liu Bao saying something.

"He's telling someone to come with him," Zhang Daiyu translated.

"It's a shame we don't have video," I remarked.

The listening devices Hua had planted were extremely difficult to detect. Cameras would have risked giving us away, but these tiny microphones concealed around the building circumvented even Liu Bao's counter measures.

There was a moment during which no one said anything but we could hear footsteps, giving us a sense of which device had the best ear on them. The hubbub of the dinner grew fainter when Zhang Daiyu switched to the listening device in Liu Bao's home office. Then a door closed and the noise of the dinner party was gone.

"I'll translate as best I can," Zhang Daiyu said as Liu took the call.

"This is Liu Bao. Go ahead, Angel, the line is secure. I have Wenyan with me. You're on speaker."

"The Americans grabbed me," Angel revealed. "The personnel at Private have connections to the US Government and had me arrested. I have become a liability here. They are sending me home."

Zhang Daiyu carefully kept the tone of her translation even and didn't capture the anger in Angel's voice.

I heard Liu Bao curse and didn't need that translated, such was the venom he put into the words.

"You were supposed to discredit them," he said. "You were supposed to kill his friends."

Fang Wenyan cut in here. "Careful what you say."

"It's a secure line," Liu Bao snapped at him before addressing Angel. "Your failure will complicate things. The downfall of Private was part of the deal."

He hit or kicked something.

"We will speak more when you get here. The brotherhood does not appreciate failure," Liu went on angrily.

There was a moment of silence and I assumed Angel had hung up.

Fang spoke up then. "Use Shang Li to draw Jack Morgan into the open. Aren't you glad we kept him alive? Use him to bring Morgan to you. Our friends will be satisfied if we kill him. They will honor the deal if we bring them the head of Jack Morgan."

CHAPTER 66

I WAS IN shock.

Shang Li was still alive. His wife had been right. Zhang Daiyu too. She looked at me tearfully, smiling with relief.

"He's alive."

I nodded, scarcely able to believe it. My friend and business partner had survived the attack that had been used to frame David Zhou and was being held hostage by these evil men.

As my mind reeled at the wonderful revelation, another part of me struggled to come to terms with the implications of what we'd just heard. My agency had been part of some sort of trade. We were the price of one of Liu Bao's corrupt deals. But with whom? I thought of all my friends and colleagues who had suffered and died, and wanted to leave the van, walk the block to his building, and beat the truth out of him.

The call had tied Angel to Liu Bao and both men to Fang

Wenyan, and we had recorded them revealing they were holding Shang Li prisoner and plotting my murder.

"Jack," Zhang Daiyu said, suddenly becoming somber. "I'm so sorry. I can't help crying with relief, I'm just so happy he's alive. But I should have been more thoughtful. They're coming for you."

I understood her fear. I had become a target of the Guoanbu, one of the most feared intelligence agencies in the world, in its home city. The odds of me making it out of Beijing alive had just lengthened significantly.

Fang Wenyan's cynical words were still reverberating in my mind when my phone rang.

It was Justine.

"Jack," she said, when I answered, "you've got to leave Beijing. Angel called someone there and they are planning to kill you."

"I know," I replied. "We heard the call. It was to Liu Bao and a Chinese State Security official called Fang Wenyan. How do you know about it?"

I didn't care about maintaining secrecy at this stage; I had already been marked for death. If anyone intercepted this call, at least the names of the conspirators would be on record somewhere.

Justine wasn't quite so reckless.

"I'm with some friends of the man you saved in Nevada. They will make sure the information reaches the right people."

She was talking about Secretary of Defense Eli Carver. I was glad she was with good people. They must have had ears on Angel.

"That's reassuring to know."

"You need to leave, Jack," she said. "Let other people take this now. Your friend has the resources to handle it."

"But Shang Li is alive," I countered. "I can't abandon him."

"They want to kill you, Jack," she protested. "You've got to get out."

"A lot of people have tried to kill me over the years, but I'm still here."

"This is different. You're in their backyard where they control everything."

"Not everything," I replied. "We have good people here too."

I looked at Zhang Daiyu, who nodded.

"I know this is hard, but I can't leave Shang Li. I must get him back, and the people behind all this need to be punished for what they've done."

There was a long pause.

"You're a stubborn man, Jack," she said at last.

"Determined," I responded. "How are things there?"

"Rafael is in custody. The DA is figuring out what charges to bring."

"What do my Nevada friend's people plan to do about Angel?"

"I don't know," she replied. "They had to let him go."

"Are they with you?"

"Uh-huh."

There was a brief pause and then a man came on the line.

"I can't give you my name," he said.

"I don't need it. I want to know if you're planning to let a man who murdered one of my colleagues, and put another in hospital, just leave the country."

"He's protected by diplomatic status, sir."

"You and I know that's meant for parking tickets, not murder."

"I can't comment on such things, sir. Not on this line. But rest assured, America always seeks justice."

"That's all I need to know," I replied.

The line went quiet for a moment.

"Jack?" Justine said.

"Can you trust that guy?" I asked.

"I think so," she replied.

"Then give him whatever help he's willing to take. Ask Sci and Mo-bot to get on it."

"Okay." She hesitated. "You sure you won't come home?"

"I can't, Jus. I can't."

It was hard to explain, but I was driven by an innate sense of duty. People either experienced it themselves and understood it, or they had no idea, in which case my actions would seem alien, possibly irrational. Thankfully Justine knew exactly what motivated me.

"Okay. Just be careful. Make sure you come back in one piece."

"I'll do my best," I replied. "I love you."

"Love you too," she said, her voice breaking.

This was hard on her. Well, it was hard on us both.

I ended the call to discover I had a voicemail message from my Los Angeles service. I returned the call and my skin crawled when I retrieved the message and heard Liu Bao's voice.

"Mr. Morgan, call me at your earliest convenience. It seems I have something you want."

CHAPTER 67

"HE'S TRYING TO lure me into his trap," I said to Zhang Daiyu. "But he's created an opportunity for us. I want you to get Hua and his team back here. We're going to put everyone on Liu Bao."

She nodded and stepped outside the van to make the call.

I phoned Mo-bot, who answered after three rings.

"Jack, Justine was just filling me in on what happened."

"We've got a chance to save Shang Li," I told her.

"So I understand. I'm all ears."

"I need to call a bad guy and I don't want him tracing my location."

"Give me the number," she said. "I'll route you off this call."

I gave her the number Liu Bao had left in his voicemail.

"The line will go dead for a while. Then you'll hear the normal ringing tones and, hopefully, whoever you need to talk to."

"Thanks," I responded.

"Good luck, Jack," she said.

I plugged my phone into one of the van's sound recorders, and soon afterwards the line went dead. The muffled noises of Zhang Daiyu talking on her phone came from outside; every so often they faded into the background cacophony of the city.

After a few moments, I heard the ringing tone and the call was answered.

"Mr. Morgan," Liu Bao said. "You're ready to trade?"

"What do you want?" I asked.

"Any evidence you've acquired in your investigation," he replied.

I knew what he really wanted, but he needed a reason for us to meet that didn't involve revealing his true intention was to kill me.

"I want copies of anything you have and your word that the originals will be destroyed," he said.

"And in exchange?"

"You get your business partner."

"The police think he's dead. How do I know you have him?" I asked. "I need proof of life."

"Give me a number and I will arrange for him to speak to you."

"A number you can trace?" I suggested. "A recording you could have made any time? No, that's not how this works. You go to his location, and in two hours I will call you and you will repeat a confirmation phrase and tell him to repeat one too."

"What phrase?" Liu Bao asked

"'The sun shines brightly on the Pacific,'" I said, quickly thinking up a unique combination of words that couldn't be anticipated in advance. "And his phrase is: 'The moon shimmers on the Atlantic.'"

"Okay," Liu replied. "But this won't happen in two hours after you've had the chance to prepare surprises for me. You're a fox, Jack Morgan, but this time you're facing a wolf. Call me in twenty minutes and you will have all the proof you need."

He didn't wait for my agreement but hung up. He was smart but not infallible. He thought we needed time to set up surveillance, but we were already on him. Even so, we were going to have to improvise.

I pulled open the side door of the van and signaled to Zhang Daiyu.

"We need to move. It's happening right now."

CHAPTER 68

"IT WILL TAKE Hua at least thirty minutes to get here," she told me. "We should call the police. Chen Ya-ting is a good man."

She was referring to her former colleague in the Beijing Police who was heading up the investigation into the deaths of the three Private agents.

"We can't take the risk of him reporting it to his superiors," I replied. "If Liu Bao's allies in Guoanbu or the government find out, all our lives would be in danger. You take the van. I'll find a cab. Liu needs to go to wherever Shang Li is being held to give me proof of life, and if he's given himself twenty minutes it must be close, so we follow him and then figure out our next move."

I could tell Zhang Daiyu didn't like the improvisation, but it was all we had so she nodded her agreement and climbed into the van.

I hurried down Tuanjiehu Road and reached Chaoyang North,

which ran in front of Liu's building. I walked along a little, heading away from the tower block, and saw a taxi coming toward me in the steady flow of traffic. I glanced over my shoulder to see Zhang Daiyu roll the van to a halt at the intersection.

Diagonally across from her, a convoy of three vehicles emerged from the underground parking garage beneath Liu Bao's building. There were two red BMW M5s and a silver Range Rover, all with blacked-out privacy glass, but we didn't need to see the occupants. These were his people.

Zhang Daiyu turned right to follow them and I hailed the cab and jumped in the back.

"Follow those cars," I said.

The driver's blank look made me regret my decision to take a taxi. I should have been in the van, and Zhang Daiyu should have been in here.

I lost valuable seconds entering the words into Google Translate and using the audio function to play the driver the translation. He nodded, muttered something and got going.

Over the many vehicles ahead of us, I could just about make out the top of the LDV surveillance van Zhang Daiyu was driving,

The cab driver, a sharp-looking man in his early sixties, said something that was lost on me.

I typed, "My friend wants me to follow her to make sure she gets home safely. She has some expensive tools with her that might interest thieves. She's in the black LDV 9 van. Could you try to keep it in sight?"

I played him the translation and he gave me a momentary look of disbelief before he nodded. He moved into the outside lane, which was for faster vehicles, and we made up some ground. I could just see Liu Bao's convoy up ahead of Zhang Daiyu, racing through the brightly lit city.

The convoy came to a busy intersection and the cars turned left, heading north on Qingnian Road. Zhang Daiyu followed, and a few cars later so did we.

When we turned the corner, I was shocked to see the two BMWs flanking the van. They had slowed and the driver of one rolled down his window to shout something. Had they made Zhang Daiyu? It certainly looked that way.

I received a text from her.

I'm done. They're warning me off. Telling me not to follow. Sorry. Let me know your location.

My fears were confirmed. Liu Bao's security team were good. They'd spotted a potential threat and neutralized it. The van's brake lights flared and it slowed right down. I was worried Liu Bao's men might recognize her and take more violent action, but the M5s peeled off and accelerated rapidly. After weaving through the light traffic on the dual carriageway, they joined the Range Rover.

I typed, "Follow the two red BMWs. The ones that just spoke to my friend in the van," and played the translation for the cab driver.

He nodded and we passed Zhang Daiyu turning into a side-street. I nodded at her but she didn't notice me. Her face was a mask of frustration and anger. She was not taking her exposure well.

I returned my attention to the convoy which was now about

fifty yards ahead. The skyline around us was changing as we moved from an upscale residential neighborhood into an industrial area. High-rise blocks were replaced by warehouses and furnace chimneys. I was heading into unknown territory, following one of the most dangerous and well-resourced men I'd ever encountered, and I was doing it alone.

CHAPTER 69

WE TURNED OFF Qingnian Road and followed Liu's convoy into an industrial park. There was less traffic now, so I used Google Translate to ask the driver to keep back.

He said something in a tone that was universally recognizable: He was frightened.

I used my phone to tell him I would pay him an additional bonus of 3,000 Yuan, roughly equivalent to 450 bucks, and that seemed to calm his nerves a little. We'd fallen back too far and lost sight of the convoy as they went round a bend, which curved for about six hundred yards following the perimeter of a warehouse complex. When we cleared the bend there was no sign of Liu Bao anywhere.

I looked in every direction. There was a rail terminal to our west, more warehouses to the north, and a large container yard to our east. The yard was packed with shipping containers stacked four or five high. There was still no sign of Liu and I started to fear we had lost our chance to rescue Shang Li.

The cab driver said something and pointed to a spot at the heart of the container yard. Liu Bao's convoy had pulled up beside a stack of large blue steel boxes.

I saw him climb out of the Range Rover and head toward the bottom container. A couple of men in black trousers and matching T-shirts opened the doors from the inside. One of them had a large triple dragon tattoo on his forearm.

The doors were closed swiftly and the angle of the container was such that I couldn't see what was inside, but I did notice the air vent and cooling system that had been fitted to the outer panel.

I opened the map on my phone, dropped a PIN in my location, and sent it to Zhang Daiyu, who replied instantly.

On my way.

I used my phone to tell the driver he could drop me off, paid him his bonus and received exclamations of relief and grateful thanks.

I got out and watched the taxi pull a U-turn and speed into the distance. I took a better look at the container facility. It was a lot of about ten acres with long alleyways that cut through the stacks. Peering down one, I could just make out the posts supporting the fence on the other side of the compound. The fence on this side was capped with barbed wire and there were automated security cameras by the main gate. One was at a height to capture vehicle registration and the other set at a suitable level to photograph visiting drivers.

A sophisticated fixed-crane system ran high over the road and was used to take the containers from the yard onto trains. There were gates either side of the giant crane system, used to stop traffic when containers were being moved, and I went over to the nearest. It was set flush against the perimeter fence. I used it to conceal myself from the view of anyone inside the compound.

I waited with a growing sense of impatience. I had nine minutes before I was supposed to call Liu Bao. Once he had given me proof of life, there was every chance he'd kill Shang Li. I couldn't risk trusting that Liu had the sense to bring his hostage to our meeting.

Zhang Daiyu arrived six minutes later and pulled to a halt at the curb beside me. I jumped in the passenger seat. We had less than three minutes before my call.

"They are in a container in there," I said, indicating the yard.

My brain was working furiously, trying to figure out a way to safely rescue my partner. The odds were stacked very much against us.

We were prohibited from carrying any weapons in China, whereas I had little doubt Liu Bao and his men would be armed. I had no idea how many people we would be up against and still didn't have confirmation Shang Li was even in there.

"Any ideas?" Zhang Daiyu asked.

I shook my head and checked my watch. Two minutes until I was supposed to call Liu Bao.

"You?"

She pursed her lips before speaking, indicating she didn't particularly like what she had to say. "We could force them to move him. Put in a call to Beijing Police and say we think we saw Liu Bao being abducted. His Guoanbu contacts will warn him before the police are even dispatched. He won't want to be caught here with the hostage. Even with his protection, it would just complicate things, so he will probably move Shang Li."

"And we intercept them when they do?" I suggested.

She was right to be skeptical about her idea – it wasn't the strongest, but it was the best we had.

"Okay," I said. "Let's do it."

CHAPTER 70

ZHANG DAIYU NEVER got the chance to make the call. The rattle of machine gunfire cut through the still night, and one of our rear tires burst as it was shredded by bullets. Another volley took out the other back tire. The van shuddered as it settled on the wheel rims.

Desperation makes people dangerous. I knew what lay in store for us if we were captured. I leapt from the cabin and was confronted by one of the men I'd seen open the container doors for Liu. He was the one with bare forearms, sporting the distinctive triple-dragon tattoo. A couple of inches shorter than me, he was well-built with a face twisted in anger and hatred.

He shouted something and brandished his gun at me, but I knew I was dead if I surrendered so kept moving toward him. He was as surprised as any man who waves a weapon around expecting people to do what they are told.

He fired a warning shot above my head and the crack of the report set my ears ringing. It didn't slow me down. I rushed at him. He tried to clock me with the butt of the QBZ-95 assault rifle, but he was too slow. I got my hands on the gun and yanked hard.

The sudden movement caused him to pull the trigger. Muzzle fire flared as a volley of bullets sliced through the air by his face. He stepped back instinctively and let go of the weapon. I took firm hold, flipped it round and thrust the butt into his face, knocking him down and out.

I ran round the van to see two more gunmen forcing Zhang Daiyu into the back of one of the BMW X5s, which had parked just on our tail. I couldn't open fire for fear of hitting her and one man took advantage of my hesitation. He pointed his gun at me and pulled the trigger.

I stepped back behind the tail of the van as a volley of bullets rattled and whined through the air where I had been standing.

I heard a screech of tires and saw the BMW shoot backwards, aiming for the gates. It swung round violently. The wheels spun, fighting for purchase, before they bit into the asphalt and sent the powerful vehicle into the container yard.

I knew I had to move fast because once Liu had his hands on Zhang Daiyu, I suspected he would kill either her or Shang Li. He only needed one of them to coerce me into obeying him.

I slung the QBZ-95 over my shoulder and ran at the chain-link fence. I hauled myself up and over, ignoring the pain as barbed wire cut into me at the top, and dropped into the container yard.

I could see the BMW reverse and start to race along the service road, passing behind the stacks of containers so it was only ever visible for an instant. I couldn't let them reach Liu Bao before I got to him. So I dropped to one knee, pulled the gun from my shoulder, and took aim.

It made a poor long-range weapon, but the rapid fire meant my aim didn't have to be perfect. I just had to ensure I didn't hit Zhang Daiyu in the back of the car. I pointed the muzzle at a gap between the containers, just ahead of the BMW, and as the car raced into sight, I squeezed the trigger and tracked the air just in front of the vehicle. Bullets chewed the ground around the wheels, and a few struck the front driver's side tire, which burst.

I didn't wait to watch the crash but was on my feet as the BMW veered out of control, sprinting by the time it hit the closest stack of containers. I was breathing heavily and my legs were burning when I saw one of Zhang Daiyu's captors drag her from the back and set off on foot. They were followed by a man I recognized; the same one who had planted the bombs in the Private Beijing office.

This was the guy who had been trying to kill us since the day we first visited David Zhou in prison.

I was spurred on by the sight of him. He'd got the better of me twice. Not this time. I raced through the container yard, bouncing off the high metal stacks as I sprinted further into the maze. It was a hot and humid evening and I was sweating by the time I got a clear line of sight on the container Liu Bao had entered.

Two of his men stood by the doors, guns raised. I shot them before they could open fire, rapid burst for each. The first went down yelling, caught in the leg, and the second was hit in the chest and fell silently.

I saw Liu Bao come racing out. He shot wildly in my direction before trying to close the doors.

Fortune had smiled on me. The men I'd shot had both fallen in front of the container, blocking the doors and preventing Liu from sealing himself inside.

Zhang Daiyu and her two captors were about thirty yards to my right, but I was going to beat them to the container. I opened fire on Liu and hit the door nearest to me. The barrage of sparking, ricocheting bullets had the desired effect and forced him inside.

The assassin shot at me from my right, but I couldn't return fire for fear of hitting Zhang Daiyu. I was almost at my target. Ignoring the volley of shots chasing my heels, I rounded the near-est door and found Liu Bao waiting for me, gun raised. Behind him I saw Shang Li tied to a chair.

Liu hadn't counted on my momentum or the fury I felt. I kept sprinting forward and barreled into him, knocking him flat.

His weapon fell to the ground and discharged. The bullet ricocheted off the roof of the steel container and hit Liu in the right thigh, which set him crying out in agony.

I aimed the barrel of my gun at his head and turned to see the assassin and his accomplice dragging Zhang Daiyu into view.

"Any false move and your boss dies," I told them, and meant every word of it.

CHAPTER 71

WE STAYED THERE, me panting heavily, the assassin and his accomplice gauging me, trying to figure out if they could take me down before I killed Liu. He lay with his hands clamped above the hole in his thigh, eyeing me with hatred. Zhang Daiyu looked defiant. I glanced over my shoulder to see Shang Li, disheveled, dirty, and slick with sweat. I felt immense relief to be reunited with the friend I'd feared dead. He looked as though he'd been beaten and battered by days of captivity, but he was alive.

I kept my gun on Liu. The assassin who'd bested me twice was alternating between targeting me and menacing Zhang Daiyu, while his accomplice kept his gun trained solely on me. Their wounded colleague in the doorway was still crying out in agony, adding to an extremely tense situation.

Time seemed to slow as we faced down each other. My perception became heightened as adrenaline surged through my body. The assassin's fingers curled around the trigger, and his accomplice developed a tic in his right eyelid. I noticed Liu Bao looking pointedly at his men, doubtless trying to communicate something. The longer this went on, the worse my odds.

I needed to break the deadlock.

I waited until the assassin swung his gun on me then brought my own round to shoot his accomplice. The man went down as a volley of bullets hit him in the gut.

Zhang Daiyu used the sudden violence to turn on the startled assassin and wrestle him for possession of his weapon.

I yelled, "Zhang Daiyu!"

She glanced back and understood my intent instantly. She let go of the man and stepped back.

He realized he was exposed and tried to bring his gun round to shoot me, but I already had him in my sights and squeezed the trigger, unleashing a short burst that caught him in the chest.

He staggered back, dropped his gun, clutched at his heart, and fell to his knees. An instant later, he collapsed face-forward and there was a sickening crack as his skull hit the concrete base outside the container.

I rounded on Liu Bao, who was fighting the pain to try and pull himself toward his weapon. He stopped and raised his hands.

Zhang Daiyu grabbed the assassin's gun, ran over to Shang Li, and removed his gag.

"Jack, Zhang Daiyu," he croaked. "Thank you. Thank you so much."

His voice was dry and rough like sandpaper. I dreaded to think how he'd been treated by these people.

Their cruelty only fueled my anger.

"Why did you target us?" I asked Liu, closing on him. He forced himself to his knees, and I raised my gun and pointed the barrel directly at his head. "Answer me!"

He glanced at his dead henchmen and fear filled his eyes.

"I'll make you a deal," he said. "Don't kill me and I will tell you everything."

CHAPTER 72

"YOUR LIFE ISN'T in my hands," I replied. I looked pointedly at Shang Li, who took what were likely to have been his first steps in days. It was his team who'd been killed, and he'd been the one taken hostage.

"I couldn't save them," Li said, tears glistening in his eyes. "Kha Delun, Ling Kang, and Jiang Jinhai. Those were their names. They were my friends. And you killed them." He grimaced as though fighting an inner demon, then wheeled round suddenly and punched Liu in the face.

The gangster reeled backward and almost lost consciousness. He cracked a bloody smile as he regained his senses.

"Their deaths were necessary. As necessary as breathing. I ordered them gone with a single breath."

Li seethed in the face of these cruel taunts.

"Will you do what's necessary?" Liu asked. "Will you breathe?"

I saw the conflict on my friend's face. He wanted vengeance so desperately, but he was fundamentally a good man. In the end his anger subsided and he sighed in resignation.

"I'm not like you," he said. "I'm not a killer."

Shang Li was a good, moral man. One of the many reasons I had chosen him to be my business partner in Private Beijing.

"Use him. Get what you need from him," said Li, heading for the world beyond the container.

"Looks like we have a deal," I told Liu Bao, who wiped his bloody mouth. "Your life for what you know." He struggled painfully to stand on his wounded leg, but I gestured with the gun. "Stay down."

He nodded slowly, eyes full of hatred, but he knew it was over for him.

"Start talking," I said, as Zhang Daiyu came to stand beside me. I glanced out of the doorway at Li, who was squatting on his haunches, head in his hands. "We should call his wife," I said to Zhang Daiyu.

She shook her head, glancing at the traumatized man. "Not yet."

She turned to Liu then and said something to him in the most derisive, hostile tone I'd ever heard from her.

He grunted and turned to me as he said, "I am a member of the Three Dragons. It is a network that reaches from the street to the government. People like me, people in government, politicians, news media. Those with power. True power for change."

He pulled down the collar of his shirt to reveal the insignia of the three dragons emblazoned near his heart, denoting membership of this secret society.

"We are going to build a new China," he went on, "powerful enough to reshape the world. We have forged an alliance with a faction in Moscow."

My heart skipped a beat when he said that word. I already suspected what was coming.

"Our new friends in Russia demanded the destruction of Private as a demonstration of our power and loyalty," he revealed.

So this had been revenge for the interventions I'd made in Moscow, and likely also in Afghanistan. I had been warned I'd angered some powerful people in the Kremlin, but this went beyond anger. This was pure vindictiveness, and innocent and blameless colleagues of mine had suffered as a result

"You failed," Zhang Daiyu countered.

Liu Bao looked at her insolently.

"There is no failure," he said. "I am just a piece in this game. There are many others. They will succeed where I have not."

"Or perhaps you will try again?" I suggested. "I can see what you're thinking."

His sly glance at me told me I was right. "It is a long road between here and the airport," he said menacingly.

"You lost. You will always lose because you're nothing. All your money and power can't change that. You're a criminal, and I break people like you for a living," I responded. "Who's the Russian contact?"

He shook his head. "You think I would tell you even if I knew?"

"That wasn't our deal," I said, brandishing the gun. "Your life for everything you know."

"Fang Wenyan," he said, referring to the young Guoanbu agent. "He's the connection. He will know who ordered Private destroyed."

"You should have killed me," I said.

"I would have, long ago," he replied. "But he wanted you alive to watch the destruction of your empire and the deaths of those you love. It was a stipulation of the deal. And now, knowing what kind of man you are, I see he was right. You don't fear death or pain. You are only moved by the suffering of others."

Fury flooded my body and I struggled to contain it. "Everyone who was part of this will pay," I seethed.

"How?" Liu Bao sneered. "You have no idea of the power you face."

"The power of evil, cruelty, greed? That's not real power. Working to bring about justice and truth—that is where real power lies."

"And how will you achieve such things?" he sneered.

"Technology helps," Zhang Daiyu replied, pulling her phone from her pocket. She held it to her ear. "You get that?"

I sensed movement behind us and looked over my shoulder to see Huang Hua enter the container together with Chen Ya-ting, Zhang Daiyu's Beijing Police contact. We'd just given him Liu Bao's confession to murder.

"We got everything," Hua said.

Chen started speaking in Mandarin and I recognized the tone of a police officer making an arrest. Zang confirmed my educated guess.

"Liu is being arrested for murder, kidnap, and treason," she said as further officers arrived. "I hope you don't mind. I called Hua while we were separated and he suggested we record every-thing. I asked him to contact Detective Chen and use my phone to track our location."

I smiled. "You did good, Zhang Daiyu. Very good."

She beamed. "Now I'm no longer using my phone to record, we can call Su Yun and let her know her husband is alive and safe."

CHAPTER 73

SHANG LI MADE the call himself, just outside the container where he'd been held captive. Zhang Daiyu, Hua and I gave him some privacy, while Detective Chen and his men dealt with Lu Bao and the others. I watched Li speak to his wife for the first time since his disappearance and saw him break down, crying with relief and joy.

After he'd told Su Yun he was coming home, he came over and hugged us all in turn. He wasn't usually a demonstrative man, but he'd been through a life-changing experience. He rained praise and thanks on us as he held us. It felt good to have my old friend back.

Following our reunion, we used Huang Hua's van, another LDV 9, to drive Shang Li to his apartment in Mingguang Village, a beautiful modern neighborhood with green spaces and playgrounds between the tastefully designed apartment blocks.

Su Yun was waiting on the street when we pulled up in front of their building, and Li almost tumbled out of the van into her arms.

Hua, Zhang Daiyu, and I got out and stood a respectful distance away while husband and wife kissed and hugged. Mai and Han emerged from the apartment building and flew down the path to join their mother and father in joyful reunion.

A lump formed in my throat as I watched their pure unadulterated happiness pour out. It was impossible not to be moved and I saw Hua and Zhang Daiyu crying tears of joy.

"Mr. Morgan," Su Yun said to me as she stepped away from her husband and children. "I knew you would restore my heart to me. You have brought us happier times." She took both my hands. "Thank you."

This was a win. One of the good moments that makes all the hardship worthwhile.

"You're welcome, Su Yun, but I didn't do it alone."

"Thank you all," she said to Zhang Daiyu and Hua. "You brought my husband home."

"Thank you," Li added. "I owe you everything."

"You owe us nothing," I replied. "You take time with your family and rest." I turned to Hua and Zhang Daiyu. "We've got work to do."

"I should help," Li said. "I want to get the people who did this."

He stepped toward me, but Su Yun put her hand on his arm and looked at me with grave concern. I recognized the look because I'd seen it on Justine's face from time to time. She had almost lost him and wasn't prepared to go through that again. At least not yet.

"You're exhausted," I said to my friend. "You've been through a mental and physical ordeal. Stay with your family. Trust us. We'll finish this."

Shang Li nodded and Su Yun smiled at me gratefully.

I watched her lead her husband and children toward their building.

"What now?" Hua asked.

I looked at Zhang Daiyu, who already knew what I was going to say.

"We need an address," she remarked. "We need to know where to find Fang Wenyan."

I nodded and she stepped away to make a call. Detective Chen did us a huge favor. He ordered his men to keep quiet about Liu Bao's arrest and said he would book him under a false name when he took him in for processing. It was as much for Chen's benefit as ours, because he needed time to gain his superiors' support, to ensure Liu was not immediately released once powerful allies began to apply pressure on his behalf, but we appreciated the favor nonetheless. We had work to do, work that involved Liu's co-conspirators believing he was still in play.

I moved a few paces clear of the others and took out my phone. I needed to speak to Justine. Not just for professional reasons. I wanted to hear her voice. After what I had just witnessed with Shang Li and his family, I wanted to hear from mine. Justine answered after two rings.

"Jack, are you okay?"

"Yes. We rescued Shang Li."

"Oh, thank God! That's so good to hear."

"We got him back and took down Liu Bao."

"I can't tell you how relieved I am," she replied. "I can't wait to see you."

"You're going to have to wait a little longer, I'm afraid. I need you to call Dinara Orlova," I said, referring to the head of the Private office in Russia. "Tell her I'm coming to Moscow."

"Moscow? No, Jack. You can't go there. Not after what happened."

"It's because of what happened that I have to go back," I replied. "It seems I have unfinished business with old enemies."

"Oh, Jack. Please don't do this," she protested.

"I must. We'll never be safe otherwise."

"I can't talk you out of it, can I?"

I didn't respond.

"Promise me one thing," she said. "You'll come back alive."

"I promise," I replied, although I knew my fate would be out of my control.

"And when you get back, we'll spend a month together. No distractions. We'll take a long vacation."

It sounded like bliss to me. "Deal," I replied.

"Be careful, Jack," she said.

"I will," I replied, before hanging up.

I went over to Zhang Daiyu, who stood waiting with Hua.

"Everything okay?" she asked.

I nodded.

"We have an address for Fang Wenyan," she revealed. "From Fen. It's an apartment in Zizhuyuan Subdistrict."

Hua whistled.

303

"Problem?" I asked.

"He is whistling because this Fang's area is where half the government lives. It's for party members with power. Those with real connections," Zhang Daiyu replied.

"Then we better make sure we don't upset anyone," I said, climbing into the van.

Zhang Daiyu and Hua exchanged hesitant looks before following me into the vehicle. Hua said something in Mandarin as he slid behind the wheel.

I looked at Zhang Daiyu expectantly.

"It's better I don't translate that word for word. It's enough for you know he asks questions about your sanity."

I smiled. "He's not the first," I said, as Hua stepped on the accelerator and we drove away.

CHAPTER 74

WHEN WE ARRIVED at Zizhuyuan Subdistrict we saw that the place oozed wealth and power. Even the night couldn't obscure it. From the expensive European SUVs and sports vehicles glimpsed in private parking garages to the perfectly manicured public areas, plush canopies over the grand apartment-block entrances, LED street lighting . . . a sense of opulence pervaded everything.

It was late and the streets were quiet. There were lights in the windows of many of the high-rise buildings around us, and at the top of each penthouses that glowed like dwarf suns.

Hua stopped outside Fang Wenyan's building, an impressive black skyscraper that resembled a giant aftershave bottle with gold trim here and there.

Hua peered toward the entrance, and I followed his gaze to see a man in a black suit seated at the desk in the lobby.

"How do you want to do this?" Hua asked.

"Too risky that way. I don't want Fang to know we're coming. Drive around," I said. Hua put his van in gear and moved on.

The building occupied its own block and was surrounded to all sides by landscaped grounds extending to the street. There were no sidewalks, just a path from the road to the main entrance, and at the rear of the building a driveway leading to a service entrance and underground parking garage.

"What do you think?" I asked.

"It's an infrared remote," Hua said, gesturing toward the grille that covered the entrance to the garage. He pulled over near the start of the driveway and went into the back of the van. "Hold on one minute."

I heard him rummaging through things and looked at Zhang Daiyu who shrugged.

Hua emerged with a device covered in buttons.

"It's a universal remote," he revealed, and pointed it at the grille while pressing a button.

The metal barrier started to rise almost immediately. He steered us onto the drive and down into the garage.

The vast space was full of expensive imported sedans, sports models, and motorbikes. We parked in a delivery spot near the elevators and climbed out of the van.

"We'd better hurry," Zhang Daiyu said. "They will have good security."

"Better than average," Hua noted, pointing at the alphanumeric keypad above the elevator call button.

"Can't you use the universal remote?" I said light-heartedly, and he replied with a frown of disapproval.

I knew full well there was no way to access the elevators without physically inputting the correct access code, likely personalized to lead direct to your own floor.

"We'll take the stairs," Hua said, gesturing to a door a few feet away leading to a metal stairwell. Access was controlled by a key-card reader. He pulled a credit-card-sized device from his pocket as he approached the door and ran it over the reader. I saw some red and green lights flash on the device. After a few moments the door buzzed open.

"Come on," Hua said with a smile.

Zhang Daiyu and I followed him into the stairwell and we started up the first flight. According to the information we had from Fen, Fang Wenyan lived in the penthouse on the twenty-fifth floor. It was a long and tiring climb, made worse by the humid, close conditions in the stairwell. By the time we reached the top, we were breathless and sweaty.

I took point and listened at the stairwell door. Nothing but silence, so I lowered the handle and pushed gently. The door swung slowly open and I stepped into a bright marble lobby. Zhang Daiyu and Hua followed me toward the solitary door that stood opposite the bank of three elevators. The door was black and double-width, set in a matching black wall. It looked ominous.

Zhang Daiyu produced a set of lock-picking tools from her pocket and went to work on the door.

A minute later, I heard the lock snap open and she pushed the door ajar. The sound of a television came from inside. Zhang Daiyu crept forward, widening the gap between door and frame.

My stomach lurched when I saw a hand grab her outstretched arm and pull her into the apartment.

CHAPTER 75

"YOU CAN COME in, Mr. Morgan," a man's voice called from inside the apartment. I couldn't see anything beyond the black door.

I looked at Hua and gestured for him to return to the stairs.

"And your friend too. There will be no escape for Mr. Huang," the voice went on. "Miss Zhang Daiyu is my guest now. You have until the count of five to come in and join her. One . . ."

I glanced around, wondering how they could see us. There were no obvious signs of cameras.

"Two . . ."

I looked at Hua, who shrugged.

We didn't have much choice.

"Three."

I walked into the apartment.

Like the rest of the building, black was the dominant color.

The huge space had a polished obsidian floor, black couches, abstract monochrome photo prints, and sculptures that matched the bleak color scheme. Beyond the expansive windows, the lights of the city added the only touches of color.

Fang Wenyan was standing by the windows, two heavy-set men in dark suits flanking him. The one to Fang's left was holding Zhang Daiyu and had a gun to her head.

"Did you really think you could break in here?" Fang reproved me. "I have security you can only dream of. You're persistent though. I can understand why you made enemies in Moscow."

"Who hired you to kill me?" I asked.

"Hired?" he responded derisively. "I don't work for anyone but China."

"You made a trade. My life and my friends and business for an alliance. There was an agreement and a price. That makes you a hired gun in my eyes."

I could see I was getting to him, which was good. I might be able to force a mistake.

He smiled, but the expression looked strained and he was clearly masking deep anger.

"You think what you want, Mr. Morgan. Using your employees' murders to imprison David Zhou has created many new opportunities for me and my allies. We are consolidating our power now, so what I have done to you and your business is in my own interests. I'm a patriot, helping China take its rightful place in the new world."

"You're a greedy extremist. I've met people like you before. Your ambition gets people killed—my friends and colleagues among them." I allowed him a glimpse of my own anger. "You will answer for their deaths."

"No, I won't," he sneered. "All three of you will die here tonight. The girl first." He indicated Zhang Daiyu, who looked back at him defiantly. "You broke into my home and killed this woman and her colleague to cover up your involvement with the criminal Liu Bao. He will be sacrificed to protect our objective, and your dreams of justice will die with you. The circumstances of your death will destroy Private's reputation and the company you've built will be ruined, fulfilling my arrangement with the Russians."

I stared at him, wondering how I was going to prove him wrong.

There were twenty feet between me and the large man holding Zhang Daiyu at gunpoint. I had no chance of reaching him before he shot her. The second bodyguard produced a pistol, which he levelled at me. Hua and I were easy targets, and I think Fang Wenyan realized I'd understood how badly the odds were stacked against us because he beamed broadly.

"You see, don't you? You've lost. This is the end for you, Mr. Morgan. Kill them."

He repeated the command in Mandarin, and Zhang Daiyu's captor pressed the barrel of the gun against her temple.

She struggled and cried out, but he held her fast.

Zhang Daiyu was about to die.

CHAPTER 76

A CRASH BEHIND me made me start. It had the same effect on Fang Wenyan and his men. The apartment came alive with the thud of boots, the clatter of heavily armed men and the commands of those in authority.

The place was being raided.

Fang Wenyan looked lost, but his initial disbelief was soon replaced by indignation. Zhang Daiyu's captor moved the gun away from her temple to point it at the squad of Special Forces operatives who were storming into the apartment.

At their head, wearing a bulletproof vest and carrying a Type-67 submachine gun, was Ma Fen, Zhang Daiyu's Guoanbu contact. Fang's indignation turned to anger as he recognized her and shouted something to his men.

They immediately opened fire on Fen and the officers with her. My ears rang as pistol shots cracked at close range. Fen and her squad responded with shots of their own as they took cover behind Fang Wenyan's opulent furniture and sculptures.

His bodyguards faced an answering hail of bullets, but the suicidal attack had achieved what Fang Wenyan wanted. It bought him time to grab Zhang Daiyu and drag her at gunpoint behind a column set to one side of the room. He placed his hand against the black wall next to it and a section of the shiny surface retracted, revealing a secret entrance.

As bullets thudded into the column shielding him, Fang managed to pull Zhang Daiyu inside and the door started closing behind them. I rushed across the room as Fang's bodyguards fell to the ground, dead, and just made it through the gap before the secret entrance closed. I heard a locking mechanism seal it shut behind me.

I realized this wasn't a panic room but a staircase leading up. I heard Zhang Daiyu struggling with Fang and caught a glimpse of them on a landing above. He was heading for the roof.

I sprinted after them and was met by a couple of gunshots that ricocheted off the iron stairs around me. I heard the stairwell door open and slam shut. Moments later I burst through onto the roof myself and saw Fang Wenyan dragging Zhang Daiyu toward an AC311 helicopter that stood idle on a landing pad. I guessed like me he was a chopper pilot.

He brandished his gun at me, which was a mistake because Zhang Daiyu elbowed him in the neck and, when his grip loosened, took a swing and punched him in the face. He staggered back, waving his gun around, and I seized the opportunity she had created to rush him.

I caught him with my shoulder, which hit him in the gut and knocked the wind out of him He dropped the gun as he fell onto his back, and I gave him a couple of jabs to disorientate him.

"Tell me who ordered you to do this," I growled. "Tell me who ordered you to do this to us."

He looked up at me and laughed. Something in me snapped. I grabbed him by the collar and hauled him to his feet. I pushed him toward the edge of the roof and might have thrown him off if I hadn't needed the identity of his Russian contact. He dug in his heels, resisting with all his strength.

"You won't kill me," he said. "I know who you are, Jack Morgan, you're the all-American hero."

His tone suggested he thought that the worst thing a person could be. I was about to tell him he was wrong when Zhang Daiyu joined us and spoke before I got the chance.

"He might not kill you but I will." She leveled the pistol he'd dropped at his face. "You're a murderer who has betrayed this country."

Fang Wenyan locked eyes with her and she hit him with the butt of the gun, opening a gash on his face.

"Don't look at me. Your eyes belong in the gutter. Give us a name."

"Tell them," Ma Fen said, emerging from another stairwell with three of her Special Forces operatives. "Your crimes are undeniable, Fang Wenyan. No one can protect you anymore. The people you've been collaborating with will abandon you. You must think about yourself. Give them up. Give up the names of everyone you've been working with. Cooperate and it will be reflected in the severity of your sentence."

Fang looked at me and smiled sadly, an expression of resignation and defeat. Then there was defiance again.

"My life is over," he said. "If I betray my brothers there is no way they will let me live. The Three Dragons reach everywhere. There is nothing you can threaten me with. And as for you, Jack Morgan—you're as dead as me. There is no point in me not telling, you will find out soon enough. The Director of the SVR himself, Valery Alekseyev, put the mark on your back. And he will find his target in the end."

Fang Wenyan raised his head to the heavens, took a deep breath, yanked himself free from my grip, and stepped off the roof.

CHAPTER 77

FANG'S APARTMENT BECAME the epicentre of a major police and intelligence operation. The streets around the building were cordoned off and packed with vehicles. Police vehicles, forensics trucks, and ambulances lined up alongside unmarked saloons, vans, and a large command center located in an unmarked trailer. Hua, Zhang Daiyu, and I were interviewed separately, each of us three times by different men and women in plain clothes. They presented no identification but I guessed they were Guoanbu officers. Even after they had finished talking to us we were told not to leave. We loitered by the command center under the watchful gaze of two uniformed cops who'd been tasked with guarding us. It had been a little over three hours since Fang Wenyan had jumped, and I was tired and impatient to reach Moscow.

Zhang Daiyu was on the phone making the final arrangements with the charter firm for the private jet that would take me from Beijing to the Russian capital. I reflected on Fang's revelation that the current director of the SVR—*Sluzhba Vneshney Razvedki*—Russia's foreign intelligence service, was out to get me. I'd foiled a major intelligence operation in Moscow, bringing down a previous director, Yevgeny Salko, and had followed it up by exposing an incredibly sophisticated Russian encryption tool after rescuing a US military pilot from Afghanistan. I'd been told I'd made enemies there but had never expected a response quite so extreme.

I used our period of captivity outside Fang Wenyan's building to access Private's secure server and research SVR Director Valery Alekseyev. I wanted to know more about the man who was out to destroy me.

There wasn't much on him. Colonel in Russian Special Forces before moving to intelligence operations. Rumored to be a hard-liner with a strong belief in military expansionism. There were two decent photographs. One taken from a distance showed a tall, muscular middle-aged man standing in swimming trunks next to Vladimir Putin while on holiday in the Black Sea. The second image was an official army photograph. It showed a man with close-shaved jet-black hair, a lean face, and hard eyes that seemed to be attempting to burn the camera lens. He looked like someone who saw the world as being naturally full of enemies; there was no sense of humanity.

He looked cruel, determined, and cold-hearted.

I saw Ma Fen round the rear corner of the building. She'd been with the team examining Fang's body.

I had mixed feelings about his death. He'd escaped justice, but would he ever have served a day in prison for his crimes? He'd foreseen the future ahead of him, most likely killed at the order of one of his fellow Three Dragons conspirators.

"I'm not surprised he jumped," Fen said as she approached us. "His death protected the identities of the traitors he was working with. That's all he cared about. It's going to be much more difficult to identify them now, but we will try."

"How much longer do you think you'll need us?" I asked.

"You're free to go," she said. "I heard the name he gave you, so I imagine you have a plane to catch."

I nodded.

Behind me, Zhang Daiyu relayed instructions to the charter firm.

"The People's Republic cannot condone intervention in another sovereign country, but given what has happened here, I would like to wish you every success in your endeavors."

I was surprised she was expressing support and it must have showed on my face

"Fang Wenyan and the fools working with him didn't realize they were being made tools of Russia, importing ideology and methods that have no place in China," Fen explained. "If they had been successful, they could have caused division and instability that threatened China's security. We were aware of a power play by this cabal, but until you arrived had no idea how well developed it was or that it involved a foreign state. Your investigation exposed these things, and for that reason your agency will always be welcome in China. As will you."

She offered me her hand and I shook it. She said something

in Mandarin to Hua and Zhang Daiyu and they replied in grateful tones.

"Your flight leaves in ninety minutes," Zhang Daiyu said to me. "Are you sure you don't want me to come with you?"

"You need to stay here and help Shang Li rebuild," I responded. "Can you let Dinara Orlova know what time the plane will arrive in Moscow?"

She nodded.

"I would never have been able to do this without you, Zhang Daiyu. Thank you." I turned to Huang Hua then. "And you, Hua. I appreciate everything you've done."

He nodded. "Delun, Kang, and Jinhai were my friends too, Mr. Morgan. I had to help avenge their deaths."

My phone rang and I saw Justine's name flash on-screen.

"Hey, Jus," I said when I answered.

"Jack?" I was on edge immediately. I sensed fear in her voice. "I've been trying to reach Dinara like you asked, but I can't get hold of her. Or Feodor Arapov. I can't reach anyone at Private Moscow. It's as though they have all disappeared."

CHAPTER 78

MY HEART SANK. There could only be one explanation for this. I took a moment to digest the news and collect my thoughts.

"Jack?"

"It's Alekseyev," I responded. "He must know what's happened here in Beijing and has taken them for leverage."

"Oh, Jack, you can't go there," Justine protested. "Not after last time."

Under any other circumstances I would have said she was right, but I owed my life to Dinara and Feo, and if Alekseyev had taken them, they needed me more than ever. None of us would ever be safe again with a man like him targeting us.

"I have to," I replied. "I want you to call Erin Sebold. She is the Agency head of section at the embassy in Moscow. See what kind of help they can give us."

"Jack . . ."

"I have to go, Justine. I can't leave them."

It sounded as though she was crying.

"I know, Jack. I know you can't leave them, but you are taking a piece of my heart with you."

"I love you, Jus."

"Love you too," she replied before hanging up.

"What's up?" Zhang Daiyu asked as I slid my phone into my pocket.

"The entire staff at Private Moscow are missing," I replied.

"Alekseyev?"

I nodded grimly.

"I'm sorry, Mr. Morgan," said Fen.

"Can you see if your people have heard anything useful in Moscow?" I asked.

"We don't have operatives in Moscow," she said firmly. "But I'll see what I can do," she added with a conspiratorial smile.

"You ready?" I asked Hua. He nodded.

We said goodbye to Fen, who thanked us again before allowing us to take the van out of the underground parking garage and cross the police cordon.

Hua took us to the workers' hostel where I collected my stuff before we headed for Beijing Nanyuan airport to the south of the city, a military base that also offered commercial facilities. I could see a fleet of executive aircraft on the stands surrounding the large terminal.

I don't know whether it was Zhang Daiyu's doing or if Fen had pulled some strings, but we were waved through the gate at the edge of the airfield and told to proceed directly to stand 47, where we found a Gulfstream G650 waiting. The pilot stood by the aircraft, not far from a customs officer behind a collapsible table. When we pulled up and stepped out of the van, the officer called me over, checked my passport, and performed a fingertip search of my holdall. When she was satisfied, she waved me on.

The pilot, a cheerful man in his late forties, had an air of easy confidence, the calm of someone who'd been flying for decades. He greeted me warmly before climbing the airstairs to complete his pre-flight checks. I turned to face Zhang Daiyu and Hua, who had waited a short distance away.

"You sure you don't want me to come?" she asked.

"I'm sure. You're needed here. I have friends in Moscow who will look after me."

"Not as well as us," Hua countered.

"Maybe not." I smiled. "Thank you for everything you've done. Both of you. I'll call you when I've found Alekseyev."

"Say hello to him from me," Zhang Daiyu said.

"And our three friends," Hua added.

I nodded and headed for the jet. I climbed the airstairs as the pilot ran through his engine checks and found the co-pilot waiting for me in the cabin. She was a quiet woman in her early thirties, who like the pilot gave off an aura of competence.

"Mr. Morgan, welcome aboard," she said. "We were told you didn't require service tonight, so it's just you, me, and Captain Tengfei for our flight to Moscow."

Nervous acid flushed through my stomach as she named the city. My last trip to Moscow had almost killed me.

I stowed my bag and took my seat in a plush armchair halfway along the cabin. The co-pilot went into the cockpit, and the pilot broadcast a short welcome and safety announcement, but I wasn't really listening. I was thinking about what I'd face in Moscow and rehearsing various scenarios.

Worry for my Russian friends and colleagues, compulsive visualization of how I'd handle each scenario, and unwanted flashbacks to the trials I'd previously faced there kept me on edge throughout take-off, but about an hour after leaving Beijing the adrenaline ebbed away and fatigue got the better of me.

With nothing but the low drone of the engines and the stars outside my window keeping me company, I finally drifted off to sleep.

CHAPTER 79

JUSTINE FELT ANGRY and she couldn't understand why. It was an internalized anger that clawed at her, a grim sense of frustration with no outlet. She knew from professional experience that such feelings were neither healthy nor productive, so tried to understand where they had come from.

Was it delayed anger and grief for fallen colleagues? Was she tired of being thrust into danger by malevolent people? Was she angry at Jack for the cavalier way he hurled himself into these perilous situations, regardless of the odds? All these issues came to mind, so Justine suspected they played a part in the fire that seemed to start in her chest and spread up her spine to the very top of her skull.

She sat back in the executive chair and stretched. She was alone in the small meeting room in the Private office overlooking Madison Square Park. Mo-bot and Sci had been elusive ever since

Angel had been released. She had told them about her experiences with Tate Johnson and the team spying on the Consulate and related what Jack had said about helping the DoD contractor find a way to bring Angel to justice.

She was happy to hear Shang Li was alive and relieved for his wife and children, but the good news had been followed by bad. Now Dinara, Feo, and the rest of the Private Moscow team were missing.

There had been a time when Justine had been jealous of Dinara, while she and Jack had been working closely together in Moscow, but Justine's feelings had been grounded in a fear of losing him that proved to be unfounded. She had since come to know Dinara as an extremely competent investigator, and was genuinely concerned about what had happened to her and her team.

There was a knock at the door and Mo-bot entered. She was in blue jeans and a green T-shirt emblazoned with a screen print of bolting ponies.

"Any word from Moscow?" she asked.

Justine shook her head. "No. Jack's on his way there now."

Mo-bot whistled softly. "Does he know what he might be walking into?"

"Yes. That's why he's going," Justine said. "He wants to put an end to this and get his team back."

"I'm sorry, Justine," Mo-bot responded. "This can't be easy for you."

"It's the job," she replied.

They both fell silent for a moment.

"You didn't come in here for a gloom session with me," Justine remarked at length. "What have you got?"

"Am I that transparent?"

Justine recognized Mo-bot's knowing smile; some scheme was brewing. She nodded.

"Well, we do have something as it happens," Mo-bot said. "Let me show you."

Justine got to her feet and followed her along the corridor to the large conference room where she and Sci had set up a couple of workstations. Sci was at his, sipping from a paper cup.

"Morning," he said cheerfully.

Mo-bot shut the door behind them and took a seat at her workstation. Outside, the midday sun was making the city shine, but the conference room was just the right side of chilly.

"What's going on?" Justine asked, taking the seat next to Mo-bot's.

She saw them exchange a look.

"Didn't sit well with us that Angel gets shipped back to China," Sci revealed. "Jack was right to want to bring him to justice."

"I agree," Justine said.

"The set-up Tate and his people had at the Consulate inspired us," Mo-bot said. "We bugged the place with devices even the Chinese won't find."

"More advanced than the Pentagon's?" Justine asked.

"No," Mo-bot replied. "Just more creatively deployed."

She indicated her screen, which brought up an image of an office ceiling. Justine could see strip lighting and the very top of a whiteboard.

"We hacked the phones of a number of embassy staffers, turning them into surveillance devices," Mo-bot revealed.

"How?" Justine asked.

"Well, once you know who they are, it isn't that complicated," Sci replied. "That's what she says anyway." He nodded at Mo.

"I built a device that hijacks the Bluetooth connection to install my software patch. It's more complicated than he's making out," Mo-bot said.

"Really?" Sci scoffed.

"Anyway, they are moving him tonight," Mo-bot went on. "He's booked on a private jet from Newark. We can tell Tate Johnson the license plate and the time of departure."

"Do you think they'll be able to hold him this time?" Sci asked.

"I hope so," Justine replied. "We now have proof he was spying. We didn't have that before. Liu Bao's recorded confession changes things. Angel has clearly been engaged in espionage activity against the United States. Carver's people must be able to hold him for that."

Mo-bot nodded. "Sounds good to me."

"Okay," Justine said, hoping she was right. She would really like to see Lewis's killer face justice. "I'll make the call."

CHAPTER 80

TATE JOHNSON HAD been very interested in the new evidence Justine had presented. Normally the State Department would have begun proceedings to secure Angel from the Chinese authorities so he could face prosecution, but with the information Sci and Mo-bot had obtained about Angel's imminent departure, Tate said he wouldn't involve State, but would instead take a discreet, more direct approach to get Angel in front of a judge.

Justine was unclear of Tate's exact role as a contractor with the Department of Defense, but he seemed to have a great deal of authority. Within a couple of hours he had established an ad-hoc command center on the third floor of the FBI building in Federal Plaza in the south of Manhattan. Justine, Mo-bot, and Sci had been invited to attend as observers, but they were more than that—at least Mo-bot was. She gave Tate's technical team access to the feeds she was picking up from the embassy staffers' phones. There was no talk of warrants or illegality, and Justine couldn't figure out whether that was because Tate's team were independent contractors or if they had already taken care of the necessary legal procedures.

The FBI building was located on the corner of Worth Street and Broadway, towering above the neighboring structures. It was set behind concrete barriers to prevent vehicle assault and security was tight. They were scanned and searched on entry, and each floor and every room was assigned a security rating from sensitive to top secret. Only people with the relevant clearance were allowed in those areas. The large windowless conference room that was Tate's base of operations was rated secret.

There were thirty-four people in the room. Justine knew because she had counted them all once she had managed to get hold of Erin Sebold to tell her Jack was on his way to Moscow. There wasn't much else for Justine to do, so she watched Tate and his team preparing for the task that lay ahead.

There were fifteen field operators, distinguishable by their body armor and weapons: six women and nine men. Fifteen analysts and support personnel staffed computer and communications terminals, and then there was Tate plus the three observers from Private.

The plane had filed a flight plan to Beijing with a 5 p.m. departure time, and it was a fifty-minute journey from the embassy, so Angel had to be leaving at any moment. The room was quiet in anticipation, as though thirty-four people were simultaneously holding their breath.

"I've got him," someone said, and Justine turned to see one of the analysts pointing at her screen. "Micro-drone camera in the underground garage."

Tate's people had bolstered Mo-bot's surveillance with some gadgets of their own. Justine saw the hitman walking through a garage with a couple of handlers. He was taken to a large SUV.

"He's getting into a silver Escalade, license DCM0089," the analyst announced.

"Okay, people," Tate said. "We've got our target. Move."

The field operators hurried from the room, Tate following.

"We'll let you know when we have him," he said to Justine before he left.

The room fell quiet again as the analysts turned their attention to the surveillance and pursuit operation that was now underway.

Justine noticed Mo-bot and Sci get to their feet.

"Where are you going?" she asked.

"We've never been good spectators," Mo-bot replied.

Sci nodded. "After what this guy did to us, to Jessie and to Lewis, I want to see the whites of his eyes when they put him in irons."

CHAPTER 81

THEY HAD PARKED a blue Nissan Rogue Private staff vehicle in a garage on Leonard Street, a block from the FBI building, and Justine hurried to keep up as Sci and Mo-bot headed there.

"How are we going to find them?" she asked.

"I slipped a tracker in Tate's body armor," Mo-bot replied. "And I put a camera and mic in the operation center."

Justine was impressed but not surprised. Mo-bot was known as the detective agency's mom partly because, like all good mothers, she made sure things got done.

Justine was sweating by the time they picked their way through the crowded city and reached Leonard Street. They hurried into the parking garage, found the Nissan Rogue, and Justine got behind the wheel. Sci rode shotgun and Mo-bot sat in the back.

"Where to?" Justine asked, starting the engine.

"Newark," Mo-bot suggested, firing up her laptop. "Tate said they wouldn't take him in the city. Too many opportunities to escape. They'll get him close to the airport."

They headed through Manhattan and took the Holland Tunnel west, following a stream of late-afternoon traffic that clogged the confined space with pungent fumes. When they emerged from the tunnel, they continued for a while before turning south through the Ironbound, a suburban neighborhood that lay north of the airport.

"Tate is about three hundred yards ahead," Mo-bot said, checking the signal being displayed on her laptop.

Justine peered over the tops of the vehicles in front of her and saw three black SUVs going south. She recognized one of them as the vehicle that had been used to collect her from the hotel. She stepped on the accelerator, pulled into the outside lane, and closed the gap. When she got to within fifty yards, she caught sight of the silver Escalade they'd seen from the operations room.

"There's Angel," Justine said, and Sci and Mo-bot craned forward to catch a glimpse of the vehicle through the heavy traffic.

Justine kept her distance and followed the three SUVs as they tailed their target.

They took the next turn-off, leaving the Expressway for Port Road, a quiet service route that offered access to the freight and private terminals.

When the Escalade was two hundred yards from the Port Road perimeter security gate, and there was nowhere for it to go other than into the airport, the convoy of black SUVs accelerated and caught up with the Chinese Embassy vehicle.

Two of the SUVs got in front of it and blocked the road,

forcing the Escalade to a halt. The third of Tate's vehicles moved to within inches of the Escalade's rear bumper, thwarting any escape. The squad of heavily armed field operators emerged from the trio of SUVs, guns trained on the windows of Angel's vehicle.

"Get out of the vehicle!" Tate yelled, raising an AR-15. "Step out now!"

Justine pulled over and she, Mo-bot, and Sci watched the tense scene unfold.

"Get out," Tate yelled as his team surrounded the car.

The front doors opened and the driver and passenger, both in black suits, emerged nervously. They were the men Justine had seen on-screen in the operations room, escorting Angel into the vehicle.

"Diplomats!" the driver yelled. He pointed at the plates clearly displayed on the Escalade. "We're diplomats."

"You in the back," Tate said, moving forward, "get out!"

Two of his operatives grabbed the driver and passenger, forced them onto their bellies, and cuffed them.

"We're diplomats," the driver protested. "You can't do this."

Both men yelled angrily and struggled against their restraints. There was still no sign of Angel.

Justine watched Tate creep toward the back door on the driver's side, his gun high, reaching for the handle.

He grabbed it and pulled the door open.

"It's empty," he said, stepping back. "Empty. He's not here."

"Impossible," Mo-bot muttered from the back seat. "We saw him get in the vehicle."

The sound of sirens made Justine jump. The road rapidly filled with airport police. A convoy of eight vehicles, engines roaring, sped toward the Escalade. Tires screeched as they shuddered to a halt.

"Drop your weapons," the officer in charge yelled as he leapt from his car.

He was soon joined by his colleagues, who drew their pistols and targeted Tate and his team.

"We're diplomats," the prostrate driver yelled. "These men are terrorists who have illegally detained us."

"Brilliant," Sci remarked. "They probably knew we were watching them. Led Tate and his people into a trap. They've made sure Angel gets away and created a diplomatic incident China can exploit."

"So he's gone?" Justine asked, as she watched Tate place his weapon on the ground and raise his hands.

His team followed suit.

"Looks that way," Sci replied, as the cops moved in to cuff Tate and his team. "I don't know how they did it, but Angel is in the wind."

CHAPTER 82

THEY SAT IN the Nissan Rogue a couple of hundred yards north of Tate and his team, who were in the process of being arrested. Justine was despondent to think that the man who'd caused them so much harm would go free, and when she looked at Sci she saw he shared her feelings.

Mo-bot was busy in the back, tapping away on her laptop, while further along Port Road, the police took custody of Tate and his team.

"I know how they did it," Mo-bot said, turning her laptop so Justine and Sci could see. She zoomed in on one of the screens in the operations room at Federal Plaza. "This is from the camera I placed in the ops room. The resolution is terrible because I'm really zoomed in, but look what the dashcam of Tate's vehicle picks up when they stop at this intersection on Route Nine."

Justine peered at the screen but just saw the silver Escalade in a line of traffic.

"I don't see anything," she admitted.

"I got it," Sci said.

"Look at the gap between the lines of vehicles to the left of the Escalade," Mo-bot suggested as she rewound the video.

She pressed play and Justine kept her eyes fixed on the shadowy space between two blurry lines of traffic. And then she saw it: a ghost figure moving between the two streams of vehicles, crouching and furtive, running quickly from one line to the other.

"He switched vehicles," Mo-bot said. "They must have had another one shadowing them."

"Or a number of them," Sci suggested.

"And the cops on speed dial to ensure there was a big scene, so Tate and his people couldn't pick up another trail," Mo-bot added.

"You think Angel made the flight?" Justine asked.

Mo-bot shook her head. "I don't think they'd risk it. If they knew they were being watched, they'll know we know about the flight and would be likely to stop it."

"Back to the embassy?" Justine suggested.

Mo-bot considered the idea. "I don't think so. They won't want to do this again. Besides, we're weakened. Tate is down and we're blind. This is the best time to get him out. I think there's another flight."

"From where?" Sci asked.

"It won't be from here. Not with all this heat around," Mo-bot remarked, gesturing at the police presence up ahead. "Go back toward the Expressway."

She returned to her laptop and got to work.

Justine pulled a U-turn and glanced in her rear-view mirror to see Tate and his team being forced into the back of police vehicles while the Chinese diplomats were released.

Mo-bot worked furiously as Justine drove toward the Expressway. They could see the southbound lanes starting to slow as the airport traffic backed up with travelers trying to make rush-hour flights. The northbound carriageway looked pretty clear, so if they had to go to JFK or LaGuardia they would have a reasonable run until they hit the city.

"Turn around again," Mo-bot instructed. "Call Carver. Tell him to stop flight PY 984, leaving from Linden Airport."

Sci took out his phone while Justine did exactly as instructed and turned south.

"There are three private jets leaving for China this evening. Two from JFK and one from LaGuardia. Both airports are on the other side of the river, which puts them at least two hours away at this time of day, but this fourth plane is heading for Seattle. No big deal except in the past six months it's made fifteen Seattle-to-Beijing flights and back. And Linden Airport is only twenty minutes from here." She typed another command and her eyes widened. "The aircraft is owned by Golden Journeys Aviation, which in turn is owned by Liu Investments. This is the one."

"Secretary Carver," Sci said. "Seymour Kloppenberg, sir . . . No, sir . . . Your friends ran into trouble. They were picked up by airport police. It seems the man we want pulled a switch and is leaving from Linden Airport. Flight PY 984. Our resident computer nerd wants you to stop it . . . Yes, sir."

Mo-bot was glaring when Sci hung up.

"Computer nerd?" Her tone was frosty.

"I didn't want to use any names."

"You used your own," she noted.

"I didn't want to put you at risk," he said with a cheeky smile.

"You just wanted to tell the Secretary of Defense I'm a nerd." Mo-bot grunted her displeasure but said no more.

Justine took less-travelled back roads south and was soon on Edgar Road, cutting through the small town of Linden. The rush-hour traffic slowed to a crawl as they passed the stores and malls that lined both side of their route. The parking lots were filling up with vehicles and people crowded into stores. Justine found every minute they had to wait sheer torture.

Finally, they turned left onto the airport approach road.

"There!" Mo-bot announced, pointing.

Justine pulled over and the three of them got out to see a green Jeep Cherokee parked beside a Gulfstream jet. Three police vehicles surrounded the aircraft and Angel was being held down on the hood of one of them by two very large officers. He was about one hundred yards away, sufficiently close to register Justine, Sci, and Mo-bot watching him through the chain-link fence.

He frowned when his eyes met Justine's, but she didn't feel triumphant, just satisfied there was a chance Lewis's killer would now face justice. There was a roar as a small commercial jet came in to land.

As its wheels touched the runway, Angel broke free of his captors and tried to make a run for it. One of the cops pulled his Taser and shot the big man in the back. He went down, convulsing. The other officer walked over, removed the barbs and handcuffed him.

"Well, I'm glad I got to see it," Sci remarked with an unmistakable air of satisfaction.

"You did more than see it," Justine replied. "This wouldn't have happened without the two of you."

"I think she's right," he observed.

"We just did what any good citizens would have done," Mo-bot replied, and Justine got the distinct impression the two of them were mocking her.

"Well, if you can't take a compliment," she countered.

"That was a compliment?" Sci asked.

Exasperated, Justine turned away and headed for the Nissan.

"Did you know that was a compliment?" Sci asked Mo-bot.

"Quit it, Kloppenberg," Mo-bot told him. "She's taking it to heart. Come on, Justine, we were just fooling around. We love you, kid."

"I know," she replied, turning back with a big smile on her face.

"She suckered us," Mo-bot said to Sci.

"This is why I don't trust profilers," he replied. "They know too much about how we all tick. Get out of my head, Justine Smith."

"Come on," she said. "Stop goofing around. I know you're excited at a job well done, but Jack's still out there facing who knows what. Let's get back to the city."

Mo-bot and Sci dropped the double act immediately. They got into the Nissan and Justine drove them back to Manhattan.

CHAPTER 83

THE LAST TIME I had come to Moscow, I had almost been killed by people determined to ensure Russian global supremacy. I looked down at the glittering city beneath the jet with a sense of foreboding. Most people would have run. They would have gone home and hoped the authorities fixed the problem, but I knew no authority could touch someone like Valery Alekseyev. He was far too powerful, and political systems are designed to protect those with power.

He had come up with an intricate plot to make me suffer in revenge for what I'd done in Moscow and Afghanistan, but his ultimate intention was to kill me. He'd come after Justine again, or Sci or Mo-bot. Angel had already tried and failed to kill them with the bombs in New York. Alekseyev would simply send another Angel at me and my friends, and another, and another, until one of them achieved his objective. The only way to truly end this was to neutralize the general giving the orders.

Our descent into Sheremetyevo International Airport was bumpy, with gale-force gusts of wind swirling in the night air. A shudder ran through the plane when we hit the runway. As I looked out the window, the lights of the hangars, emergency-response buildings, and terminals emerged from a moving blur when the aircraft came to a stop.

"Sorry about that," the captain said, emerging from the cockpit.

"No problem," I replied. "I used to fly Sea Knights. Those crosswinds were nasty, would have tested any pilot."

He nodded, opened the door and lowered the airstairs.

I grabbed my bag and headed for the exit. Warm air and the sweet smell of a new city hit me. I saw two guys in short-sleeve shirts and black pants standing beside a black Toyota Landcruiser.

"Mr. Morgan," the taller of the two said, "I'm Mark Espiner. This is William Powell. Erin Sebold sent us to pick you up."

"Good to meet you," I said, shaking their hands.

"Let me help you with that," Mark said. He took my bag and put it in the trunk.

I climbed onto the tan leather back seat and Mark got behind the wheel. William took the front passenger seat.

"Erin said you'd run into trouble in Beijing," William said, glancing over his shoulder. "Is that why you're here?"

Something about the question bothered me. Would Justine have been so careless? Would Erin? I really doubted it. Neither of them would have divulged the reason for my visit, and genuine embassy or CIA staff would have known better than to quiz a subject they'd been sent to collect.

"You guys give me a minute?" I said, producing my phone. "I promised my girlfriend I'd call her as soon as I landed."

I dialed a number, but it wasn't Justine's. I called Erin Sebold, who answered after a couple of rings.

"Hello?" she said groggily.

"Hey, honey. I'm down safely," I replied. "Yeah, Erin sent two guys to meet the plane."

"I didn't send two guys," she said, suddenly alert. "They're not mine, Jack."

My stomach lurched.

"Thanks, honey, that's good to know."

I heard her try to tell me something else, but I wasn't listening and hung up. I was reeling. I had to get out of this vehicle before it left the airport, and we were almost at the gate.

"Everything okay?" the man who'd introduced himself as Mark asked.

I nodded. "You know how it is on these long business trips." I paused. "You know what, guys? I think I forgot my laptop on the plane. You mind if we go back and check?"

The look they exchanged was unmistakable. They were both wondering whether they'd been made.

"You wanna check when we get through the gate?" "Mark" asked. "Take a look in your bag. I can pull over just up ahead."

He gestured to a layby beyond the gate.

If they were Russians, their American accents were extremely convincing, but his suggestion told me everything. They knew as well as I did that with its enhanced security my best chance was to stay in the airport. They needed to get me into Moscow proper.

"Just pull over and I'll have a look now," I suggested.

The guard was outside the gatehouse and had activated the mechanism that opened the barrier. I could see the gates swinging toward me, exposing the road, which felt like a dark and ominous place.

"Just pull over here, by the gatehouse," I said.

"That isn't going to happen," "William" said, producing a pistol and training it on me.

I kicked out immediately and the gun went off, shooting a hole in the Landcruiser's roof.

"Mark" accelerated rapidly. I launched myself forward and beat the man calling himself William, lashing out with my fists and catching him repeatedly around the head. I glimpsed the gate guard, who looked shocked to see the mayhem in the vehicle as we raced past him.

"William" tried to get the gun on me, but I grabbed his arm and twisted it round. We were locked in a struggle, each trying to make the other the target, but I was stronger and the barrel of the gun was inching toward his face.

"Mark" swung the wheel and we bounced onto the airport access road. We raced toward an intersection as "William" and I fought, but I could feel the vehicle slowing. If we stopped, the other man could get involved in the fight, and then I'd be facing two adversaries instead of one.

I put everything into defeating "William," watched him grimace as the airport perimeter fence flashed by in a blur.

Then, from the other side of the road, I heard a roaring engine as we went through the intersection, and a huge black pick-up truck bore down on us and hit the driver's door at speed.

There was the crashing, crunching, grinding sound of a serious collision, and we were flung about violently. The airbags deployed and I was hurled against the one that shielded the passenger-side rear door. The Landcruiser spun wildly out of control and finally came to a halt when it hit the perimeter fence.

Groggy and disoriented, I awaited certain death.

CHAPTER 84

THE PASSENGER DOOR opened and I felt hands grab me under my arms and haul me out. I tried to resist but was dazed and weak. I became vaguely aware of words beneath the ringing that filled my head.

Then I understood them.

"Jack! Come on! We've got to get out of here."

I thought I recognized the voice, but my memory couldn't place it. When I looked up I saw a face I definitely recognized.

Master Gunnery Sergeant Marlon West.

The lean, muscular Marine was in civilian clothes—a dark hooded top and black jeans—and pulled me clear as the driver and his passenger started to come to their senses.

I tried to make my legs work and found some purchase.

West half carried, half dragged me to his pick-up truck, a large Ford F-350. By the time we reached the vehicle, I was able to haul myself into the passenger seat. He ran round to the driver's seat and started the engine, which growled reassuringly beneath the crumpled hood.

I saw a dazed "Mark" reaching for his phone as West put the truck in reverse and stepped on the gas. When we cleared the intersection he pulled a sharp U-turn and raced north, scanning the road, which was empty in both directions.

"Sorry about that, Mr. Morgan," he said. He was talking fast, his adrenaline high, but I was having difficulty focusing and took a moment to process his words. "Erin sent me to meet you, but when I arrived those two goons were already there so I had to improvise. You okay?"

I nodded and the world swam.

"We don't have long," he said. "If they want you as badly as I think they do, they're going to set half of Moscow against us."

West and I had worked together during my investigation into Karl Parker's murder. My old friend had been assassinated as part of an attempt to cover up a massive Russian Intelligence operation. West had successfully smuggled me out of the US Embassy when the Russians had been tearing Moscow apart looking for me. I knew him to be smart, dependable, and fiercely brave.

"We need to get you to the embassy, sir," he said.

I tried to reply, but my words were mumbled and indistinct.

"Excuse me, sir," he replied. "I didn't catch that."

I took a breath and composed myself.

"I said, call me Jack."

"Will do, sir—I mean Jack."

He smiled and I tried to smile back, but I had a horrible

feeling it was a grimace. My chest and back were aching with the pain of the impact.

I took a moment to get my bearings and realized that rather than taking us away from the airport, West was following the approach road to the main terminal building.

He must have sensed my concern.

"We need to ditch the pick-up," he explained. "They will be looking for it. A taxi will be better."

I nodded, relieved the gesture didn't spark another explosion of pain. My muscle control and nerves started to feel as though they were returning to normal. Hopefully there hadn't been any serious damage from the impact.

West steered the F-350 into one of the airport parking lots and we hurried out to catch a taxi from the deserted rank.

The driver, a taciturn middle-aged man with a perpetual scowl and a cigarette hanging from his lip, nodded when West told him our destination and we set off for home turf.

CHAPTER 85

"WE'VE GOT A problem," West said as we made our way into the city. "Over there." He pointed beyond the taxi driver.

Through the windshield I saw a line of traffic, red tail lights flaring as the drivers slowed. Their vehicles crawled toward a Moscow Police checkpoint.

"We're two blocks from the embassy," he said.

The Russians were nothing if not predictable. This was exactly what they'd done when I was last in Moscow. They'd encircled the embassy and used checkpoints to try and catch me.

"I'm going to tell him to pull over so we can walk from here," West said.

I nodded and he spoke to the driver in Russian. The man's scowl deepened and he tutted as he signaled and pulled out of the line of traffic.

He stopped by the sidewalk, which ran in front of some

apartment blocks, and West paid him. We clambered out of the bright yellow Skoda Octavia, and I was grateful my injuries seemed to have downgraded from intense pain to dull aches.

"Foot patrols," West said, nodding toward a trio of uniformed Moscow police officers who were milling around near the vehicle checkpoint. "We need to be careful."

"Hey!" I heard the taxi driver yell, and turned to see him leaning out of his window, addressing the trio of cops.

He said something in Russian and West cursed under his breath.

"He just told them we're Americans and wanted out when we saw the checkpoint."

"Hey!" one of the officers yelled in English. "Stop!"

"Can you run?" West asked me.

I nodded. "I think so."

"Well, let's go then," he said, starting off at a sprint.

I raced to catch up, hearing yells and barked commands aimed in our direction.

"We're going to take the rat run," West said.

He set a cracking pace that left me struggling to keep up. Every part of me screamed with pain and I was already out of breath. The collision had taken a greater toll than I'd realized.

I heard tires screech and saw the three vehicles that had formed the checkpoint racing toward us. The trio of officers on foot ran in our direction, yelling instructions and giving hurried commands into their radios.

I followed West along a path that led to one of the large apartment blocks ahead of us. He stepped off the path and ran across a small lawn, aiming for a gap between the block and its neighbor. I saw more apartment buildings through the gap, set around a large square.

"Come on," he said, and when I glanced round I saw the reason for his urgency; there were more police officers coming from almost every direction.

We ran on, passing through the gap between the two buildings, emerging onto the square. A path edged a park that featured a small football pitch and playground.

We ran along the path for a short distance until West suddenly turned right and raced toward the entrance to one of the apartment blocks. He yanked the front door open and held it for me as I struggled to catch up.

"Thanks," I said breathlessly, but he didn't acknowledge me. Instead he sprinted across the lobby to an interior door that led further into the building.

We burst into a corridor lined with numbered doors. West ran ahead until he came to apartment 12. There were a couple of locks, but he ignored these and touched the center of the figure 2 in the apartment number.

"Fingerprint reader," he explained.

The door clicked open and West pushed it wide. As I followed him inside, I glanced down the corridor to see police officers in hot pursuit.

West slammed the front door shut and locked it. Moments later there was the hammering of fists on the other side.

"Come on," he said, leading me from a narrow hallway into a sparsely furnished living room.

He ran over to a black fabric-covered couch and lifted it surprisingly easily.

"Spring-loaded," he explained, as the wooden floor beneath the couch slid back to reveal a set of steps.

"Down," he said.

I did as instructed and hurried down a dozen steps.

He followed and allowed the couch to fall in place behind him. When he reached the bottom of the steps and the couch and hatch had sealed closed, West bolted the mechanisms into position and a light came on.

Above us we heard the thunder of footsteps and then the start of what I'm sure would be many bemused questions in Russian.

"Come on," West said as he started running down what looked like a very long tunnel.

"What is this place?" I asked, following him.

"It's the rat run. A way in or out of the embassy without being seen," he replied. "We bought the apartment and built the tunnel after all those times you had trouble getting in and out."

It was an impressive escape route.

"A few things changed after your last visit, Jack."

"The Ambassador?" I asked

"Ambassador Dussler is still here. In fact, he's waiting at the embassy, eager to see you."

CHAPTER 86

THE TUNNEL RAN in a straight line for about half a mile. Tiny motion-activated LED lights came on as we approached them, illuminating our way. West slowed to a gentle jog as we left the Moscow police behind us.

"That was a little too close," he said.

He had the decency not to blame me for being too slow. Each step was making me feel better though, and I was shaking off some of the worst after-effects of the crash.

After six or seven minutes we reached a dead end. The tunnel was capped by a concrete wall. West found a particular area near the bottom right corner and held his palm to it. An optical reader disguised as a patch of concrete scanned his handprint and the wall retracted and then descended into the floor.

We went through the newly created opening into what looked like a ten-feet-long six-feet-wide metal bank vault. Rivets peppered the walls and thin structural supports propped up the ceiling. There was no door, just a metal wall at the other end, but when the slab of concrete closed and returned to its position, the inner metal wall rose into the ceiling.

"Tempered steel," West said. "The roof is a solid block that can be dropped into the space, sealing it."

I glanced up and shuddered the thought of the heavy block falling on us.

"Simple but effective way of closing it off if anyone ever discovers the tunnel," West observed.

He took me into an embassy equipment room. It was full of emergency gear: torches, medical supplies, and flight cases lined up on neat racks. I watched the wall close, concealing the tunnel, and West went to the door and tapped a code into the keypad beside it.

A buzzer sounded and he pulled the door open, leading me into a basement corridor.

A uniformed Marine was waiting for us there.

"The Ambassador is here, Master Gunnery Sergeant," he said.

He took us through a maze of identical corridors until we reached a bank of elevators. He escorted us to the top floor, hand just touching his sidearm the whole way. He knocked on the door to Ambassador Dussler's office and opened it for us.

West and I stepped inside to find Dussler leaning against his desk talking to Erin Sebold, who sat on a couch on the other side of the room. Dussler hadn't changed since our last meeting, and was still as confident and suave as ever, except in contrast to his usual tailored suit, today he wore navy sweatpants and a grey hooded top. Erin Sebold was in jeans and a thin sweater. The casual clothes looked out of place in the very traditional office but were the result of the lateness of the hour. There was the obligatory photograph of Dussler with the President, and framed artwork that dated from shortly after the Revolutionary War hung above antique furniture that was carefully arranged to impress visiting dignitaries.

"Jack Morgan, you sure know how to make a dramatic entrance," the Ambassador said, stepping forward to offer me his hand. "Good to see you."

"I wish it was under better circumstances," I replied.

"What happened at the airport?" Erin said, getting up to greet me.

"Two guys tried to abduct him," West responded. "FSB probably."

"How did you stop them?" Erin asked.

"I improvised," West remarked. "I'm going to need a new vehicle by the way."

"That's some improvisation," Erin remarked.

"It was," I said. "He saved my life. I owe you," I told West. "I won't forget it."

"I reckon we're even from before. The country owes you a debt," he countered.

"So, what's happening, Jack?" Dussler asked.

"A faction of Chinese nationals struck a deal with Valery Alekseyev to work together to advance their strategic interests. Private was the intended target. A secret Chinese group led by a guy called Fang Wenyan was supposed to destroy my business, kill my people, and, when I'd suffered enough, kill me."

"On Alekseyev's orders?" Dussler asked.

"Yes, sir," I replied. "I'm guessing it was supposed to be revenge for what I did here and in Afghanistan."

"Alekseyev is bad news, Jack," Erin observed. "It would explain what our sources told us. Yesterday morning, raids took place on the Private office here and the homes of every member of its staff. All your people were arrested and incarcerated somewhere."

The thought of Dinara, Feo, and the others being held captive filled me with anger.

"I need to find them. And then I need to put Alekseyev out of action."

Dussler and Erin exchanged a concerned look that indicated the sensitivity of the situation.

"We cannot be seen to be aiding a vigilante mission against a member of the Russian Government, Jack," Dussler said. "Even if America's strategic interests would be served by the removal of that man. I'm afraid we can only provide moral support."

I was deflated. "I have to help my people."

Erin eyed me sympathetically, but she and Dussler seemed resolved.

"Sir, ma'am, I have some annual leave due," West responded. "I'd like to use it now to show Mr. Morgan around Moscow. Take in some sights."

"Sights?" Dussler asked.

"Yes, sir, sights," West replied.

Erin murmured approvingly. "That's not a bad idea. Maybe

you could borrow a camera and any other gear you might need for sightseeing from the armory," she suggested.

"I was hoping you might say that, ma'am," West replied.

It was clear what was happening. The US Government was going to support me through West, while retaining plausible deniability. It was an elegant lie, and fine by me. I would have single-handedly torn Moscow apart, stone by stone, to recover my team and get two minutes alone with the man who had been responsible for so much evil.

Having West by my side would make the task a great deal easier.

CHAPTER 87

HAVING SLEPT ON the flight from Beijing, I was ready to go, but West needed some rest. After I'd been checked over by the duty medic who'd pronounced me battered but essentially fit, we each took one of the embassy staff bedrooms. Mine was on the third floor, located in a small residential wing away from the offices, on the western edge of the building. It was simply furnished, with a single bed, closet, desk, chair, and small bathroom.

I wanted to call Justine to reassure her I was safe. I knew how worried she was about me coming to Moscow but given the amount of surveillance the embassy was subject to, decided the risk would be too great. Once I'd used the bathroom, I lay on the bed, expecting restless impatience to be my companion while I waited for morning, but I had underestimated how exhausted I was. Days of relentless pressure in Beijing and the after-effects of West's collision with the Russians combined to send me to sleep. I didn't even realize I had gone until I woke to find bright sunlight streaming through the window.

"Feel better?" West asked.

He was seated at the desk. I'd been so far under I hadn't even registered him come in.

"Yeah," I replied, rubbing my face.

"Ready to go?"

Had he feigned the need for rest for my benefit?

"I've packed a truck, so we're ready when you are," he added.

Whether intentionally or not, the enforced rest he'd given me had made me feel so much better. I got to my feet and stretched, energized and more like my old self.

Ten minutes later we were in one of the embassy Land Rover Defenders, concealed in a secret compartment beneath the flat-bed. Next to us was in assortment of weapons West had borrowed from the armory, and above us were flight cases of gear that wouldn't raise eyebrows during a search. Comms equipment, torches, and other field supplies.

And the flight cases were searched, twice, at two checkpoints near the embassy, but the secret compartment did its job and soon the Land Rover made it out of the danger zone.

After a while twisting and turning through Moscow, the Marine driver pulled over and gave us the signal to open the compartment. We climbed out to find ourselves in a derelict industrial site.

"I made sure we weren't followed, Master Gunnery Sergeant," the Marine said.

"It's just Marlon today. I'm officially on vacation."

"Some vacation," I remarked with a smile.

"There are worse ways to R and R," West replied. "You going to be OK getting back?" he asked the Marine.

"There's a cab rank about a mile east of here."

"Well, get going," West suggested.

"Enjoy your vacation, sirs," the Marine replied before jogging away.

West took the wheel of the Land Rover and I climbed into the passenger seat.

"Where to?" he asked.

"I think we start at Dinara's apartment. See what we can find out about this raid on her and the others."

He nodded, started the engine, and headed out of the deserted lot.

I gave him directions and forty minutes later we were in Yermolayevskiy Lane, opposite a small park. West drove the Land Rover into a bay alongside the green space.

It was 8:30 a.m. when we arrived, and we only had to wait a minute or so before one of the residents opened the front door of Dinara's block and allowed us in while he headed out for work. We passed through a simple lobby and climbed some dingy stairs to the fourth floor.

As we walked toward the apartment, I was surprised to see an old woman sitting in the corridor, reading a book. She was on a battered old folding garden chair, had a mismatched table beside her and was surrounded by pot plants.

"Going to make it tricky to break in," West observed. "Maybe I can distract her?"

I nodded, but the woman made it clear there was to be no distraction when she started yelling at us angrily.

West replied in Russian, his tone soothing and conciliatory.

"She says we better not be here for more trouble. The last gang smashed Dinara's door in and broke this lady's chair."

"You are Americans, yes?" the woman said in broken English. "They smash my chair. I don't like this one so much."

As we came closer, I saw the door frame was splintered, and a roughly fitted padlock secured the door to it.

"Did you see the people who did this?" I asked.

"Your name?" the woman replied haughtily.

"Jack Morgan. Dinara works for me."

"Then you are a very bad man," she said, rising indignantly from her rickety chair. "This woman needs a husband and babies, not to be working all God's hours."

"Did you see the men who did this?" West asked.

She fixed us with a disapproving stare.

"Dinara is in danger," I said. "We're the only people who can help her."

She hesitated and then sat down and reached under the chair for her phone.

"I have photos," she revealed. "After they broke my chair and took her away, I got pictures of them and their transport from my window so I could make a police report. But the police don't want to know. Maybe you can help."

She opened her phone and swiped through a series of photos that showed two grey UAZ Patriot SUVs and a matching UAZ-452 van with blacked-out windows parked not too far from where we'd left the Land Rover. A group of half a dozen men were crowded around Dinara, who was in restraints, and a series of sequential pictures showed her being forced into the back of the van.

"Can I have copies of these?" I asked.

The woman shrugged and I AirDropped them onto my phone.

I pointed out a detail to West.

"License plates," I said.

He nodded.

"If you find Dinara, tell her Mrs. Minsky helped," the old woman said.

"I will. Thank you, Mrs. Minsky," I replied while hurrying toward the stairs. "We've got faces and plates," I said to West, who jogged alongside me. "We can find these guys."

CHAPTER 88

WE RETURNED TO the Land Rover, and West reached into the glove compartment for a communicator that looked like a satellite phone. I guessed it was an Echelon machine, used by the CIA for secure comms, and wondered whether he was just a Marine or whether he moonlighted for the agency. Was he moonlighting now?

He placed a call which was answered moments later.

"Mom, me and Cousin Lenny have got some great souvenir photos. Do you know anywhere that could process them?" he said.

He listened for a moment.

"The store in Kuzminki? Great idea."

He hung up and turned to me.

"That was Erin Sebold. She wants to meet us at one of the Agency's facilities. She can help with the photos."

I nodded and he started the engine, pulling into the slow-moving rush-hour traffic that was circling the park.

"How long have you been stationed here?" I asked as we drove through the city.

"Six years," West replied. "It's my last posting. Assuming I don't re-up. You were in the Corps, right?"

I nodded. "While back."

"You know you're a legend?" he remarked, and I shook my head. "Seriously, even if you were a flyboy, a millionaire hero Marine is a role model for so many."

"I don't know who that guy is, but he sounds cool." I smiled. "And I won't take offense at you calling me a flyboy."

"None intended," he scoffed.

"I just see a problem and need to fix it," I said more seriously. "Everything else is noise."

"Did you always know you wanted to start a detective agency?"

I shook my head. "It was my dad's. I took it over after I left the Corps. That was something I never expected, but after what happened in Afghanistan, I couldn't stay. I lost people. Buddies."

"I feel that. It cuts deep," West replied.

We sat in silence for a while, and I reflected on those I'd lost.

"What do you think you'll do if you don't re-up?" I asked.

"Who knows? Maybe close protection. Maybe I'll start my own detective agency."

"Ha! Well, if neither of those works out, look me up. There will always be a job for you at Private."

"Thank you, Jack," he replied.

He seemed genuinely touched. Maybe he wasn't as connected to the CIA as I had thought?

We talked about our military experiences and traded war stories as we crossed the Russian capital. Finally, when we were in the south-east of the city, West turned onto a narrow sidestreet full of old warehouses and storage facilities.

He parked outside a rundown yard where dozens of ancient trailers and trucks were stored.

"Come on," he said, and we got out.

The gate wasn't locked and he led me into a graveyard for huge trucks, trailers, and containers that would once have transported tonnes of goods around Russia. We went deep into the yard, navigating the maze of rusting metal machines and containers, until we reached a Soviet-era ZIL truck.

West knocked on the back door and it opened slowly to reveal an empty container. As I looked closely at the interior, I realized something wasn't quite right and then the far wall rose. It wasn't a wall at all. It was an LED display a few feet from the door, showing an image of an empty trailer. It retracted into the ceiling, and in the gap beneath it I could see a glimpse of workstations and surveillance equipment.

West climbed in and crouched to go through the gap. I followed. Once we were inside, the door swung shut and the screen descended.

The container was about thirty feet long, eleven wide, and twelve tall. There were six workstations but only two were occupied. The analysts were a couple of women in their thirties who were focused on their screens.

Erin Sebold was supervising them. She turned to welcome us as we approached.

"Mr. Morgan, Master Gunnery Sergeant, how can we help you?" she asked.

"We've got photos of the men who took my country manager, and the license plates of the vehicles they used to abduct her," I replied.

"Quick work for a couple of holiday makers," she replied. "Can you give them to Cecily?"

The older of the two analysts turned and held out her hand for my phone.

"I've unlocked it," I said, passing it to her.

She gave me the withering look I'd seen on Mo-bot's face numerous times.

She connected the phone to one of the devices at her station, and soon my photo library was displayed on a large screen that formed one side of the container. Cecily highlighted all the photos I'd retrieved that day and scrolled through them.

"We should be able to acquire the vehicles on Hawkeye," Erin suggested, and Cecily nodded.

"Hawkeye?" I asked.

"A few years ago, the Agency realized we often only appreciated the significance of an event long after it happened, so we changed the way we approach satellite data. High-resolution, near-constant surveillance and long-term storage. We keep a permanent record, a history of everything that has happened," Erin explained. "And we do this on a global level."

Cecily took the timestamp and geolocation data from

Mrs. Minsky's photos and input them into the Hawkeye program.

A moment later, an overhead satellite image popped onto the big screen and I recognized it as Dinara's neighborhood. I could see her building and the park opposite. And, more importantly, the three vehicles that had taken her away.

"We can tag them and the AI will follow them through the city," Cecily said as she used the cursor to attach markers to three target vehicles.

She typed a command and the image changed, jumping forward a few seconds. The vehicles were now on the road. Then it changed again and they were partway round the square, and then again and the system had picked them up in a different neighborhood. The intervals between these images shortened as the AI got better at processing their route. We followed it on a series of high-resolution satellite images of Moscow that had been taken more than twenty-four hours ago.

"We lose them on the edge of the city," Cecily said, drawing my attention to a country road beside thick forest.

I couldn't believe what I was seeing, but next to the last image we had of the SUVs and van that had taken Dinara, I saw the distinctive wreckage of two crashed vehicles. I had driven past that very spot on my last trip to Moscow.

"I know this place," I said.

"Can you pick them up again?" Erin asked.

Cecily shook her head.

"I've been there before," I remarked, drawing close to the screen and studying the very last image we had of the convoy.

"Ma'am, there's something I think Mr. Morgan should know about Valery Alekseyev," the younger analyst said.

"Go ahead, Kate," Erin replied.

"Alekseyev isn't his real name," Kate revealed. "That's his mother's maiden name.

"Alekseyev's father's name was Salko. He is Yevgeny Salko's half-brother. His elder brother. Our intel suggests Alekseyev recruited Yevgeny into the SVR."

The news left me reeling. Yevgeny Salko had been a director of the SVR with responsibility for the Bright Star program. I'd destroyed his life's work and his career during my investigation into Karl Parker's death.

"Our sources indicate Salko might have been executed after your intervention," Erin revealed. "He was certainly disavowed and no one has seen or heard anything from him since."

I studied the satellite image of the van, picturing Dinara inside the vehicle, alone and frightened, and as I looked at the picture I realized I was scared too. This wasn't about geopolitics or espionage. This was personal. I'd unwittingly ruined Alekseyev's brother, and possibly cost him his life. This man would go to the ends of the earth to make sure his brother got justice.

"This is a vendetta," I remarked. "It isn't about what I did to Russia, this is about what I did to Valery Alekseyev's family."

I looked once more at the satellite picture of the two wrecked vehicles by the side of the road, and recalled my previous journey north out of Moscow.

"I know where he's taken them," I said. "I know where they are. Back where all this started."

CHAPTER 89

"YOU THINK THIS is revenge for Bright Star?" Erin asked.

"I'm almost certain of it," I replied.

"We need to—" she began, but didn't get any further.

"We've got movement outside, ma'am," Kate cut in urgently.

She brought up the feed from surveillance cameras located around the yard and surrounding area, and the screens filled with images of Moscow Police and unmarked vehicles flooding the property.

"This location is compromised," Erin said. "We have to assume your vehicle or ours was tracked here."

My heart sank. The Land Rover contained all our gear. Could the Russians have marked and tracked every embassy vehicle? In the era of big data and AI surveillance, anything was possible.

"You need to leave now," Erin told us. "The truck three to our north with the red container. Access code is seven-six-three-four.

Inside are four Kawasaki motorbikes, fueled and ready to go. Get out of here. Use the blue route and go to the old bakery on Fadeyeva Street in Lefortovo District. The Red Man has the key to everything you need. Just tell him you need bread. Go!"

West moved toward the exit as the false wall rose. I followed. We crouched to step beneath it. When I glanced back, I saw Erin, Cecily, and Kate priming explosive charges to destroy all the gear in the container.

The door opened and West and I jumped onto asphalt and ran north toward the red container. I saw flashes of vehicles between the parked trucks as police and unmarked vehicles raced through the yard. We didn't have long. The roar of approaching engines set my heart pumping. As we neared the red trailer, I understood what Erin meant by the blue route. There were blue butane canisters scattered around the yard but when I looked closely, I saw they weren't placed at random. They indicated an escape route.

West climbed onto the red container and tapped the code that Erin had given us into the keypad. The doors clicked open and he swung them wide to reveal four powerful dirt bikes, each with a helmet perched ready on the seat.

"Can you ride?" he asked.

I nodded and hauled myself into the container. I grabbed the black bike and West took the silver one. We each put on a helmet that matched our bike.

I jumped on, pressed the ignition, revved the engine, kicked down into first gear, and shot forward, jumping out of the container and hitting the road. West followed and we both took a hard right, aiming for the furthest blue butane canister we could see.

Behind us, two police vehicles and an unmarked saloon gave chase. I kicked up through the gears and twisted the throttle to put some distance between my bike and our pursuers.

My heart leapt into my throat when I heard a loud explosion. I glanced over my shoulder to see a huge fireball over the tops of the vehicles chasing us and the surrounding containers. The three spies had destroyed their operations center.

We raced on, wheeling and turning to follow the route marked out by the canisters, and soon the road ran out and our wheels were chewing up dirt.

One of the pursuing police vehicles broadcast commands over its loudhailer, and the passenger in the unmarked saloon started taking pot-shots at our wheels.

West and I weaved around, trying to stay clear of the bullets as we raced toward what appeared to be a dead end—a line of containers set against the perimeter fence.

I thought we'd been led to disaster until I saw two butane containers either side of a tiny, barely visible gap between two of the containers. It was just wide enough for a motorbike and rider.

I raced toward it and lined myself up as best I could. There was no chance to slow down with the pursuit almost on us, and if West and I got this wrong, hitting one of the containers at 60 m.p.h. with no body armor would be devastating.

I roared toward the gap, held my breath, and shot between the two containers. West made it too. I heard the screech of brakes and the crunch of dirt as the vehicles behind tried to stop. One of them couldn't and hit the container to my right, which shuddered as I cleared the end and passed through a gap that had been cut in the perimeter fence.

We joined the road beyond the yard and raced east. My thundering heart only started to quieten when we'd put half a mile between us and our pursuers. I was in awe of the planning and preparation that went into making Agency locations secure.

West and I finally slowed when we reached the gas station about two miles away. We pulled into the forecourt, stopped the bikes side by side and raised our visors.

"Holy hell, that was close," he said.

I nodded and exhaled deeply. "I hope they made it out okay."

"Chief Sebold is a pro," he assured me. "They'll be fine."

"I guess we need to go to Lefortovo District," I remarked.

"And find the Red Man," he added. "Follow me."

He lowered his visor and I did likewise before trailing him out of the gas station, heading north through Moscow.

CHAPTER 90

I REMEMBERED THE Lefortovo District from my last time in Moscow. Dinara Orlova and I had encountered Madame Agafiya, the proprietor of a brothel, in the impoverished quarter when we'd been on the trail of an old friend of hers. Not much had changed since my last visit and daylight showed more of the neighborhood's flaws. The tall blocks that dotted the area were crumbling and covered in graffiti. Discarded food containers, empty bottles, nitrous canisters, and needles were scattered in the gutters. This rundown area was once intended by the Soviets to be a residential utopia. It had forgotten once capitalism reached Russia, then left to deteriorate by politicians who saw no benefit in restoring the old place.

The bakery was on Fadeyeva Street, a road of dilapidated apartment blocks and empty shops. Most of them had been boarded up, including the old bakery, a single-story detached building about the size of a tennis court that lay between two low-rise apartment blocks. The place would once have been a community hub, providing bread and sweet pastries to the neighborhood, but now it was still and silent, slowly decaying like the buildings around it.

West parked in a spot in front. As he took off his helmet, I pulled up next to him.

"No sign of the Red Man," he said.

"Let's take a look around," I suggested, removing my helmet.

He nodded and we dismounted. We walked along the pot-holed road, crossed the broken sidewalk, and I followed him down the driveway that ran between the bakery and the adjacent block.

We entered an open space that must have been the old delivery yard. There was a set of steel double doors that looked newer than the rest of the building. Mesh covered the rear windows, but even so some of the panes behind the protective metal grilles were cracked and broken.

Weeds were growing in the yard, particularly around an ancient bakery truck that stood on bricks.

"Any sign of the Red Man?" West asked, and I shook my head.

The yard was overlooked on three sides by a trio of five-story apartment blocks with small square windows. Most were dirty, some were cracked, and a few looked as though they were about to come away from their frames.

A booming voice shouted something in Russian and I turned to see a huge man with a thick head of red hair and a matching bushy beard yelling at us from the ground-floor window of the apartment beside the driveway.

"I think that's our Red Man," I remarked.

"He's not happy," West said, before replying in Russian.

The man's mood softened at the sound of West's words, and we walked over.

"What did you say to him?" I asked.

"I told him we need bread," he replied.

A three-feet-high fence separated the driveway from a narrow stretch of scrubland beside the block, and we stopped beside it.

"Americans?" the Red Man asked.

He was bare-chested, giving off a wild, unstable vibe.

"How can you tell?" West asked.

"Your clothes. Your accent. You never get it quite right," he replied. "How is it I can do Alabama," he said in a perfect Mobile accent, "but you folks can never nail Moscow?"

West scoffed. "Maybe we don't eat enough *pelmeni*?"

The Red Man reverted to his Russian accent. "Start eating more. Then you grow up big and strong like me."

He stood tall, revealing that he was naked. I was glad when he leant against the windowsill again.

"You're not here for bread, little American liar. You were sent to collect a vehicle," he remarked. "I received a message."

West nodded and the Red Man tossed him a set of keys.

"The small key is for the door. The other is for the Volkswagen Transporter. There are three in there. Take the blue one. It has what you need in the back. There is an inventory in the glove box. Make sure you close the door when you leave."

"Thanks," I said.

"No need," he replied. "Now be ready because I'm going to swear at you in Russian."

And he did. Loudly and violently, obviously for the benefit of his neighbors. Nothing like hiding in plain sight.

West yelled something back and the Red Man smiled.

"Not bad, American," he said quietly. "You can swear like a Russian even if you can't talk like one."

West flashed him a grin and we headed for the bakery. He opened the double doors to reveal three Volkswagen Transporters in the large storeroom.

He got in the blue one, started the engine, and rolled into the yard.

I shut and locked the double doors then jumped in the passenger seat.

"Check the glove box," West suggested.

I opened it to find the laminated inventory list.

"What have we got?" he asked.

"Everything," I replied. "There's enough artillery in this thing to launch an assault on the Kremlin."

"Hopefully it won't come to that."

"Don't go getting soft just because this is meant to be your vacation," I suggested, and we both smiled.

He put the Transporter in gear, drove us out of the yard, and headed north.

CHAPTER 91

THE LAST TIME I made this journey there was thick snow every-where and the bitter winter had covered everything in frost. This time the countryside north of Moscow was rich with color: the green of trees and grass, the white, pink, and yellow of wildflow-ers, and the blue of a cloudless July sky. But it might as well have been monochrome. I was impervious to it, lost in contemplation of the task that lay ahead.

My people had been taken by Valery Alekseyev, a man con-vinced I'd wronged him and his country. His position suggested he was powerful and his actions told me he was vindictive, which meant he was unlikely to surrender Dinara and the others with-out a fight. His power gave him resources that would stack the odds against us, which made our prospects grim.

"Are you sure you want to do this?" I asked West when we were about an hour north of Moscow. He was closer to home than to danger, and I wanted him to have the chance to turn around.

"No, I'm not sure," he replied. "Is anyone ever sure? But I'm staying the course."

"Why?" I asked.

"Because if I don't, it's more likely the bad guys will win. Call me sentimental, but I was raised on apple pie, *Sesame Street*, and the belief good triumphs over evil. You and I both know that's a lie, but good can triumph over evil sometimes, and for that to happen, men and women like us need to stand up."

I nodded. He glanced in my direction.

"Why are you here? You could sit stateside counting your money and pretend you'd done your part by calling the Moscow Police."

"I was raised on *Sesame Street* too," I replied. "And these particular bad guys have my team, which makes it personal."

"I could tell you were a *Sesame Street* fan," West joked, but his smile didn't last, and neither did mine, and we continued our journey lost in our own thoughts.

We took turns behind the wheel, switching every couple hours. I was driving when we passed the wreckage of the two vehicles which I'd seen all those months ago. This time they weren't buried in snow, so their rusting twisted chassis were completely exposed. They made me think of the rotten, corrupt network we had exposed, linking Russia and China, and how it too was a blight on the world, polluting everything it touched.

The sun had dropped beneath the horizon and we were traveling through the glow of the last embers of the day by the time we reached Volkovo, almost ten hours after we'd set out from Moscow.

I was driving and slowed as we went through the town, past the simple houses and the bakery where Leonid Boykov, a good and kind man who had worked for Private until his untimely death, had once bought pastries for Dinara and me. I pictured him smiling, trying to push sweets on us. His loss still weighed heavily on me, but all I could do was remember and mourn him as I did so many of the departed.

I took us north and found a trail two hundred yards south of the dirt track that led to Boltino army base. I drove along this and parked behind some trees that would shield the vehicle from view.

"The base is about two miles north-east of here," I said. "Not long now."

CHAPTER 92

THE BACK OF the Transporter contained four flight cases full of gear and there was a secret compartment beneath the flatbed that held a cache of weapons.

We used a micro surveillance drone to survey the base. The drone was silent and dark, nothing more than a tiny shadow against the night sky. West used a remote control with an infrared display to pilot the device up through the trees that concealed us and over the forest that ringed the base.

The buildings were much as I remembered them. A collection of bunkers, hangars, silos, and barracks, all crumbling and rusting, the legacy of a military might long gone. In the center of the base was the command block where I'd questioned Maxim Yenen and forced him to admit his involvement in the Bright Star program—a deacades-long initiative designed to subvert America's political system and power structure.

Apart from the lack of snow, the only other difference was the collection of vehicles parked between the command block and the largest hangar. There was a large forward-operations truck. It didn't have any military markings but was decked out in grey-and-black camouflage. Next to it were two troop carriers and a dozen SUVs and ten vans.

There were four men patrolling the vehicles, each armed with a machine gun, each sporting night-vision goggles. There were another three stationed outside the large hangar, who were similarly equipped. Two more men stood outside the command block.

West piloted the drone around the large building. We couldn't be sure how many people were inside, but the artificial lights coming from within meant he was able to switch from infrared to optical camera, and through holes in the walls, we counted a minimum of three guards patrolling the interior. West flew the tiny aircraft through one of the holes and found a makeshift operations center in what looked like an old communications room. Six men and two women stood in front of computers that had been placed on old concrete plinths that were designed to be blast-proof. Some of the men and women were talking on their phones.

"They are hunting us," West translated the audio picked up by the drone. "They're coordinating a massive search of the blocks around the embassy where we disappeared."

And overseeing it all was Valery Alekseyev, operations director of the SVR. He wore a black pullover and pants, looking every inch as cruel and ruthless as he had in his photograph. This was the man responsible for the deaths of the three Private agents in Beijing, for killing Lewis Williams and putting Jessie Fleming in hospital, destroying Private Beijing, abducting Alison Lucas, making a traitor of Rafael, and trying to kill yet more of my friends and colleagues in New York and Moscow. I understood the depth of the anger Alekseyev felt toward me for causing his brother's ruin because now I returned it many times over.

And then he was gone, swept off the screen as West piloted the drone around the rest of the command block. We didn't find anything else.

"Let's check out the hangar," I suggested.

He nodded, switched back to infrared and flew the drone over the vehicles and high above the roof of the huge hangar. It was pocked by large holes and West took the device down through one at the heart of the building. The hangar was dark so he stayed on infrared, but we didn't need light to spot the cluster of twenty-three blindfolded, gagged, and bound people huddled in the center of the vast space: Dinara, Feo, and the rest of the Private Moscow staff.

We had found Alekseyev's hostages.

"I count six hostiles," West remarked, pointing out half a dozen large men who brandished what looked like ShAK-12 urban assault rifles, extremely powerful short-range fully automatic machine guns.

I nodded. "Heavily armed and likely very well trained. You still sure you want to do this?"

West smiled. "What better way to spend my vacation?"

"Let's get ready then," I said, my stomach churning and adrenaline setting my body alight at the prospect of what was to come.

CHAPTER 93

MASTER GUNNERY SERGEANT Marlon West was no stranger to combat, but he had never faced odds quite this bad. He checked his watch, the luminous dial gently lighting the digits to tell him it was four minutes to midnight. Jack Morgan would be in position now, and it was West's job to neutralize the guards outside the hangar so the hostages could be rescued.

West inched closer to the edge of the treeline and lowered his night-vision scope, which was attached to the headset that also supported his field radio.

"Go," Jack said, and West peered at the corner of the hangar and saw the green glow of Morgan's scope by the back wall.

West broke cover and ran for the vehicles parked in the yard. The four men guarding them had moved to the other side of them. West crouched, moved silently, and slowed as he approached so they wouldn't hear his steps in the dirt.

He could hear them though. They were talking in Russian, discussing the situation in Ukraine, complaining that Russia should be taking stronger action. West crawled alongside the camouflage operations truck until he reached the hood. He leant over it to see the men with their backs to him. He targeted the tallest of the four with his HK416 assault rifle fitted with a custom suppressor.

He lined up his sights and applied pressure to the trigger.

The rattle and crack of automatic gunfire sent his heart into overdrive as bullets hit the ground and truck beside him. West turned and saw one of the guards from the hangar was off position and had caught sight of him. The guard was shooting from fifty yards away, which was the only reason West hadn't been killed instantly.

He was about to return fire when he saw muzzle flash from the rear corner of the hangar. Jack Morgan felled the guard instantly.

There were shouts and commands barked across the base, and West heard movement behind him as the taller of the four men jumped over the hood. West wheeled round and opened fire instinctively, catching the man in the chest as he tried to raise his own gun. He fell forward, tumbling to the ground inches from where West stood. His comrades raised their weapons but West was already on them and squeezing the trigger. The HK416 sprayed a burst of bullets that put them down.

West didn't even wait to watch them fall. He started running toward the hangar, aware of shadows and shapes moving around the base. He had to neutralize the guards by the entrance if Jack was to have any chance of rescuing the hostages. Thanks to him, the first guard was already down. West passed his motionless body as he drew level with the hangar.

"I'm almost at the target," he said breathlessly into his radio. "The four by the vehicle pool are down."

"Copy that," Jack replied via the earpiece.

"I owe you."

"Don't mention it. Let's get this done."

"Copy that."

He ran along the edge of the hangar, which curved like the side of a bell, so that he was obscured from the view of anyone at the entrance. West saw armed figures running toward the vehicle pool and knew he didn't have long.

He slowed to a walk and then a creep as he reached the apex of the curve. He raised his rifle and—

There were two incoming shots. The first hit the hangar beside his head and the second caught him in the shoulder, missing his body armor and tearing through the bulb of flesh at the top of his arm.

He cried out.

"West?" Jack said urgently. "West?"

"I'm hit."

"I'm coming."

"No!" he replied, pressing his hand to the wound.

He saw three men across the yard. They were heading away from the command building and one of them had his gun on West.

He tried to raise his weapon but his arm wouldn't work, so he grabbed the rifle with his left hand and lifted it to take aim.

He was about to fire one-handed when he heard a noise behind him. One of the hangar guards had got the jump on him. He drove his rifle stock into West's face.

West went down like a derelict building being demolished and blacked out an instant later.

CHAPTER 94

WEST HAD LEFT his mic open so I heard voices speaking in Russian as they carried him away. I prayed he was still alive and wondered whether I should go for him or stay on mission. If he was dead, I'd be wasting my energy and risking complete failure. If he was alive, I could rescue him later. Making the correct decision felt straightforward.

I hurried over to my ingress point, a section of hangar wall directly behind the main entrance. West was supposed to engage Alekseyev's men in a frontal assault while I used the cover of the hostages to attack from the rear, but the plan was in tatters now. I'd have to improvise.

I took a canister of nano-thermite foam from my equipment belt, sprayed the contents in a thin arc from the ground to an apex about six feet above it, and then back down again. The explosive foam expanded and took on a more solid texture as it clung to the hangar wall. I primed a small detonator, stuck it in the foam near the top of the arc and backed away a dozen paces. I turned my back and covered my ears as there was a staccato blast from the thousands of tiny explosive charges that made up the foam, detonating in rapid succession.

The moment the noise subsided, I ran toward the hole I'd made, raised my HK416 rifle and went through.

The interior was gloomy but I had my scope. Through the smoke I saw two figures by the main door and three more by the hostages. There were shouts, commands barked in Russian, and the men turned toward me, guns raised.

The first cracks of gunfire broke out. Bullets whistled around me. I picked out my first target and squeezed the trigger. The bullet hit him in the chest, and I had moved on to the second man before the first dropped.

Headshot.

The third guy made the mistake of moving away from the hostages, so I ran toward him at an angle. The space he had created between himself, Dinara, Feo, and the others meant I didn't have to be so careful with my aim. As he opened fire and tried to compensate for the speed and direction of my movement, I sprayed a volley in his general direction and a cluster of bullets caught him in the knees and thighs.

He went down screaming.

The two men by the door were firing wildly now and one or two of the bullets went into the assembled hostages. I heard grunts, nothing more because they were all gagged, but I knew someone had been injured. I had to take those guards out, so I pulled an M67 grenade from my belt, released the spoon, and threw it over and past the hostages.

The green metal ball travelled the eighty or so feet separating me from the two men. When it hit the ground between the pair of them, they stopped shooting and tried to dive clear, but they weren't quick enough and were caught in the blast, which picked them up and hurled their broken bodies through the main entrance. I'd judged the distance well so that, although buffeted by the blast wave, the hostages weren't affected by the fireball or full force of the explosion.

I raced over to them and found Feo, the former Moscow police officer who now worked for Private. He was easy to pick out because of his enormous size. I used my tactical knife to cut his bonds and he removed his blindfold and gag.

"Jack Morgan, you magnificent immortal!" he boomed, and followed it up with something equally expressive in Russian.

"We don't have much time," I said. "Cut the others loose while I watch the door then take them out the back. There's a blast hole. Head west through the forest. I'll find you."

"What about you?" Feo asked.

"They've taken a friend. I need to get him back," I replied. "And I have to find Alekseyev."

"Valery Alekseyev?" Feo's eyes widened.

I nodded. "He's behind this. He gave the order to have you kidnapped. He needs to answer for this and everything else he's done."

He nodded and I handed him my knife.

I ran to the door and watched the yard and command building

opposite. There was no movement. No guards swarming toward me. Everything was still and the only sounds were those of Feo and the people he'd freed, working to free others. The lack of response was unnerving and I couldn't understand why Alekseyev wasn't sending his men at us.

The two guards who had been caught by the grenade lay in the dirt, their bodies scorched and twisted, and I wondered why their comrades hadn't come to avenge them.

"Jack."

I turned to see Dinara Orlova hurry toward me. Anna Bolshova, the officer from Moscow Police who had joined Private soon after the Bright Star investigation, was with her. Behind them, most of the hostages were free and on their feet. I could see two team members I didn't recognize being helped by others. They had both been caught in the crossfire, but their injuries didn't look life-threatening and they were able to walk.

"Thank you for coming," Dinara said. "*Thank you* so much."

I noticed she and Anna were carrying guns taken from the men I'd shot. Good.

"Take the staff out through the back and go through the forest. Head west and I'll find you."

"We're coming with you," Dinara responded. "Feo says Valery Alekseyev is responsible for all this."

"Yes," I replied. "He's taking revenge on me. On us. Yevgeny Salko is his brother."

Dinara understood the implication immediately, and Anna sucked in a sharp breath of disbelief.

"Feo says he has one of your friends," Dinara remarked.

"Marlon West from the embassy, but you need to go. You're not in any shape—"

Dinara cut me off. "And what shape are you in? You look tired, battered, no better than us."

"She's right," Anna added. "We're coming with you. I'd like to see Alekseyev myself."

"Don't waste time arguing with them," Feo said, walking over with a ShAK-12 in his hands. "Or with me. The others will tend to the wounded and take them to safety."

I looked over his shoulder and saw the rest of the Private Moscow staff making their way out of the hangar through the blast hole. I knew there was no point arguing with these three.

"Come on," Feo said. "Let's go get your friend."

CHAPTER 95

WE CROSSED THE yard between the hangar and the command block, and I marveled at my friends and colleagues. Anna looked as though she'd been abducted from bed. She wore a pair of tight leggings, which were filthy, trainers that seemed too big and an oversized jumper riddled with holes. Her hair was tangled and matted, her face dirty. Dinara and Feo were in similar condition, but were at least wearing proper clothes: jeans, boots, Feo a leather jacket, Dinara a thick sweater. They looked exhausted and shaken by their ordeal but they kept going, prepared to risk their lives to be by my side. I was grateful to have such loyal friends.

I took point and kept my rifle ready as we neared the command building. The first shots came when we were within yards of the entrance, careless and wide. The shooter had appeared from behind a balustrade on the roof.

I replied with a volley and was joined by all three of my

colleagues. The building was old and unstable. The balustrade collapsed under the barrage, sending the shooter, who had been leaning against it, tumbling two storys down along with a mass of rubble. He landed on his head and there was a sickening crack that left him motionless.

We ran over the fallen man, picked our way through the rubble and went into the building. I recalled the dank, decrepit lobby from my previous visit and checked the doorway leading off it.

I gave the others a thumbs up to indicate it was clear. We crept slowly and carefully through the lobby in file formation, toward the wreckage of the interior doors. I remembered from my last time in the building that there was a corridor branching left and right with rooms off it to either side. The old command offices and operation rooms lay to the right.

I entered the corridor and checked left. Nothing.

And then right. Also clear.

I signaled to Anna, Feo, and Dinara and we went right, moving silently along the corridor. The floor was damp and the walls pockmarked and crumbling. The place was dimly lit by moonlight shining through the holes in the roof. I kept my scope on; the others were forced to pick their way through the gloom.

We were nearing the operations room where West had flown the drone and we'd seen Alekseyev commanding his subordinates. I slowed, held my breath and dropped to a crouch as I neared the pool of light coming through the doorway. I lifted my scope as I got to within inches of the opening and peered round one side. I could hear the electrical static, computer fans, the hum of a radio receiver . . . but there was no sign of anyone in the room.

Then I heard a rattle of gunfire and a scream. I turned to see Anna fall, wounded in the leg. She clutched her thigh and cried out as I ran back to her.

"Get her inside," I said to Feo.

He took one arm and I grabbed the other. We dragged her into the operations room while Dinara laid down covering fire. Her muzzle spat fury to our left, but there was a burst of gunfire from the right and Feo was caught in the arm. He yelled a curse and dropped Anna.

I pulled her into the operations room by myself, then turned and grabbed Feo before he toppled over. He took three stumbling steps to get inside and collapsed on the floor next to Anna.

"I shouldn't have given them such a big target," he said with a faint smile.

"Put pressure on it," I told him, indicating the wound in his arm.

Dinara raced through the doorway, frantic with fear.

"They're coming!" she said. "Four of them. Two from each side."

"Help," Anna said weakly.

She was bleeding badly from the wound in her leg.

"She needs medical attention," Dinara remarked, crouching beside her.

"She needs a tourniquet," I said. "Here."

I opened a pocket on my gear belt and produced a field first-aid kit that included a tourniquet. I gave this to Dinara.

"I'll cover us," I said.

She opened the kit and got to work. Anna's skin looked pale and clammy by the white glow of the field lights in the corner of the room.

I turned to face the door and raised my rifle.

"Jack Morgan," a Russian-accented voice said through a speaker somewhere down the corridor, "you know who this is. You have come here to die, Jack Morgan, but first you will watch me kill your people."

CHAPTER 96

I HAD NO doubt the booming voice over the speaker was Valery Alekseyev's. I glanced at Feo, who was badly injured. His face was ashen and he was bleeding heavily from the arm. He gave me a look of defiance and clasped his rifle in his good hand. Anna was in a bad way also. Dinara tightened the tourniquet and gave me a concerned look. We weren't much of a fighting force anymore, and I knew if Alekseyev's men got in here it would be a slaughter.

I glanced around the operations room. Eight workstations and comms gear had been placed on top of the old legacy computer terminals, which had been built into concrete consoles approximately three feet high and two wide. They were arranged in two rows down the center of the room.

"Move," I told Feo. "Behind the terminals."

I ran over to Anna and helped Dinara drag her behind the nearest concrete console. Dinara and I dropped behind the ones to either side as the first of Alekseyev's men peered through the doorway.

There were two of them and they were clad in grey-and-black camo gear, ski masks, and each carried a ShAK-12 assault rifle. I glanced around to see Feo had made it behind the console furthest from me.

What I was about to do was foolhardy, and if the concrete didn't hold, it would be suicidal. We each had a console in front of us and another behind. I prayed they'd hold as I took two grenades from my belt, released the spoons, and held them for two seconds to give our assailants minimum reaction time. The two seconds seemed like a decade.

I threw the grenades at the doorway and ducked as I heard Alekseyev's men cry out in Russian. I covered my ears as a loud blast shook the building and a fireball engulfed the corridor and spilled into the room. The shockwave hit the consoles and chunks of concrete were blown off them. Parts of the ceiling started coming down as the fireball licked over the top of our shields.

I thought the fire would consume us, but the flames receded and I checked on Dinara, Feo, and Anna. They all looked dazed and were covered in dust and chunks of concrete, but they were alive and that's what mattered.

"I'm going for West," I told Dinara. "Look after these two. Get them out of here and to a hospital."

She nodded. As I was about to leave she took hold of my arm. "Thank you for coming for us, Jack."

I got to my feet and went to the doorway. The smell of scorched flesh, burnt hair, and smoke filled the air. I lowered my scope to my eye and the darkness immediately came alive in shades of green. I saw four bodies near the door, all badly disfigured by the blast, none showing any signs of life.

I hurried left along the corridor past the old bunk rooms where the children who had been part of the Bright Star program used to sleep.

I reached a dogleg and went left again until I came to one of the old classrooms where the children had been taught. I peered round the doorway and lifted my scope as I saw the room was lit by a field light connected to a mobile generator.

Part of the roof was missing, but the remains of the desk and the chair on which Maxim Yenen had sat as I'd interrogated him were still there.

At the far end of the room, seated in a leather armchair, was Valery Alekseyev. Marlon West had been hogtied and laid on the floor to Alekseyev's right. Two masked men in night camo held West. One was crouching, holding the point of a large combat knife to the prisoner's neck. The other was standing. He kept the muzzle of his ShAK-12 aimed at West's head.

He had been badly beaten and his face was covered in blood. There was more blood around the wound in his shoulder, but his eyes blazed defiance.

"Kill them, Jack," he yelled, before the man with the knife punched him.

"Mr. Morgan isn't here to kill us," Alekseyev said in flawless English. "He's here to die."

CHAPTER 97

"MY BROTHER DIED six months ago in disgrace," Alekseyev told me. "Not even your intelligence agencies know, because I wanted to hide his shame. Shame that you caused." Giving way to anger, he jumped to his feet. "You brought about his ruin. I hold you solely responsible."

"Then why not face me like a man?" I asked. I noticed he was keeping his distance on the other side of the room. He likely thought me dangerous. Rightly so. "If you hold me solely responsible, why involve all these innocents?"

"Innocents!" he almost spat. "There are no innocents in this world. You ruined so many lives here. Not just my brother's. Don't blame me for involving others. They are suffering because of your actions. They are dying because of you."

"If you let my friend go, I won't kill your men," I said.

He challenged, "And will my life be spared into the bargain?"

"No," I replied coolly.

"You seem to be under the misapprehension that you hold the power here. I propose a different deal. Put down your weapon and surrender, and I won't kill your friend."

The knifeman underlined Alekseyev's threat by pressing the point of his blade into West's neck.

"You know I'm not bluffing. Put down the gun."

"Don't do it!" West said. "Shoot them."

I weighed my options. Shoot the knifeman and the guy with the gun drills a hole in West. Shoot the gunman and the knifeman goes to work.

I did the only thing I could.

I lowered myself to the ground and put down my rifle.

CHAPTER 98

ALEKSEYEV YELLED SOMETHING in Russian, and the knife-man stepped away from West and started toward me.

"Lie down," the SVR director instructed me. "Flat on your belly."

I locked eyes with West, who looked disappointed and shook his head slowly.

I watched the knifeman carefully as he approached. He had a Makarov MP-71 pistol in a holster at his hip and was reaching into his pocket for something. He produced a coil of high-tensile cable.

"Hands behind your back," Alekseyev said. "He will tie you like your friend."

My hands were beneath me. I shifted to free them, and as I did so the knifeman crouched to reach me. I grabbed my tactical blade, rolled toward him and drove it into his neck. Before he moved, I took his Makarov pistol from its holster, flipped onto my back and shot the gunman in the chest. He fell to his knees clutching the wound, while the knifeman made horrific gasping sounds and toppled onto his back.

"Don't move," Alekseyev said.

I glanced round to see him grab an SR-2 Veresk submachine gun from beside the armchair and aim it at West.

"Drop it or I will shoot your friend," he commanded. "Drop it!"

I wavered. He was going to kill us both anyway. I might as well take a shot.

"Don't be stupid, Mr. Morgan. Your friend's life is in your hands."

I looked at West and saw him nod almost imperceptibly. He was telling me to take the shot.

"Put down the gun, Mr. Morgan," Alekseyev said. "You don't want to be responsible for another death."

I was on my side with the gun pointed at the space above West. I would have to roll onto my back and adjust my aim significantly to target Alekseyev. He would have ample time to shoot West.

I lowered the pistol and put it on the floor beside me.

"People like you never have what it takes," Alekseyev told me. "This is for my brother."

He swung his gun toward me, but before the barrel completed its arc, his chair and the floor around him splintered under gunfire. The volley sounded like thunder breaking.

Alekseyev yelled in pain. He'd been hit in the lower leg, but like a wounded wild animal, he could still run. He managed to get through the hole in the wall and escape into the night.

I looked behind me and saw the source of the gunfire.

Dinara Orlova stood in the doorway, the barrel of her machine gun smoking.

"You might not have what it takes to be a psychotic killer, but at least you have friends," she said.

I smiled. "Shouldn't you be with Feo and Anna?"

"I thought you could use some help," she replied. "Besides, Feo has rallied. He's helping Anna outside."

"Cut West loose and get him to safety with the others," I said, grabbing the pistol and getting to my feet.

Dinara nodded. "Be careful, Jack. He's wounded and that's going to make him even more dangerous."

As she hurried over to West, I ran through the hole in the wall, following Alekseyev into darkness.

CHAPTER 99

I LOWERED MY night-vision scope and saw him almost imme-diately. He was making his way along the edge of the command building. He looked back and fired a couple of wild shots in my direction before limping around the corner.

I sprinted after him. I knew he was heading for the vehicle pool, and that if I didn't get him now, I might never have another chance. Back in Moscow, in normal circumstances, he'd be an extremely hard target to reach.

My legs pounded out the yards and my chest heaved with each gasping breath. I heard the roar of an engine being started when I reached the corner. I ran the short width of the crumbling old building and saw a gray UAZ Patriot SUV start to move away from the vehicle pool, gathering speed.

I dropped to one knee, stabilized myself, and raised the pistol. The shot was thirty yards and the distance lengthening. It would be asking a lot of me and the gun, but I didn't have much choice. I squeezed the trigger again and again, but the bullets missed their mark and the Patriot kept going.

I was out of ammunition so I sprinted toward the vehicle pool to find something fast enough to catch Alekseyev's SUV, but when I reached the corner of the building I was startled by the sudden appearance of a green mass in my night-vision scope. I lifted it to see Feo lit by the moonlight.

"Try this," he said, handing me his ShAK-12.

I took it, raised it to my shoulder, and targeted the Patriot's front left wheel as it headed along the base access road. Another fifty yards and I would lose it behind the thick forest.

"I'd take the shot myself, but you know, my arm," Feo said. "I'll be quiet now."

I didn't need his silence. I'd taken shots like this in the heat of combat, amid the noise of mortars, grenades, gunfire, and the screams of the wounded.

I squeezed the trigger and the first bullet travelled two hundred yards and blew out the front tire. I adjusted my aim as the Patriot started to shimmy uncertainly. This time I targeted the rear wheel. I took the shot, and an instant later the back tire burst and Alekseyev lost control of the vehicle completely.

It veered off the access road, ploughed through a field, and smashed into a tree at the edge of the forest.

"Not bad," Feo said.

I looked past him to see Anna leaning against a wall. She smiled weakly. West and Dinara emerged from the main entrance.

"Get them to a hospital," I said, nodding to Feo and Anna, then I ran toward the forest.

I rounded the badly damaged Patriot with my gun raised. Alekseyev, dazed and bloodied, was trying to get to his feet. He had managed to open the driver's door but couldn't get his legs to work.

I moved closer and saw he had his SR-2 Veresk in his hand. I kicked it and it dropped to the ground. He looked at me, his face covered in blood, eyes unfocused like a Saturday-night drunk.

"Well, go on," he said. "Kill me. Avenge your friends."

I stared at him down the barrel of my rifle and my finger curled around the trigger.

"Kill me," he said.

I wanted to take the shot. I wanted to take it so badly, but I couldn't. I wasn't that man. I wasn't a cold-blooded killer.

"You're just like me." There was a note of triumph in his voice. "I see it in your eyes. I've read your record. I know death and destruction follow you everywhere. That's because you like them. You seek them out."

I was horrified by the thought I was anything like this twisted, evil man.

"No," I replied, lowering my weapon.

It took him a moment to register what was happening.

"Why?" he asked. "I killed your friends. Kill me."

"I'm not like you. I value life. Someone like you isn't afraid of death, you welcome it, because you don't value life," I said. "Your punishment is going to be much worse. You won't be given the easy way out, Director Alekseyev. You're going to suffer."

CHAPTER 100

ANNA WAS TAKEN to Rybinsk General Hospital along with the other two Private staffers who had been caught in the crossfire during the rescue. The hospital was located about twenty miles south of the defunct military base.

True to form, Feo had insisted a doctor patch him up just enough so he could come with us, and West, equally stubborn, had followed his example. So twenty minutes after depositing the wounded at the hospital along with four members of Private staff to keep an eagle eye on them, Feo and West joined Dinara and me in the Volkswagen Transporter, heading south toward Moscow.

Dinara had used the company account to lodge the rest of the team in a motel in Rybinsk until we were able to reassure them it was safe to return.

She drove for the first leg and sat behind the wheel looking shellshocked. I was in the passenger seat, and Feo was dozing behind Dinara. West sat next to him looking grim-faced.

Our valuable cargo lay bound and gagged in the back of the Transporter, with all our gear.

"Thank you for rescuing us," Dinara said.

"You'd have done the same," I replied.

She nodded. "I hope so. What now?"

"How are you getting on, Master Gunnery Sergeant?" I asked.

"They're going to meet us at the Red Man's place," he replied, glancing down at a secure communicator he'd pulled from the gear cases when we put Alekseyev in the back. "Eleven a.m. Can we make it?"

Dinara nodded. "We'll make it."

She drove like the wind, cutting through the Russian landscape as though devils were chasing her. After four hours, I took over and kept up a similar pace. The roads were deserted, giving us a clear run. The other three dozed while I drove.

The quiet gave me time to think and process what had happened these past few days. Had Alekseyev been right? Was I more like him than I cared to admit? Had I been changed by the years I'd spent inhabiting the world's underbelly? They say a person is shaped by the environment around them. Was I destined to end up like the men and women I'd brought to justice? Would I become like Valery Alekseyev?

The fact I hadn't killed him at Boltino suggested there was still clear water between me and him, and the nature of my life when I wasn't dealing with villains told me there was still a chance that things would stay that way.

I looked at the faces of those around me: Feo, Dinara, and West. I thought of Hua and Zhang Daiyu, and Sci and Mo-bot, and waiting for me somewhere in New York was my heart, Justine.

I had a sudden urge to be with her. I knew she kept my moral compass on the right heading. More simply, I missed her. But there was still work to be done to ensure Alekseyev faced justice, and I was glad to see the sun rising over the horizon as we neared Moscow.

Mid-morning traffic meant it took two hours to reach the bakery once we'd entered the city. We sat in heavy queues, surrounded by bored, frustrated, or patient Muscovites. I was envious of their lives. Regular, predictable and mundane. I didn't think I'd ever have an existence like that.

When we finally rolled along the potholed driveway beside the bakery, everyone was awake and glad to be at our journey's end.

There were no other vehicles in the yard and no sign of the Red Man, so I parked near the loading-bay doors. I jumped out and opened them—to find myself staring down the barrel of a gun.

CHAPTER 101

"EASY, PHIL," ERIN Sebold said.

He was a member of her six-man security team, and lowered his weapon after his principal gave the okay.

"Mr. Morgan, Master Gunnery Sergeant West says you have a gift for me," Erin said.

She was standing by a black Ford Excursion SUV, one of a trio of such vehicles parked next to the two Volkswagen Transporters in the bay.

"Bring it in," I said, waving at West.

He hopped into the driver's seat and drove our Transporter inside, stopping near Erin's security team. Dinara jumped out while West and Feo climbed in a more gingerly fashion. Both men were feeling their injuries.

"They're wounded," Erin remarked. "Why aren't they in hospital?"

"You try telling them that," I replied.

"I'm almost as stubborn as my American friend here," Feo said, nodding at West, and Erin laughed.

"At least his sense of humor seems healthy enough," she remarked. "And what about you, Master Gunnery Sergeant West? How are you feeling?"

"I've been better, but the rest on the journey back did me good."

Erin turned toward me. "So where is this gift?"

West moved to the rear of the truck and I joined him. I opened the back door to reveal Valery Alekseyev, bound and gagged, lying on his side between the equipment cases. He looked at us fearfully and tried to talk, but his words were nothing more than muffled grunts.

I climbed inside, grabbed him and dragged him out. West and I frogmarched him across to Erin, who was stunned.

"Valery Alekseyev, Director of the SVR . . . How?" she asked in disbelief.

"He made some bad choices," I replied.

"We can't . . ." Erin began. She hesitated. "Can we?"

"Director Alekseyev is going to defect to the United States," I told her. "He's worried that if he stays in Russia, his life will be in danger. Isn't that right, Director?"

Alekseyev nodded.

Before we'd put him in the back of the van, Feo and West had made it clear there were dozens of people in Russia with motive and means to want him dead, most of them among the Private personnel he had abducted.

"Director Alekseyev isn't asking for an expensive package," I went on. "He'd like to share what he knows about Russian Intelligence in exchange for a simple home in the Midwest that might feel a little like a prison."

"Director Alekseyev wants *that*?" Erin asked.

I saw him hesitate.

"Or we can bring him before a court the moment we get him stateside and he can rot in a supermax prison."

Alekseyev shook his head.

"See? He's got at least four of my colleagues' murder on his hands, and he will answer for that one way or another," I said.

Alekseyev looked sheepish and nodded.

Erin glanced from me to him and back again. She finally settled on me.

"Can I speak to you for a moment?"

I nodded and followed her, while Feo, Dinara, and West gathered around Alekseyev menacingly.

Erin and I stopped near the open door to the old kitchen.

"Are you seriously suggesting we abduct Valery Alekseyev?"

"Not abduct. Assist him to defect," I replied.

Her skeptical look would have withered most people.

"He knows the alternative is death if he stays here." I wasn't exaggerating. Private's Moscow staff was made up of former police officers, Special Forces, and intelligence operatives. Some of them would be far less forgiving than I was. "And he gets prison in the States if he refuses to cooperate and I manage to get him in front of a judge. Defection is the least bad option."

"So you're giving us the director of the SVR?" Erin asked.

I nodded.

"And you're happy with him being allowed to live?"

I hesitated. "I'll be honest—a large part of me wanted to kill him, but that wouldn't have brought anyone back. And a man like this doesn't fear death. But treachery, to be known as Russia's most infamous traitor, to go from patriot to villain . . . that will make him suffer for the rest of his life."

Erin gazed at Alekseyev whose eyes betrayed his fear and distress.

"Alright, Mr. Morgan," she said. "We just need to get him out of Moscow before the Kremlin shuts down Russia to find him."

CHAPTER 102

ERIN WENT INTO what must once have been the manager's office and shut the door to give herself privacy as she made some calls.

West and I returned Alekseyev to the back of the Transporter and he looked at me with defiance as I set him down on his side.

"Keep looking at me like that and I'll get Feodor in here. He took an armful of lead from your goons. I'm sure he'd like to share his pain with you."

Alekseyev turned away. I checked his gag wouldn't stop him breathing, climbed out of the truck, and slammed the doors shut.

"It's a bold move," West remarked as we walked round to the front of the Transporter. "Kidnapping the director of the SVR."

"Helping him defect," I countered.

"Yeah," West scoffed. "He's defecting."

Feo and Dinara were chatting quietly in Russian when we joined them.

"I heard what you said to him," Feo told me. "And I would very much like some time alone with the director."

"Not going to happen," I replied. "You need to go to hospital. Get yourself some proper medical attention. Promise me you'll take him," I said to Dinara.

"I promise. We would have left already if he wasn't so stubborn," she replied.

"I don't trust these American Marines if there's trouble," rumbled Feo. "They don't look very robust." He stared at West, who wasn't amused. "No offence meant."

"Plenty taken," West said. "But I'm going to let it slide because I'm sure it's just the morphine talking. I'm feeling quite hazy myself."

"You had morphine? Huh. I had no painkillers, American," Feo responded. "Just antiseptic. I wanted to be sharp."

West looked confused, unable to tell if Feo was joking or not. I wasn't totally sure either, but it wouldn't have surprised me if it were true. I had experienced Feo's unbelievable toughness before.

Erin Sebold emerged from the musty office and joined us.

"I take it you want to deliver the defector in person?" she asked me.

I nodded. "I'll need a ride home."

"Well, you've got your work cut out. The Kremlin is in uproar. My sources tell me they found quite a scene at the military base up north in Boltino. They don't have our satellite capabilities, but their human intelligence is good. They'll track you to Moscow soon, if they haven't already done so."

She moved toward an SUV.

"I've arranged for one of our company jets to be waiting for you at Vnukovo Airport. Master Gunnery Sergeant West knows the way there," Erin said. "Do you feel up to running Mr. Morgan to the airport?"

"Yes, ma'am," he said.

"If you hit trouble, I want you to head for Kuzminki Park. I can't guarantee anything, but I'm trying to set up a little surprise for anyone who causes any problems."

She climbed into the largest SUV as her security team got ready for departure. "We need to go now. Good luck, gentlemen."

"Thank you," I said. "For everything."

"You don't ever need to thank me, Mr. Morgan. You pull this off and the country will owe you an even greater debt of gratitude."

She shut herself in the SUV. The Marine nearest the bakery doors opened them and Erin's convoy streamed out. The man by the doors jumped in the last vehicle, which sped away on the tail of the others.

"We're coming with you," Feo said, when they were out of sight.

I walked over to the huge Russian.

"No. This is where we say goodbye. Get the medical care you need. Lay low till Alekseyev is Stateside and his power over Russian Intelligence is well and truly ended."

"I—" Feo began, but I cut him off.

"You've done enough, Feodor Arapov. More than enough. Look after him, Dinara."

"I will, Jack."

"Thank you for saving us," Feo said. "Both of you."

"Alekseyev would have killed us once he had what he wanted," Dinara added. "We owe you our lives."

I am never comfortable receiving thanks for what I've done. I always hope if I wasn't around, someone else would be standing in my place.

"We look out for each other," I replied. "That's what we do."

"You be careful," Dinara said. "Both of you."

I nodded and followed West into the Transporter.

"You ready?" he asked as he started the engine.

"Let's do this," I replied, and we rolled out.

CHAPTER 103

WE NEEDED TO head south-west to the airfield. The first couple miles passed without incident. West and I were silent, on edge, and alert. We had forty miles to go, and I hoped we'd be as lucky for the remainder of our journey.

We weren't. As we turned onto Volgogradskiy Avenue, a busy dual carriageway lined with offices and shops, we saw the first roadblock.

There were long lines waiting to make their way through two checkpoints. There were another two on the opposite side of the street, and traffic was also backed up in that direction. The uniformed cops were thorough, checking identity papers and searching each vehicle. We had no doubt they were looking for us.

"Take the alleyway," I suggested, pointing to the narrow street to our right, which cut between two office blocks. I couldn't see where it went, but it had to be better than certain capture.

West nodded. Once he had crawled forward enough to clear the metal barriers either side of the mouth of the alleyway, he made the turn. We drove between the two office buildings and reached a T-junction. West went right, which took us toward 11-Ya Tekstilshchikov Street.

"We'll go one block further and try to cut south from there," West said.

He made a right turn onto 11-Ya Tekstilshchikov Street, and we immediately saw a problem ahead. Moscow Police were setting up another checkpoint at the intersection with Lyublinskaya Street. The noose was tightening.

"Bluff, fight, or run?" West said. "Those are our only three options."

"I don't see us bluffing our way out. Not with a bound and gagged guy in the back," I said.

"Me neither."

"And I don't like the odds of fighting Moscow's finest for forty miles."

"Neither do I," he responded. "So that leaves run."

"Yeah," I said, buckling my seat belt.

I bent into the footwell and picked up Feo's rifle. "Maybe with a little fighting."

"Okay then," West replied, gripping the steering wheel tighter.

Establishing the roadblock had caused traffic to build up in both directions, which created a gap on the other carriageway as vehicles were held back while the cops got ready to start their checks.

"Hold on," West said, as he swerved across the outside lane

and cut over the median onto the empty stretch of road on the other side.

He stepped on the gas and the van roared forward. The cops at the checkpoint were startled and slow to react. They didn't manage to get their weapons drawn before we were on them. They had to dive clear as West crashed through the gap between two of the vehicles. The Transporter hardly slowed, but the buckled cop vehicles spun wildly as we raced by.

West hopped the median and bounced onto the right side of the road, eating up a clear stretch as we gathered speed.

I heard sirens behind us and glanced in the wing mirror to see the undamaged police vehicles screech clear of the checkpoint and start to chase us.

"Forty miles, you say?" West asked as we shot straight across a roundabout, bouncing over the kerbs and chewing up grass.

"Yeah," I replied.

He frowned. "Long way."

He swung the wheel and took us right onto Saratovskaya Street, but to my dismay I saw this single-lane road, which cut through a popular retail district, was completely closed. Police vehicles blocked access in both directions. They were obviously trying to divert traffic to the main checkpoints.

I saw four cops draw their pistols and crouch behind the hoods. Soon we would be all over the radio and every cop in Moscow would be looking for us. It looked as though there was no escape.

CHAPTER 104

WEST MOUNTED THE sidewalk and accelerated. There were no pedestrians, which meant we had a clear run, but fortune can cut both ways. The cops were able to shoot freely. The van took heavy fire as we raced to the barricade. West caught the rear end of one of the vehicles, parked to block the sidewalk, and there was an almighty crash and crunch of metal as the Transporter's weight and momentum carried it past the barricade. Bullets pierced the chassis, thudding into the side panel, and shattered the square windows at the back of the van.

West and I were unscathed but we still had a long way to go. I heard sirens, lots of them, and glanced in the wing mirror to see a swarm of police vehicles buzz into the mouth of the street.

West jumped the kerb back onto the road and we raced toward the next intersection with a growing convoy of police vehicles on our tail.

There was a dip in the road and the van took off as we went down the slope, heading for the intersection. We saw police vehicles directly ahead. West pointed to a side road where there were more liveried vehicles speeding toward us.

"They're cutting us off," he said.

"We need Erin Sebold's miracle," I replied.

"If she's pulled it off," he countered.

"We've got nothing to lose."

He nodded and swung the wheel left. The Transporter screeched round the corner onto Saratovsky Proezd, a broad road lined with large shops.

"Damn it," West said, and I saw the reason for his dismay.

Another roadblock, this one properly prepared. Five police vehicles were positioned to form a barrier across the street and sidewalk. They were arranged so the hood of each was behind the tail of its neighbor, making it harder to batter the rear end out of the way. The Russian cops were upping their game. Uniformed officers were positioned behind the center of each vehicle, aiming their rifles over the roofs. These men were more heavily armed than our previous opponents and unleashed a barrage of bullets as we approached.

The Transporter's windscreen shattered, turning the world a frosty white.

"Kick it out," West yelled.

I leant back in my seat and stamped the broken glass out of the way. It tumbled over the hood and slid onto the street. I could feel the wind on my face, and the sound of semi-automatic gun-fire was even louder now we were exposed to the world.

We were about fifty feet away from the barricade and West was showing no sign of slowing. Instead, he bumped onto the sidewalk and, to my amazement, drove the van into the window of a store on the corner.

Glass shattered and sprayed everywhere, falling on my lap through the open windshield. We crashed through some kind of clothes boutique, which hadn't opened yet, knocking down mannequin after mannequin until finally we smashed through the window on the far side of the store. Another storm of shattered glass and West swung the wheel left as we crossed the sidewalk and bounced back onto Saratovsky Proezd after the barricade, but our luck wasn't going to hold. The cops were already in the driver's seat, breaking up the barricade and joining the pursuit.

West pushed the van to its limit, racing up a rise to see Kuzminki Park ahead of us.

The leading police vehicles were gaining on us as we sped toward the park gates.

"If you're going to use that thing, now's the time," West said, nodding at the ShAK-12.

I opened my window and leant out. West cut diagonally across the street to give me an angle and I opened fire, shooting hot lead at the tires of the pursuing vehicles. The response of automatic gunfire was deafening, and the street behind us erupted until I found my mark and took out the tires of the lead vehicles. Two vehicles veered out of control and another went into a violent spin.

I'd bought us a few vital moments' respite while another wave of pursuers took point.

"I'm almost out of ammo," I said. "I'm going to have to use it wisely."

West nodded. We had a large armory but it was in the back of the van, which I couldn't access without stopping.

We were moving fast, at least 90 m.p.h., when he steered us into the park. We smashed into the metal gates, which flew off their stone pillars.

I leant out of the window and targeted the wheels of the lead police vehicle.

More rattling and cracking of gunfire and the front tires exploded, sending it crashing into one pier and blocking the gateway.

There were people in the park but West didn't slow. He sped along the pedestrianized driveway as they dived clear.

Behind us, I saw the massive police convoy stop and officers jump out and try to remove the smoking vehicle that was blocking the gate.

We raced along the carriageway, whizzing past specimen trees and shrubs.

"Any sign of anything?" West asked.

"I don't know what we're looking for," I replied. "But I see trouble ahead."

I pointed to more police vehicles, about a dozen of them, streaming through the gate on the far side of the park, joining the carriageway, coming toward us.

"Damn!" West said, and turned right, taking us between two venerable conifers and onto an expanse of grass. "I'm not sure we're getting out of this."

My heart sank. I knew what capture would mean for both of us. Valery Alekseyev was not a forgiving man.

Then I heard a low rumble, a familiar sound that made my heart soar. An Ansat light helicopter buzzed us, flying low over the van as it charted a course for the center of the lawned area.

West swerved and set the van on an intercept course.

"This is going to be close," he said, flooring the accelerator.

The van shot forward, chewing up the ground between us and the chopper. To our left, a dozen or so police vehicles were speeding round the perimeter of the park, trying to reach us. Behind us, cops were clambering over the one that had blocked the gate and running in our direction. West was right, this would be tight.

The pilot set the helicopter down a hundred yards ahead of us, and I saw a man in a dark suit open the side door. His face was covered by a ski mask. He beckoned to us.

"Thank all that's good and holy!" West declared.

We seemed to cover the distance in an instant. West stepped on the brakes. The van shuddered to a stop a few feet clear of the rotors. I jumped out and turned to face the oncoming cops, rifle in hand.

"Get Alekseyev," I yelled. "I'll cover you."

"On it," West shouted back as he ran to the rear doors.

I opened fire on the first police vehicles as they tried to cross the grass, slowing them down. West appeared moments later, dragging Alekseyev. I emptied my magazine, but it was no use. There were too many of them by now, a police convoy racing over the grass toward us.

I grabbed Alekseyev too and joined West in forcing the reluctant SVR director forward.

West and I hurled him into the chopper, but before I jumped aboard I asked the man in the ski mask, "Who sent you?"

I'd been stung by an impostor before.

"Erin Sebold," he replied. "She said I should tell you the Red Man used to bake great bread."

The roar of engines was loud now as the cops drew closer.

"All good?" West yelled above the sound of the rotors.

"All good," I confirmed, jumping in.

He climbed aboard and the masked man gave the pilot a thumbs-up. We rose into the sky with such speed I was knocked into the seat next to Alekseyev's.

"Enjoy your flight, Director," I said, settling back and breathing a little more easily as a small army of angry, frustrated cops stared up at us getting away.

Alekseyev's trademark scowl was gone. He looked smaller somehow. Broken and defeated.

CHAPTER 105

AMERICA HAD NEVER looked so beautiful. Manhattan was gleaming in the sunshine. The chopper had delivered us to the CIA Gulfstream jet that had whisked us out of Moscow. The sleek aircraft began its descent into Teterboro Airport, New York at 2 p.m. local time. As we descended toward the city, even the East River shone like a magnificent ribbon of mercury.

Alekseyev was sitting opposite me. We had taken off his gag but cuffed his arms and legs. He had his hands on the walnut-veneer table between us. The cuffs clanked and clattered every so often as he moved his wrists. He had slept for much of the nine-hour flight, or at least pretended to.

I hadn't needed to make any such pretense and slept soundly for the first five hours before I woke to take the second shift watching him. West slept just as soundly as I had for the remainder of the flight.

"I underestimated you, Mr. Morgan," Alekseyev said.

They were his first words since we'd left Moscow.

"It's a common mistake," I responded coldly. "People only realize the truth when it's too late."

I leant across the aisle and gently shook West awake. He rubbed his eyes, peered out of the window and beamed when he saw New York's distinctive skyline.

"Boy, it's good to be home," he declared.

"Some vacation," I said.

"Hey, anything that gets me stateside is alright with me."

A few minutes later we were on the ground, taxiing to our stand. When the aircraft had come to a halt, our pilot, who had introduced himself only as Bobby, emerged from the cockpit in the same black sweatpants and T-shirt he had been wearing when we boarded.

"End of the line, folks," he said, opening the passenger door and lowering the airstairs.

I grabbed Alekseyev and marched him out. West followed. As we went down the stairs, a convoy of three Chevy Suburbans approached.

I pushed Alekseyev across the tarmac toward them. Secretary of Defense Eli Carver stepped out of the second vehicle, and his close-protection team emerged from all three vehicles to assemble around him.

Two of the team, large Secret Service agents in dark suits, stepped forward and searched Alekseyev to ensure he didn't pose a threat to Carver. When they were satisfied, they waved us forward.

"Director Alekseyev, welcome to America," Carver said. "We can't tell you how grateful we are you decided to defect."

Alekseyev snorted derisively.

"Take him," Carver commanded, and two of his detail grabbed Alekseyev and marched him toward the rearmost Chevy.

"You've outdone yourself this time, Jack. A rogue Chinese and Russian network. We've had back-channel thanks from the Chinese Government, which isn't something that happens very often," Carver said. "The Russians aren't so happy, at least not officially, but Alekseyev has made many enemies over the years, so their diplomatic protests might be for show only. Many of the higher-ups will secretly be glad he's gone. You did good. Real good."

"Thank you, sir," I replied. "I hope he's a useful source."

"Cut this 'sir' crap, Jack. I've told you before, it's Eli," he said. "And are you kidding? The director of the SVR? He'll be very useful. In ways he can't even begin to imagine. What now for you?"

"I need to find my team," I replied.

"Where are they?" he asked.

"In the city somewhere."

Carver turned to one of the Secret Service agents. "Take Alekseyev for processing. We're going to give Mr. Morgan and Master Gunnery Sergeant West a ride."

"Yes, sir," the agent responded crisply, before heading for the SUV that contained Alekseyev.

We watched it pull away.

"Come on," Carver said, turning for his Suburban. "Maybe we can finally have that beer together?"

CHAPTER 106

"JACK?" JUSTINE ASKED in disbelief.

"Yeah. It's me. We just landed in New York. At Teterboro."

I heard sobs of relief down the phone.

"Jack, oh my God," she said. "Are you OK?"

"I'm fine."

"Are you sure?" She sounded happy beyond reckoning, and I was too.

"I'm fine. Feeling so much better now I'm home. Hearing your voice."

"Me too, Jack. Me too." She was crying now, but they were tears of joy.

"Where are you?" I asked, eager to see her.

"Sci, Mo-bot, and I just sat down for a late lunch at the Edition. Near the office."

"The Edition Hotel," I told Carver, who was beside me on the back seat of the Suburban.

"You get that?" he asked his Secret Service driver, and the man nodded.

"We'll be there in twenty minutes," I said.

I'd waited to make the call until we were on the edge of the city.

"I can't wait," Justine replied, her voice alive with excitement.

I hung up and looked across at West, who had coped admirably with his shoulder injury.

"I hope you'll take my offer seriously," I said. "If and when you leave the Corps."

"Are you trying to poach a Marine in front of the Secretary of Defense?" Carver asked jokingly.

"I wouldn't say poach. I'm just giving him options."

Carver smiled.

"Thank you," West replied. "I appreciate it."

We made it through the gleaming city in record time and reached the hotel in fifteen minutes, where we found Sci, Mo-bot, and Justine with plates of sandwiches.

Justine's had hardly been touched. She got up, hurried across the room and threw her arms around me the moment we walked in. Carver's arrival set the busy bar abuzz, but he didn't pay it any mind and sat down with West, Mo-bot, and Sci while Justine and I kissed.

"I've missed you so much," she said.

"Me too," I replied.

"I was so worried."

"It was touch and go at times," I acknowledged.

"Don't tell me that," she said, and took my hand. "Come on. You must be starving."

I nodded. I couldn't remember the last time I'd eaten.

I pulled up a seat between Justine and Carver. He was getting prompt attention from the server, a starstruck woman in her early twenties. She kept smiling uncontrollably, much like Justine and me.

"A beer for me, please," Carver said. He turned to me and asked, "Beer?"

"Yeah. I'll have a beer," I replied. "Thanks, Eli."

CHAPTER 107

A WEEK LATER, Justine and I were standing in the garden of Jessie Fleming's parents' home with some of the Private New York team. Sam and Ellen Fleming looked small and fragile, diminished by the trauma of the past couple of weeks and the near loss of their daughter. There were some members of her extended family there too, and school and college friends. We were all waiting to welcome her home. She had come out of her coma the day after I'd returned to New York but was only being discharged today.

Justine and I stood apart from the main group and sipped cold lemonade on the warm August afternoon, enjoying the sounds and smells of rural upstate New York. The Flemings clearly spent a great deal of time on their garden, and everything from the magnificent pine trees to the tiny delicate wildflowers looked well cared for.

Justine glanced at me and smiled. We hadn't been able to get enough of each other since my return from Moscow. I'd visited Jessie every day, grateful to see her strength returning, and Justine had insisted on coming with me. When she had needed to attend to paperwork, I'd sit in the same room and catch up on my own admin. We were happiest being around each other.

I smiled back at her, expressing the warmth and contentment I felt. Maybe one day she would get me to make that promise to stay by her side and let others rush into danger. The draw of being with her was strong enough.

My phone rang and alerted me to a Beijing number I didn't recognize. My heart skipped a beat. I half expected bad news when I answered.

"Hello?" I said tentatively.

"Jack, it's Shang Li," my business partner said, much to my relief.

Across the garden, I saw a community ambulance pull up beyond the gate. The driver jumped out and ran to the back.

"And Zhang Daiyu," she said. "You're on speaker."

"Save this number," said Li. "This is the new Private Beijing office line. We just wanted to let you know."

"That's great," I replied. "How are things over there?"

"Fortune smiles on us," Shang Li replied. "David Zhou was released from prison. I don't know if he spoke to his allies about us, but we've been approved for government contracts. We can expand the scope of our work considerably. And my wife says I must thank you again."

"Thank Zhang Daiyu," I replied. "I couldn't have done it without her."

"Of course," he said.

I looked across the garden and saw Jessie being pushed toward us in a wheelchair by a nurse.

"Listen, Li, I need to go. Let's catch up properly at our next monthly Zoom meeting," I said.

"Look forward to it," he said.

"Talk soon, Jack," Zhang Daiyu added.

"Count on it," I replied, before hanging up.

A crowd had formed around Jessie, with her parents at the heart of it. There were tears in their eyes as they greeted their daughter and welcomed her back to her childhood home. She looked gaunt and exhausted, but her doctors said she'd make a full recovery.

Justine and I edged our way toward her. She looked up at me and smiled.

"Good to see you, Jessie," I said.

"You too, Jack," she replied, her eyes brimming over.

Justine took her hand. "We missed you."

Jessie nodded and we backed away to give others a chance to talk to her.

"Do you think she'll be okay?" Justine asked when we were some distance from the group.

I knew the toll these things took, often felt most profoundly in the mind. We had been to Lewis Williams's funeral a few days prior, and I'd seen unending grief in his parents' eyes. They would never recover from the loss of their son. Jessie at least had a chance.

"With time," I replied. "With time."

Justine took my hand and we walked beneath the high trees for a while.

Fifteen minutes later, I saw Sci and Mo-bot enter the garden and greet Jessie. She was so overwhelmed she was crying now. They left her after a minute or so and came to join us.

"Good to see her out," Mo-bot remarked.

Justine and I nodded.

"The DA is still figuring out how to prosecute Rafael," Sci said. "It looks likely he'll face conspiracy to murder."

I shook my head. Rafael's role in all this was one of my greatest disappointments. He could have come to any of us. Instead, his life and those of so many others had been ruined. My thoughts turned red every time I thought about his betrayal of Private, but there was sadness for him too. He'd been taken advantage of by an evil man. I would never forgive Rafael, but I would probably never stop pitying him either.

"You think West will take you up on your offer?" Mo-bot asked.

"I hope so. Carver arranged for him to have two weeks stateside to visit family and then he's going back to Moscow."

"For now," Sci remarked.

"For now," I agreed.

"So, are you ready?" Mo-bot asked. "We've got a plane to catch."

"I think so," I replied, looking at Justine.

"Perfectly ready," she said. "Let's go."

She took my hand and we started our journey home.

ACKNOWLEDGMENTS

We'd like to thank our editor, John Sugar, editorial coordinator, Katya Browne, and the team at Penguin for their excellent work on this book. We'd also like to thank you, the reader, for joining Jack Morgan and the Private team on another adventure, and hope you'll return for the next one.

Adam would like to thank James Patterson for his continued support and guidance. He'd also like to thank his wife, Amy, and their children, Maya, Elliot, and Thomas, for being such great inspiration, and his agent, Hannah Sheppard, for her diligence and good counsel.

ABOUT THE AUTHORS

JAMES PATTERSON is one of the best-known and biggest-selling writers of all time. His books have sold in excess of 400 million copies worldwide. He is the author of some of the most popular series of the past two decades – the Alex Cross, Women's Murder Club, Detective Michael Bennett and Private novels – and he has written many other number one bestsellers including stand-alone thrillers and non-fiction.

James is passionate about encouraging children to read. Inspired by his own son who was a reluctant reader, he also writes a range of books for young readers including the Middle School, Dog Diaries, Treasure Hunters and Max Einstein series. James has donated millions in grants to independent bookshops and has been the most borrowed author in UK libraries for the past thirteen years in a row. He lives in Florida with his family.

ADAM HAMDY is a bestselling author and screenwriter. His most recent novel, *The Other Side of Night*, has been described as ingenious, constantly surprising and deeply moving. He is the author of the Scott Pearce series of contemporary espionage thrillers, *Black 13* and *Red Wolves*, and the Pendulum trilogy. Keep up to date with his latest books and news at www.adamhamdy.com.

Have you read them all?

PRIVATE
(with Maxine Paetro)

Jack Morgan is head of Private, the world's largest investigation company with branches around the globe. When his best friend's wife is murdered, he sets out to track down her killer. But be warned: Jack doesn't play by the rules.

PRIVATE LONDON
(with Mark Pearson)

Hannah Shapiro, a young American student, has fled her country, but can't flee her past. Can Private save Hannah from the terror that has followed her to London?

PRIVATE GAMES
(with Mark Sullivan)

It's July 2012 and excitement is sky high for the Olympic Games in London. But when one of the organisers is found brutally murdered, it soon becomes clear to Private London that everyone involved is under threat.

PRIVATE: NO. 1 SUSPECT
(with Maxine Paetro)

When Jack Morgan's former lover is found murdered in his bed, Jack is instantly the number one suspect, and he quickly realises he is facing his toughest challenge yet.

PRIVATE BERLIN
(with Mark Sullivan)

Mattie Engel, one of Private Berlin's rising stars, is horrified when her former fiancé Chris is murdered. Even more so when she realises that the killer is picking off Chris's friends. Will Mattie be next?

PRIVATE DOWN UNDER
(with Michael White)

Private Sydney's glamorous launch party is cut short by a shocking discovery – the murdered son of one of Australia's richest men. Meanwhile, someone is killing the wealthy wives of the Eastern Suburbs, and the next victim could be someone close to Private.

PRIVATE L.A.
(with Mark Sullivan)

A killer is holding L.A. to ransom. On top of this, Hollywood's golden couple have been kidnapped. Can Private prove themselves once again?

PRIVATE INDIA
(with Ashwin Sanghi)

In Mumbai, someone is murdering seemingly unconnected women in a chilling ritual. As the Private team race to find the killer, an even greater threat emerges . . .

PRIVATE VEGAS
(with Maxine Paetro)

Jack Morgan's client has just confessed to murdering his wife, and his best friend is being held on a trumped-up charge that could see him locked away for a very long time. With Jack pushed to the limit, all bets are off.

PRIVATE SYDNEY
(with Kathryn Fox)

Private Sydney are investigating the disappearance of the CEO of a high-profile research company. He shouldn't be difficult to find, but why has every trace of evidence he ever existed vanished too?

PRIVATE PARIS
(with Mark Sullivan)

When several members of Paris's cultural elite are found dead, the French police turn to the Private Paris team for help tackling one of the biggest threats the city has ever faced.

THE GAMES
(with Mark Sullivan)

The eyes of the world are on Rio for the Olympic Games, and Jack is in Brazil's beautiful capital. But it's not long before he uncovers terrifying evidence that the Games could be the setting for the worst atrocity the world has ever seen.

PRIVATE DELHI
(with Ashwin Sanghi)

Private have opened a new office in Delhi, and it's not long before the agency takes on a case that could make or break them. Human remains have been found in the basement of a house in South Delhi. But this isn't just any house, this property belongs to the state government.

PRIVATE PRINCESS
(with Rees Jones)

Jack Morgan has been invited to meet Princess Caroline, third in line to the British throne, who needs his skills (and discretion) to help find her missing friend. Jack knows there is more to this case than he is being told. What is the Princess hiding?

PRIVATE MOSCOW
(with Adam Hamdy)

Jack Morgan is investigating a murder at the New York Stock Exchange and identifies another killing in Moscow that appears to be linked. So he heads to Russia, and begins to uncover a conspiracy that could have global consequences.

PRIVATE ROGUE
(with Adam Hamdy)

A wealthy businessman approaches Jack Morgan with a desperate plea to track down his daughter and grandchildren, who have disappeared without a trace. As Jack investigates the disappearances, the trail leads towards Afghanistan – where Jack's career as a US Marine ended in catastrophe . . .

Discover the next thriller from James Patterson . . .

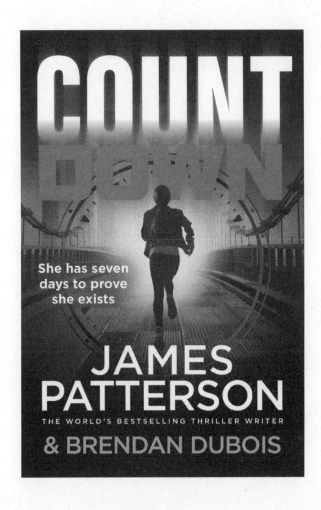

CHAPTER 1

I CHECK my watch and if all goes well, the killing will begin in less than two minutes.

I'm hiding with two other members of my sniper team in the barren mountains of northeastern Lebanon, just a few klicks away from the Syrian border. Jordan Langlois is the shooter and Santiago Sanchez is his spotter. Jordan is from the mountains of Kentucky and Santiago is from East LA. From the way they joke and work together, you'd think they were raised in the same orphanage.

No, not really. Just the Marine Corps and eventually the CIA.

I'm originally from Maine, then went into the Army, and now I'm the lead officer for this squad of the CIA's highly classified Special Activities Division—a very bland name for a very dangerous job. We go in way behind enemy lines, kill bad guys, then get the hell out. Along the way, we work very, very hard to ensure that our names and activities never appear in the newspapers.

Considering I'm married to a journalist, that can sometimes be a challenge.

Today we're waiting for a convoy to appear below us on a narrow, rugged dirt road, carrying a number of al-Qaeda fighters and leaders traveling into Syria for a summit meeting. Hypothetically my new place of employment could rain down thunder and fire from any one of half a dozen drone platforms to wipe out the entire convoy and any lizards or buzzards in the vicinity, but the rules of engagement have recently changed.

There's been too much embarrassment and too many scathing news stories (and accompanying editorials) over killing wedding parties and other innocents traveling in convoys in remote parts of the Middle East and Asia during the past few years. Now it's up to a small killing unit like us, sent into the field under secrecy, doing our job directly and quickly, so that mistakes are kept to a minimum and not instantly broadcast around the world.

Plus it's cheaper to kill a terrorist with a 99-cent round through his forehead than with a $115,000 Hellfire missile from a stealth drone—especially if the host country allowing us airstrip access doesn't want to be ID'd as helping out the infidels who are incinerating jihadists.

It's a new rule I'm comfortable with, because I know from sad experience the bone-dead feeling you get when you realize that a squeeze of your finger on a trigger in an air-conditioned room in Kentucky killed half a dozen innocents seconds later.

My spotter, Santiago, thankfully breaks up that dark memory: "Got dust on the westbound approach of the road, Amy."

"Roger that," I reply.

Santiago has a very powerful and highly classified optics system, set on a bipod, that allows him to "see" through the supposedly impenetrable black-tinted windows of SUVs in this part of the world, along with a laser facial-identification system that will ensure our target inside the SUV is indeed our target.

Next to him, Jordan is scanning the road with his weapons system, a high-powered military-issue-only Remington .308 bolt-action rifle whose aiming system is similar to Santiago's. Whereas Jordan is focused on the approaching target, Santiago—as the spotter—keeps a wider view of the target and any emerging threats our sniper can't see.

Me, the superior officer in this group, I'm muddling along with an off-the-shelf German-made pair of Zeiss 10x50 binoculars. Rank sometimes doesn't have its privileges.

I'm spotting the dust cloud now, moving right along in our direction.

According to our latest briefing, there should be four SUVs in the convoy, and we have two targets: hard men from the Abu Sayyaf terrorist group in the Philippines. Once upon a time great men and women thought that with the fall of the Berlin Wall and the rise of Facebook, we'd all live in one harmonious world.

That didn't quite work out, now did it?

A British male voice comes through the earpiece secured to my left ear.

"Zulu Lead, Zulu One here," he says. "We've acquired our target. You?"

Across this narrow canyon is another sniper team, on loan from Britain's famed MI6 intelligence service. The shooter is Jeremy Windsor and his spotter is Oliver Davies, both former SAS troopers. It's Jeremy's cultured British voice I hear in my left ear.

We've worked with them twice before, and despite the usual complaints and competition about the empire versus the colonials, the team has clicked, successfully completing Classified, and later Highly Classified, missions.

Or *successfully killing a number of men who deserved to be killed.* Take your pick.

"Jordan," I ask, turning my head. "How long?"

"About another fifteen seconds, Amy."

I toggle the microphone switch at my lapel; it's connected to the classified Motorola Saber-X radio strapped to my side. "About fifteen seconds, Zulu One."

I hear a *click-click* as Jeremy toggles his microphone in reply.

I keep my chatter to a minimum. I'm dressed like Santiago and Jordan, in a combination of northern Lebanese tribal pants and overcoats, along with sniper veils and gillie suits that allow us to blend into the rocky background. About the only difference between the two guys and me is the elastic bandage wrapped tight around my torso, to keep my boobs under control.

Nearly a year ago, in training at the CIA's Camp Peary—a.k.a. The Farm—some clown suggested I should stuff a cucumber in my crotch to complete my disguise. That made a lot of folks laugh, including me—right up until that night in the mess hall, when I secured a cucumber from the kitchen and shoved it halfway down his throat.

Also, there's the matter of firearms. Jordan has his sniper rifle, and Santiago and I have 9mm Heckler & Koch MP5 submachine guns with a 40-round magazine, with each of us carrying extra magazines. All three of us are also packing 9mm SIG-Sauer P226 pistols, along with a variety of other killing tools. Our rucksacks contain rations, water, extra ammo—nearly every necessity to survive in this hostile part of the world.

The pale blue sky overhead is clear of our drones, so it's just us kids. The CIA recently learned that our supposed allies have been locating our drones and passing along the information to the terrorists, so the fact that the convoy is on the move this early in the morning means they're confident all is safe.

Cue a deadly lesson proving otherwise.

In my binoculars, the four SUVs emerge from the dust about thirty meters below us, clearly heading in our direction. One Abu Sayyaf leader is riding in the second SUV, the other in the rear SUV. The vehicles all seem to be black GMC Suburbans with tinted windows.

"Target acquired," Jordan says.

I toggle a switch on my coat collar. "Zulu One, we're acquired."

"Same here, Zulu Lead," Jeremy replies.

"Go," I say, loud enough for both Jordan and Jeremy to hear.

There's a muffled thump next to me as Jordan fires his suppressor-equipped rifle. "Clear hit," says Santiago. "Driver is covered in blood, bone, and brains."

Jeremy radios to me, "Clear shot, clear results."

I look down at a multiple collision. The second SUV slams into a gray boulder, then another SUV rams it in the rear. Doors pop open and armed men bail out, bees flying out of a tipped-over hive, and Santiago whispers, "Oh, Amy, I would love to stay up here for a few more minutes. Look at all those lovely targets."

Jordan says, "Don't tempt me, Bro."

"No temptation, no nothing," I say, stowing my binoculars in my nearby rucksack. "Time to fly."

I toggle my microphone one more time. "Zulu One, time to break. See you at the rendezvous."

"Absolutely, Zulu Lead," he says. "Zulu Two and I are on the move."

Get the job done, and get the hell out.

I check my watch.

We should be picked up and safely out of here in thirty-five minutes.

But it takes only seven more minutes for disaster to strike.

CHAPTER 2

WE QUICKLY break down our gear and go down a trail we hadn't used before, because any repetition will get you noticed. Santiago is in the lead, Jordan is in the middle, and I'm Tail End Charlie.

I look at my watch once more. Analogue, old-fashioned, reliable. It will never need a battery at the wrong time, doesn't beep to give away your position, and has no electronics to fry in case somebody tosses a nuke into the air someday. It doesn't tell me the date, which is fine, because I know it's May 22.

The path we are on is narrow—broken rock and gravel—and seems too rugged even for goats. Yet we move with confidence and speed toward the safety at the other end of the trail. Like me, Santiago is carrying his MP5 in his arms, head always moving: left, right; left, right. Jordan has his pistol out and is doing the same. As the one bringing up the rear, I have to move and look over my shoulder at the same time.

Jordan says, "This sun is starting to fry me. Where are all the cedar trees? I thought Lebanon was full of 'em."

Ahead Santiago says, "Bro, King Solomon had them cut down, years and years ago."

Then I brake to a halt and loudly whisper, "Hold!"

Santiago and Jordan turn to look at me. I put my left hand to my earpiece.

I press my fingers together on the transmission button clipped to my collar. "Zulu One, go."

Some static, then "...have a bit of a problem, Zulu Lead."

"What is it?"

I turn my head and close my eyes so I can focus on what I'm hearing.

The strained but polite voice of Jeremy quickly comes back.

"It seems we have about two dozen hostiles chasing us."

"Zulu One—"

I hear the rattle of gunfire.

"Chat with you later," he says. "Quite busy now."

I turn and Santiago and Jordan stare at me.

"The Brits are in trouble," I say. "They've made contact with about two dozen bad guys."

"Shit," Jordan says.

Santiago says, "I thought this place was relatively safe. Boss?"

I motion with my left hand, though something dark and heavy has started growing in my chest. "We keep moving."

About ten minutes later, Jeremy comes back on. In a louder voice he says, "I'm afraid the buggers have us pinned down at the moment."

I can hear gunfire in the background.

I swear, trying to remember our location in the mountains and where the Brits might be after leaving their shooting spot. "Hold tight," I say. "We're on our way."

"No, don't do it," says Jeremy. "Trust me...you won't get here in time. Ollie! That bastard over there!"

I hear the loud sound of a three-round burst.

"Good shot," Jeremy yells. Then his radio cuts out again.

*　　*　　*

Move along, I think, *move along.* My mouth is dry and I'm terribly thirsty, but I know that no amount of water will help. I'm thinking of the MI6 crew and how they're my responsibility, my job to lead, and now they're in the middle of an ambush.

The rocky trail gets wider, and in my mind's eye I know what's about to appear. The CIA does a lot of things wrong but a number of things right, including a detailed briefing of the mission and whatever might be of interest in the area of our operation. The trail is going to curve to the right; then, in a wide portion of a narrow wadi, there will be a stealth helicopter from the Army's 160th Special Operations Regiment, ready to pick us all up.

I have full faith in the crew of famed Night Stalkers to get us out safely.

But there's one gigantic rub in all this.

Our rendezvous time is 9:00 a.m.—0900, if you prefer—and if we're not aboard that beautiful, Sikorsky-made escape vehicle by 9:05, it's going to lift off without us.

I check my watch again.

It's 8:53 a.m.

We've got plenty of time.

These three here, I think. As for the Brits...

"Zulu Lead!" comes the loud voice in my left ear.

I skid to a halt, nearly falling over among the sharp rocks and gravel.

"Zulu One, go," I say.

I hear his harsh breathing, hear the gunshots growing louder.

Oh, God.

"It's...ah, the bastards have us surrounded."

"Where are you?" I ask, tugging at a side pouch, trying to retrieve our topo map.

"Doesn't matter," he says. "I don't think we're going to be here very long."

"Zulu One, I need your location. Now."

There's a harsh stutter of gunfire, so loud I have to take my earpiece out. Jordan and Santiago stand closer to me, and even they can hear the desperate battle going on somewhere up there in these harsh mountains.

"Zulu One."

A hiss of static, more gunfire.

"Zulu One!"

A very loud gunshot, a grunt, and a whispered obscenity.

"Jeremy!" I say, raising my voice and breaking radio protocol, as if doing so could magically make him hear.

A harsh cough.

His voice comes back, speaking rapidly.

"Zulu One and Two are signing off, destroying our equipment. A pleasure working with you all."

Before I can say anything else, there's dead silence.

CHAPTER 3

JORDAN AND Santiago stare at me—so bulky and confident in their background, their experience, and the deadliest and most up-to-date weaponry in the world—and I know they're feeling exactly what I'm feeling: utter failure.

We've lost our comrades.

I stick in the earpiece and nod. Like the pros they are, Jordan and Santiago keep moving. Ahead of us, we all hear a low hum that sounds like a leaf blower at work.

There are no leaves here.

And positively no leaf blower.

But that soft noise is our way out of here.

As the wadi comes into view, it's 8:59 a.m.—a minute ahead of schedule. But I can already sense the catastrophe that's going to echo loudly between Langley and London in the next few days. Jeremy and Oliver will shortly be captured, tortured, and probably paraded around or made the topic of a propaganda tape by whatever armed group has found them.

We've all been "sheep-dipped," meaning that whatever paperwork we carry identifies us as contract workers for Global Security Solutions. That means in the event of our capture or death, our respective governments will have plausible deniability for us mercenaries in the field.

A nice cover story, which would no doubt last about as long as it would take an al-Qaeda type to come after one of our feet or hands with a chainsaw.

We're off the trail and at the outskirts of the wadi. Santiago mutters a prayer in Spanish, then says, "There she is. Have you ever seen anything so beautiful?"

Truth is, this latest classified and stealth helicopter is one ugly bird. It has droopy rotor blades and retractable landing skids, and its current color matches the rocky slabs nearby. The fuselage, all sharp angles, has a high-tech liquid-crystal exterior, meaning that when the helicopter finally gets off the ground, its exterior will match the surrounding sky.

Radar can't see it, and bare eyes will detect only flickering shadows, like a distant flock of birds.

Oh, yeah, it's ugly, expensive, and a bitch to fly—and I want to be on it so bad I can taste it. Its engine is humming along nicely, and we move forward and the rotors start to rotate. I look behind me, tail-end Charlie, watching our six, hoping against hope that our British comrades have broken free and are now running down the trail.

No such luck.

The engine is at full power now, the sound a loud hum, the blades spinning into a blur, and I see the frame of the helicopter rise just a bit.

So close.

I check my watch.

It's 9:02.

One after another, I clap Jordan and Santiago on the shoulders.

"Hold!" I yell.

I hunker down and they do the same, all three of us looking back up the empty trail.

Waiting.

Waiting.

The seconds whizzing by.

Jordan leans into me. "Amy! They're not coming."

I check my watch.

It's 9:03.

I yell back, "We wait!"

Santiago swears, but he and Jordan stick with me. Dust is starting to kick up, biting our eyes. I blink hard and look up at the trailhead.

"C'mon, c'mon," I whisper, knowing the odds of their showing up are near zero. But you have to believe sometimes. Believe they can make it. Believe in miracles.

Santiago tugs at my shoulder, points to his watch.

It's 9:05.

"We stay!" I yell back.

Santiago looks at Jordan, Jordan looks to him, and the two of them then look at the chopper, ready to scoop us up and take us out to a Navy vessel in this part of the Mediterranean, on a routine training mission.

Routine.

That's how the deaths of Jeremy and Oliver are going to be reported, if they get killed outright, without the horror of captivity and torture: *Died while on a routine training mission.*

And me?

Lost half my crew in a foul-up.

Almost as one, Jordan and Santiago scream my name, and I look at my watch.

9:06.

The nice crew over there from the Night Stalkers has given us an extra sixty seconds, and maybe I'll live long enough to thank them. But then the helicopter lifts straight up, its landing struts retreating into its belly.

The chopper rises up out of the wadi, soars over a rugged set of rocks, and then it—

Disappears.

Just like that.

Now even its engine sound has gone away.

All I can hear is the heavy breathing of my crew, Jordan Langlois and Santiago Sanchez, who stare at me with murder in their eyes.

I stand up from my crouching position.

"Saddle up, fellas," I say. "We're going back to get our guys."

CHAPTER 4

JEREMY WINDSOR, once with the 22nd Regiment of the Special Air Service and now a member of MI6's Expeditionary Research Branch (code name E Squadron), is squatting in a corner of a dirt-floored farmhouse, wrists handcuffed behind him, rope tied around both ankles, waiting.

He hates waiting.

His head, back, and arms throb from the beatings he and Oliver Davies received after their quickly dug-out foxhole did little to delay their capture. Now he and Ollie are in this stinking room, alone.

Jeremy gives his spotter a reassuring smile. Like him, Ollie has let his hair and beard grow, but Ollie's blue eyes are darting around the interior of the small room. Their clothes are dusty, torn, and soiled. Like him, Ollie came to MI6 via the 22nd Regiment.

"Guess our intelligence boys fouled up," Ollie says. "I never thought we'd get captured."

"Occupational hazard," Jeremy says, wishing he could say more to comfort his mate. "We'll be all right, just you wait and see."

"Too bloody confident, aren't you?"

"Somebody has to be..."

From its smell and shape, this room has been a storage area for seed or grains. A couple of rough muslin bags sit in a corner. Two high, small windows—open to the air but barred and covered with chicken wire—allow light in.

When he and Ollie had been sent to work with the CIA para-military group, Jeremy initially said no. A bird leading two sniper squads into the field? But he had seen Amy Cornwall's records, saw that she had been one of the few women to pass the U.S. Army's grueling two-month plus Ranger course—and thought, *Well, she might just work out.*

And she had done exactly that on their two previous missions.

Jeremy was a pro. So he shut his mouth and went along.

But even professionals have a bad day.

"Cheer up, Ollie," he says, once again wishing he could say more to his fellow shooter and friend. "It'll all get sorted soon."

Ollie smiles, but there's a flicker of uncertainty in his face. "Remember the bagging drill?" says Jeremy. "This will be nothing in comparison, I promise."

His spotter's smile widens, and Jeremy recalls all too well the secret and highly illegal bagging drill: being suddenly and quickly stuffed into a large sack by your SAS trainers, then dumped in the barren hills surrounding their base in Hereford, leaving you to find your way back without being noticed or requiring anyone's help.

"If you're right," Ollie says, "I owe you a pint at Berber's."

Jeremy is about to say, "Make it two" when the door is unlocked and flung open.

Five men enter, and Jeremy takes a moment to eye each one. All of them save one are carrying an AK-47, and he has a memory flash of a particularly rugged exercise one rainy day in the Shetlands—and God, the rain could get cold up there—when their trainer, Burke, a scar-tissued and rugged old Scot who had served behind enemy lines from the Congo to East Germany, had made a pronouncement.

Some of you wee ones have fantasies 'bout going back in time and killin' Hitler, he had said. *If I'd my way, I'd go back an' kill that Russkie bastard Mikhail Kalashnikov. Every would-be revolutionary and rebel piece o' shite loves to kill innocents with that bugger's invention.*

The man in front seems to be their leader. He has on dark boots, gray wool trousers, and a khaki jacket. In his filthy hands he carries an AK-47, and around his thick waist is a weapons belt stuffed with ammo magazines, a Russian Tokarev pistol, and a long knife. He has a thick mustache and stubbly cheeks, with a checked kaffiyeh around his head and neck.

Three other men in the group look like they could be his brothers or cousins, for they are similarly dressed and armed. The fifth man is unarmed, older, filthy, and wearing a black robe, cotton trousers that may have been white at one time, and a black scarf around most of his face. He hacks up mucus and spits it on the floor, then goes to the wall next to the door, squats down, and starts fingering a string of dark brown *misbaha,* or worry beads.

This group bunch had been part of a much larger group that ambushed and pursued them; the five had then split off to take Ollie and him to this stinking little farmhouse.

The lead man turns and whispers to the older man, who just shrugs and spits again on the floor.

Now he's looking at Jeremy.

In Arabic, Jeremy says, *"As-salāmu ?alaykum. I apologize for my friend and I trespassing on your lands."*

The lead man smiles widely. His teeth are brown. In return he says, *"Wa?alaykumu as-salām."* Then the strong voice switches to English.

"You are British, correct?"

Ollie keeps quiet, and Jeremy says, "Yes, we are British."

He speaks quickly in Arabic—*"Get them both up, now!"*—and two of the men sling their AK-47s over their shoulders, come forward, and gently help Ollie and Jeremy to their feet.

Jeremy allows a moment of relaxation.

It seems to be going well.

The leader smiles again, as do the other men, and he too slings his rifle over his shoulder.

Now it seems to be going very well indeed.

The man taps his chest. "I am Farez."

"Pleased to make your acquaintance," Jeremy says, breathing easier. Ollie seems to sense his relaxation. Jeremy says, "Again, my apologies for trespassing. My Uncle George promises he can sort it all out."

"Ah," Farez says, "your wealthy and influential Uncle George."

He laughs and the rest of the men—except for the old man sitting against the wall—laugh as well, then Farez comes forward and punches Jeremy squarely in the face. Jeremy gasps more in surprise than pain—*the code word and acknowledgment had been used!*—and staggers back as Farez quickly removes his AK-47 and drives it into Jeremy's abdomen.

He lets out a cough and he's on the ground, and so is Ollie, and the kicks and the blows from the automatic rifles rain down, and he squirms and tries to curl into a ball to protect himself as much as possible, but the handcuffs and ropes make that impossible, and he's drifting into unconsciousness, knowing it's all gone horribly wrong.

THE GLOBAL NUMBER ONE BESTSELLER

'Like having Dolly in the room with you'
VAL McDERMID

'Will have you rooting for them all the way'
GUARDIAN

'Told with passion and sensitivity' *DAILY MAIL*

'Deserves to be a runaway success' *EXPRESS*

'This is going to be BIG' *THE TIMES*

'One great read' LISA GARDNER

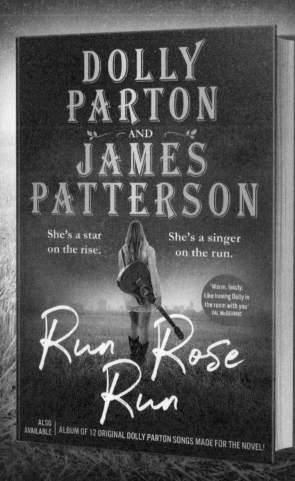

Also by James Patterson

ALEX CROSS NOVELS

Along Came a Spider • Kiss the Girls • Jack and Jill • Cat and Mouse • Pop Goes the Weasel • Roses are Red • Violets are Blue • Four Blind Mice • The Big Bad Wolf • London Bridges • Mary, Mary • Cross • Double Cross • Cross Country • Alex Cross's Trial (*with Richard DiLallo*) • I, Alex Cross • Cross Fire • Kill Alex Cross • Merry Christmas, Alex Cross • Alex Cross, Run • Cross My Heart • Hope to Die • Cross Justice • Cross the Line • The People vs. Alex Cross • Target: Alex Cross • Criss Cross • Deadly Cross • Fear No Evil • Triple Cross

THE WOMEN'S MURDER CLUB SERIES

1st to Die (*with Andrew Gross*) • 2nd Chance (*with Andrew Gross*) • 3rd Degree (*with Andrew Gross*) • 4th of July (*with Maxine Paetro*) • The 5th Horseman (*with Maxine Paetro*) • The 6th Target (*with Maxine Paetro*) • 7th Heaven (*with Maxine Paetro*) • 8th Confession (*with Maxine Paetro*) • 9th Judgement (*with Maxine Paetro*) • 10th Anniversary (*with Maxine Paetro*) • 11th Hour (*with Maxine Paetro*) • 12th of Never (*with Maxine Paetro*) • Unlucky 13 (*with Maxine Paetro*) • 14th Deadly Sin (*with Maxine Paetro*) • 15th Affair (*with Maxine Paetro*) • 16th Seduction (*with Maxine Paetro*) • 17th Suspect (*with Maxine Paetro*) • 18th Abduction (*with Maxine Paetro*) • 19th Christmas (*with Maxine Paetro*) • 20th Victim (*with Maxine Paetro*) • 21st Birthday (*with Maxine Paetro*) • 22 Seconds (*with Maxine Paetro*)

DETECTIVE MICHAEL BENNETT SERIES

Step on a Crack (*with Michael Ledwidge*) • Run for Your Life (*with Michael Ledwidge*) • Worst Case (*with Michael Ledwidge*) • Tick Tock (*with Michael Ledwidge*) • I, Michael Bennett (*with Michael Ledwidge*) • Gone (*with Michael Ledwidge*) • Burn (*with Michael Ledwidge*) • Alert (*with Michael Ledwidge*) • Bullseye (*with Michael Ledwidge*) • Haunted (*with James O. Born*) • Ambush (*with James O. Born*) • Blindside (*with James O. Born*) • The Russian (*with James O. Born*) • Shattered (*with James O. Born*)

PRIVATE NOVELS

Private (*with Maxine Paetro*) • Private London (*with Mark Pearson*) • Private Games (*with Mark Sullivan*) • Private: No. 1 Suspect (*with Maxine Paetro*) • Private Berlin (*with Mark Sullivan*) • Private Down Under (*with Michael White*) • Private L.A. (*with Mark Sullivan*) • Private India (*with Ashwin Sanghi*) • Private Vegas (*with Maxine Paetro*) • Private Sydney (*with Kathryn Fox*) • Private Paris (*with Mark Sullivan*) • The Games (*with Mark Sullivan*) • Private Delhi (*with Ashwin Sanghi*) • Private Princess (*with Rees Jones*) • Private Moscow (*with Adam Hamdy*) • Private Rogue (*with Adam Hamdy*)

NYPD RED SERIES

NYPD Red (*with Marshall Karp*) • NYPD Red 2 (*with Marshall Karp*) • NYPD Red 3 (*with Marshall Karp*) • NYPD Red 4 (*with Marshall Karp*) • NYPD Red 5 (*with Marshall Karp*) • NYPD Red 6 (*with Marshall Karp*)

DETECTIVE HARRIET BLUE SERIES

Never Never (*with Candice Fox*) • Fifty Fifty (*with Candice Fox*) • Liar Liar (*with Candice Fox*) • Hush Hush (*with Candice Fox*)

INSTINCT SERIES

Instinct (*with Howard Roughan, previously published as* Murder Games) • Killer Instinct (*with Howard Roughan*) • Steal (*with Howard Roughan*)

THE BLACK BOOK SERIES

The Black Book (*with David Ellis*) • The Red Book (*with David Ellis*) • Escape (*with David Ellis*)

STAND-ALONE THRILLERS

The Thomas Berryman Number • Hide and Seek • Black Market • The Midnight Club • Sail (*with Howard Roughan*) •

Swimsuit (*with Maxine Paetro*) • Don't Blink (*with Howard Roughan*) • Postcard Killers (*with Liza Marklund*) • Toys (*with Neil McMahon*) • Now You See Her (*with Michael Ledwidge*) • Kill Me If You Can (*with Marshall Karp*) • Guilty Wives (*with David Ellis*) • Zoo (*with Michael Ledwidge*) • Second Honeymoon (*with Howard Roughan*) • Mistress (*with David Ellis*) • Invisible (*with David Ellis*) • Truth or Die (*with Howard Roughan*) • Murder House (*with David Ellis*) • The Store (*with Richard DiLallo*) • Texas Ranger (*with Andrew Bourelle*) • The President is Missing (*with Bill Clinton*) • Revenge (*with Andrew Holmes*) • Juror No. 3 (*with Nancy Allen*) • The First Lady (*with Brendan DuBois*) • The Chef (*with Max DiLallo*) • Out of Sight (*with Brendan DuBois*) • Unsolved (*with David Ellis*) • The Inn (*with Candice Fox*) • Lost (*with James O. Born*) • Texas Outlaw (*with Andrew Bourelle*) • The Summer House (*with Brendan DuBois*) • 1st Case (*with Chris Tebbetts*) • Cajun Justice (*with Tucker Axum*) • The Midwife Murders (*with Richard DiLallo*) • The Coast-to-Coast Murders (*with J.D. Barker*) • Three Women Disappear (*with Shan Serafin*) • The President's Daughter (*with Bill Clinton*) • The Shadow (*with Brian Sitts*) • The Noise (*with J.D. Barker*) • 2 Sisters Detective Agency (*with Candice Fox*) • Jailhouse Lawyer (*with Nancy Allen*) • The Horsewoman (*with Mike Lupica*) • Run Rose Run (*with Dolly Parton*) • Death of the Black Widow (*with J.D. Barker*) • The Ninth Month (*with Richard DiLallo*) • Blowback (*with Brendan DuBois*) • The Twelve Topsy-Turvy, Very Messy Days of Christmas (*with Tad Safran*) • The Perfect Assassin (*with Brian Sitts*)

NON-FICTION

Torn Apart (*with Hal and Cory Friedman*) • The Murder of King Tut (*with Martin Dugard*) • All-American Murder (*with Alex Abramovich and Mike Harvkey*) • The Kennedy Curse (*with Cynthia Fagen*) • The Last Days of John Lennon (*with Casey Sherman and Dave Wedge*) • Walk in My Combat Boots (*with Matt Eversmann and Chris Mooney*) • ER Nurses: True stories from the frontline (*with Matt Eversmann*) • James Patterson by James Patterson: The Stories of My Life • Diana, William and Harry (*with Chris Mooney*)

MURDER IS FOREVER TRUE CRIME

Murder, Interrupted (*with Alex Abramovich and Christopher Charles*) • Home Sweet Murder (*with Andrew Bourelle and Scott Slaven*) • Murder Beyond the Grave (*with Andrew Bourelle and Christopher Charles*) • Murder Thy Neighbour (*with Andrew Bourelle and Max DiLallo*) • Murder of Innocence (*with Max DiLallo and Andrew Bourelle*) • Till Murder Do Us Part (*with Andrew Bourelle and Max DiLallo*)

COLLECTIONS

Triple Threat (*with Max DiLallo and Andrew Bourelle*) • Kill or Be Killed (*with Maxine Paetro, Rees Jones, Shan Serafin and Emily Raymond*) • The Moores are Missing (*with Loren D. Estleman, Sam Hawken and Ed Chatterton*) • The Family Lawyer (*with Robert Rotstein, Christopher Charles and Rachel Howzell Hall*) • Murder in Paradise (*with Doug Allyn, Connor Hyde and Duane Swierczynski*) • The House Next Door (*with Susan DiLallo, Max DiLallo and Brendan DuBois*) • 13-Minute Murder (*with Shan Serafin, Christopher Farnsworth and Scott Slaven*) • The River Murders (*with James O. Born*) • The Palm Beach Murders (*with James O. Born, Duane Swierczynski and Tim Arnold*) • Paris Detective

For more information about James Patterson's novels, visit www.penguin.co.uk.